"In the tradition of James Clavell's *Whirlwind*, W
us into the heart of the Middle East, makes us b
ance of a child, and touches our own spiritual journey as we travel with one family's faith and fortitude in their effort to bring a child home. A page-turner set in a contemporary world with the faith of the ancient world to sustain us and give us hope."

—Jane Kirkpatrick
Best-selling author of *A Name of Her Own*

"Tanneberg has done it again. A compelling novel that not only entertains the reader page after page, but enlightens us to the dangers we all could face. This is destined to be a best-seller!"

—Bill Carmichael
Author of *Seven Habits of a Healthy Home*

"*Vanished* is a certified page-turner backed up by the most thoroughly intricate research imaginable. You've got your history and geography so convincingly detailed, you feel like you've been there and seen that in person. You've got your theology and morality ringing through as clear as a bell. You've got your trauma-drama in graphic color that will make your hair stand on end. You're in a real world with real evil, surrounded by people with real faith and hope, fighting real spiritual warfare, but they know that Christ is the victor and to Him someday every knee shall bow. There is a prophetic quality that prevails as the story of *Vanished* unfolds. You should definitely read it!"

—Ralph Carmichael
Christian music artist

"With the observable talent of a gifted artist, Ward Tanneberg paints a compelling portrait of vulnerability in a world shrouded by the ever-present threat of terrorism. The intrigue and suspense of his imaginative palate allow him to picture a believable plot with details that keep the reader reading. *Vanished* is truly a brush of genius."

—Rev. Greg Asimakoupoulos
Pastor, author, and writer for Chapel of the Air

"I was deeply moved as I read *Vanished.* Actually, I couldn't put it down! The story of a young girl ripped from the side of her father and thrust into a terrifying life under the evil hand of Middle Eastern terrorists moved me to tears. Tanneberg skillfully weaves a story of intrigue, terror, and unrelenting faith into a spell-binding thriller. The characters in this story brilliantly match wits and spirits. The author's creativity is demonstrated as he leads us in and out of life-threatening situations while keeping it emotionally real. Tanneberg also demonstrates the rare ability to have God in the story in a natural, wonderful way. No sugar-coated God here. Tanneberg skillfully balances faith and reality without a trace of tame religiosity. When you read *Vanished,* prepare for some deep soul impact."

—Jon Sharpe
Acting Dean, Northwest Graduate School

Vanished

Vanished

Ward Tanneberg

Vanished

A revised edition of the work originally titled *October's Child* and published in 1995.

Published by Kregel Publications, a division of Kregel, Inc., P.O. Box 2607, Grand Rapids, MI 49501.

ISBN 0-8254-3850-0

Printed in the United States of America

04 05 06 07 08 / 5 4 3 2 1

To the ones still missing.

Tell it to your children,
and let your children tell it to their
children, and their children
to the next generation.
—Joel 1:3

God is love.
—1 John 4:16

Acknowledgments

As always, there are many people to whom I am indebted for their interest and assistance. Among them are several unnamed sources who have provided the author both professional and practical insights into the world of terrorism and counterterrorism.

I also owe thanks to Eric S. H. Ching, firearms consultant; Ken Moore, private investigator and airport security expert; Markku Pelanne, who introduced me to the world of commercial shipping; and Mehlika Seval, whose friendship and insights into Islam have been invaluable.

The Kregel Publications family has been wonderfully supportive throughout. Dave Lindstedt has once again come through with his masterful editing skills. Thanks, Dave. You've been a true partner on this project. And a special thanks to my agent, Joyce Hart, for being the consummate encourager.

Perhaps the most significant of all are the people who pray for me. Some of you I know. Many of you I have never met. You have simply taken me into your hearts because I needed to be there. If you are one of these eternal friends, thank you.

Of course, days devoted to research, meeting with people, traveling to places that I write about, endlessly formulating ideas, and telling the story would never be possible were it not for the encouragement and support of my family and the love of my life. I love you, Dixie.

—WT

Synopsis of *Without Warning*

There is often more going on around us than we see at first glance.

It was like that for John and Esther Cain of Baytown, California, and their children, Jeremy and Jessica.

John Cain was a man hanging onto his career and marriage by his fingernails. Disheartened by church politics, at odds with his teenage son, and despondent over the death of his eighteen-month-old daughter and the effect of that tragedy on his marriage, he had decided to resign his outwardly successful position as Calvary Church's senior pastor. He was burnt out and he intended to get out, just as soon as he led one last church tour group to Israel. After that he was leaving Calvary, and ministry altogether.

Esther was spiralling downward faster and more intensely than John. She had reached such a low that she began to consider suicide. Feelings of guilt and grief numbed her spirit. No matter what others said, she was sure Jennifer's death was her fault. She had tried to be the ideal wife and mother, and had failed. Now no desire for anything remained. She had nothing left to give John. Their marriage was running on the rims.

Life couldn't possibly get any worse, or so it seemed until the Cain family suddenly found themselves targeted by international terrorists. Marwan Dosha, an Islamic terrorist leader, had coordinated an ambitious demonstration of the power of Islamic jihad over the United States and Israel. His jihad turned a tranquil weekend in September into a cadence of violence and hatred that spread over two continents.

During Sunday worship, a well-armed team invaded Calvary Church and held the congregation hostage. On the other side of the country, a second team sought to turn Boston into an uninhabitable graveyard by releasing a biological warfare agent. And in Israel, the tour group from Calvary Church simply disappeared. Dosha intended to use them as pawns in a plot to destroy Jerusalem's sacred Western Wall and to incite international war.

The world was on notice, for these could not be random events.

Separated by ten time zones, John, Esther, Jeremy, and Jessica were each thrust into their own life-and-death struggles. They saw people they knew and loved die, and were called to tasks they would never have imagined they could do, in an effort to thwart the evil unleashed around them.

And when the dust finally settled, twelve-year-old Jessica was still missing.

Prologue

Sunday, 18 September, local time 2200
Somewhere in Israel

Why can't I see anything?

She was positive her eyes were open, but she shut them again, felt her eyelids press tightly together then opened them once more just to be sure.

It feels like I'm in bed, but . . . no, the surface is too hard for that. Did I fall out onto the floor?

Her head was throbbing.

She lay perfectly still, feeling the darkness, straining to see something. Anything.

But there was nothing.

No early morning dawn.

No afternoon sunlight.

No stars, no moon in the night sky.

Nothing.

Only the darkness.

And voices.

At first they seemed nothing more than a distant murmur. She couldn't make out what was being said. Closing her eyes again, she pushed everything to the back of her mind. The murmur, the hard surface, the darkness. Everything.

A wave of nausea roiled in her stomach. She tried to swallow, but her throat was bone dry.

I should get some water.

But she couldn't move. It felt as if she had rolled herself up in the sheets as in a tight cocoon.

If only I could see. . . .

The voices. They were there again.

Low.

Distant.

Unintelligible.

Maybe Daddy's watching television in the other room.

No, it couldn't be that. The voices were getting louder now . . . like when people quarrel. Though she couldn't understand what they were saying, she could tell they were arguing.

Then it came to her. She recognized the language.

Arabic. They're speaking Arabic.

How do I know that?

The mental cobwebs that had spun their way into the dark corners of her mind began to detach, and then one terrifying memory devoured every other thought.

The bus.

I missed the bus!

Her thoughts grew slippery again, kaleidoscopic images shifting and falling, twisting and turning, but always coming back to the same place.

The hotel. In Ein Bokek.

The bus to Jerusalem.

It was gone. It wasn't there when I came out.

Daddy left me.

Why?

How could he not know that I wasn't on the bus? I'm always right there in the front seat, nearest the door.

Her thoughts continued their sickening spin.

Why wasn't I on the bus?

Another wave of nausea seized the pit of her stomach. Then she remembered. *I was feeling sick. "Traveler's revenge." That's what the people in our tour group call it. Daddy told me to go to the restroom one last time, because it was a two-hour trip to Jerusalem, and there wasn't a toilet on the bus. I went back inside the hotel, and when I came out—they were gone.*

The same panic seized her as when she had stood in the hotel lobby entrance, staring in disbelief at the very spot where only minutes before a bus had been parked. Her bus! She'd run out into the late afternoon heat and looked to see if the bus had moved to some other place in the parking area. But it was not there. It had vanished.

Bewildered and frightened, she had hurried back inside and approached the desk clerk. When he looked up, he'd seemed as surprised to see her as she was to be standing there.

"How did you fail to take your bus, Miss?" he asked, his eyes never leaving her, as he fumbled for the handle of an open drawer.

"I don't know. I went to the bathroom, and when I came out they were gone. How could they not have missed me? What should I do?"

The clerk's demeanor had changed rapidly from startled disbelief to benign kindness and sympathy. He had assured her that she was not the first person to miss a bus, and that as soon as her absence was discovered, they would return for her. And if not, he would personally contact the tour agency representative. They would make whatever arrangements were necessary to reunite her with her father and the others. In the meantime, would she like to rest and watch TV? Well, of course she would. And he had an unoccupied room available where she could wait.

On the way to the room, he stopped to get me a glass of orange juice. I was thirsty.

It had been such an uncomfortably hot day, and a glass of that freshly squeezed orange juice had sounded great. Besides, it was probably the one thing that might stay down. Earlier, stretched out in the shade by the pool, her father had cautioned her to drink lots of liquids.

"Don't let yourself get dehydrated, sweetheart. If you do, this heat will make you feel even worse."

Now she lay in the darkness, listening to the strange voices, and struggling to remember what had come after the orange juice.

But she couldn't. Try as she might, she could not remember past the orange juice. There was nothing.

Now, fear gripped her again, clawing and flaying at her insides. She struggled to sit up, but for some reason she couldn't.

What's the matter with me? Why can't I get up? Why can't I see? Why do I feel so groggy? What is happening to me?

Questions, like pirouetting ballerinas, danced randomly across her mind, disappearing into the wings, only to reappear a moment later.

Then the awful realization hit her: She couldn't move because her arms and legs were tightly bound. She was helpless, wrapped up like an Egyptian mummy.

Now an all-consuming terror burned inside her mind like a fever. She cried out for help, but only muffled sounds escaped her lips. Tape over her mouth barricaded her cry.

The slam of a door sent new shock waves of terror through her system.

A motor started up, and with it a deep, rumbling vibration ran through Jessica's bed.

Seconds later, she felt herself moving. She was not in a room after all.

Am I in the back of a truck? Maybe that's why the air smells so funny. They are taking me somewhere. But where?

She felt herself slide as the truck started to move. Her body banged about as the truck bounced over potholes and rough pavement. In the darkness, fright played the boogeyman.

Who are these people? Where are they taking me? What are they going to do? Daddy, where are you?

But Daddy was not there. He couldn't save her now.

Her head bumped painfully against the metal truck bed. The roar of the engine, the scraping of gears, and the hum of the wheels on the blacktop filled her with such panic that she convulsed involuntarily. The darkness and the truck's erratic movement added the panic of claustrophobia. She fought back the bile that threatened to erupt from her stomach. She would choke if she didn't get control.

Don't throw up! Calm down! Concentrate.

She closed her eyes tightly, wanting desperately to open her mouth, to suck in air! But she could not. Steeling herself, she gradually brought her breathing under control, but her young heart hammered as if it were trying to escape from her chest.

Oh, God, what is happening to me? Jesus, help me not to be scared. Don't let them hurt me.

The nightmare of her predicament hit home. Her worst fears were a reality. She was always careful to stay clear of situations that felt uncomfortable or dangerous. She never got too close to strangers. Yet, here she was.

I am being kidnapped!

She thought of her home in California. Her room. It was safe there.

Please, God, I just want to go home. Oh, Daddy, where are you? Please don't leave me here. You can't let them do this to me. Come and get me. Dear God, please help me. Please get me out of here!

Tears broke free now, scalding her cheeks, streaming in rivulets into her hair and ears as the silent screams of all the world's missing children fought to escape her lips.

Daddy? Help me!

PART ONE

We say to our brothers in Palestine, that your children's blood is equal to our children's blood. Blood for blood and destruction for destruction. As the great Allah is my witness, we will not let you down until victory is achieved or we become martyrs.

—from an al-Qaeda recruiting video
seized by London police soon after the
September 11, 2001 attacks

Fight them who believe not in Allah nor the Last Day, nor hold that forbidden which has been forbidden by Allah and His Messenger, nor acknowledge the Religion of Truth, from among the People of the Book [Jews and Christians], until they pay compensation with willing submission, and find themselves subdued.

—The Qur'an
Surah 9: Yunus:29

Answer me when I call to you,
O my righteous God.
Give me relief from my distress;
be merciful to me and hear my prayer.

—The Holy Bible
Psalm 4:1

1

MONDAY, 17 OCTOBER, LOCAL TIME 1915
BAYTOWN, CALIFORNIA

Northern California's rolling hills were not their usual honey gold. Instead, they lay gray, gaunt, and cheerless, huddled like burnt ashes piled high from a million fireplaces. The record heat of the summer had finished off whatever bit of green had survived four years of negligible rainfall. Digger pine, California bay canyon oaks, yerba santa, and poison oak still dotted the parched hillsides, but any grass had long since retreated into the parched earth. Blackened trails from recent fires meandered indiscriminately through forests.

East of San Francisco Bay, nestled high in the perpetually snow-capped Sierra peaks, the Hetch Hetchy Reservoir stood at its lowest level in thirty-seven years. Wapama Falls usually pouring a steady flow all year, now showed alarming depletion. Due west of Wapama, Tueeulala Falls' gossamer display of water dropping over a sheer cliff into the reservoir had been reduced to a trickle. Great mountain streams that normally roared westward out of the snow and high glaciers had dwindled to empty beds of mud and gravel. This perpetual source of water, taken for granted by the millions of people who had depended on it for decades, was now endangered by nature's insolvency.

John Cain's mind was focused thousands of miles away on a more personal concern—Jessica—as he drained the last sip of water and stared pensively at the empty glass.

Where is she, Lord? Why did I have to leave her behind? She's only twelve years old.

He offered up a look of anguish at the black oak that reigned like a grand monarch in the far corner of the backyard patio. Through its branches and leaves, he glimpsed the fading rays of the evening sun.

First it was Jenny. That nearly tore us apart for good, Lord. And now Jessica.

Refilling the glass, he set the pitcher down on the Middle East map spread out on the patio table beside his Bible and the day's *Chronicle.*

Where could they have taken her? He leaned his head back and stared up at the sky. *God, why don't you answer? Why won't you tell us?*

Heaving a sigh of frustration, he reached for the first section of the paper, staring once again at headlines he already knew by heart. The news was not good. The lead articles were focused on the disintegration of hope for peace in the Middle East.

BOMB KILLS CLERIC, 93 OTHERS AT SACRED IRAQI SHRINE.
HOPE FOR PEACE FADES IN ISRAELI-PALESTINIAN TALKS.

Signing of Permanent Status Agreement Postponed as Both Sides Try to Patch Together Promise of Peace.

He pushed the newspaper aside and reached for his water glass.

Has she been beaten? Raped? Is she dead? Has her body already been tossed like garbage into some nameless grave half a world away? When I left her there, Lord, I asked you to protect her and help her get home safely. I trusted you. I trusted our little girl to your safekeeping. What's happening with your promise to never leave us or forsake us?

A thought repeated itself over and over in his mind: "*Do not throw away your confidence; it will be richly rewarded. You need to persevere so that when you have done the will of God, you will receive what he has promised*" *(Hebrews 10:35–36)*. John had read these words repeatedly in the past week, a biblical injunction to the faithful to persevere while passing through hard times.

Did the writer have any idea how hard the times could get? Is it possible God's promises don't cover our kind of need?

He turned the glass slowly in his hand, anguishing over thoughts that seemed too blasphemous to be spoken aloud.

Promises made can also be broken. I never thought so before. Not God's promises. But now I'm not so sure.

He lifted the glass to his lips and drank deeply. It was good water. Mountain water. One of the nice things about living in Baytown. It had always been there. But now, with the extended drought, even the promise of water might not be trustworthy. No one knew for certain.

One thing John *did* know for certain was that no lack of rainfall or water in the reservoirs could compare to the dryness in his soul.

Maybe there aren't any guarantees after all.

He stared off in the distance, wondering how this tragedy could have happened in the first place. His mind went back, as it had a hundred times, to that fateful day, four weeks ago, when his little girl had simply vanished off the face of the earth.

What sort of thing have I fallen into? What is really happening here?

He set the glass onto the table, thrust his hands into his pockets, and glanced regretfully at the map. This whole episode was insane. And as far as he was concerned, all that really mattered in life had come down to one burning question.

Where is Jessica?

2

Over four weeks had come and gone . . . twenty-nine days, or thirty if you counted today. John walked to the edge of the patio. Low garden lights cast a soft glow onto the flowers and trees surrounding the pool.

Quiet water.

The half moon reflected prismatically on the glasslike surface.

Dark water.

A repository of mixed messages.

John's eyes followed the path of light across the pool's surface. Upward into the night sky.

The moon, marked now with human footprints.

The stars.

Tiny torches in angels' hands.

The backdrop, black and cold and vast.

It all seemed to work together, giving his mind permission to open the road to the past, an act these days that did not always meet with his approval.

How many hours had he and Esther spent out here with the family? He smiled at the memory of splashing water and screams of laughter filling the air as, one by one, the members of the Cain household "cannonballed" into the pool, each attempting to outdo the other by the amount of water they displaced.

Happy hours.

A lifetime ago.

John was pretty good at it. Actually, everyone agreed that the cannonball, requiring little to no skill, was probably his best diving form. But there was never any question as to who the real champion was. Jeremy remained the consistent winner, his best efforts spraying water all the way over and onto the patio table, a feat no one else had ever accomplished.

Though his diving exploits were legendary, they were not appreciated by everyone.

Jessica liked to read her books by the patio table. She also did her schoolwork there in the afternoons until it was too cold to sit outside. Jeremy's antics exasperated her and she told him so in no uncertain terms. Of course, the more infuriated she became, the more her older brother antagonized her. Esther was the one who normally called a halt to these sibling spats before they became serious.

What usually followed was a familiar ritual.

When Jeremy's antics were brought to a halt, he would get out of the water and stretch out in the sun on a lounging chair. After a few minutes, the last droplet of water would disappear from his tanned, muscular body, as he absorbed the afternoon heat.

It would not be long now.

In the ritual, timing was everything.

Jeremy pretended to be oblivious to the approaching danger. He dozed, enjoying the warm rays of the sun, eyes ostensibly shut, yet all the while watching as Jessica made her way toward him, stealthily, on tip-toe, pitcher of ice water in hand. It was all Jeremy could do to lay still, feigning sleep.

At the most opportune moment, with a squeal of vengeful delight, Jessica would dump the icy water on Jeremy and run for the family room door. She never once made it all the way inside, nor really anticipated that she ever would. In a flash, Jeremy was up, sputtering and yelling and chasing after her. She screamed as his strong arms wrapped around her and swept her off her feet. While she squirmed and tried to get away, he carried her to the pool's edge, holding her over the water while she kicked playfully and cried out, "No, Jeremy, no. Don't do it. We're even now!"

"No," was Jeremy's relentless reply. "I managed to get a few drops on you and your book. You nearly drowned me in ice water, little girl. So, in you go!"

The culmination in this sibling ceremony came as Jeremy tossed her into the center of the pool, being careful not to let her drop near the edge. When she came up, laughing, Jeremy jumped in after her. For the next half hour, he and his little sister created memories for the two of them and also for Esther and John.

The noise would occasionally awaken baby Jennifer from her afternoon nap. Her face glowed with excitement as she waddled out in her diaper, holding tightly to Esther's finger as her feet continued adjusting to the fine art of walking. Her eyes sparkled as she watched her brother and sister splashing together in the pool. John and Esther thought it must look like great fun to Jenny, something she would one day enjoy doing with them.

It would never be.

One day, when she was eighteen months old, little Jenny managed to unlock the screen door, push it back, and wander onto the patio in search of her favorite pink and blue ball.

It was waiting at the edge of the pool.

A few minutes later, Esther came looking for her. No time at all, really, but long enough. Esther pulled Jenny's lifeless body from the bottom of the pool. That tragedy had nearly destroyed them all.

Yes, this place was indeed a repository of memories.

John looked at his watch.

Ten after eight.

That means it's ten after six, tomorrow morning in Israel. People stirring. Alarm clocks ringing. Feet slipping into sandals. Pants and open-collared shirts. Cool dresses. Shorts and tops. Military uniforms. They are feeling a pre-dawn chill in Jerusalem, but it will be pleasant and warm along Galilee's shores, and stretching further south toward the Dead Sea, all the way down to Eilat.

John's mind shifted to Ein Bokek and the Salt Sea Hotel & Spa. He felt the familiar heaviness return to his chest, as it always did when he remembered. Every detail was vivid.

Sunday, September 18, John's personal "9/11." Again without warning, the world had been reintroduced to terrorism, this time in a suburban church in California, in the grand old city of Boston, and on a bus filled with Americans on spiritual pilgrimage in Israel.

John had been sitting in the shade by another pool, with Jessica. Their shoes tossed to one side, feet dangling in the warm water. A quiet lull before resuming their journey toward Jerusalem. Time for complimenting his little girl on how well she traveled among the adults. Time for thinking how glad he was that she was with him on this trip. It would be one of their most treasured life memories.

Late afternoon in Israel.

John had planned the group's arrival in Jerusalem to coincide with sunset. It would be a spectacular sight, and he was anxious for everyone to experience it. Only Jessica was not feeling well.

John brushed at a patch of unruly hair. Every detail was fixed with a torturous clarity.

Shortly after four o'clock they had entered the hotel lobby. Everyone was there, ready to board the bus and be off. John reminded Jessica that they had a two-hour journey ahead with no toilet on board. She excused herself to go to the restroom one last time.

Then the unexpected message. David Barak, their guide, was called away to a family emergency. The hotel volunteered one of its employees to go along as an interim guide. John had assured them it would not be necessary. He could handle things until tomorrow, when either David or another guide could rejoin them. The hotel manager insisted, however, and soon John was making his way across the parking lot, his slow, sure stride keeping pace with a female hotel employee who was now their designated local guide.

John remembered the exact instant he thought of Jessica. In the surprise and concern he was feeling for David, he had momentarily forgotten about her.

Stopping abruptly, he had turned to go back.

He would never forget that first time in his life when he felt the hard reality of a handgun barrel digging into his side.

The attractive hotel employee had instantly become John's worst nightmare, forcing him across the sun-bleached parking lot and onto the bus. He remembered the pale, frightened looks on the faces of his group, huddled in their seats, as they stared at the automatic weapons in the hands of two strangers. A third hijacker had taken the place of Amal, their driver.

There had been a split second in which to make a decision.

He might live to regret his next decision for the rest of his life. Rather than bring Jessica into this calamitous situation, he had determined to say nothing.

Leave her! She would be safer at the hotel than with these armed fanatics. In the harrowing hours that followed, it had seemed the right choice.

The hostage drama in which he and his group were cast as major players had been filled with danger and at some points little hope for survival. It was no place for adults, much less a twelve-year-old girl. With each passing hour, he had been more thankful that Jessica was not involved. Not until events had played themselves out did John discover the terrible truth.

Jessica was gone. She had simply vanished!

Israeli investigators had gone to work quickly, stirring a nationwide effort to find her. In a matter of hours, they knew that a clerk from the hotel in Ein Bokek was also missing. An inside contact from among the hotel staff would have been invaluable in the plot to hijack a tour bus. After the bus had departed, that same person must have recognized Jessica as John Cain's daughter. Perhaps she even went to him for help after realizing the bus had departed without her.

John's decision to leave her behind had proven disastrous. He could hardly accept the horrible reality of this added loss.

First Jenny.

Now Jessica.

What more could possibly happen to destroy his world?

After several fruitless days spent searching in Israel, John had come home. Esther had nearly died from wounds suffered during the hostage-rescue operation at Baytown's Calvary Church, where associates of the Ein Bokek terrorists had taken the congregation captive. Jeremy had kept close watch over his mother until his father returned. The pressure of strained relationships had marked their family prior to all this. But in the aftermath of their remarkable experiences, the family had drawn new strength from each other and from their faith in the Lord.

Especially the Lord!

Over the four weeks since the ordeal, Esther had almost completely recovered from her physical wounds. She also seemed to be recovering from the emotional scars left over after Jenny's death as well. Even Jeremy had reached a higher level of peace within his young spirit. He and John were connecting as they had not for many months, if ever.

Yes, a lot has happened around this pool.

Around the world.

He looked up at the night sky one more time.

The moon and stars were blurred by the tears in his eyes, as an all-too-familiar feeling of hopelessness swept over him again.

Where are you, sweetheart?

Daddy is sorry.

So very sorry!

3

SUNDAY, 18 SEPTEMBER, LATE NIGHT
SOMEWHERE IN ISRAEL

How long has it been? An hour?

Two?

Longer?

It was impossible to know. What time of day was it? How long had she been out? She couldn't tell.

There was only one thing she knew for sure. Her body ached from bouncing around on the steel bed of the truck. Occasionally her head banged against the side wall, reenergizing the headache she'd had since she awakened. And with every twist and turn in the road, her stomach tied a new knot.

Where are they taking me? And where is Daddy? How could he just go off and leave me behind?

Anger mixed with fright. A fresh course of tears streamed into her hair as she scrambled to sort out her patchwork thoughts. Suddenly, her mind skidded to a stop.

What if something happened to Daddy? And the others, too. Maybe—

Suddenly, Jessica slid forward, banging hard against the truck's front wall, as the driver applied the brakes sharply. The truck began slowing down.

We must be stopping. Oh, please, God . . .

Jessica desperately wanted the truck to stop. She wanted to be free from the darkness, the cocoon wrap, and her musty cell on wheels. She wanted to be outside in the open air. But she was afraid, too, dreading to see whoever it was that had taken her. This could not be a nice person. No one who would do anything like this could possibly be nice.

Why would anyone want me?

She heard voices again. Men's voices. Arguing still. At least that's what it sounded like.

What will they do to me?

A name pushed its way forward in her consciousness.

Sherri Jacobs.

Panic set in again, and her mind filled with still greater fear. She remembered seeing a picture of Sherri on television. And her parents pleading tearfully for their daughter's life. There had been an "Amber Alert," the missing child information alert that was spread automatically around the United States. It didn't help Sherri. She had been kidnapped from her own home, raped, and murdered. A homeless man scavenging in a dumpster had discovered the body. Jessica remembered how everyone had prayed for Sherri at school and the shock when she'd been found dead.

Maybe that's what's going to happen to me. They're going to rape me and then kill me! Oh, God, please . . . she squeezed her eyes shut . . . *please help me!*

The truck seemed to be creeping along now. Jessica rolled onto her side as the driver took a sharp turn to the right. The tires sounded different, not like on pavement, or gravel either.

We must have turned onto a dirt road.

The truck rolled to a stop.

The engine no longer rumbled.

Jessica felt a wave of relief that the jostling was over, then apprehension as she heard the truck cab door open and the driver step down. The door slammed shut. Then she heard the cab door on the other side open and close.

She listened tensely to the sounds of people moving toward the back of the truck. Someone was fumbling to unclasp a padlock on the door. Now the door opened, but no sunlight flooded in. All was darkness, broken by the beam of a flashlight that played back and forth on the ceiling. After hours in pitch black, even this indirect light was glaring. In the distorted shadows, she noticed that at least three crates were strapped along the opposite wall. Now someone was climbing up into the truck, grunting as he stood up.

A moment later, Jessica squinted as the flashlight shined directly into her eyes. She turned her head and saw the shoes of a second man, standing behind the one with the light. He spoke, and the man with the light grunted a reply.

The second man stepped forward, reached down, and scooped Jessica up. Even through the binding tape, she sensed the muscular strength of his hands and arms. In the reflected glow of the flashlight, she glimpsed a dark beard that stretched from his chin to his hair. The man's breath was foul, and he reeked with sweat. Jessica turned her face away.

He hoisted her over his shoulder like a sack of potatoes and dropped from the truck to the ground. Jessica groaned as her stomach slammed into the bony part of his shoulder. The man moved away from the truck, an arm wrapped around her legs and the rest of her body draped uncomfortably over his shoulder. Jessica's upper body and head draped upside down next to the man's sweat-soaked back, and the rush of blood only intensified the throbbing in her head. All she could see in the night's darkness was the back of the man's body, the movement of his legs, and the dirt path.

The man continued along the path until he came to a crudely fashioned concrete slab. Stepping up, he pushed through a screened doorway.

Jessica heard another voice. *A woman! Oh, thank God. Maybe . . .*

The man swung her off his shoulder and dropped her onto an old sofa. Imbedded dust lifted from the faded green cushions as she landed. The room was dimly lit by a solitary floor lamp in the far corner. The concrete floor was good-sized and had once upon a time been painted green. Several tattered rugs were scattered about, lending the faintest hint of hominess.

The woman came over to Jessica and stared down at her. She looked old, just how old was hard to tell. Her skin was dark and leathery. Her face and eyes were difficult to make out in the diffused light, but snippets of hair poked out from beneath a scarf tied around her head. She wore the long garments traditional for an Arab woman.

Jessica's eyes pleaded with her.

The woman looked away and said something to the men who were standing off to one side, talking in low tones.

The one who had carried her in replied curtly.

The old woman's response was sharp in return.

The man grunted and then shuffled across the room. He bent over Jessica, frowning. To her surprise, he addressed her in heavily accented English.

4

"I am removing the tape from your mouth, girl. If you scream or make any noise, I will break your neck right now." His tone was menacing, and his dark eyes glared down at her. "Understand?"

Jessica blinked and gave a half nod.

"You will be quiet?"

She nodded again, afraid to do anything else.

The man tore the tape away with one smooth motion. Jessica stifled a cry of pain for fear he would do exactly as he had threatened. She breathed deeply through her open mouth, grateful for the increased supply of air. But there was another problem that needed immediate attention. How could she ask them?

Her eyes went to the two men, but they had turned their backs and resumed their discussion. She looked toward the Arab woman, who stood alone by a wooden table at the opposite end of the room, watching her. Jessica mouthed a silent word to the woman.

Please?

The woman didn't move. Jessica mouthed the word again, a look of desperation on her face.

Slowly the woman came over until she stood next to the sofa, never taking her eyes off the young girl.

"I need to go to the bathroom," whispered Jessica, feeling both embarrassed and more desperate with each passing minute.

The woman gave no response. She continued staring at the girl.

"A restroom. I need a restroom," Jessica whispered again.

Still no response.

Maybe she doesn't understand English. And the man who does said he'll kill me if I say anything.

Jessica's mind raced back over the few Arabic words and phrases she had learned on this trip. What was the word for bathroom?

"Toilet . . . *Taewaelit?*"

The woman's eyebrows lifted and a look of concern flashed across her face. She turned and said something to the men. They stopped their conversation and stared at Jessica. The man who spoke English reached into his pocket and pulled out a Swiss Army knife. He opened it as he came over to her.

"You need the toilet?"

Jessica nodded.

"All right. I will remove the tape. If you try to get away, I'll cut your throat with this. Do you understand?"

Jessica flinched as he touched the steel blade to her cheek. She nodded and whispered, "Yes."

The man slid the sharp blade through the tape that had been wrapped around her body. It came off quickly, tearing free from her clothing. Fortunately, instead of the usual shorts she had been wearing during most of the trip, she had put on a pair of pants in preparation for going up to Jerusalem. But her arms were bare and she felt the sharp sting as hair pulled away along with the tape. She grimaced, but said nothing, showing no other outward expression of pain.

Her relief at being able to move her arms and legs was overwhelming.

"She will go with you," the man said, nodding toward the Arab woman.

Jessica got to her feet, feeling wobbly and very much afraid. The room seemed to sway, her knees buckled, and she started to fall.

The old woman caught her as she fought to regain her balance. She nudged Jessica forward, pointing to a doorway at the opposite side of the room. Jessica shuffled toward it slowly, taking stock of where she was as she went, hoping against hope for some escape route to appear.

Like you would know where to run if you got out!

At the opposite end of the room was a wooden table, surrounded by four chairs. A small stove was near. Dishes and pots and pans lay stacked on open shelves of a cupboard. It looked odd. Jessica couldn't remember ever seeing cupboards without doors.

She recognized the man in a picture tacked to the wall from television news. Double chin, unshaven, looking like a soldier, with a gun strapped to his side. What was his name? She couldn't remember, but he looked menacing.

She paused in the bathroom doorway. To the left was a shower, framed in rusty metal, with a faded plastic curtain pulled partway across the opening. A stool had been plumbed into the wall next to the shower. It obviously had not been cleaned in some time. The memory of her own well-appointed bathroom at home flashed through her mind. She looked for the familiar paper roll near the seat. There was nothing. Only a bucket, half-filled with water. There was a small window above the stool and to the left.

It's open!

Her eyes darted from the top of the stool to the window, then back again, gauging the distance.

Maybe . . .

Jessica stepped into the small room and reached for the door.

"No!"

Startled at the sharp command, she turned. The man who spoke English was shaking his head now and motioning with his hand.

"Leave it open."

Jessica started to protest.

"Open," the man repeated and started toward her.

Jessica quickly removed her hand from the doorknob.

Now, instead of the possibility of escape, she faced the embarrassment of using the toilet without privacy. Taking two additional steps, she stood by the stool, her hand on the wall, then turned and looked back into the other room. The men were talking again, oblivious to her predicament. Only the old woman was watching.

Jessica's body made a last desperate call for relief. She sighed and sat down, gingerly trying to limit her contact with the seat, noting thankfully that at least the men had moved out of her line of sight. She looked around one more time for a roll of paper—paper towels, anything. The only thing within reach was the half-filled water bucket. She stared at it for a long moment, grimacing as she finally realized its purpose.

5

Saturday, 24 September, local time 0430
Somewhere in Israel

Jessica stirred, shifting her position on the filthy couch as she opened her eyes.

Emotionally and physically exhausted, she had been dozing again. How many days had come and gone since her arrival? Four? Five? She was not sure. Unbound now, she had not been permitted outside the room. She could only sit or recline on the couch. She could stand and stretch, but if she moved more than a step away, the old woman shook her finger and motioned for her to go back.

Her longest journey was the twelve steps to the *taewaelit.* She knew them by heart. She had resigned herself to the little cubicle's filth and inconvenience. And she was feeling better. Her discomfort at Ein Bokek had passed. Still, she slept hardly at all beyond what her mother called catnaps. Not until well into the second night did Jessica finally drift into exhausted sleep.

The old woman remained nearby. Although they never spoke, Jessica was reassured by her presence. Usually, one or both of the two men were also present, although they ignored her presence. Twice the woman brought her a small bowl of fruit to supplement the watery, brownish soup she ate each evening and the morning fare of plain pita bread and fresh goat's milk. She gagged on her first taste of goat's milk, thinking it was spoiled. Eventually she got it down. It might have been better cold, but no matter. She needed to eat and drink whatever was offered. Keeping her strength was important.

Stay alert. Daddy will come soon. When he does, I need to be ready.

At this moment, the man she dubbed "English," because he seemed to be the only one who spoke her language, was sitting at the table with the other man, eating a piece of cheese and drinking orange juice. He had left the house earlier. When was that? How long had she slept?

The old woman walked around the table, seeing to the needs of the two men. Noticing that Jessica had awakened, she picked up a plate and came over to her. As she extended it, Jessica saw that it held more pita bread, a substance she had grown familiar with while traveling with her father in Israel. In the last two days, it had become the staple in her diet. This time, though, it was not plain. There was something inside. What was it? Jessica reached up and took it from the woman.

"Thank you," she whispered, then remembered that the old woman spoke no English. "*Shokran,*" she added, using one of the few Arabic words she had learned. The woman's face was expressionless as she nodded and turned away.

The pita bread pocket was filled with a strange-looking mixture. Jessica examined it suspiciously, but it was food and she was suddenly very hungry. Biting into it, she chewed and swallowed, deciding that there was pickle or cucumber mixed in with something, maybe chicken. Whatever it was, it was not a Big Mac.

The woman went back to the table and took down a glass from the nearby shelf. Jessica watched as she withdrew several oranges from a basket and proceeded to cut them open, squeezing the fresh juice into the glass by hand. Still silent and unsmiling, she carried the juice over and handed it to Jessica.

The first time she had been handed a glass, one filled with goat's milk, she had wondered if it was clean. It looked dirty—at least not up to the standards she was used to at home. But when she had examined it up close, she had seen that it was only stained from many washings and was clean. As she took the glass of juice from the woman's hand, her mind flashed back to one she had been given at the hotel. Her abductors had knocked her out with that drink. Might there be something in this one, too? Jessica had become suspicious of everything and everyone.

No. I watched her. She couldn't have put anything else in without me seeing.

Finally, thirst overcame her hesitation, and she drank eagerly, handing the glass back to the woman when she was finished.

"*Shokran,*" she said again. "May I have another?"

The woman looked at her with the same expressionless stare, then turned and walked away without a word.

Jessica started as the door opened, and a third man entered the house, carrying a wooden crate. He placed it on the floor in the middle of the room and said something to the others in Arabic. The man glanced at Jessica as he reached into the box and lifted out a thin blanket roll, shaking it loose.

English said something to him. He shrugged and tossed the blanket aside. Then he took a knife from his pocket, opened a blade, and bent over the crate.

Jessica's apprehension increased as she watched him work.

What is he doing?

Her eyes widened as the other men rose and came toward her. English held a hypodermic needle in his hand. Jessica's anxiety spiked, fueled by a wrenching spasm of terror. An inner alarm went off.

"No!"

She pushed herself off the couch and darted for the door. But there was no chance.

The second man's rough hands grabbed at her, pulling her up off her feet. Jessica thrashed her fists helplessly and kicked at his shins with her heels. She thought she heard him grunt in pain—at least she hoped so—and she kicked all the harder. Her arms were pinned now and the man held her back against his belly. English stepped in and Jessica yelped as the needle sank into her arm. The contents burned as the syringe emptied into her system. Then, just as quickly, it was over.

The man holding Jessica threw her back onto the couch. Crying, with a mixture of fright, anger, and pain, she continued kicking and swinging her fists. She rolled off the couch and attempted to stand up, but slipped and crumpled to the floor instead.

I've got to get out of here. They're going to kill me. Got to run . . .

But the effect of the drug was already taking over. She fought back gamely until the room itself began turning. It was a sickening feeling, one she recognized from before. She felt someone's hands gripping her arms.

Kick. Fight them. Do . . . something . . . oh, please, God . . . Daddy!

Jessica's eyes refused to focus. She slumped forward helplessly, her chin drooping against her chest as she lost consciousness.

—~—

The old woman watched in silence, then turned and began clearing plates from the table.

"She's a little vixen," English laughed, the empty syringe still in his hand. "Here. Put her back up on the couch."

"I'll tell you where I'd like to put her," grunted the one who had held her, rubbing his shin with a free hand. "I'd like to bash her head in and drown her slowly in the Jordan."

"Just bring her here," the third man said. "The box is ready."

"Don't be such a bad sport, Ahmed," English chuckled. "A little girl bruised your shin. Maybe she has bruised your spirit, too?"

"Why do we go to all this trouble for her?" the man by the box asked as he took Jessica's limp form from Ahmed.

"Since the failure in Jerusalem, the girl is all that is left. She is the daughter of the one who led the fight against us."

The third man paused. "You mean the infidel *kafir* from America? The one who is in all the newspapers and on television? This is his girl?"

"Yes, this is his girl. She was left in Ein Bokek by accident when our people took over the bus. Our instructions are to get her out of the country. That is all I know."

"But it is dangerous. Everyone is looking for her."

"They are looking for her because she is important. If we are successful in removing her, she will be important for later negotiations."

"And if we are not successful?"

His comrade shrugged.

"So we ship her into Jordan this morning?"

"As soon as the bridge is open. We want to be there early before the line is long. The authorities often let the first trucks go through with little examination, so the line does not become bogged down too soon. The truck has been across many times in recent weeks. That should help us."

"But if they are looking for her? What if they search and find her?"

"As Allah wills. The decision is made. Ahmed, this is the most important assignment we have been given. Allah will guide us and make a way."

The man who was holding Jessica chewed his lip for a moment, thinking through the implications of what he had just heard. Then, without further comment, he picked up Jessica's limp form and lowered her into the box, turning her onto her side, forcing her knees up into her stomach. The other man knelt by the side of the crate, pulled Jessica's arms behind her, and taped them at the wrists. Next, he bound her feet. A piece of tape was placed over her mouth. He positioned her face near the small ventilation hole that had been drilled in the side.

"The lid. Bring it to me," the man said to Ahmed, "and the hammer, too. They are outside, in the back of the truck."

Ahmed returned with the hammer and the top to the wooden crate. As it was being nailed into place, the old woman busied herself at the small sink.

6

The driver glanced about nervously as the four trucks in front of his were systematically searched by security personnel. The authorities didn't seem to be in any hurry this morning. The first truck had already crossed the Allenby Bridge, but the driver of the second truck in line had just been instructed to remove an entire side of his load of oranges. Two inspectors were opening random crates and looking inside. Meanwhile, a uniformed soldier was examining the engine compartment of the third truck, looking for weapons or illegal drugs, and the fourth truck had just been motioned to the side of the road.

It did not bode well for the driver of truck number five.

After the signing of the peace treaty between Israel and Jordan, and the Palestine National Authority (PNA) occupation of the region surrounding Jericho, things had been more relaxed at this crossing. Not surprisingly, there was tension in today's early morning air, since the nearly catastrophic events in Jerusalem earlier in the week. A tour bus had been hijacked as part of a plan to blow up the Western Wall. The unusual plan might have worked, had not the hijacked tourists unexpectedly fought back, led by a Christian church pastor from California.

Little more than a one-way crossing from the West Bank to Jordan's Hashemite Kingdom, the Allenby Bridge spanned one of the world's best-known waterways, the Jordan River. No farther across than two or three truck lengths, the bridge was sandwiched between ugly block buildings on either side of the river. Only scattered palm trees enlivened the scene. And everywhere, plenty of sand and dirt underfoot.

At one time, this had been the only crossing point between Israel and Jordan. In recent years, however, another had been added in the north and a third to the south.

The area was, for all practical purposes, a no-man's-land between Israel on the west bank of the river and Jordan on the east. Sandbags were piled high, shielding a machine-gun nest in which two soldiers sat, casually observing the familiar chaos of the scene below. In a small office at the side of the bridge crossing, border guards shouted and strutted back and forth, looking and feeling a good deal more important than they really were. At least that's how the driver of the fifth truck in line saw it, as one of those soldiers strolled up to his door.

"*Sabah ael-kher,*" the Israeli greeted the driver in Arabic. *Good morning.*

"*Toda, boker tov,*" the Arab replied politely in Hebrew. *Thank you and good morning to you.*

"Please, get out and open the gate of your truck."

Reluctantly, the driver pushed open the door and stepped down. Tiny dust clouds puffed from under his feet with each step as he moved to the back of the truck and unlocked the rack. The orange crates were stacked on top of each other, surrounded by a wooden, open-slat rack.

"Take that one down from up there. Yes, that one, on the right. Open it, please."

The driver proceeded, without protest, to remove the lid. When the oranges inside were visible, the soldier ran his hand down into the crate, feeling for concealed weapons or other contraband. He found nothing.

"Over there, please. Yes, that one next."

The driver and the soldier continued this security ritual for the next twenty minutes. All in all, thirteen crates were randomly selected, removed, opened, and examined. Nothing out of the ordinary was found. Everything was routine. The guards were familiar with this truck, which crossed the border every few days. Even though this was not the regular driver, his papers were in order.

"Where is the man who normally drives?"

"He is sick."

"Too bad. Hope he's better soon," said the soldier, checking to see that the appropriate stamps and signatures had been placed on the man's documents.

"*Naharak sae'id.*" The soldier handed the papers to the driver and stepped back. *Have a good day.*

"*Shokran. Ilael liqa,*" the driver smiled, climbing up into the truck. *Thanks. See you later.*

He started the truck's engine and released the brake. Soon he was inching across the narrow bridge toward the Jordanian checkpoint. An hour later, he was back on the highway, making his way slowly up the long, winding grade toward the capital city of Amman with a truck loaded with crates of the finest Jaffa oranges, ready to be delivered to the marketplace.

Every crate was loaded with oranges except one.

7

Jessica's eyes felt too heavy to open. Totally disoriented, her head was spinning and a wave of nausea swept over her. She fought to open her mouth, certain that she was going to throw up. By the time she recognized the now all-too-familiar feeling of tape over her mouth, the nausea had passed.

She closed her eyes and opened them again. It was so dark. A brief ray of sunlight penciled its way across her vision, the laserlike brightness causing her to squint momentarily. Just as quickly, it disappeared.

Where am I?

She could hear the roar of the truck's motor, the downshifting of gears, the sounds of wood scraping against wood.

Where are they taking me?

She tried to stretch her legs but couldn't. Wedged in so tightly, her hands bound and helpless behind her back, there was no room at all to maneuver. Her ankles were taped together, too. The feeling of claustrophobia pressed down like a heavy weight.

The box at the house. They must have put me in the box!

As the reality of her predicament intensified, she continued sucking for air through her nose as best she could—but she was so frightened that her lungs would not release. Desperate, she concentrated on controlling her breathing.

Breathe deeply. Force it out the same way. It's so stuffy and hot. I need more air. I need to get out of here!

Her mind was swirling with fright. She pushed desperately against the end of the box, but there was no way to gain leverage. It only hurt her neck and back when she pushed. She tried changing positions, but the right side of her face was pressed against the bottom of the crate, with her shoulder curled underneath. Spasms of pain answered every bounce over a rut or pothole. With a muffled groan and a twisting motion, she finally shifted her shoulder out from beneath her so that she rested partly on her chest, with her face pushed up against the small hole that the light had come through. It was her only source of air.

Are they going to bury me alive? Does anybody know where I am? Of course they don't. Oh, Jesus, I'm so scared!

Jessica jumped involuntarily at the blast of an air horn and felt the truck veer sharply. The engine seemed to be testing its limits on a steep uphill grade. The truck swayed with frequent sharp turns.

—w—

A tour bus filled with Americans, most members of the Merryweather Baptist Church of Savannah, Georgia, worked its way down the steep two-lane highway leading to the Jordan River. Whenever their guide was not pointing out an interesting sight or offering up a bit of local history, the talk among these Christian pilgrims turned to media coverage of another group of tourists, who had become the heroes of the hour for thwarting a terrorist plan to destroy the Western Wall. Especially celebrated was the tour's leader, Reverend John Cain. The story had become almost surreal when coupled with reports of potentially devastating attacks back in the United States—one in Boston and the other a hostage situation at Cain's own church in California. The events had provided these tourists with no end of exciting conversation. This was a good day to be an American in Israel, and in another hour or two, they would be there themselves.

In the front seat nearest the door, Pastor Harvey Drake sat in silence, withdrawn from the animated discussion and speculation. His thoughts drifted ahead to Jerusalem, where the same John Cain, a colleague in ministry, was searching anxiously for his missing daughter. He did not know the man—had never heard the name before it hit the news—but he could not get Cain off his mind.

What must he be going through? His wife is still in critical condition, hovering between life and death. His church has been shot up, with people he has pastored lying dead or seriously wounded. He's under a doctor's care himself in Jerusalem after being beaten while a hostage. Now his daughter has vanished. The man must be going crazy.

Pastor Drake stared out the window toward the Jordan River far below and covered in a sultry morning haze. At the thought of what it would be like to stand in John Cain's shoes, his eyes moistened. He closed them in silent prayer while the bus continued down the steep grade.

Lord, I am so deeply moved right now for my brother. Please undertake for this man's wife and young daughter. Let your healing flow through Mrs. Cain there in the hospital in California. And be with Pastor Cain and his group, for all the trauma they've gone through. Undertake for each one of their needs. Especially, Lord, be with that little girl, wherever she is. If she's really been kidnapped, then watch over her. Only you can do that. Keep her safe and bring her home to her family once again. They've all been through much too much. Thank you, Jesus.

Pastor Drake looked up just in time to see a truck loaded with crates creeping around the corner, its wheels well over the middle line. The bus driver honked the air horn, stepping on the brake as the truck veered back across the line. The other driver waved apologetically as the two vehicles squeezed by each other.

"Stupid farmer!" muttered the bus driver. Pastor Drake chuckled, somehow feeling relieved of the prayer burden he had experienced just moments before. He turned to watch the truck as it passed.

"Oranges," he called back to his fellow tour group members. "Those are Jaffa oranges. Some of the best in the world. Maybe we can get a case in Jericho. That sounds good, doesn't it?"

A chorus of happy voices echoed through the bus.

He turned back again, facing toward Israel's desert hills, which loomed ever larger as the bus continued its descent into the Jordan Valley. The orange truck was quickly forgotten as the pastor reached into a leather pouch for the crossing papers that would be required once they reached the border separating Jordan and the West Bank.

8

It was nearly noon when the truck turned off the main highway and trundled along Amman's suburban streets. Whitewashed apartments lined both sides of the rocky hillside street. Once again, the driver checked the receiving address on the invoice. Minutes later the marketplace came into view.

Situated on a corner crowded with shoppers and hagglers, the market was a mélange of colors, smells, and sounds. Varieties of fruits, vegetables, and herbs were stacked on top of rickety wooden tables, displayed in rows on the street in front of a two-story building. Pickled foods and pita bread, offered at bargain prices. Persimmons and star fruit piled alongside more prosaic fruits like bananas and oranges. Everything a family needed was there, under the sun.

Off to one side, a man squatted in the dirt, planting a seedling of some sort. His shirtsleeves were rolled above his elbows and dark-rimmed glasses gripped his ample nose. A cloth cap perched askew on top of his graying hair fended off the sun's rays. As the truck rolled to a stop, the would-be gardener stood and wiped his hands. His friendly smile revealed unusually white teeth for someone in this part of the world, where teeth were often permanently stained by tobacco juice or simply from lack of personal hygiene.

"You made it," he shouted over the combined sounds of the marketplace and the truck motor. "No problems?"

"None at all," the driver grinned as he jumped down from the truck, relieved to be at his destination and ready to transfer his cargo.

"Is she all right?" the jovial-looking man asked, his voice lower now.

The driver shrugged.

"I don't know," he replied, his voice lowered as well. "She was drugged when we left. The soldier that checked me at the border came within one case of finding her. I thought for sure he was going to open her box and we would all be history. Allah was with us, however, and I made it through. I've been on the road up from the valley ever since. There was no place to stop to check on her."

"Then let's hurry," said the older man. His grandfatherly face hardened and his eyes narrowed into steely slits. "I don't want to have to bury her here from suffocation. Quickly now. Which one is she?"

The two men walked to the side of the truck and the driver pointed to a crate that was sandwiched in at the bottom, about midway back.

"That's her."

The pair worked quickly to remove the wooden rack. The driver climbed up and began handing down crates of oranges to the other man. These were stacked along the ground beside the truck. In a matter of minutes they reached the bottom crate. The man from the market observed that this box was slightly larger than the others, but he said nothing. A sharp-eyed border guard would have noticed.

He let the driver take the lead in dragging the box to the edge of the truck bed before jumping to the ground. Then each man took one side of the box and lowered it. They paused briefly to catch their breath and adjust for a better hold. Picking up the crate, they carried it through a large, open door located just behind the display of exotic fruits.

Inside, they climbed a narrow flight of stairs, making their way along a hall to a door that opened into a small flat. They set the box down in the center of the room and quickly closed the door behind them.

From a drawer in the tiny kitchen, the older man retrieved a sturdy-looking knife and began working on the box's lid.

A matter of seconds was all it took to break it loose.

Dropping the knife, he removed the cover and peered inside.

The girl was wedged in tightly, her hair matted with sweat, clothes soaked through, her face drawn and pale. She did not move.

Her mouth pressed against the solitary air hole, but there was no indication of breathing.

The man from Amman swore softly as he shook his head, throwing a hard glance at the driver.

The little girl had not survived.

He reached in and lifted her lifeless form from the box.

9

The delicious feeling of damp coolness spread across her face and body, easing Jessica back to consciousness. Slowly she lifted her eyelids to take in an unfamiliar world in which the walls and ceiling swirled in a slow, sickening circle. She squeezed her eyes shut, then opened them more slowly, trying to still the feeling of motion. Her head was pounding and her tongue felt thick and dry. The rotation of the room slowed at last and then came to a complete stop.

An attractive young woman, obviously Arabic, was bending over her. The woman was dressed in a blue, one-piece cloak that covered all of her body except her hands, feet, and face. Jessica remembered seeing women in similar costumes, but usually they had been black.

What is it called? A châdor?

"*Aehlaen*, Jessica." The woman spoke softly. Her teeth were even and white, her smile warm and friendly.

Jessica lay quietly, staring at the woman's face.

How does she know my name?

Her mind kept turning pages, trying to find the right one, something that would help her remember. But there was nothing. All the pages were blank.

"Hael taetaekaellaem arabi?"

Jessica moved her head to signal that she did not speak Arabic. This slight movement caused her to wince in pain. She grasped at the sides of the cot as again the room dipped and swayed like a drunken dancer. The combination of the earlier drug dose and dehydration while being transported in the orange crate had left her with a blinding headache. The woman seemed to know this. Gently, she placed her hands on each side of Jessica's head and held her steady, pressing in on her temples ever so slightly, moving her fingers in a circular motion.

Oh-h-h, that feels good.

"If you do not speak Arabic, you must listen to my poor English," the woman spoke softly. "Do not move your head just yet. You have been very ill, Jessica. The others thought we had lost you. Almost we did, but you are strong. You came back to us. You have need to rest now. And you must drink liquid. Here is some water. I will lift you slowly so that you can take some."

Jessica felt the woman's hand slip beneath her head and neck. As she lifted, a bottle was pressed to her lips. She tried to swallow, but most of it ran down the corners of her mouth and onto her shoulders. That's when she noticed her blouse had been removed. In its place, a damp towel had been draped across her chest.

Another sip.

This time, more water ran cool down her throat.

The woman took the bottle away and lowered Jessica's head until it was resting again on the cot.

"Where am I?" He own voice sounded strange somehow and far away.

No answer came.

Instead, the woman gently spread a cool, moist cloth over Jessica's face.

Pictures flashed across her mind.

A blanket. A box. Men staring at her. One had a syringe. He . . . he . . .

Shards of recent memory pricked her consciousness. Jessica flinched involuntarily. Then, without thinking, she lunged to one side, throwing her feet onto the floor, instinctively scrambling to escape.

The woman's hands were on her immediately, restraining her, forcing her gently back on the cot.

"Please, Jessica, try to remain still. You are safe now." The woman's words were soft, reassuring.

Jessica settled back, trying to remember what came next . . . after the man with the needle. *Darkness. A truck motor. Can't move. A hole with light coming in. So hot. Not enough air. The hole. Bouncing. The truck is rolling. Press against the hole. I'm going to suffocate! It's so hot. I need air. Oh, God, please help me! More darkness.*

Jessica clinched her fists and struggled to control the panic in her stomach.

The woman took away the facial cloth and lifted her again, ever so slightly, placing the bottle to her lips, letting the water trickle over Jessica's tongue and down her throat.

Minutes passed. Exhausted, Jessica lay back and closed her eyes. Moments later, she slipped into fitful sleep.

PART TWO

There are but two powers in the world, the sword and the mind. In the long run, the sword is always beaten by the mind.

—Napoleon Bonaparte, while in exile

As to America, I say to it and its people a few words: I swear to God that America will not live in peace before peace reigns in Palestine, and before all the army of infidels depart the land of Muhammad, peace be upon him.

—Osama bin Laden, videotaped statement
first aired on October 7, 2001

And ye shall know the truth, and the truth shall make you free.

—inscription in the lobby
Central Intelligence Agency headquarters
quoting the Holy Bible, John 8:32 (KJV)

10

TUESDAY, 18 OCTOBER
BAYTOWN, CALIFORNIA

During his first week home from Israel, John had been inundated with requests for news interviews and television appearances. Network magazine shows clamored for attention. *Good Morning America* and the *Today* show featured interviews with John in their prime viewer time slots. *Sixty Minutes, Dateline,* and every other news show, it seemed, worked the story with features surrounding the events. *Newsweek, Time,* and *U.S. News & World Report* each sought an exclusive angle. *People* magazine put Jessica on the cover. All funds received were deposited in the "Bring Jessica Home Fund" that had been hastily established by Baytown community leaders with the assistance of the local bank that served Calvary Church.

Although the media as a whole were sympathetic to the plight of the Cain family, John occasionally found himself facing interviewers who were not particularly enamored of his profession or his Christian faith. It had happened most recently on the *Greg Lauring Show*. Lauring was the rising young actor who hosted a popular Bay Area talk show. His reputation for asking probing, sometimes embarrassing questions touching all aspects of life, including politics, religion, and personal lifestyles, had made him a "must-see" for many of the Bay Area's under-thirty crowd. John thought this particularly interesting in light of the fact that Lauring and his sister were Baytown natives and had attended youth camps sponsored by Calvary Church in years gone by. Now, Greg's show was being considered for national syndication. The last he had heard, Lauring's sister was attending seminary.

John made a mental note to call the Laurings and ask about her. He wondered what Lauring's parents thought about their son's ultraliberal—at times Machiavellian—views. His father pastored a small and very conservative fundamentalist church on the other side of town.

During the interview, John could tell by the caustic edge to Lauring's questions that if the subject was not a missing child, John would most likely have been treated to a full dose of postmodern religious cynicism. There was no doubt that Lauring was sharp. It was just too bad that the Christian message had not captured his heart. John wondered what had happened.

Initially, John had not wanted to accept money. It didn't take long, however, before he began to consider the significant costs being incurred for printing and mailing posters to countries throughout the Middle East, North Africa, and Europe. Their small personal savings was quickly being eaten up, with no end in sight, but keeping Jessica's plight before the world's conscience was crucial to any positive outcome. It was expensive, but out there somewhere an innocent twelve-year-old girl had become the unwitting victim of international terrorists. And not just any girl. This was John's girl, and he would get her back, whatever the cost.

The media attention had continued well into the second week following Jessica's abduction, with Calvary Church's telephone lines jammed by news reporters seeking information, well-wishers offering heartfelt condolences, and the usual crank calls. By the time Esther was released from the hospital, the home telephone was taking voicemail only. Volunteers from the congregation took turns collating calls and determining how best to answer them.

Esther continued to convalesce at home under the watchful eye of John, Jeremy, and a task force of women from the church who cooked, cleaned, answered mail, and did whatever else the family required. Their presence freed John to use and to be used by an interested media, keeping Jessica's story in front of the world.

Turning their quiet home into a beehive of activity, however, had removed the last vestige of refuge from the public eye. The physical and emotional stress was taking its toll. John needed to get away, to the beach or the mountains. He needed time off for the sake of his own recovery, let alone Esther's. But there was no opportunity for that now. He knew that and kept driving himself. Too much depended on the moment.

As with every story deemed worthy of round-the-clock attention by the world's news organizations, the impact of the recent rash of terrorist activities launched against Americans reached its crescendo quickly. And just as quickly, attention began to wane. September's high-tension drama, fueled by the all-consuming coverage of national and international television and chronicled by daily newspapers and weekly magazines, gave way to a rash of new crises that fed the public's voracious appetite for news.

By the beginning of week three, the telephone calls had started to subside.

John sensed that their window to the world was closing. By the end of week four, only occasional calls from the media came in. Volunteers from the church still came by daily to check on the Cains and bring a hot evening meal, and two women came each Thursday to clean house and wash and iron clothes. Then, sensitive to the drain that even a helping presence caused, they told Esther to call when she wanted them.

Today was John and Esther's first full day alone since early September. They spent most of it in the backyard, near the pool. At one time the yard had been their favorite place. Now, in some undeclared way, both were trying to recover that feeling of family wholeness.

John relished the thought of being alone with Esther. Yet he was nervous as well. Though almost fully recovered from the ordeal he had survived in Israel, he was thoroughly exhausted from the nonstop tension of the past few weeks as the search for Jessica continued. However, as the afternoon grew warm, the tight muscles in his neck and back gradually loosened and his set jaw relaxed. He and Esther catnapped in the warm October sun, sipped iced tea, their hands touching now and again as if reassuring one another that they were still there, that somehow this nightmare would end. The morning's light conversation had eventually given way to long periods of silence, and a strange awkwardness remained between them.

When they had first reunited in Esther's room at the hospital, they spoke reassuringly of their love and devotion for each other. It was easy for John to see that Esther had experienced a profound change. She seemed possessed by a much greater peace with herself, which was no small miracle, considering their present circumstances. The depression had not disappeared, but it had retreated below the surface, and in its place appeared a fragile serenity.

It was different for John. He didn't know what he felt, other than an overwhelming sense of responsibility and loss where Jessica was concerned. But there was no opportunity to deal with personal feelings. All his energy had been focused on the crisis at hand. There would be time enough later, when this was over, to care for himself.

"Where do you suppose Jessica is?" Esther's soft voice broke the long silence. She hesitated before continuing. "Do you think she's still alive?"

"I do," John said quietly. "I can't explain it, but I have a sense that she's okay. Well, not *okay,* you know; but I think she's alive. At least I'm still hoping."

"I have that same feeling, and I think it's from the Lord. . . . I feel so helpless, but I guess we just have to trust him. What else can we do?"

Now that the ice had been broken, their conversation lasted through dinner, which they ate out on the patio. Jeremy had gone to Allison's for the evening, so they were able to speak at length about Jessica, trying to imagine where she might be and what she was doing.

Toward the end of the evening, Esther excused herself and went into the house. She surprised John a few minutes later by returning in her swimsuit. Without a word, she extended her hand to John and led the way into the pool. They swam together for the first time since Jenny's death.

Later, they showered and went to bed.

John was mindful of Esther's freshly healed bullet wounds and the scars still tender to the touch. His lips brushed each wound lightly as an awesome awareness washed over him: His wife had narrowly escaped being killed in their own church building by terrorists. He felt as he if was holding something rare and exquisite, something that might easily be broken with a careless move on his part.

They lay quietly, cradled in each other's arms as moonlight filtered through the window across the room, illuminating their bed with a soft glow. John cherished the look of his lover's face, resting inches from his own.

Her eyes were closed.

I love you so much.

His lips silently shaped his declaration of devotion.

But he knew. The tensions that had been set aside earlier were there still. They had not disappeared. They lurked, like demons in the shadows, ready to sap his energy and drain away his hope.

Why?

He breathed again the fresh scent of her hair, loosely fallen across her shoulder. He felt the warmth of her body next to his.

What is it?

Her physical injuries he could see and avoid hurting. That was easy enough. But there was more—so much more uncertainty.

What about the other scars? The emotional lacerations that I can't see? John knew that these were the truly frightening wounds, the ones that tore not simply into flesh but into the soul and spirit as well.

Ever since Jenny's drowning, they had hardly been able to touch each other, much less be intimate. The pain of her loss had plunged them both into depression. Esther had been ravaged by her grief, swept up in a massive whirlpool of guilt. John had been unable to reach her. His own wounds were too deep, too all-pervasive, sucking the very life out of their relationship. He'd had nothing left to give.

A tender truce had finally prevailed between them, upon which their very survival seemed to depend. John did not know exactly what it was they were waiting for, but he hoped there was something.

There had to be.

Otherwise, their marriage was never going to make it.

11

WEDNESDAY, 19 OCTOBER, SUNRISE
AMMAN, JORDAN

The call to prayer was blaring from a nearby mosque.

Jessica had no choice but to listen to the mystical cadence, but she was growing accustomed to the regular sounds of the minaret.

I used to think there was someone actually up there in the tower calling the people of the city to prayer.

She remembered the first time she had heard these unfamiliar sounds of the Middle East and how her father had explained that, in most cases, the prayers were prerecorded and played back automatically at the appropriate hours. In any event, she had discovered that these unintelligible appeals to the Almighty helped her keep track of time, both the hours and the days. She awakened each morning at sunrise to the call to prayer. Before long, she learned that the call was repeated each day at noon, and her food was delivered shortly thereafter. In the middle of the afternoon, she wasn't sure exactly when, the third call to prayer was offered. Next was at sunset. Last of all, came the evening prayer. Five times a day, every day.

The whole process seemed amazing—depressing, sad, and beautiful, all at once. So many feelings that fused in her mind.

Looking at the collection of tiny marks, near the boarded window, she could see that nearly a month had crawled past, day by ever slowly creeping day. Each morning, at first prayer, Jessica scratched the block wall with a tiny stone she had found in a corner of the room. Four scratches. A fifth crossed through the other four. Then, four more. She recounted just to be sure.

Twenty-seven!

She figured that two or three days were probably missing from the beginning of her captivity, when she was still weakened from her near-death experience. She couldn't be sure.

The kind woman in the *châdor* came every day, but whenever Jessica asked her name, she simply smiled and shook her head. Occasionally she arrived at mealtime, but not always. Once a week, she stood guard at the door of the toilet while Jessica took her shower. Gratefully, she scrubbed with soap and ran the towel over her body when finished. She had asked for a toothbrush and toothpaste and had received it on the side of her plate at the evening meal.

The woman had gathered up Jessica's clothes the first time she had showered, and in their place had presented her with a *hejab.* It was made of dark blue cloth that draped loosely on her body and formed a hoodlike covering over her head, leaving only her feet, hands, and face unconcealed. She looked to anyone who might take note of her, like a young Muslim girl.

Jessica had assumed that her own clothes were gone forever. But the next day, the woman returned them, washed and folded, placing them at the foot of her cot.

One day, soon after Jessica had regained most of her strength, she heard someone talking over a loudspeaker. This voice continued considerably longer than the usual prayers, piquing Jessica's curiosity. She had discovered that one of the men who took turns guarding her door and bringing her food spoke a little English, so she asked him what was happening. He told her it was Thursday, and every Thursday a sermon was delivered at the mosque. It was the longest conversation she had had with any of her captors, and now she at least knew what day of the week it was.

The next day, at Friday morning prayers, another lengthy address boomed across the loudspeaker. She wished that she understood Arabic. *Or that they would just speak English!* The sermon and prayers made her think of her father. She yearned to be home again, to hear his full, rich voice fill the sanctuary as he led the congregation in prayer or asked them to "join with me today in the reading of God's Word." Every Thursday evening and Friday morning, it was the same routine, which became the confirmation of her calendar scratches.

One day, Jessica asked for a book to help her learn Arabic.

No. There would be no book.

Next, she asked for books or magazines in English.

Nothing.

The days stretched out interminably, and because she was not chained or bound in any way, she walked. Each time someone came into her room, she studied his or her face, inscribing every feature in her mind. She wondered about their willingness to let her see them. Surely they knew that she would be able to identify them later. That is, of course, unless they knew there would be no "later."

Across from where she sat, Jessica stared at the boarded-up window. Light filtered through the cracks between the boards during the day. But they were too narrow to see through. She was certain the mosque had to be somewhere nearby. At times, she overheard voices, unintelligible and distant. Was it a school? No, it sounded more like voices jumbled together. A plaza, perhaps, where people gathered? Or maybe a marketplace?

The handle on the inside of her door had been removed. A single lightbulb hung down from the center of the room, its pale glow the only nighttime illumination in the otherwise gloomy surroundings that had become her personal prison cell. That's the way she viewed it, at least. It was not home, that's for sure. Nor was it a hotel room. It *was* a prison cell, nothing more, nothing less. She remembered her visit to the Anne Frank House in Amsterdam with her father on their way to Israel. She thought about the annex where Anne and her family had hidden from the Nazis and wondered how Anne would have passed the time without her diary.

At least she had someone to talk to.

Then she remembered that the Franks had been captured and that Anne had died before the end of the war.

But if they're going to kill me, what are they waiting for?

She was grateful that at least she was not bound. Circling the room, she paced it off, measuring its length and breadth. She even tried to calculate how many times around the room she would need to walk to complete a mile.

At home, she had walked with her mother, not every day, but now and then. The route that they normally took was about two miles in length. It had never taken them more than thirty minutes. Now, however, her watch was gone. She assumed that her captors must have stolen it. Counting from one to sixty as she walked, she attempted to establish the length of one minute. She kept track of the "minutes" until fifteen of them had been counted.

Six times around the room in a minute. Ninety times equals one mile. Go forty-five times one way, then reverse direction.

Sometimes she walked two miles in the morning. Other times it was one in the morning and another before going to bed. But every day, she walked.

Every day.

The cell was musty and surprisingly cold at night. Jessica had taken to wearing the *hejab* over her own clothes, and she wished she had her suitcase with all her things in it.

The cot was a piece of canvas stretched across a wooden frame. On top of it was a foam rubber mattress and a thin blanket. When Jessica complained to the woman about being cold, an additional blanket, in much better condition, had been provided, along with a small pillow.

The men who took turns guarding Jessica generally left her alone. She could not tell their ages, but the oldest one had gray in his hair and few good teeth. The guards usually smiled and nodded to her—except for the youngest, who was always sullen—but they rarely spoke more than a word or two at a time. That was okay with Jessica. She didn't want to talk with them anyway. She looked forward to the daily visits from the woman with the kind face, even though she did not talk a great deal, either. It was all very perfunctory. No real conversations.

The times when Jessica needed to use the toilet were the worst. At first, she was embarrassed to tell the men what she wanted. Eventually, she outgrew that hesitation. Necessity forced her to become bolder and more assertive where her personal needs were concerned.

She learned to pound on the door in earnest.

A key would turn in the lock, and the door would open.

She was always relieved when it was one of the two older men.

"Sit," they would say.

She sat.

"Why you make noise?"

"I need the toilet."

"Not make noise."

"If I don't make noise, you won't open the door."

"No noise."

"It's urgent. I need toilet."

"Later. Not now."

"No. Now. I need to go now!"

This argument took place on a fairly regular basis. The exceptions were the times that Jessica needed the toilet when the woman was there. She permitted access without question.

The guards always followed her down the hallway and stood outside while she went in. The door could be closed, but was always left ajar. When she finished, they followed her back to her cell. As soon as she walked through the doorway, it closed behind her and she heard the sound of the key turning in the lock.

Today, she pounded on the door. After a minute, the key turned. When it opened, the youngest guard was standing there, his automatic weapon slung over his shoulder by a single strap. She was surprised to see a grin on his face.

"Sit."

She sat.

"Why you make noise?"

"I need the toilet."

The guard let his eyes roam up and down Jessica's body. She had folded the *hejab* at the foot of the cot and was wearing her own clothes today. She immediately wished that she had put on the long, shapeless garment. His stare made her nervous.

"Not make noise."

"It's urgent. I need the toilet."

"Later. Not now."

"No. Now. I need to go now."

"All right," the guard said reluctantly, his eyes still roaming over Jessica. "Go."

He did not back away from the doorway.

Jessica bit her lip. She wished she could hold it until one of the other guards was on duty. But her bladder was full and she needed to go. Desperately.

"Excuse me."

The young man didn't move.

"I said, excuse me."

He continued blocking the doorway.

Jessica started past him. Turning sideways, she pressed her back against the doorjamb as far as she could. There still was not enough room to get through without touching him, so she put her hands in front of her and nudged him away. Up close, the young man smelled and she wanted to gag.

Suddenly, he grabbed her wrist and pulled her back into her room. He twisted her arm, causing her to drop to her knees.

"You're hurting me. Stop it!"

"How badly do you need to go?" the young man stood over her, laughing at her discomfort.

"I said, quit it. You are hurting me!"

"American whore!" He kicked the door shut with his heel and leaned his rifle up against the wall. Dropping to his knees, he yanked her forward until her face was next to his and tried to kiss her. His mouth was wet and his breath bad. She felt his hands pressing and fumbling over her shirt as she twisted and struggled to push away.

Then his mouth was on her lips again.

This time she bit him.

With a cry of pain, the guard fell back.

Jessica scrambled to her feet as the guard felt his lip and looked ruefully at the blood on his fingers. Angry, frightened, and without thinking, she aimed a well-placed kick at his groin. It hit the mark causing him to double over with a groan. As she turned to run, he reached out and grabbed her ankle. She screamed as she fell to the floor and began thrashing her other foot to keep him away. He was on his side, yelling obscenities, one hand around her ankle, yanking her toward him, the other hand shielding his head from her kicks. Jessica rolled onto her stomach, her face to the floor, as she struggled to get away. She could not see what was happening, but she heard other sounds, and then as quickly as it had started, it was over. The young man let go and Jessica rolled to one side.

The woman with the kind face had jerked the young man backward, sending him sprawling across the floor. Her face flushed with anger as she stooped to pick up his weapon, which had fallen over during the struggle. Jessica began to scoot away slowly on the seat of her pants, but the woman did not point the gun at her. Instead, she aimed it at the guard.

The young man said something and reached for the weapon.

The woman replied angrily, shaking her head.

The guard began to rise, still arguing with the woman, but he sat back down when she brandished the weapon in a way that clearly indicated she knew how to use it.

After a tense moment of silence, the young man pushed himself to his feet, glaring sullenly at the woman and then at Jessica. Without a word, he turned, walked out into the hallway and disappeared down the staircase.

The woman turned and looked at Jessica.

Jessica stood up unsteadily, shaking and crying at the same time.

"Are you all right?" she asked.

"Ye–yes," Jessica stammered. "I just need to go to the toilet."

"Go."

Jessica turned and ran to the end of the hall. At the door, she paused and looked back. The woman had not moved. She still held the guard's weapon. With her head, she motioned for her to go in. Jessica went inside and closed the door. Tightly. For the first time, she was alone. She had not been this far from her guards since they'd brought her here. Her breath was coming in short, heaving bursts. Looking down at her shirt, she saw that the top two buttons were missing. She shivered at the thought of what had just happened.

When she was done, she opened the door and stepped back into the hall. The woman was still standing in front of the door to the room, talking to someone that Jessica had never seen before. The stranger looked over as she came out, then returned to his conversation with the woman. As Jessica approached, he took the rifle from the woman and turned toward the staircase.

The woman extended her hand to Jessica. In it were the two missing buttons. Jessica took them, and the woman guided her back into her quarters.

"Are you all right now?" she asked.

Jessica nodded.

"You are certain? He did not hurt you?"

Jessica looked up, tears rolling down her checks.

"He twisted my arm and tried to . . . to kiss me. I bit him! Then he called me a name, and started putting his hands all over me."

"He touched you? Where?"

"Here," Jessica motioned with her hands.

The woman's face clouded over in anger.

"And he called you a name?"

"Yes. He said I was an 'American whore.' He frightened me. But *that* made me mad!"

The woman suppressed a smile.

"Yes. I could see that you were mad. And I saw what the boy was doing. He will not return. They know you were not trying to escape. No one will bother you from now on as long as you are here. I have seen to that."

Jessica crouched down on the edge of her cot. She was still quivering. The woman with the kind face moved closer and placed a hand on Jessica's head. Jessica leaned forward, releasing a surge of emotion, as she buried her face in the folds of the woman's *châdor* and wept uncontrollably. Then the woman did something that Jessica had not experienced in weeks.

She put her arms around her and gently rocked her back and forth.

12

WEDNESDAY, 19 OCTOBER, LOCAL TIME 0900
BAYTOWN, CALIFORNIA

The morning sun seemed almost apologetic as it caressed the few remaining flowers that had survived the heat of summer. John cleared away the fruit bowls and coffee cups from the table. He returned to find that Esther had moved away from the patio table and into the sunlight, letting its warmth cut the cool edge that lingered in the morning air.

"Feel like going for a walk?" John asked, smiling.

Esther nodded, releasing a deep sigh.

"We don't have to, if you don't feel up to it."

"It's okay. I want to walk," she said, stretching out first one leg and then the other. "I need to walk. All this lying around and being waited on hand and foot has got to end sometime. I'm getting lazy."

"The day you can be classified as lazy, we'll both check into the old folks home," John responded, taking her hand as they walked through the garden gate. They made their way along the side of the house and onto the sidewalk.

"If we live that long."

Esther's words were pensive. At another time, they would have laughed and joked about getting older, about hot flashes and memory lapses just around the corner, about John's graying hair above his ears. Then, Esther would break into a run, calling back over her shoulder, "Come on, old man, let's see if you can keep up!"

But not today.

Today, they walked slowly, staring off into the distance. A car drove past, windows open, radio booming unintelligible noise from a hip-hop station.

"Think that guy is hard of hearing?"

John watched the car slow for a stop sign then speed around the corner and disappear.

"If not now, soon," Esther replied.

John's hand pressed against Esther's, palm flat, fingers touching, but not intertwining. They had touched like this for years. Not always. Sometimes they held hands like ordinary people. But now and then they would walk like this, letting the palms of their hands feel the slight movement of the other. A sensual feeling. A message to each other in a crowd.

You are not holding me.

Nor I you.

You can leave if you want.

I know.

But you won't, will you?

No. I am here with you by choice. And you?

Yes, here by choice.

Esther looked over at John and smiled. They continued walking in silence for several minutes.

"Last night was wonderful," John broke the silence. "Thank you."

Esther hesitated for a moment, then said, "No. Thank you."

More silence.

"It's been a long time, hasn't it," she continued, finally.

John felt her hand move and her fingers intertwine with his.

"It's been a hard time," John answered. "For both of us."

They walked along Creston Field, a small neighborhood park with slides and tables and benches, designed for young families.

"Can we sit down for a few minutes, John? I need to rest."

"Sure. Would you like for me to get the car? You shouldn't overdo it."

"No. I don't need the car. I just need to rest . . . and to talk."

They walked across the grassy field to a picnic table and sat down on the wooden bench. Esther touched the scar from the bullet wound along the side of her head. Early on, it had been the most dreadful looking of her injuries. Now, it was well on its way to healing, though a scar was sure to remain. She was letting her hair grow and styling it to cover almost all of the mark.

"Does it hurt?"

"Not so much."

John watched as she moved her hand away, brushing an imaginary fleck of something from her denim skirt. Then, she folded her hands together in her lap.

When she looked up at him, he wondered what was coming. Her face was a mask of sadness. He started to reach for her, to reassure her that somehow everything was going to be all right. Somehow . . .

She held up a hand and he stopped short.

"I don't know exactly how to begin this, John. Actually, I'm so terribly embarrassed and ashamed, it is hard to put it into words, especially to you." She paused and looked away across the field of grass. Then her gaze returned to John. "I did something while you were gone. I know Jeremy hasn't told you anything, because I asked him not to. Believe me, I wish I didn't have to tell you this, but . . . well, we've never had any secrets before, and I can't start living with them now."

John did not move, paralyzed with anticipation of what might be coming. He already understood by Esther's tone of voice and pale face that the news would be serious.

She looked down and swallowed, her fingers nervously twisting the corner of her shirttail. When she looked up again, her eyes were rimmed with tears. But her voice was steady.

"I tried to kill myself."

Her words hit him with the force of an explosion. And a flood of memories burst across his mind as though a dike had broken. The heartrending wail when the fireman confirmed that Jenny was dead. The endless blank stares as Esther sat by her favorite window. The look in her eyes last month when they had said good-bye at the airport.

"Please, John," she was crying softly now. "Don't hate me. I need you not to hate me. It wasn't your fault."

John closed his eyes tightly, stunned by what he was hearing. When he opened them again, she was still sitting in front of him, head bowed, shoulders drooped, tears falling freely onto clenched hands that continued twisting the ends of her shirttail into tight little triangles—a little girl caught doing something very bad.

"I'm sorry," she said simply. "I'm so very sorry."

"Oh, dear God," John whispered in shocked disbelief, "what have I done?"

He folded Esther into his arms, pulling her off the bench and down onto the grass. They clutched each other tightly, losing track of time, huddled together in the warm autumn sun. John brushed away her tears and then his own. He listened while Esther retold her story of inner pain and the overwhelming depression that had followed. They spoke softly to each other, words of comfort and healing and forgiveness.

And gradually, a wonderful thing took place. For the first time in a long time, John felt himself begin to relax. It was so noticeable that he was physically conscious of the change coming over him. With Esther's head against his chest, he listened to how Jeremy had taken John's role of healer in his absence and how God had used even the awful events at church to bring Esther back from the edge. Still, John felt incredible sadness as Esther tried to explain how her thoughts of Jenny had jumbled with feelings for the one female terrorist.

Then it was John's turn to talk. He implored Esther for forgiveness for not being there emotionally and spiritually for her in her time of trial. He could see now how he'd been an unwitting contributor to her despair. How could he have missed it? All the signs had been there. Yet, immersed in his own grief over Jenny's death, his broken relationship with Jeremy, and his decision to resign as Calvary Church's pastor, he had failed to help Esther. He spoke of his continuing feelings of guilt over Jessica's disappearance. As John had assured Esther that Jenny's drowning was not her fault, so Esther spoke gentle words of comfort and forgiveness to John.

You could not have known.

You did what you thought was best for her.

This whole thing is unimaginable.

We can't go on blaming ourselves for what has happened, can we?

Where is God in all of this?

Just before lunchtime, they rose from the lawn and slowly retraced their steps homeward. Near the entrance to the park they moved aside as two women approached on a late morning stroll. John and Esther were so intent on each other, so lost in their thoughts, they didn't return the greeting that was offered as they passed.

—m—

It was nearly four-thirty when Esther reached over to turn the nightstand clock so she could read it. She smiled at John, absorbed in the warmth of his gaze. It was the most satisfying look of love she could remember. This had been an unforgettable day. Desire and devotion had merged as she and John had searched for each other in a multilayered healing of emotions, in the unimpeded restoration of passion. Esther could not remember having felt like this before.

She relished the blissful feeling.

When was the last time they had done something like this?

Their afternoon together had left her feeling beautiful and whole, as if at long last the two of them were truly one again, not just in name, but in every respect. She knew it now with such certainty. This was not like first love. It was better, so much better. And the feeling she had toward God seemed fresh and new and somehow different. In the mysterious and wondrous expression of human love, her soul had touched the divine heart as well.

"What?" John smiled questioningly, looking at Esther's glowing face.

"Nothing," she replied.

Then, laughing, she kissed the tip of his nose. "Nothing, my dearest darling. And everything."

She rested her head against his chest, listening to his heartbeat and feeling her own at the same time.

Contentment.

When was the last time we did something like this?

As she pondered the question, a smile came to her lips.

I can't remember the last time—but I do remember one *time.*

One October afternoon, thirteen years ago.

The day they had created a child named Jessica.

PART THREE

Terrorism appeals as a weapon of the weak; a way to assert identity and command attention; and as a way to achieve a new future order by willfully wrecking the present.

—John Arquilla, David Ronfeldt, Michele Zanini,
Countering the New Terrorism (Santa Monica, Calif.: Rand, 1999)

Seize them and slay them wherever you find them: and in any case take no friends or helpers from their ranks.

—The Qurʾan
Surah 4: Nisa:89

Listen to my cry for help.

—The Holy Bible
Psalm 5:2

13

WEDNESDAY, 19 OCTOBER, LOCAL TIME 1605
CHARLES DE GAULLE AIRPORT, PARIS, FRANCE

An old man shuffled slowly across the concourse, stopping every so often to catch his breath and lean on his cane. Eventually, he reached a telephone, where he waited patiently for a young man to finish setting up a date. As near as the old man could tell from the one-sided conversation, the woman on the other end of the line was giving the young man a deadline.

Hanging up the receiver, the young caller bolted away from the phone, brushing past the older man in an obvious hurry to get on with his plans for the evening. The old gentleman watched him go for a few seconds before stepping up to the phone. He hooked his cane over the edge of a metal tray that held a very thick telephone directory, reached into his pocket and retrieved a folded piece of paper on which a series of numbers had been hastily scrawled. Taking the phone receiver in hand, he listened, dialed the number, inserted the appropriate coins, and waited.

"*Bonne après-midi,*" a male voice answered at the other end. "Good afternoon."

"*La nuit est somber,*" said the old man. "The night is dark."

"*Le soleil ne brille pas dans le nuit,*" came the cryptic reply. "The sun does not shine at night."

"*Seule le croissant de la lune peut allumé notre chemin.* Only the crescent can light our path."

"*Ça c'est certaine, Gloire á Allah.* This is certain, Allah be praised!"

"We are booked on Aeroflot, tomorrow, at 0930 hours. I have the tickets with me."

"Do you know for certain that they can provide us with a sufficient amount of what we need?"

"Yes. The first shipment has already gone. It went a month ago. They expect payment for the final purchase when we meet tomorrow evening. You are ready?"

"Of course."

"Good. I will join you in front of the passport control at 0800. Listen for the name *Contaviani*. And bring your long underwear. Where we are going, it will be cold."

"I will be there."

Without saying good-bye, the old man hung up the phone and started shuffling toward the beltway.

14

SATURDAY, 22 OCTOBER, LOCAL TIME 1735
AMMAN, JORDAN

"Why?"

The woman with the kind face did not smile and said nothing.

"Do you know why they brought me here? What is happening? Where is my father and the rest of the people from our church? It has been over a month. If you know, you should tell me." Jessica's voice wavered a little, though she tried very hard to sound grown up.

"Do you have any idea at all?" the woman countered at last. "Have you not overheard the men speaking?"

Jessica shook her head as she sat down on the edge of her cot.

"I don't even know where I am. I know there must be a city outside, but where? Are we in Jerusalem? No one will tell me anything. Please, I deserve that much at least, don't I?"

The woman was silent for a moment. Then she turned and knocked for the door to be opened.

"I will return shortly, child, with your dinner."

The guard poked his head around the doorjamb and grinned at Jessica. As quickly as his face appeared, it was gone and the door closed. Jessica threw herself down on the cot, overwhelmed with feelings of despair.

She stared at the boarded window, the bare walls, the door. Everything felt hopeless. All she wanted was to get out of this place and find her father and go home. Then everything would be all right.

Where is he? Has something happened to him? Did they take him prisoner, too?

The totality of her isolation was closing in on her.

So was the reality of emotional and physical exhaustion.

Her eyes closed and she fell into a restless sleep.

—~—

At the sound of movement at the door, Jessica opened her eyes and watched as the woman entered, carrying a food tray. The guard reached around and closed the door behind her.

Jessica wasn't hungry. She rolled onto her side, facing the wall.

"Eat, child."

Jessica didn't move. She lay staring at the cracked, dirty stucco, an ache building in her stomach as she hovered near the breaking point of total desolation.

"Jessica."

Jessica ignored her.

"Jessica, I have something for you."

Jessica rolled slowly onto her other side and looked at the woman. She withdrew something from beneath her *châdor*.

Curious, Jessica pushed herself up on one elbow.

The woman held a finger to her lips, with a knowing glance at the door as she handed her the folded paper.

Jessica threw her feet over the edge of the cot and sat up, unfolding what appeared to be a piece of torn newsprint. She let out a cry of surprise at what she saw.

"Shh," the woman whispered anxiously. "You must be quiet."

Jessica looked up into her eyes, back at the paper, then up again. She was awestruck. It was a news article torn from the front page of an English-language edition of the *International Herald*, a newspaper she remembered her father purchasing each morning at the newsstand in their hotels. With the article was a picture of her father, shaking hands with another man that she did not recognize.

Her hands began to quiver.

"It's my father," Jessica exclaimed excitedly, looking up at the woman.

"Read it quickly, child. If we are discovered, it will not go well for either of us."

"Oh, please, let me keep this."

"No. It is too dangerous."

"But you can't take it from me," Jessica pleaded, clutching the paper to her chest. "It's about my father. I'll hide it. I promise."

The woman hesitated, gazing sympathetically at Jessica.

"Put it under your mattress when you are done. Fold it tightly and place it here." She lifted the edge of the thin mattress, near where Jessica would lay her head. "If they come for you, do not carry this on your person. Do you understand?"

Jessica didn't really, but she nodded.

"Are they taking me somewhere?"

Again, she saw the woman hesitate.

"Soon," she answered finally. "I'm not sure when. But soon, you will leave this place."

Jessica felt a twinge of apprehension.

"Where are they going to take me? Are they releasing me? Are they taking me to my father?" She glanced down at his picture.

"No, you are not going to your father. I'm not sure where you will be taken. All that I know for certain is that it will be far away from here."

"Why? What have I done?"

"You have done nothing, child. But your father has done something. The leaders of Hamas, the Islamic Jihad, and al-Qaeda are powerful men. And they are very unhappy with what your father has done. The story is there. Put it away now and eat. You can read it after I have gone. But you must be careful. Do not let the guards see you with this. Understand? You will take great care, Jessica?"

"Yes, I will. *Ana mamnoon*. Is that not the way I say, 'I am grateful'?"

The woman stared at her, then smiled nervously and nodded. "How do you know this?"

"I have nothing to do but listen. And sometimes I ask one of the guards how to say things in your language."

The woman said nothing but her eyes never left Jessica's.

"This is dangerous for you, isn't it?" Jessica asked. "I mean, bringing me this newspaper story."

The woman remained silent, but looked down.

Jessica carefully folded the precious paper and slipped it under her mattress. Her appetite was gone, but she forced herself to eat. She knew that the woman would not leave until she was done. She nibbled at the roasted chicken and picked her way through a side dish of raw onion, chilies, and olives. Finally, she pushed the tray back.

"*Shokran*," she said, in a loud voice.

The woman smiled briefly at Jessica's attempt to express thanks in Arabic. "*Afwan*," she replied, and reached for the tray. As she did, Jessica's hand moved to the place on the mattress just above the hidden newspaper. The woman did not miss the significance of the gesture. Their eyes met for a long moment.

"*Shokran*," Jessica said again, this time whispering softly, "*Ana mamnoon*." She *was* grateful, more than words in any language could express. Her eyes brimmed with tears.

A look of concern flashed briefly across the woman's face. She started to say something, appeared to think better of it, then turned and walked to the door. Without looking back, she knocked. The door opened and she disappeared into the hallway.

15

22 October, local time 2315

The sound startled Jessica from her sleep. She clutched the blanket around her shoulders and scrunched herself into a ball as a light from the hall cut a path through the open doorway and into the darkness of her cell. She lifted her head slightly and made out at least two shadowy human silhouettes. One reached for the pull chain on the bare lightbulb hanging from the ceiling. Now more light filled the room, dispelling shadows. She was right. There were two of them. Squinting, she recognized the one. It was the same man she had observed the woman speaking to in the hallway following her attack by the young guard. The other man was a stranger.

To her relief, the woman entered the room behind the men, and stood by the door.

"Get up," ordered the man she had seen before.

"What do you want?"

"Get up!" The man started toward her and Jessica scrambled out from under the blanket. The floor felt cold to her bare feet.

"What do you want?" Jessica asked again, mustering up as much defiance in her voice as she could. "Where are you taking me?"

"Shut up," the man growled.

"I want to . . ." Jessica stopped in midsentence as she caught a glimpse of the syringe in the man's hand. She shrank back onto the cot. "Please, no more of that stuff. I'll be quiet."

The woman passed in front of the man and wrapped a woolen jacket around Jessica's shoulders. She turned to the man and spoke to him in English, for Jessica's benefit.

"The last time she was given a shot like that, she almost died. Our instructions are to keep her alive until she can be delivered to Marwan Dosha. I will instruct her that she must behave—or we will give her the shot. She will obey. I am certain."

The man hesitated, looking over at Jessica, and then responded to the woman in Arabic with what seemed to be a question. She nodded quickly and turned to Jessica, who was by this time standing on top of the cot, all the way back against the wall.

Delivered to Marwan Dosha. I don't know where that is.

"Child." The woman's voice was stern, but the look in her eyes was one of concern. "If you do not wish to be put to sleep, you must promise to be absolutely quiet. Will you do this?"

Jessica nodded silently, never taking her eyes off the syringe.

"You must do exactly as you are told."

She looked over at the woman and nodded again.

"Your life depends on your obedience, Jessica. This is not a game. Do you understand?"

"I understand," she answered. She started to ask a question, but stopped short.

"Do you want something?" the woman asked.

Jessica nodded.

"What is it? Speak up."

Jessica glanced nervously at the man with the syringe.

"May I go to the toilet before we leave?"

"Of course. But hurry."

The man with the syringe turned and walked over where his partner was standing by the door. The two men began talking to each other in Arabic, for the moment paying no attention to Jessica. She slipped her hand under the mattress and withdrew the telltale news story. The woman started, her hand moving involuntarily to her lips as she observed what Jessica was doing. In an instant, the paper was hidden inside the sleeve of her woolen jacket.

Slipping into her socks and shoes, Jessica walked past the men and down the hallway, turned on the light and closed the door. Reluctantly, she pulled the crumpled newsprint out from her sleeve.

There it was. The familiar face of her father. His smile. The story of his heroism. She had gazed at the picture for hours since she had received it, and had reread the story at least a dozen times.

She stifled a sob.

I love you, Daddy.

Tears splashed down onto the picture.

I love you so very much!

Everyone she loved was gone. And now, this too.

A last look.

Jessica brought the photo to her lips and kissed the inked imprint of her father's face. For a brief moment she hesitated, then crumpled the paper and dropped it into the water.

Her hand pulled the flush chain.

She watched to be sure it disappeared.

Wiping at her eyes, she opened the door, turned out the light, and walked to where her captors stood waiting.

—∾—

Twenty minutes later, Jessica sat in the open back of a truck, shivering from apprehension and the early morning chill.

She was relieved to see the woman climb in beside her.

Moments ago, coming out of the building, the feeling of fresh, cool air on her face had been indescribable. According to the last tally on her wall-scratch calendar, she had been held prisoner in that room for over a month. She had forgotten how good a breeze could feel. The outdoors gave her a sense of freedom, even though she knew that she was far from free. The night air seemed to breathe new hope and courage into her. She glanced around quickly at her surroundings.

Empty tables.

I knew it sounded like a marketplace.

Lights in the distance.

It's a city of some kind. I need to remember to watch for signs. Maybe they will tell me where I am.

A tower across the alley.

That must be the mosque.

The truck was a single-seat affair, green, its sides caked with mud. It looked a little like a Jeep. The carrying space behind the cab was covered with canvas across the top and open at the sides. She guessed it would be about the size of a small pickup truck back home in California.

Home.

California!

How long had it been since she admitted thoughts of home into her mind? The overwhelming depression that followed them was so painful that she had begun to shut out her former life. All at once this morning, they were back with hurricane force, threatening to sweep her away on a riverbed of dreams and longings that were altogether too painful to think about.

As Jessica waited, huddled in the truck bed beside the woman, one of the men carried a cardboard box around to the back and dropped it inside. The box flaps were open and she was able to catch a glimpse of the contents: packages of potato chips, crackers, and bottles of water. From the rounded shape of one item wrapped in butcher paper, she guessed it to be cheese.

At least they don't intend for us to starve.

"Here, girl, put this on." The man handed Jessica a dark, wrinkled pile of cloth.

Jessica looked at the woman, inquiringly.

"It is a *châdor*, Jessica. You need a black one where we are going. Here, I will help you."

"Where *are* we going?" asked Jessica. "I heard you say *Marwan Dosha*, but I don't know where that is."

The man looked startled for a moment, but when he understood Jessica's confusion, he simply shook his head.

"Hurry up and put it on," he ordered impatiently, standing by the driver's door. "And don't try to attract attention or get away."

Jessica slipped into the *châdor* and sat down on the floor of the truck next to the woman. The woman sat with her legs crossed, as if sitting in front of a campfire. Jessica, watching her every move carefully, followed suit. The man leaned over the edge and looked at them. Grunting his satisfaction, he spoke to the woman.

"Sultana."

She looked at him steadily.

"You must keep an eye on the girl," he said in English.

The woman nodded.

"And you, Jessica Cain, had better behave." The man's voice was low and threatening. "I am leaving you unfettered. But if you try anything, I will put you back in the box. Is that understood?"

Jessica nodded, conjuring up memories of the dreaded box. But her mind was also racing in an opposite direction.

Sultana. Had the man called her by name, or was this just another Arabic word? Sultana!

As Jessica absorbed the significance of this unexpected revelation, which had eluded her all these weeks, the two men climbed into the cab and started the motor. Soon they were bouncing along the poorly paved streets, heading toward the lights at the center of the city.

After a few minutes, Jessica decided to test her new knowledge.

"Do you know where we are going, Sultana?"

The woman glared at her, obviously displeased that Jessica had picked up on her name. After a moment's hesitation, she answered.

"We are at the western edge of Amman. We are going through the city and into the desert."

"Where is Amman? Am I still in Israel?"

"No. You are in Jordan, but not for long."

"Where are we going?

"Be quiet. It does not matter. Soon enough you will find out."

Jessica tried to control the fear. Her stomach felt like a caldron on fire.

"Do you have the paper?"

What paper?

For the moment, Jessica had forgotten about it. Then she remembered.

"No."

"Where is it?"

"I threw it away."

"Where did you throw it? Will anyone find it?"

"No. I flushed it down the toilet."

It was one of those moments that come about unexpectedly.

Sultana's gaze seemed to slip past Jessica's eyes and into her heart. The silence that followed between them was disturbed only by the sounds of the city and of the truck as it rolled through Amman's dimly lit streets.

Jessica was the first to look away, her spirits lifting when she saw a familiar red and white sign—a reminder of another world.

Kentucky Fried Chicken.

Sultana looked at Jessica and smiled.

"Yes, we have them here, too," she said.

They turned left onto Sulleman an-Nabulsi Street, the truck jerking forward as the driver gunned the motor, grinding his way through the gears. After a while, Jessica noticed an impressive-looking building off to the left.

Sultana saw her staring as they passed by.

"It is the *qasr,* the palace," she volunteered, motioning with her hand. "It reaches back to the early eighth century, though no one seems to be able to say for certain what its function was."

The truck banged its way through another huge pothole, jarring the two women, who had only a folded blanket between them and the metal flooring.

"Look over there." Sultana pointed off in the distance. Jessica noticed fencing, cranes, and rubble, outlined in the shadowy combination of moonlight and streetlight. "That is the temple to Hercules. You have heard of him?"

Jessica shook her head.

"A group from the United States has worked to restore it to its former glory. They will have spent over $600,000, U.S., to restore a portion of it. The ancient columns and parts of the temple walls that are standing date from the reign of the Roman emperor Marcus Aurelius, in the second century."

"You know a lot about things," Jessica said, taking in the sweeping views of the theater and the center of town. There were countless backyards, some draped with last night's wash and others full of rubble and debris. "Are you a teacher? A guide?"

Sultana blinked, but did not answer.

After a while, the lights of the city faded into the distance, becoming an ethereal glow along the skyline. The truck was headed east now, and the stony desert plain opened in anticipation of swallowing up the three Jordanians and their young prisoner.

During what seemed an endless night, while the sky was still dark and dotted with stars, Jessica noticed that traffic was increasing. They began passing huge trucks that were rolling along the desert highway. Most vehicles seemed to be going in the same direction as their truck.

"Where are all these trucks headed?" Jessica asked, thinking that an answer might give her some further idea of where she was going. To her surprise, Sultana answered.

"Most are going from Aqaba to Iraq."

"Aqaba? What is that?"

"It is our seaport, in the south. Initially, it was thought you might be sent there. Eventually, however, the desert route was chosen. The trucks you see are part of a major supply effort, ever since the first Gulf War. An embargo was levied against Iraq, but people there must continue their lives. Families must eat and heat their homes. Most of their supplies have come through this backdoor route. Since the second Iraqi war, the supply line continues and is augmented now by supplies entering through the Gulf—from Great Britain and the United States, mostly, but other countries, too."

"Is that where we're going? Iraq?" asked Jessica. Hope and fear began to mingle in her heart. There were Americans in Iraq, but also fighting and unrest. She chose to place her hopes on the positive possibilities.

Maybe they intend to turn me over to the Americans that are there helping rebuild the country. Maybe they just want to get rid of me and let me go home.

16

SATURDAY, 22 OCTOBER, LOCAL TIME 2345
MOSCOW, RUSSIA

This late in October, most of the leaves had already fallen from the trees lining the city streets. Their stark branches intertwined along deserted sidewalks in a suburban neighborhood of run-down row houses. The night sky was clear, the air crisp and cold, as a solitary automobile slowly rounded the corner and coasted to a stop in the darkness just beyond the streetlight. The headlights were turned off, but the driver left the motor running, the exhaust curling upward in wispy, cloudlike patterns behind the car.

About a hundred feet farther down on the opposite side of the street, Marwan Dosha and his companion, François Genet, had been waiting long enough to become uncomfortably cold. It was impossible to tell how many passengers were inside the other vehicle. The two stayed put as one minute passed, then two, scanning the surrounding area for a sign of trouble, anything that was where it should not be. For the past fifteen minutes, everything had been quiet. It remained so now. Nothing seemed out of place.

"Okay," said Dosha, opening the passenger-side door, "watch. Keep me covered."

Genet opened the driver's side door and got out, resting one arm on the top of the open door. In his other hand he held a 9mm PM Makarov pistol far enough above the door frame so that the other car's occupants could see it. Dosha took a few steps around to the front of the automobile, then stopped and waited.

The dark-colored car pulled away from the curb and moved forward slowly. Its headlights were still darkened as it drew alongside. The left side windows, front and back, rolled down simultaneously, revealing the driver and three additional passengers. Dosha walked over and bent down to look inside.

"You have the money?" the nearest rear-seat passenger peered at Dosha as he spoke, his English heavy with a thick Russian accent.

"Have you completed arrangements for the shipment?" Dosha replied, his face impassive.

The front-seat passenger emerged from the other side and came around the back of the car, waving his hand slightly as he passed through the exhaust fumes and walked toward Dosha. This man was obviously not Russian. His features were distinctly Arabic. "I have confirmed with my own eyes, Marwan. The shipment is on the way."

The two men smiled as they greeted one another in traditional Middle Eastern fashion.

"*Marhaba*, Wafa."

"*Marhaba*, Marwan. *Keef halek?*"

"I am fine. It is good to see you again, Wafa. It has been a long time."

"Indeed. Too long, my friend."

"There is no chance of there being any problem with the shipment?"

"I assure you, there is none.

"It is going by rail?"

"Yes. Just as we agreed last month. We acquired three surplus tankers and prepared them. Three tractors for these tanker trucks have been leased by our people in Canada. We also managed to get a sufficient amount of boron nitride. It is a hard crystalline ceramic and can be formed into shapes by pressing powder and sintering."

"What is its purpose?"

"They have been shaped into tiny rings to prevent nuclear criticality reactions by absorbing neutrons."

"I still do not understand," said Dosha as he fumbled for a cigarette.

"Each one of these rings is a small glass pipe about the length of your thumb. There are thousands of them and they cost us a good deal more than the tankers, I might add. We poured these glass pipes into each tanker unit. Over time, they absorb neutrons and become radioactive. Their purpose is to enhance the shelf life of our product so that it does not deteriorate before we are ready to use it. Without them, it is also possible to accidentally start a chain reaction. It would be like dropping a bouncing ball onto a floor covered with fifty thousand mousetraps. There would be mousetraps snapping everywhere. Only, instead of mousetraps we would have a big, blue flash."

"An explosion?"

"Not an explosion, a fatal flash of nuclear energy that would kill everything and everyone nearby in a few hours."

"If such a thing were to happen, would it be seen?"

"If there was nothing to obstruct your view," Wafa answered with a grin. He was obviously enjoying this. "If there was, say, a concrete wall in between you and the flash, then you would not see it. The wall would not stop it from killing you, however. And the plutonium would remain every bit as deadly after the flash as before. It would be useless for our purposes, however."

Dosha's hands were getting cold. He rubbed them together briskly, noting that Wafa was taking pleasure in his moment of professional triumph as a terrorist with an unusual set of skills. Staring at the exhaust vapor rising from the car, he listened as Wafa continued.

"There is a modified PUREX process that produces significant amounts of plutonium nitrate solutions. My scientist friends here have worked with that process at Complex 300 in Majak. I doubt you have been there?"

Dosha shook his head.

"Few outsiders ever have. It has always been one of Russia's closed towns, quite a ways southeast from here. It is close to Lake Karatsay, but you wouldn't want to spend your summer vacation there. They have dumped liquid radioactive waste into that lake for years, and it is still one of the most radioactively polluted areas in the world. For sure, if we need more of this stuff, there is plenty to go around. Over the last several weeks, our friends here were able to shunt approximately two thousand curies of the plutonium isotope 239Pu into each of the three tankers. That's six thousand curies altogether, my friend. Believe me, it is more than enough to do the job."

"Are you certain it will arrive safely?" asked Dosha, growing impatient to be on his way. He glanced around to be sure they were still alone on the street.

"No problem. The three tankers have been placed on railcars and leave early this morning. Their route takes them north to Severodvinsk and then to then to Murmansk where they will be loaded aboard a ship. From there it is in the hands of others."

"One thing. Tell me, how can you be certain it will not be discovered along the way?"

"We poured a layer of diesel fuel on top of the plutonium. This is like oil and water; it does not mix. Officially, each tanker is carrying five thousand gallons of an experimental bio-diesel fuel, derived from a crop that grows well in cold climates. It is to be tested on American semi-trucks and locomotives that must pull loads up steep grades. The shipment is designated to go to a Union Pacific locomotive fueling depot at Sparks, Nevada. Once it is inside the United States, we can take it wherever we want, to await the target date.

"They would have to use a Geiger counter or some such detection device before having any chance at discovering the plutonium. It is highly unlikely that they will be so thorough. Even since our great September 11 victory, Allah be praised, only about 2 percent of all cargo entering a port city is really checked. We will ship through Canada, then cross into the U.S. by truck. Relax, my friend. It will succeed."

"You have done well," Dosha replied, patting the man's shoulder. "And your friends in the car?"

"These scientists are too honest to betray us." Wafa chuckled at his little joke, winking at Dosha. "Or too stupid. And they are sufficiently afraid for their own welfare. They will not be a liability to us. They just want to get rich and get out."

Dosha turned to the car's other occupants, while reaching inside his coat.

"Gentlemen, I thank you for your help," he said, handing the nearest rear-seat passenger an envelope. "Inside is the number to your new bank account in Zurich and a receipt. The agreed upon amount has been deposited according to the instructions that you gave to us. You have received verification, I am sure. Yes?"

The man nodded.

"Then you are three very rich men. It is what you wished?"

The man did not smile or look directly at Dosha as he took the envelope. He opened it quickly, glanced inside, and then nodded.

"We are done here, Wafa," said Dosha, patting his friend on the shoulder. "I have some news that will sweeten things even more, I think. We have unexpectedly come into possession of yet another item that should help us break the resolve of our enemies. If you will join me for the ride back to the hotel, I will tell you about it."

"I will be delighted." He turned to the three Russian scientists. "It has been a pleasure doing business, gentlemen. *Schastlivo. Do svidaniya.*"

None of the Russians said a word. Nor did they look happy as their car pulled away. With the economy in the tank, the Cold War ended, and their skills no longer in such demand, these $50-a-month professionals had just sold their souls, and perhaps the lives of countless thousands. The only question remaining was whether two million dollars each would be enough to assuage their consciences for placing in the hands of known international terrorists six thousand curies of deadly plutonium nitrate.

17

SUNDAY, 23 OCTOBER, LOCAL TIME 0645
MURMANSK, RUSSIA

A gray jungle of booms, masts, antennas, and cold steel hulls fringed by icy waters lay exposed by an early dawn that pushed against the stubborn darkness. Ships were lined up on either side of an aging, rusty freighter, each awaiting its turn under the loading crane.

Around the *Grodno,* a rancid potpourri of smells—oil, dead shellfish, escaping steam, and rubbish—hovered in the cold air as dock workers toiled over a random patchwork of cables and hoses strewn across the wooden planks. Tractors rumbled past one another, their drivers hunkered against the stiff northerly wind. Bells clanged in the distance as the last of the cargo was lowered into the ship's hold.

From inside the ship, over a radiophone, the crewman in charge of cargo placement instructed the crane operator to shift the load farther to the right.

". . . a little more . . . there. Now, down one more meter. Good. It is done."

Cable hooks were released and the crane swung slowly away from the ship, leaving its last deposit directly in front of the ship's side hatch. The crewman glanced down at the manifest in his hand and nodded. Five hundred cases of Red Star beer.

A short distance away, workers were tying down the last of three scrap tankers, in preparation for the long voyage. According to the manifest documents, each was loaded with high-tech diesel fuel.

18

SUNDAY, 23 OCTOBER, LOCAL TIME 0645
AZRAQ, JORDAN

A little over 100 kilometers east of Amman, the wide shallow valley of the Wadi Sirhan stretched southward toward Saudi Arabia. In previous centuries a major caravan route, today, it lay shrouded in silent desolation, traveled only by memories of past glories.

The sun was beginning to rise on the jumble of shabby buildings that make up the tired, little oasis community of Azraq. The lifelong desert dwellers of Azraq were beginning to stir and make preparations for facing the inevitable heat of another day. To a truckload of travelers passing through the night before, its small town streets seemed to be in a never-ending process of being dug up to make way for new roads in front of the dreary buildings and cracked sidewalks.

Early rays of light crept across the landscape, like fingers feeling for signs of the only water source in this barren region of the eastern desert. At one time, Azraq's early morning skies had been filled with birds migrating between Africa and Europe. But no longer. Also gone were the water buffalo, bear, deer, cheetah, ibex, and gazelle that once lifted their heads to greet the dawn.

During the past several decades, large pumps had sucked water from nearby wells to supply city dwellers in Amman. Lush swampland had been reduced to an oasis that was little more than a muddy pond. Most days, the sun seemed bent on vaporizing every last vestige of life from this desert. The birds now flew over, without stopping to rest, on their way to the Sea of Galilee in Israel. The sounds of their flight drew a few upward glances, followed by a collective sigh of human resignation.

Still, there was hope.

Workers could be seen leaving their modest homes and making their way to the nearby Shaumari Wildlife Reserve, as they had most days for the past thirty years, carrying out the nation's belated attempt to reintroduce wildlife that had all but vanished. These men were the vanguard of the future; the heroes of hope for a land in its death throes.

In the center of it all stood the massive, Qasr al-Azraq, lifting its stolid, impassive face to the sun. The present structure had been built out of black basalt in the thirteenth century, but inscriptions in Greek and Latin identified earlier construction on the site dating as far back as AD 300. Some of the castle's original three stories lay in crumbled stone heaps, shaken loose by an earthquake in 1927, remaining as a mute testimony to both the unrelenting will of the desert and the unwillingness of man to succumb to its power.

As the sun broke over the horizon, the castle's elderly caretaker put a cigarette between his lips and reached for a match. This was his turf, his charge for as long as anyone could remember. Some locals swore he was older than the castle itself. There might not be many visitors today, but Majid ibn Asim intended for those who did come to have a memorable experience. As on every other day, he would regale them with his stories of Lawrence of Arabia, the same stories he had heard from his father, who had, in fact, been one of Lawrence's Arab officers.

As he approached the old castle, he was surprised to see a green truck parked nearby, caked with mud and dirt. It was unusual for any vehicle to be out this early in the morning, and it aroused his curiosity. He stopped a few feet away and called out.

"*Sabah al-khayr.*"

From inside the truck, he heard someone stirring. A man poked his head through the driver's side window. "*Sabaah an-noor.* Where are you from?"

"Amman," the driver replied, stretching, as he opened the door and stepped out. He rubbed sleep from his eyes and squinted into the rising sun, then back at the old man. "We arrived too late last night to get rooms at a hotel. Who are you?"

"I am Majid, the guide here at Qasr al-Azraq. I was surprised to see your truck, as I do not normally find people here ahead of me."

Another man stepped down from the passenger side of the vehicle and walked a few paces away, lighting a cigarette.

Hearing movement in the back of the truck, Majid glanced in that direction in time to see a woman's face come into view. As she adjusted her veil, it was obvious that she, too, had been sleeping. Then a second face appeared, this one much younger. Both women were dressed in traditional dark *châdors*, and only the eyes, nose, and upper part of the older woman's mouth could be seen. Although the younger one's head was covered, her face was entirely visible.

Just a girl, barely come of age, thought Majid. He ignored the woman and smiled at the child.

She did not return his smile, but neither did she look away.

"Ahlan wa sahlan. Kayf haalik? Hello. How are you?" Majid asked the young girl. It was not the usual custom for an Arab man to speak so casually to a young woman without first being introduced. But Majid was old enough to be the girl's grandfather, though he had never married. He was used to talking to children in his line of work.

The girl's gaze was steady, but she said nothing in reply.

The driver gave a curt order to the older woman, who in turn spoke softly in the young girl's ear. Majid could not hear what was being said, but the child slowly disappeared below the side of the truck—never taking her eyes off the old man until she was gone from view.

Strange, Majid thought.

"We must be on our way," the driver announced. "Can you recommend a place to eat that has good food, but where it is not expensive?"

"The Al-Zoubi Hotel is the best for you. About one kilometer south of the old junction road on the way to Saudi. You are going in that direction?"

"Aiwa. Shokran jazeelan. Yes. Thank you very much."

"Afwan. You are welcome."

The two men stepped up into the vehicle and the older woman settled down in the back. Majid watched as they turned the truck around and headed away from the castle.

Strange. Very strange indeed. If they intended to cross the border this morning, why did they stop here instead of getting into line last night? And that young girl. . . . What was different? Something. Why did she not smile when I spoke to her? Was she just shy? Perhaps I am losing my touch with young girls.

Majid's face broke into a broad grin, revealing several missing teeth.

He walked to the southern door of the castle, a single massive slab of basalt. Later today, someone was certain to pass by here and he would tell them how Lawrence declared that this very door "went shut with a clang and a crash that made tremble the west wall of the castle." Majid loved quoting that historic line.

He continued toward the small mosque, located in the middle of the courtyard, thinking how much he truly loved this place. All at once, he stopped, scratching his beard as he stared at the mosque.

That's it! That's what was different.

He started toward the storerooms, opposite the entrance.

The girl's face. Her skin was so much fairer than the woman's.

He paused.

No. That's still not it. There was something else.

Majid turned and stared thoughtfully out through the castle entrance and out into the empty desert.

And then it came to him

It was her eyes. Her eyes were green. Like emeralds!

19

The number of trucks and cars lining the road at the border crossing was moderate today, but there was still a considerable backup. The drivers had come prepared. Each truck had a well-stocked food box attached to the side, complete with teapot and gas stove. The men came together in groups of three or four, making a brew and telling road stories while sitting out the wait.

Sultana and Jessica remained in the back of the truck under the canvas. Already, the early morning coolness was giving way to what promised to be an onslaught of desert heat. Earlier, while they stopped at a cluster of *falafel* and *shawarma* stands near the Al-Zoubi Hotel, one of the men had purchased additional food for the journey ahead. Some of these supplies had been passed back to the women, the rest placed in a small bag under the seat in front. Jessica ate quietly, surprised at how hungry she was and that the food tasted as good as it did.

By now, she had become familiar with *falafel,* a Jordanian staple served at breakfast, lunch, or dinner. This morning, it was filled with deep-fried balls of chickpea paste, mixed with spices and wrapped in pieces of *khobz,* an unleavened bread. The operator of the *falafel* stand had inserted a few pickled vegetables and tomatoes as well. Jessica washed down the simple fare with bottled water stored in the cardboard box next to Sultana. The water was not cold, but it was clean, and Jessica drank deeply.

Don't let yourself get dehydrated, sweetheart.

She had made a habit of rehearsing her father's words each time she placed a bottle of water to her lips. It was comforting, somehow. It would have been hard for Jessica to describe, but there came a feeling of belonging whenever she did it. She did not belong here. Not here in this truck. Not with these men. Not in this godforsaken place.

She belonged at home with her mother and father, with Jeremy and her friends at church and school.

Staring over the side of the truck, she thought once again of how unbelievable her situation was.

What am I doing here anyway? How can this possibly be happening to me? What do you suppose Mom and Daddy are doing to get me back? I'll bet they're sad. They miss Jenny so much. Mother has never been the same since she died. And now they've lost me too. But what can they do? I'm sure they don't know where I am, or even if I'm alive. I don't even know where I am.

I wonder if Jeremy will be on the starting team again this season. I hope so. I should be there to see him play. It's his last year. I'll bet Amy and Shawna are at school. No, wait. It's probably nighttime where they are. I wonder if they'll still be my best friends when I get back? Maybe they've already found someone to take my place. School has been going for two months now. My first year in junior high. I've missed so much, I'll never catch up. But then, it may not matter. I may never get back anyway.

Jessica reached up and brushed a tear from her check.

"What's wrong, child?" asked Sultana.

Jessica said nothing.

"Is the food not to your liking?"

"The food's okay."

"Then why are you crying?"

"I'm not crying," Jessica replied sharply. "Just leave me alone."

Sultana sat quietly, watching Jessica. A few feet away the two men crouched, drinking hot tea and making conversation with three truck drivers whose vehicles were parked in front of theirs.

"Perhaps you are homesick?"

Jessica looked at Sultana. Her lip quivered as she tried to steel her emotions against the unexpected power of those four words.

"I'm not homesick," Jessica retorted, biting her lip. "I . . . I'm . . ."

Words failed, but the tears came all too easily.

Sultana reached over and took Jessica's hand.

"I'm sorry, child."

Jessica didn't move for a long minute. Then she dropped the remaining piece of *falafel* on the floor of the truck bed and buried her face in the folds of Sultana's *châdor*. Her shoulders heaved with uncontrolled, heavy sobs. Sultana put her arms around her and drew Jessica against her breast.

Hearing something, the driver looked over at the truck. He stood up, drink in hand, to get a better view. Taking a few steps closer, he saw the girl huddled in Sultana's embrace. He could easily hear her sobbing. Sultana looked across at him and shook her head. *No need to come closer. Leave us alone.* He turned back to the circle of drivers, squatted once more on the ground, and resumed his conversation.

Nearly two hours later, the green truck and its four passengers passed through the border crossing. First, on the Jordanian side, and again at the entry checkpoint into Saudi Arabia. Vehicle registration, driver's licenses, passports. Everything was in order. Nothing out of the ordinary.

The fact that the registration papers, passports, even the vehicle's license plates were forged or stolen escaped the scrutiny of the disinterested border guards. The two men heaved a sigh of relief as they headed out into the vast open desert, on the road to Riyadh. All that money for false documents had paid off.

20

For the next two days, the exhausted quartet traversed the Arabian desert, making their way through a land the likes of which Jessica had never dreamed existed.

For the most part it remained flat and uninteresting. At other times, huge sand dunes welled up like golden waves of water, seemingly ready to swallow up their tiny, desert ship. The vastness of the terrain grew monotonous, however, and before long she was staring listlessly at a stretch of hard, rocky earth, wishing it would all go away.

Will it never end?

The daylight hours were unbearably hot. The temperature soared mercilessly, and all four travelers consumed water in large quantities. The men periodically stopped the truck and walked a few steps away to relieve themselves.

The first time they stopped, Sultana motioned to Jessica and climbed out of the truck. Jessica followed after her as Sultana walked away from the men to the opposite side of the truck and proceeded to relieve herself. At first, Jessica stood there, appalled, casting embarrassed glances toward the truck and the men just beyond. Then, necessity overcame her reluctance and she did what she had to do. At least the *châdor* preserved a modicum of modesty.

Jessica lost track of time long before they stopped at a gasoline station. As they pulled in, she sighed with relief. *A real restroom!* A small boy and his sister followed her around the corner of the shabby, sand-colored building. They waited, curious, smiling shyly at her. Jessica looked at the hole in the ground and the surrounding filth, and promptly decided that the desert was without a doubt the lesser of two evils.

When Jessica returned, Sultana handed her a warm soft drink with a straw sticking out of the glass bottle.

"Use the straw, child," admonished Sultana, when she saw that Jessica had removed it.

She looked at Sultana questioningly.

"It is clean," she said simply.

Jessica put the straw back in the bottle, at the same time wondering how long these bottles had been sitting out in those wooden crates.

Don't let yourself get dehydrated, sweetheart.

As they continued on, Jessica could feel the others slipping into the rhythm of the desert. The quietness. The loneliness. The stark landscape. The effort required for survival. It appeared to be so natural for her grown-up captors. She wished that she could say the same. Still, she had to admit that being out of her dreary cell in Amman was an improvement.

And as evening approached, the desert sky gave way to the most spectacular sunset that Jessica had ever seen.

Thank you, God! I needed a reminder of your presence.

They drove well into the night with the headlights out, making their way by the brightness of the moon. The nights were the total opposite of the days, so cool that Jessica shivered in her *châdor*. She pulled the blanket up around her chin and huddled against Sultana for warmth. A bond of sorts was forming between them, but Jessica sensed that it was important to resist it, not to give in completely. Still, she needed somebody.

I wonder how old she is? Probably about Mom's age. How old is that? Was it last year or the year before that Daddy had friends over for her fortieth birthday?

Jessica tried to sleep, but the desert stars left her wide-eyed with wonder. The first night out, as she lay staring up at the sky, her mother's face appeared. Jessica imagined watching her run a brush through her long hair, over and over. A hundred strokes, she always said. Her eyes were radiant, dancing with merriment, and she tossed her head the same way each time. She was the most beautiful person in the world. At least she had been before Jenny died. After that, she always seemed to be . . . somewhere else.

She used to look at me. Even into me. Now she just looks past me.

The memory became mixed with anxiety over what might be happening with her parents back home. She knew lots of kids whose parents were divorced. It was hard to imagine this happening to her mother and father, but the unspoken possibility had worried her for some time. All the signs were there.

Jessica trailed the moon across the velvet darkness, its cold light illuminating her dark despair.

Tonight she was empty. Abandoned by everyone and everything she knew. Numb with repressed fear about the home she might never see again, about wherever in the world she was right now, about what might happen to her. . . .

She pressed her body closer to Sultana and drifted off to sleep.

21

During the second day, it was easy for her to guess the direction they were traveling by watching the sun's position as it inched its way across the heavens. Sometimes east, but mostly south, she estimated. Not that knowing this would do her any good. Jessica didn't have a clue where she was headed, but that fact was as much a blessing as a curse. Somehow, it permitted her mind to remain free. She couldn't really explain it. But where could she possibly run? She tried to remember the maps in her geography class at school. Recalling the days her class spent studying the events of the Iraqi War gave her some perspective, albeit a hazy one. But one thing she knew: There was no place to run. Not here. Not yet, anyway.

East of Jordan. Okay. Just keep your eyes and ears open, Jessica. And pray.

We must be in Saudi Arabia. Iraq is somewhere around, but I would have known if we had gone there. Wouldn't I? Wouldn't there be American soldiers there? No, I don't think we're going to Iraq. The only thing I'm sure of is that home is west, and we're traveling east. That means I'm farther away from home today than I was yesterday.

Jessica occasionally observed a large pipeline and periodic clusters of oil derricks. These were familiar sights to her from California's central and southern oil-producing areas. Only here they were multiplied, many times as many as she had ever seen. She pictured the Standard Oil refinery, only twenty or so miles from her house, and visualized the huge oil tankers that plied San Francisco Bay. Had they been transporting oil from these fields that surrounded her here?

Jessica dozed off and on, physical exhaustion merging with the heat and the ceaseless movement of the green truck as they cruised across the sea of sand.

Late in the afternoon of the second day, they arrived at yet another border crossing. This one, too, was clogged with vehicles of various kinds, but they moved along more rapidly than last time. Jessica checked the road signs, but they all seemed to be in Arabic. Looking away from the signs, she quickly sat up straight and stared out over the edge of the truck.

Water!

As they drew closer, she became convinced that this was no mirage. Nor was it simply a pond or lake. It was larger. Much larger.

Maybe it's the ocean.

Sultana had not awakened at the border checkpoint. She looked as exhausted as Jessica felt. Soon they were driving along a stretch of well-kept roadway, within continuous eyesight of the beach and the shimmering water just beyond. The sun was almost directly behind them now.

We must still be headed east.

The sunlight was brilliant on the water, forcing Jessica to look away every once in a while. Still, she was drawn back to its contrasting beauty as the shore scenes rushed by. After a few miles, she could see that they were entering a city, larger than anything she had seen since Amman. People were strolling along the beach, looking very much the way people did back home. There were paved streets. Office buildings. Hotels. Restaurants. Civilization.

A Sheraton! Hey, that's an American hotel. There's one in San Francisco. And we stayed in one of those on our vacation. . . .

The truck slowed down as Jessica continued peering over the edge.

If I could get to the Sheraton, they would help me.

Her body, stiff and sore from the day's journey, tensed as she saw a traffic signal ahead. She might never be closer to freedom than this.

Yellow . . . yellow . . . red. Yes!

She glanced over at Sultana.

Still sleeping.

Go for it!

As the truck rolled to a stop, Jessica made her move. Instinctively, like an animal discovering an open gate, she scrambled over the side, dropped down onto the street, and began running.

She stumbled, regained her balance and dodged between two cars.

A horn blared.

Then another.

The door of the green truck flew open.

She had reached the sidewalk by the time the man shouted.

She heard racing footsteps behind her.

Another horn was sounding.

Run, Jessica! Run for your life!

PART FOUR

These youths love death as you love life. They inherit dignity, pride, courage, generosity, truthfulness, and sacrifice from father to father. They are most steadfast at war.

—Osama bin Laden's second fatwa, February 1997

And kill them wherever you find them, and drive them out from whence they drove you out, and persecution is severer than slaughter, and do not fight with them at the Sacred Mosque until they fight with you in it, but if they do fight you, then slay them; such is the recompense of the unbelievers.

—The Qur'an
Surah 2: Baqara:191

The name of the LORD is a strong tower;
the righteous run to it and are safe.

—The Holy Bible
Proverbs 18:10

22

TUESDAY, 25 OCTOBER, LOCAL TIME 1735
SHARJAH, UNITED ARAB EMIRATES

Syd Hershey spotted the Sheraton just three blocks ahead. His pulse quickened at the thought of a cool shower and a warm evening out by the pool. It was the beginning of a four-day holiday away from Kuwait's oil fields.

Syd was from Texas. The first time he had come to Kuwait, he had signed up to fight the terrible fires set by Iraqi raiders during the Gulf war. He had been here almost a year that time before returning home. Then, when the bottom dropped out of the Texas economy again, he had returned to Kuwait.

It was good money. He'd told his wife, Helen, that he would be in and out before she knew it. But the promise of a raise if he stayed a while longer convinced him to extend his contract. Room and board was included. The countryside was so remote that there was no place to spend what he was making, which was more than twice what he could make back home, even when the economy was favorable. It would be worth it to stick around. Only he hadn't counted on the boredom factor. No amount of videos and books could make up for it. Now, he was counting the days until his contract was up and he could get out.

Ever since coming over, Syd had heard about the United Arab Emirates. It had quite a reputation among his working buddies, and what he'd heard sounded pretty good right now. He'd heard all the stories about high-priced European call girls, who were flown into the Emirates on a regular basis and readily available to anyone with money enough to buy their services. It had been a long time since he and Helen had been together. A very long time. So Syd had decided to visit the Emirates and see for himself.

When it came to the morality of his holiday plan, Syd was more of a pragmatist than a theologian. Religion had really never fit into his thinking all that much. However, one could never avoid being confronted by the effects of religion in this part of the world, and he was often amused at its contradictions. How, for example, could this sort of behavior be tolerated in the middle of some of Islam's strictest cultures? The whole thing seemed to him at best a dualistic, chauvinist morality, a kind of religious parenthesis that provided a socially acceptable moral gap for the male sexual appetite.

Still, while it seemed there was little, if anything, that kept Muslim men from dalliances with non-Muslim women, it was crucial to a foreigner's well-being to avoid taking similar liberties with a Muslim woman. At the very least, it could result in deportation. The end result could also be far worse.

Thus, it was a familiar sight in the city of Sharjah to see Western workers prowling the hotel district, looking for liaisons with European prostitutes.

Let the infidels lie with their own kind, and not with our Muslim women. That was the code, and Syd intended to abide by it during his four-day holiday.

The waters of the Persian Gulf were off to the left as he scanned the boulevard through the open side window of his pickup truck. The street was modern and well kept, as were the surrounding buildings. He was within constant view of the beach now, with the sun directly behind him, and a dirty, green truck just ahead. In the back of the truck, there were two women clothed in dark *châdors*. One looked as if she was sleeping, her head slumped forward, chin against her chest. The other one looked like a scared rabbit, her head shifting from side to side, as if looking for a way out of a cage.

The truck was slowing now as it neared the intersection.

The light turned yellow . . . then red.

The "rabbit" glanced furtively at the woman who was sleeping.

Suddenly, as the truck rolled to a stop, she leaped over the side, dropped onto the street, and began running.

Syd slammed on the brakes to avoid hitting her.

The woman stumbled, reaching out a hand out to brace herself against the front of his pickup. He saw her face clearly for an instant as she regained her balance and dodged between his pickup and the next car.

She's young—and white as a sheet!

A horn blared.

Then another.

The door of the green truck flew open.

A man jumped out and chased after the woman.

As Syd watched the strange scene unfolding in front of him, the part of the *châdor* covering the woman's head fell away, letting her hair drop free as she ran. It was long and light chestnut in color, its reddish highlights flashing in the sun. Syd caught his breath.

It's just like Helen's. Same color. Same length.

A sharp wave of guilt overwhelmed him.

The woman reached the sidewalk. The man was shouting for her to stop, calling out in English.

English? That's strange.

Another step and he had her. His hand flashed in the sunlight and Syd flinched as the man hit the woman hard on the back of her head, sending her sprawling onto the sidewalk. He bent down and grabbed her by her hair, yanking her to her feet again. Twisting her around, he headed back toward the green truck, dragging her by the arm. Syd got a good look at her as she passed in front of his pickup. His eyes grew wide at what he saw. It was not a woman at all. It was a young girl, and she was fair-skinned, her features more European than Arabic.

The guy must have knocked her senseless when he hit her. Now, that makes me mad! And everyone just sits around and lets him do it. If we were back home . . . in Texas. . . .

A symphony of horns sounded as the light turned green.

The man was standing by the truck now, glaring at the woman in the back, who was crouched on her knees, gripping the side of the vehicle with both hands. He said something to her that Syd couldn't hear. Then he pushed the girl inside the cab and climbed in behind her. The light turned yellow again, and then red, just as the truck roared through the intersection and disappeared down the street.

Syd waited for the light to turn green and then continued on toward the Sheraton. His mind was no longer on high-priced European women. He couldn't shake the image of the young girl and the man who had hit her. And the fact that nobody seemed to care.

What kind of a world is this anyway?

Minutes later, he was inside the hotel, leaning against the registration desk, watching as the clerk checked him in. He fingered his blue-covered passport.

The good old U S of A!

A dull ache had begun pressing directly between his eyes.

She was there in his mind.

The young girl with the fair skin and the long, chestnut-colored hair.

Helen's hair.

23

LOCAL TIME 1840

The ceiling was white.

The room was large—at least it seemed so from her vantage point.

Her head throbbed. Her left cheek and jaw were especially tender. She remembered the man twisting her around and seeing his fist above his head . . . coming down at her. Thankfully, that was all she remembered.

She turned her head, ever so slowly. A large picture window filled her view. Outside she could see blue sky.

Nice room. Looks like a nice view.

It was nicer than anything she had seen since being taken captive.

How did I get here? We were in the street. I was running . . . then he hit me . . . He must have carried me back. . . .

She tried to sit up.

With the motion, a rope noose around her neck began to tighten, choking her. She tried reaching for it, only to discover that her wrists were bound by another rope running underneath her body. She could not raise them higher than her waist. She tried moving her feet. They were tied to the foot of the bed.

"Please . . . help me," she gasped.

Sultana was on her feet, reaching for Jessica, when one of the men pushed her back.

"Let her alone!" he snapped in Arabic.

He walked over to the bed and watched as Jessica struggled to get her breath. Reaching into his pocket, he pulled out a cigarette and casually lit it, blowing the smoke toward Jessica. He watched as her face began turning a dark red.

"Help her!" Sultana was on her feet again. "Amal, that's enough!"

The man watched a moment longer, then reached down and indifferently loosened the noose.

Jessica coughed repeatedly as she gasped for air.

"How do you like that, Jessica Cain?" The man spoke to her in heavily accented English. His voice, at first far away, seemed to come closer with each word.

Jessica tried to respond, but broke into spasms of coughing again. She twisted forward as she coughed, causing the rope to choke her once more. This time, the man moved quickly to loosen the knot.

"Do not move, girl!" the man said roughly. "If you move, the noose will tighten. It will not release itself when you stop. It will remain tight. The more you move, the tighter it gets. Unless someone releases it, you will choke to death. Is that clear?"

"Yes," she whispered, forcing herself to settle back onto the bed.

She was utterly helpless. She felt it, and it was clearly what he wanted her to feel. But there was more. Despondency and fear had controlled her emotions and actions for the past seven weeks. Now something else was stirring deep within her. Something terrible and dangerous. She felt it, but didn't understand it. It was completely out of character, a secret darkness she had never known.

The man leaned over, breathing another cloud of smoke in her face. "What you did out there on the street was stupid. You're lucky we did not kill you on the spot."

Jessica turned away, but even that slight movement caused the rope to tighten again. Feelings of desperation threatened to overwhelm her. She wanted to scream or cry out, but something held her back.

And then she snapped.

From deep down beneath the layers of despair, fear, and anger, the darkness broke to the surface. Jessica's eyes blazed with hatred and her voice was a throaty snarl.

"You are a . . . a . . . an animal!"

She spit out the words, her entire body quivering as it had many times before. Only this time, it was not fear that caused her to tremble. It was indignation, fueled by the fires of an intense, out-of-control rage. Jessica was as astonished as anyone at the outburst.

The man slapped her face with his open hand.

"You're not a man. Not like my father. You're a pig!"

Jessica screamed out her anger, incapable of holding back.

Things she had never said before.

Not on a dare.

Not to spite anyone.

Not ever.

Until now.

The second blow hit her with enough force to cause her neck to pop as her head twisted sideways. Her upper body lifted off the bed, just for an instant, but it was long enough to draw the noose tight again, choking off her air. She fell back, but it was too late. The man was angry now. He hit the opposite side of her face with his other hand and stepped closer to hit her again.

As she saw the man bending over her, Jessica spit what little saliva she had left directly into his face.

He flinched as the spittle found its mark.

Jessica saw his fist double. She clenched her eyes shut, tensing to receive the blow she knew was coming.

She heard an angry shout and opened her eyes in time to see the driver wrapping his arms around the other man, dragging him back out of her line of vision. Sultana was at her side a second later, loosening the rope around her neck. Jessica fell back, gasping for breath, exhausted from the physical violence and the aftermath of the emotional volcano that had so unexpectedly erupted from within her.

Now everyone seemed to be yelling at once. Jessica tried to settle her frayed nerves and stop shaking. She didn't care anymore. She couldn't understand them anyway. One new fact burned its way into her memory, though. As she lay, panting for breath, she now knew a second name in her trio of abductors.

Amal. The man who hit me. His name is Amal.

The two men and Sultana continued to argue for several minutes. Finally, Amal turned away without a word and walked out of the room, slamming the door behind him.

The other man went over to the window and gazed silently out toward the sea, where sailboats danced across the water, pushed along by a warm evening breeze.

24

WEDNESDAY, 26 OCTOBER, LOCAL TIME 0730

Syd woke up the next morning alone in his seventh-floor room. The rising sun was streaming through the window as he stepped into the shower. A half hour later, dressed for the day, he locked the door behind him and walked along the hallway to the elevator.

The gift shop was on his left as he stepped out of the elevator. There was a stack of *International Heralds* on the floor by the door. Syd was not really a great one for reading, but it had literally been weeks since he had taken time to look through a newspaper, so he picked one up anyway, paid the clerk, and folded it under his arm as he walked across the lobby toward the restaurant.

The maître d' smiled and led Syd to a table by a window overlooking a large, freshwater pool. Already, a few hotel guests were settling down at poolside. Three young children splashed in the water, reminding Syd of his two kids in their younger days.

Now, Josie's married and Dan is off to college, generating the last of the big bills that climax the child-rearing experience. All the more reason for me being over here, I guess.

Syd sat for a moment, appreciating the ambiance of the place. The high windows overlooking the pool, with a view out toward the sea. The attractively displayed breakfast buffet. There was even a tablecloth. How long had it been since he had been served on a tablecloth? He smiled contentedly.

This is nice. I think I'm going to enjoy this place.

He dropped the newspaper onto the tabletop, pushed back his chair, and sauntered over to the buffet.

Toast. Cereal. Hard-boiled eggs. Some scrambled eggs. Cucumbers and fresh tomatoes. Yuck. Is that yogurt?

After filling his plate, he returned to the table, arriving at the same time as the waiter, who held a carafe of coffee.

"It's fresh, sir."

"Good. And I'd also like cream, thank you," Syd said as he sat down.

He broke open a hard-boiled egg, added a dash of salt and pepper, and relished the first bite.

Picking up the *Herald*, he scanned the first page.

Arafat in Jerusalem despite the breakdown in talks . . . Two suicide bombers killed fifteen and injured dozens more . . . the president meeting with Britain's prime minister . . .

"Same old same old," Syd snorted in disgust. "That's why I don't bother reading the newspapers . . ."

He pushed the remainder of the egg into his mouth and turned the page.

What the—!

He stared in amazement at the picture on page three. It was the girl from yesterday.

That's her! That's the one that jumped out of the truck yesterday—and got whacked for her trouble.

Syd's eyes quickly shifted to the caption: "Twelve-year-old Jessica Cain has not been seen since 18 September when she was kidnapped from a resort hotel in Ein Bokek, Israel." He read the accompanying story about the Reverend John Cain's daughter, who had been missing now for over a month. Cain was the pastor from California who had thwarted a terrorist attack in Israel in September. Syd had heard the story but had quickly forgotten it.

He ran his fingers over the printed image of the girl's features, still finding it hard to believe what he was seeing.

It's her, all right. I got a good look and I'll never forget that face. It's the same girl. She was right there in front of me!

Hurriedly, he read the rest of the story, which was datelined Azraq, Jordan. An elderly Jordanian caretaker at the Qasr al-Azraq had reported seeing a young girl answering the description of the missing Jessica Cain. The guide, a man named Majid ibn Asim, indicated that it had been the girl's fair skin and green eyes that had caused him to be suspicious. As it happened, he had been following the story on local Jordanian television. Authorities believe that she may have been taken into Saudi Arabia. They were last seen traveling in a green truck, outfitted for desert travel.

Fair skin. I couldn't see her eyes, but she did have fair skin. And, it was a green truck, too. It was her!

By now, Syd had forgotten about his breakfast. He had also forgotten his reason for being in Sharjah in the first place. Excitedly, he scooped up the paper and rushed out of the restaurant to the registration desk.

"May I help you, sir?"

"Yes. How do I dial 9-1-1 in this country?"

"Sir?"

"I need to speak to the local police!"

"Is there something wrong, sir?" asked the young lady behind the counter, a look of concern crossing over her face.

"Yes, there is. There certainly is. Now, hurry, please."

26 OCTOBER
DEPARTMENT OF STATE

SENSITIVE

SHARJAH, UNITED ARAB EMIRATES. INFORMATION RE MISSING CHILD. NAME: JESSICA CAIN, AMERICAN CITIZEN, MISSING IN ISRAEL SINCE 18 SEPTEMBER, BELIEVED TO BE POSSIBLE TERRORIST KIDNAP VICTIM.

SOURCE: MR. SYDNEY HERSHEY, US CITIZEN, AGE 47, OIL WORKER.

INFORMATION QUALITY: GOOD.

26 OCTOBER, MR. HERSHEY REPORTED SEEING YOUNG, FAIR-SKINNED FEMALE JUMP FROM THE BACK OF A TRUCK AT AN INTERSECTION NEAR THE SHERATON HOTEL IN SHARJAH, UAE, THE PREVIOUS EVENING, 25 OCTOBER. DESCRIPTION MATCHES THAT OF JESSICA CAIN. GIRL WAS PURSUED AND CAUGHT BY THE DRIVER OF THE TRUCK, WHO STRUCK HER AND DRAGGED HER BACK TO THE VEHICLE. SUBSEQUENT DIRECTION AND DESTINATION OF GREEN TRUCK UNKNOWN.

MR. HERSHEY MADE POSITIVE ID OF JESSICA CAIN FROM PHOTO IN INTERNATIONAL HERALD, 26 OCTOBER.

INTERPOL, CIA, AND MOSSAD HAVE BEEN NOTIFIED.

25

WEDNESDAY, 26 OCTOBER, LOCAL TIME 1025
BAYTOWN, CALIFORNIA

As soon as the last of the groceries were put away, Esther reached for the telephone. While at the store, she had decided to call John as soon as she got home. Earlier, she had sensed his depression as he was leaving for the church office.

I'll just see how he's doing. Maybe we could sneak away later for an early dinner at Hunter's. I can see if they'll give us a table in the back corner where no one will bother us. It's one of John's favorite places.

Picking up the receiver, she heard the familiar *beep-beep,* indicating that messages were in the voicemail box. Hesitating for a second, Esther tapped in the numbers that opened the box. There were times when she hated this task, but it did avoid a lot of otherwise missed messages.

The automated voice said, "You have one new message . . ."

Oh, good. Only one.

Esther pressed the number to replay messages and prepared to jot the information down on a notepad.

". . . received today at 9:23," declared the familiar recorded female voice. The next voice was that of a man with a deep southern drawl.

"I'm calling for the Reverend or Mrs. Cain. It's about 12:25 here in Washington, D.C. Please return this call as soon as possible to Charles Rodeway at . . ."

Esther continued listening as she scribbled down the name and number as fast as she could. "We have some information we'd like to discuss with you. Good day."

Esther's heart skipped a beat. She stood staring at the receiver in her hand, then at the freshly written note.

Information? It's Jessica. It's got to be!

Esther listened for the dial tone, then tapped in the direct dial number to John's office.

"Hello. This is Grace speaking. How may I help you?"

"Hi, Grace. Is John there?"

"Oh, hello, Esther. No, he's not. How are you?"

"I'm fine—but I need to talk with John." Esther knew there was an impatient edge to her voice, but she didn't bother trying to cover it up.

"He's with the staff right now. Would you like for me to buzz him?"

"Yes, please. And hurry, Grace. I need to speak to him right away."

"I'll get him, Esther. It'll just be a moment."

Esther did not normally like to bother John when he was counseling or with the staff. On the other hand, he had always made certain that Esther and the children knew they could call him, even if it interrupted something important. It was one of the ways he tried to compensate for the long hours and numerous evenings spent away from the family.

"Hi, hon," John's voice greeted her.

"John, there was a message on the telephone when I got home from the store. It's from a Charles Rodeway."

"The name doesn't ring a bell. Are we supposed to know him?"

"He's calling from Washington, D.C."

Silence.

"Did he leave a number?" John's voice had taken on a cautious tone.

"Yes, he did. He called just over an hour ago." Esther repeated the area code and phone number.

"Okay. I've got it."

Esther hesitated.

"Honey, are you all right?" asked John.

"I'm . . . okay. But would you come home, please? Let's make the call here together." The apprehension was clearly evident in her voice. "I . . . I don't want to be alone right now."

"I'm on my way."

26

In under fifteen minutes, John walked through the front door. Without a word, he took Esther in his arms. They held each other tightly. She pressed her face against his chest.

"How are you doing?"

"I'm okay. No, that's not true. Actually, I'm frightened. Petrified. Scared to death."

"The message didn't contain any other information?"

"No, nothing. But it wasn't from a secretary. He called directly."

Slowly, they withdrew from each other, their eyes on the telephone.

"Well, okay, let's do it," John said, lifting the receiver. "Get on the extension. Maybe this is good news." He flashed a thin smile at Esther.

Forcing a weak one in return, she hurried into the other room. Moments later the phone was ringing through.

"Charles Rodeway's office. Whom may I say is calling, please?"

"This is John and Esther Cain. We're returning a call received earlier this morning from Mr. Rodeway."

"Thank you, Mr. Cain. One moment."

Her voice was pleasant enough, but John had the feeling they had just stepped into a different world. Was this the State Department? FBI? CIA?

It doesn't really matter, he thought. *There probably isn't that much difference between them all anyway.*

"Hello, Rodeway here," boomed a voice with a southern drawl.

"Hello, Mr. Rodeway. This is John and Esther Cain. We're returning your call."

"Oh yes, thank you for calling back, Reverend Cain. You say your wife is there with you?"

"That's right."

"Good. Well, first of all, let me add my congratulations and admiration to that of the rest of the world for the way you both conducted yourselves last month. You are heroes. Our country—actually the whole world—owes you a debt of gratitude. We're all walking a little taller around here in Washington."

"Thank you, Mr. Rodeway," John responded, a tinge of impatience in his voice. "But I'm sure you had something else on your mind when you called earlier?"

"Right you are, Reverend Cain. Actually, something has turned up. We're not a hundred percent certain as to its validity at this point, but I wanted to let you know. Before I go on, though, would you mind confirming for me again the color of your daughter's eyes?"

"Her eyes are green," John said guardedly, his heart in his throat. "But would you please tell us what it is you're talking about?"

"Certainly. As I'm sure you're aware, we have had hundreds of possible sightings of your daughter reported, ever since she disappeared. These sighting have come from everywhere in the world you can imagine, and we've been able to dismiss most of them as unsubstantiated and probably false. However, in the past two days, we have had two separate reports that have a high probability of being legitimate. The first is from the caretaker of an old castle—a tourist stop—out in the Jordanian desert. He reported seeing a young woman with fair skin—though she was dressed in the traditional Arabic clothing—traveling with two men and a woman. What really caught this man's attention was that the young woman had green eyes. 'Like emeralds,' he said."

Esther gasped. "That's Jessica! She's been seen? Are you saying she's still alive?"

"Well, ma'am, all I can tell you is what the report says. It's a possible sighting, and it's unconfirmed."

"Yes, but you did say 'a high probability of being legitimate,'" John broke in. "Why would you call unless you thought it would be good news?"

"Well, sir, I wanted you to know that we are making some progress in tracking down her whereabouts, but I also must make you aware—if these sightings are indeed legitimate—that your daughter's situation could get very complicated."

"Complicated—what do you mean? What are you saying?" Esther said. "What about the second sighting? You did say there were two. . . ."

"Yes, ma'am. This second one came in earlier this morning. And that's where it gets complicated. Yesterday evening, in the United Arab Emirates, an American oil worker saw a young woman traveling in the back of a truck. Once again it appears it might be your daughter. Could be the same green truck the old caretaker reported. The American noticed her when she jumped out of the truck and tried to run. Unfortunately, she was captured by the driver of the truck and taken away."

John and Esther groaned in unison, and Esther choked back a sob. "Oh, my poor baby. She must be terrified."

Rodeway paused while the Cains gathered their composure. "I'm sorry, folks. I know this has to be very hard."

"It's all right," Esther said. "Go on, please."

"Well, the location of this second sighting, in the United Arab Emirates, raises the question of where they intend to take her. It could be they'll try to get her onboard a ship out of the Persian Gulf, or they could try to slip her across the Strait of Hormuz into Iran. If that happens, I don't think I need to tell you that the situation gets a lot more complicated. I'm sorry to say that Iran is one of the most difficult places on the globe for us to get at."

"And you're certain that this girl that was seen is Jessica?" John asked.

"It's a possibility. We can't be absolutely certain at this point, but I wouldn't be here talking to you if we didn't think that it was likely your daughter."

"Iran," John repeated. "Are you serious? Why Iran?"

"We've known for a long time that the Iranian government is one of the chief financial backers of world terrorism. And one of the groups they love to help sponsor is the Palestinian Islamic Jihad. That's the group that claimed responsibility for all the activities of this past month that you and your family have been involved in. I guess you both know them better than I do at this point."

"But Iran?" Esther echoed. "Why? What would they do with her there?"

"We aren't sure of anything, Mrs. Cain," Rodeway's voice softened a little. "Look, I know how difficult this must be. I have a ten-year-old son. I can only imagine what you folks must be going through."

"If it is her, where in Iran would they take her?" John persisted.

"We don't know. We're just beginning to call in some of our markers on this case now. They've been watching for her in Israel, Jordan, and Egypt. And our military people in Iraq have had a watch out at the borders there. The fact is, she could be anywhere. When we find out anything further, we'll let you know."

"Yes, of course. Thanks very much," John said.

"Yes, thank you, Mr. Rodeway." Esther chimed in. "Good-bye."

John hung up the phone, his mind racing in all directions at once.

Iran. I can't believe it. Dear God. When will all this madness stop?

Esther's steps were slow as she returned to the kitchen.

"She's alive," her voice cracked with emotion as once more they held one another tightly. "I've been trying to keep believing that. But it's been so hard. Oh, darling, it has to be her. Jessica is still alive."

John was silent, lost in a mental scramble.

27

THURSDAY, 27 OCTOBER, LOCAL TIME 0800
SHARJAH, UNITED ARAB EMIRATES

The next morning, Sultana awakened an emotionally exhausted Jessica, untied her, and told her to put on her *châdor.* After a brief and uneventful breakfast—during which no one spoke, Sultana walked over to where Jessica was sitting and picked up a black scarf that was lying on the bed.

"Turn around," she said.

When Jessica complied, Sultana quickly and expertly wrapped the scarf around Jessica's head, deftly tucking and folding to make sure that none of her hair was showing. She left enough fabric at the end to drape across Jessica's face, leaving only her eyes exposed.

When everyone was ready, the driver said something to Sultana. The woman nodded and then grasped Jessica's arm roughly, turning her until their faces were mere inches apart. The look in Sultana's eyes frightened Jessica.

"Listen to me carefully," she said. "We are going for a short walk. If you know what is good for you, you will stay right next to me and say nothing. If you try to run or draw attention to us, these men will kill you on the spot. Do you understand?"

Jessica nodded solemnly, her eyes wide.

Amal and the driver led the way, followed by Sultana and Jessica dressed in their *châdors.* As they left the room and walked down a hallway, Jessica recognized that they were in a hotel. Her heart sank at the realization that all this time she had been close to potential rescuers but unable to call for help.

The green truck, caked with layers of dust on top of mud, was left parked on a side street. The four of them walked down to the corner, turned right, and headed toward the dock. A ferry boat was tied up at the end of the pier, lying quietly on the calm sea. As they approached a small crowd of waiting passengers, Sultana checked again to be certain that Jessica's *châdor* was close around her face, showing none of her hair. For the first time since leaving Amman, the two men were wearing *jalabiyyehs,* the full-length garment often preferred by fundamentalist Muslim men.

A short distance from the group of people waiting to board the vessel, the driver stopped and turned to Jessica, his eyes hard. There was no trace of a smile.

"Do you remember what Sultana told you?"

Jessica nodded.

"If you do anything to draw attention to you or us, I will kill you first. Is that clear?"

Jessica swallowed and nodded.

"I will shoot you in the head with this revolver," he said, pulling a black handgun just far enough out from under the *jalabiyyeh* so that it could be seen. A second later, he produced a short dagger. "Or, I may choose to drive this into you and tear your heart out. Understand?"

"Yes," Jessica answered, her voice strained. She glanced at Sultana, her eyes clearly revealing the terror she was feeling.

"You must do as he says, Jessica," Sultana spoke quietly but firmly. "You have no other choice. Do not try to run as you did yesterday. All right?"

Sultana placed her hands on Jessica's shoulders and stared directly into her eyes.

"You will promise?"

Jessica bit her lip and her shoulders sagged in resignation.

"I promise."

"Good. Stay close beside me. If you must say something, whisper it in my ear. No one can hear you speaking in English."

They continued walking toward the dock. As they drew near, Amal produced tickets and handed them to a man standing at the foot of the gangplank. He took them and waved the four travelers aboard.

At the top of the gangplank, the man whose name Jessica did not know spoke to a passing crew member. "*Momkin tasif li at-tariq daraja awla?* Can you direct me to first class?"

"*Aelæ tul,*" the crew member responded, pointing along the narrow walkway. "Straight ahead."

"*Shokran.*"

A few steps farther, they pushed open a door and entered a small private cabin. Amal immediately went to the solitary round window and pushed it as far open as it would go. If there was air-conditioning on board, which was doubtful, it certainly wasn't working. The room was already sweltering. Sultana motioned for Jessica to sit. A worn seat, designed to accommodate two persons, was attached to each wall. A fold-down table resting on a wobbly chrome leg separated them.

Jessica watched as drops of perspiration formed on the men's faces. The man without a name said something to Sultana, and then both men turned and left the room. The door shut securely behind them.

Sultana and Jessica sat quietly for a while, feeling the throb of the ferry's engines as the boat moved slowly out into the Strait of Hormuz. Finally, Jessica broke the stifling silence.

"Where are we going?"

Sultana remained silent, looking away, toward the porthole.

"Sultana?"

Slowly, she turned and faced Jessica.

"It has been a long journey, hasn't it?" she responded, ignoring Jessica's question. "Would you like something to drink?"

"Yes, please."

Sultana produced two small bottles of water from a cloth bag she had carried on board. She opened one and handed it to Jessica, keeping the other for herself.

"Sultana, I want to know where we are going."

"Will it make any difference to you if you know?"

"How would I know? I'm not even sure where I've been. I think we are somewhere in Arabia or something. Is that true?"

Sultana paused, taking a deep drink of water. Then, with the look of someone about to make a momentous statement, she put the bottle down on the tabletop and folded her hands ceremoniously in her lap.

"For the past two days, we have traveled across Jordan and Saudi Arabia. Yesterday, we came into the United Arab Emirates and stayed in a city called Sharjah. This morning, child, we are in the final stage of our journey. When we have crossed the channel, we will dock in a city called Bandar-é Abbâs."

"Is this in Arabia, too? Or, the United Arab whatevers?" asked Jessica.

"No."

Sultana waited, then went on.

"There is something else," she said. Her face took on a look of sadness that gave Jessica a fresh twinge of apprehension.

"What is it?"

"I will be leaving you today. When we arrive, our orders are to turn you over to the people who will meet us. They are expecting you."

Jessica fell silent. Sultana had become more than an enemy to be overcome. She represented what little safety Jessica had been granted in an otherwise frightening and hostile world. She was the only person in the last seven weeks who had acted toward her with any degree of civility and kindness. Jessica had felt at least some sense of security with her, no matter how tenuous it might actually have been. And now the woman with the kind face was telling her that she would be leaving.

"Who are these people?"

Sultana said nothing.

"Where am I going?"

Sultana looked away for a moment in silence. When her eyes returned to Jessica, there was a hint of regret in her voice.

"We are taking you to Iran."

28

THURSDAY, 27 OCTOBER, LOCAL TIME 0630
BAYTOWN, CALIFORNIA

Early morning light finally overcame the darkness that had tormented John for most of the night. He was wide-eyed as he lay staring up at the ceiling, and had been for hours. Ever since the call from Charles Rodeway, he had been consumed with thoughts of Jessica and Iran. He felt so helpless and so distant. His little girl, on the other side of the world, undergoing who-knows-what kind of hardship and terror, and there was nothing he could do about it. He didn't even want to think about it, but his mind would not stay away.

Then there were his responsibilities at the church. Outwardly, last weekend's services had gone reasonably well, but John knew he had not been at his best. And the thought of having to finish up his sermon for the coming Sunday was almost more than he could bear. The kind of concentration needed for the task was impossible to come by. Jessica was at the forefront of his mind, not any message from God's Word to the people. Normally, he could put distractions aside, no matter how significant they might be. But not this week; especially not after Rodeway's phone call. Try as he might to lay thoughts of Jessica aside, he could not. It was too much to ask.

He rolled over and stretched. As he did, one of the knots in his back cramped sharply. With a groan, he leaped from the bed, placed both hands against the wall, and stretched again, this time to control the pain. As the cramp slowly subsided, he tried to relax.

Esther leaned forward on one elbow.

"Are you all right, hon?"

"Yes. I'm okay. Go back to sleep."

"What happened?"

"Just a cramp. Sorry I woke you. Had to move fast."

"That's all right. Tense, huh?"

"That's an understatement."

"Here. Lie down and let me rub your back."

"No. It'll be okay."

"Lie down. Don't be so stubborn. John, you've been moody all week—even before that phone call yesterday. You're acting like it's still Monday, the day every pastor resigns from his church."

Esther stood and pulled back the covers until only the fitted sheet over the mattress remained. John stretched out on the bed and closed his eyes, again trying to relax. Esther climbed over him and straddled his waist. Her strong fingers began working their magic.

"Goodness, John. Your back has more knots than a Boy Scout rope."

"Tell me. I've been tying those knots all night."

She stopped for a moment and touched his hand.

"Loosen up, sweetheart."

John realized for the first time that his hands were clenched into tight fists. He relaxed his grip and breathed in deeply.

"That's more like it," Esther said.

29

John wasn't sure how long Esther's relaxation program had gone on, but all at once he realized that he was alone.

Must have dozed off.

Ten minutes? An hour? He looked at the digital clock by the bed. *Oh great. It's nearly eight!*

John started to get up, just as Esther came in with a cup of coffee in each hand.

"Here you go," she said brightly. "A little pick-me-up."

Setting the cups on the nightstand, she fluffed the pillows. John sat up and leaned back. Esther settled in across from him in her favorite reading chair.

"So, is it just Jessica, or is it something else?" Esther said.

John stared vacantly across the room, concentrating on an imaginary spot.

"I mean, the services went well enough on Sunday," she continued. "People have left us pretty much alone so far this week. The coffee's your favorite blend. And we're good for each other, aren't we?"

John smiled and turned slightly to include Esther in his line of vision. Her hair fell, uncombed, around her shoulders. The sunlight through the window behind her seemed to greet each tumbling strand with a golden kiss.

"You're beautiful, you know it?"

"Don't change the subject. I know you're as obsessed about Jessica as I am, but is there something else?"

John took another sip, his brow furrowing as the hot liquid burned across his lips and tongue.

"It's everything, I suppose—but Jessica's enough. You're right. I can't get her out of my mind. And Sunday's services *weren't* all that great. I did a lousy job. Every time I tried to focus on the message and the people, there was Jessica. And the last two days at the office have been the pits. We've got some problems that need solving at the school. The bills for repairing the damage from the attack in the sanctuary are in and they're higher than we first thought. The insurance company is reviewing our coverage. They say they're not certain that 'acts of terrorism' are covered by our policy. The board is anxious about security now, with all this publicity, and rightly so. And me? All I can think about is the last time I saw her at Ein Bokek."

Esther put her cup on the lamp table by the chair. "Darling, look at me."

John raised his head and looked her straight in the eye.

"I'm fully aware of how careful you've been, John, ever since you got home, when we're talking about Jessica." Her voice was flat and low. "At first I thought it was because you weren't sure if I could deal with it. That's really not the case, though, is it?"

John didn't answer.

"Is it?" Her voice rose slightly, edged with determination.

John looked down again. It was obvious that the time had come. He knew Esther well enough to know that when she spoke in that tone, nothing but the whole truth would suffice. There would be no getting out of it this time.

He let out a deep breath.

"No, it isn't."

"So what's the problem? Haven't we talked this all through? Just what is it that you are carrying around, John?"

Esther waited, her eyes never leaving him, her coffee cup forgotten completely.

"It's . . . well, . . . it's just that I . . ."

". . . you can't bear to think that she may be undergoing the same sort of treatment that you experienced in Israel?" Esther finished his sentence. "Imprisonment? or worse? You're afraid they might . . . beat her, rape her, or even kill her. That's it, isn't it?"

Esther's words scraped like fingernails on a chalkboard across John's raw emotions. *Rape? Kill? Please don't put those words in the same sentence where Jessica is concerned. But that's what they did to that woman who worked for Jim Brainard, isn't it? So how can we really think that they will treat Jessica any differently? They are evil monsters. What do they want with a little American girl anyway? Is it about what I did in Israel to thwart their plans and prevent them from destroying the Wall?*

When he started to speak, his voice cracked in hoarse response.

"Yes. I am afraid. I'm afraid of all those things." John cleared his throat. "These people are killers, Esther. Fanatic killers. They think they're going to purge the earth of evildoers in the name of Allah. They are certainly not representative of every Muslim in the world, but life doesn't hold the same value for the fanatics as it does for us. They're using Jessica as some kind of pawn. I don't know why. A tiny, helpless pawn in a game that we don't really understand. They've draped it all in politics, but there's more. They've fueled it with hatred and with religious fanaticism. No one understands it, except maybe that Marwan Dosha character."

It was Esther's turn to sit in silence. She moved her toes back and forth, smiling wanly.

"Thanks. I need you to talk to me, John. I know we've discussed this before, but we can't stop talking now. If we do, things begin to build up. The hurts, the anger, the fears—believe me, I live with them every single day, just like you. The same demons that you wrestle with, I'm fighting, too. At times, I don't think I can bear it.

"That's why I need you to keep talking to me. The worst words must be said, at least to each other. We have to own them. They describe the reality of our situation. I know it is even possible that she . . . won't come home." Esther's voice faded into a plaintive whisper. "I know it. And I need to be able to talk about all this to someone. I guess you're elected."

They came together then, wordlessly clinging tightly to each other in an embrace tinged with a fierce desperation.

"We're all we've got right now, along with Jeremy and Jesus," she added tearfully. "So, go take your shower and get dressed. By the time you're finished, breakfast will be ready. Maybe we can continue this conversation then."

John nodded and started for the shower. Just before rounding the corner, he stopped and turned.

"I love you. Do you know that? And I'm sorry."

"Sorry? That you love me?"

"No, of course not." His voice grew husky. "I'm just so sorry that I came home without her."

Before she could respond, he disappeared around the corner.

Esther didn't move. Seconds later, she could hear the water running. Silently, she headed for the kitchen, head down, remembering the guilt she had carried for so long over Jenny's accidental drowning.

Now John is feeling the same over Jessica.

A sharp hurt twisted deep inside her.

Dear God, help us. He's going through the same agony of feeling responsible for Jessica's kidnapping that I have been suffering over Jenny's death. Lord, is there no end to this? I need to help him. But how? What should I do?

Esther reached into the cupboard and pulled out a cereal box, her mind far away from the task of serving breakfast.

What do you suppose is happening to her right now? God, do you know where Jessica is? Sorry. Foolish question. Of course you know. You always know where we are. So, please, Lord, I'm begging you. Let us know, too, so that we can bring her home. Meanwhile, keep her safe until we find her.

A tear dropped onto the counter.

Oh God, please . . . please keep her safe!

30

THURSDAY, 27 OCTOBER, LOCAL TIME 1130
BANDAR-É ABBÂS, IRAN

Standing in the cabin doorway, Sultana stared at the approaching skyline of the busiest port city in Iran, which stretched along a narrow coastal strip looking out on the Straits of Hormuz. Even on this late October day, the sweltering heat and humidity were relentless.

"Why am I being taken to Iran?"

Sultana turned to look at Jessica.

"Isn't that the country that once held a bunch of Americans hostage?" Jessica asked, recalling a lively discussion in her history class last year. She couldn't remember the details, but Iran did not sound like a place in which she wanted to be left alone.

"Please. I need to know why. What you all are doing is not right. I don't deserve to be here. But you know that, don't you?"

Sultana remained silent.

"I don't understand any of this, Sultana. All I want to do is go home!"

"Hush, child. You are not going home. You must stop thinking about home. You'll only make yourself more miserable." Her look was stern now. "If you want to survive, you must be strong."

Jessica stared at Sultana as the words sank in.

"What do you mean? How can you say I'm not going home?"

"Because it is true. Get used to it. You are a hostage. Do you understand what that means?"

"Of course. I'm not stupid. You are holding me here against my will. But surely you can't believe that what you are doing is right."

"It may not seem right. But it's a fact of life. You are a little girl whose father got in the way of an important mission for my people."

"You mean destroying the Wall in Jerusalem? That's your idea of an important mission?"

Sultana looked away.

"I know about the Wall, you know. I read the story about what happened in that newspaper article. My dad did a good thing. He helped save your people from going to war. He saved the lives of my friends back home. He—"

"Be quiet."

"No," Jessica retorted. "I will not be quiet."

Sultana's hand flashed with rapier swiftness, stinging Jessica's face. Jessica flinched at the blow, instantly fighting back tears.

Sultana watched the girl wipe her eyes and saw the set of her jaw. She regretted letting Jessica's defiance upset her and wanted to apologize, but then decided against it. Outside the stifling cabin, the mournful sound of the ship's horn signaled that docking was only minutes away. Soon it would be over and Jessica would vanish like so many others.

—~—

Jessica stood close to Sultana, watching as the other passengers disembarked. The crowds milling about on the dock were a sea of dark-skinned faces. There did not appear to be a single Caucasian anywhere—but Jessica was growing more and more used to that. She could think of no reason why any white person in their right mind would be here anyway. At the moment the thought registered, she caught it. It was the first time she could remember thinking in terms of color where people were concerned.

Back home, I never gave the color of a person's skin a second thought. In fact, I've been taught to treat everybody the same way all my life.

Edgar and Jill Anderson, from church, were two of her favorite people. They were like family. The fact that they were black and she was white had never been an issue. They had always treated her like one of their own grandchildren, and she loved them dearly. Now, however, she was suddenly very conscious of race.

I'm the oddball here. The hated minority. It does make a difference in the way you feel about things when you're the one that feels unaccepted or second class. If I . . . when *I get back, I'm sure going to see others differently than before. First off, I'm going to tell the Andersons just how much I love them!*

Now that the ferry was no longer moving, the oppressive humidity hung even heavier in the air. Wooden docks and vessels of all shapes and sizes lay clustered along the shoreline. Jessica could see low, barren hills behind the city, and Esklelé-yé Shahid Bahonar, the main docking area, could be seen off to the west.

"What is this place called?" asked Jessica.

"Bandar-é Abbâs. *Bandar* means port or harbor. Shah Abbâs founded the town in the seventeenth century."

"How big is it?"

"It is approximately two hundred . . . how do you say it in English?"

"Two hundred? Oh, you mean thousand? or million?"

"Yes. I think about two hundred thousand."

Amal and the other man were back again, standing a few feet away, waiting their turn to walk across the gangplank. Jessica noticed several of the passengers being greeted by waiting relatives, a kiss on both cheeks, hands eager to help with tattered luggage and cardboard suitcases.

Contrary to Sharjah's distinctly modern look, most of the women of Bandar waiting on the dock appeared conspicuously plain and tentlike in their black or dark blue *châdors.* Only two women, among the many who were waiting, wore more conventional long skirts and long-sleeved blouses. All were careful to have their heads covered.

A few of the men wore shirtlike garments in a variety of colors, mostly faded pink, purple, or white, that hung below the knee, over their trousers. The majority, however, were wearing clothes that to Jessica looked like poorly made Western fashions. Several wore jeans.

Even some of the younger girls on the dock were wearing jeans, albeit almost entirely hidden under their *hejab.* Many were barefoot; others wore loose-fitting sandals. Jessica saw no shorts being worn by anyone, and all the men were dressed in long-sleeved shirts done at the wrist, even though the dock area was sweltering in the heat.

Jessica caught herself searching the crowd for her father, even though she was resigned to his not being there. There was always the chance. . . . There *must* always be the chance. . . .

"Come."

Sultana's hand was on her shoulder, propelling her forward as they followed the two men across the gangplank and onto the wooden dock. She flinched as the sound of a nearby ship's horn startled her, looking up just in time to see another ferry moving slowly away from the dock as it headed out to sea.

"Where is that one going?" she asked.

"Jaziré-yé Gheshm," Sultana replied.

"Where's that?"

"It doesn't matter. You're not going there," answered Sultana, her hand pressed against Jessica's back, pushing her forward through the crowd.

31

The line through customs moved fairly quickly, but the sticky heat made it feel like forever. Amal showed passports and the necessary visa permits. Jessica had a strong feeling that the papers were false and she hoped someone would notice and raise questions. But the man in uniform glanced up only briefly, his hand busy stamping an empty page on each passport. Moments later, they were through. He never gave Jessica a second look.

On Jaddé-yé Eskele, they paused while Amal purchased sodas from a street vendor. They were warm, but Jessica took hers appreciatively, drawing deeply on the straw as she drank.

Don't let yourself get dehydrated, sweetheart.

From out of the heavy flow of traffic, a dusty blue van pulled up alongside and stopped. Jessica saw the man without a name hesitate for a moment as he scrutinized the driver. Then, opening the side panel door, he motioned for the others to get in. He shut the panel door and then climbed into the front passenger seat, next to the driver, as the van moved out into the traffic.

"*Salâm,*" said the man without a name.

"*Salâm aleikom. Esmam Sardar-é. Hastam dust-é Massumeh,*" the driver answered. "Peace be upon you. My name is Sardar. I'm a friend of Massumeh."

The driver stepped on the gas as he squeezed the van between one of Bandar's few taxis and a local bus filled with unsmiling commuters. Just as quickly, he pumped the brakes to keep from hitting the rear of yet another bus.

Jessica remembered a television movie she had once seen, in which the heroine kept an eye out for street signs as her captor drove her through a strange city. Later, when the heroine escaped, she was able to call her fiancé and direct him to her location. Jessica watched out the window for signs. Unfortunately, even when she saw one, she could not read the lettering. Thwarted, she tried instead to encapsulate landmarks in her mind. Before long, a forlorn feeling swept over her. It all seemed so hopeless.

She recognized numerous larger-than-life posters of the late Ayatollah Khomeini. It was a face that Jessica remembered from school and from looking through her dad's old *Time* magazines. Heavy eyebrows, glowering face full of deep lines, and a thick beard, all under a turban-style head covering. *What a sinister-looking man! He wasn't much of a happy camper, that's for sure.* There were other faces, too, of other men. She did not recognize them. One was smiling and had a white beard. *Definitely not Santa Claus.*

For the first in a long time, Jessica felt herself start to smile. The smile quickly faded, however, as she turned her attention back to her surroundings. An office building. A mosque. More office buildings. Straight ahead, she saw what looked to be a large fruit market and bazaar.

The van turned left and moments later stopped in front of a building that looked considerably older than the others surrounding it. The drab sign in front read Hotel-é Homâ.

"Come," the man without a name motioned to Jessica and the others. "Move quickly."

They stepped out of the van and walked toward the hotel. Jessica did not turn to look, but she heard the vehicle pull away, merging with the traffic as it continued up the street.

The hotel lobby was relatively empty, giving the impression, whether true or not, that rooms were plentiful and guests were few. Jessica looked around distastefully. It was nothing like the hotels back home. In fact, the worst hotel she had ever been in was a palace compared with this.

This has to be a "no-star" hotel, she thought.

After Amal went to the registration desk and signed them in, they crowded into an antiquated lift and rose to the fourth floor. They exited into a musty-smelling hallway with bare electric lightbulbs dangling loosely over their heads. Amal proceeded to open the door to a room and entered, the others following after him in single file. Here, as in the lobby and the hallways, the paint was flaking and the fixtures looked worn and cheap. Jessica went straight to the lavatory, only to discover that the stool had no seat. Amal fiddled with the air-conditioning controls, but it did not appear as if guests had much control over air circulation.

When Jessica emerged from the lavatory, she walked past the others, who were sitting about talking and drinking lukewarm bottled water. She stared out the window. Across the street and beyond were countless rooftops draped over drab buildings. Farther beyond were the glistening waters they had just traversed. Below the window were a swimming pool and some tennis courts off to one side. It all had a sadly run-down appearance. There was an air of past elegance, but no longer could this establishment be considered a luxury-class facility.

Jessica sat down on a well-worn cloth-covered chair, and waited. She sensed, by the way the others were acting, that this must be the destination site. *But for what?* Tired of the long journey, she was relieved to think that the end was at hand, yet her anxiety level kept building.

What is going to happen next?

"Amal and I are going out for a while," the man without a name said to Sultana in Arabic. "We'll find Massumeh and make the necessary arrangements. When we come back, we'll bring food."

Sultana responded only by wiping perspiration from her forehead with the back of her hand.

"Amal, tie up the girl," the other man ordered.

Amal reached inside the cloth bag he had been carrying and withdrew a roll of tape. Jessica's eyes widened as she realized what he was about to do. Prying the end of the tape from the roll, he moved around behind her, pushed up the cloth of her garment until her arms were exposed, then roughly twisted them backward, wrapping them with the tape.

"Wait," said Sultana, looking at the man without a name. "She needs to bathe. Let her be free to do that. Then I will bind her."

Amal paused, his eyes on the other man. Jessica wished she could understand what they were saying.

"No. You almost lost her in the street yesterday. I cannot trust that you will be able to control her by yourself."

"That was *not* my fault," Sultana protested.

The man ignored her.

"Hurry up, Amal. The sooner we leave, the sooner we get back. We've only been in this miserable place for a few hours, but I am already anxious to leave. Let's do what we have to do and get out of here."

Amal finished taping Jessica's arms from wrist to elbow. He proceeded to twist tape around her ankles. As he bent in front of her, Jessica fought off temptation. She wanted to kick his face but knew she was helpless and that retribution would be swift and brutal. He concluded his task by tearing a final strip of tape and pressing it over her mouth.

Amal smiled at her wickedly. The fear she had battled in past weeks was now back in full force. She wanted to scream. She squeezed her eyes shut while trying to regain control of her surging emotions, swallowing the bile that once more threatened to erupt from her stomach. She opened her eyes when she heard the door close. Sultana was busy locking it behind the men, who had just left.

She turned and gazed at Jessica for a long moment.

"I am sorry, child. I cannot disobey his orders."

Jessica furrowed her brow and made unintelligible sounds as she attempted to plead through the tape.

Sultana stood in the center of the room, rubbing her hands nervously, watching. Finally, she came closer.

"I do not think anyone can hear you, even if you try to cry out. And, believe me, child, even if they could, no one would care. Not in this place. You must promise, however, that you will not cry out if I remove the tape from your mouth."

Jessica nodded her head vigorously.

"You promise?"

Jessica nodded again.

"This may sting."

Jessica felt the woman's finger tug gently at a corner of the tape. Then, with one swift motion, she peeled it away. Jessica flinched.

"Thank you," she exclaimed breathlessly.

"Don't ask me to do any more," said Sultana, her voice low and her countenance dark with worry. "This, in itself, is enough to cause me great trouble."

"Sultana, I know your name and the name of that evil man, Amal. But who is the other one? What is his name?"

"You should not know any of our names, child," Sultana responded. "You would be much better off not knowing."

"Well, I do know them, so nothing can be done about it. But how is it that you can be alone with these two men? I thought, from what Daddy told me, Arab women are never to be alone with men other than their husbands. Is that true?"

Sultana nodded affirmatively.

"Then how can you . . . oh." Jessica paused as it dawned on her. "Do you mean the other man is . . . is your husband?"

A weak smile crossed Sultana's face. "Yes."

Jessica lay back on the bed, trying to assimilate this new piece of information. She was totally surprised.

"But you are never alone together. You do not act like a husband and wife toward each other."

"He is my husband. Being a wife in my country is sometimes a very complicated thing, child. In our culture, it is permissible for a man to have as many as four wives."

"Are you serious?"

"Yes."

"Why would anyone want to be married to a man who had three other wives?"

Sultana shrugged. "There are worse things."

"Does your husband have four wives?"

"No." She smiled, giving Jessica the distinct impression that she was relieved. "Generally speaking, it is only the very rich or the very poor that have more than one wife."

"Why is that?" Jessica pressed the question, temporarily setting aside her own circumstances, as she tried to understand what she was hearing.

"The Qur'an teaches that each wife and her children must be treated equally. They must be accorded the same worth and value. This may mean an extra tent for the very poor man or an extra palace for the very rich. The middle-class man cannot usually afford more than one wife under those conditions."

"But why doesn't he ever talk to you like a husband? He doesn't kiss you or treat you like a wife. I've never even seen him touch you. He orders you around and treats you like a servant."

"In our country, each wife is subject to her husband's authority in every aspect of life. Your own Bible talks about women being submissive to their husbands. But Christian women don't practice this, as we know."

"How would *you* know what the Bible says? You don't know anything. My mother lives that way with my father."

"She may be the exception. We, too, have such a teaching in the Qur'an. However, we are not like you in America. We live out our belief in Allah, and we practice what the Prophet Muhammad has taught us. We do not show affection publicly. We do not kiss or hold hands where we will be seen by others. A few young people are beginning to do this when others are present, but it is generally considered highly improper. Even immoral by some. It is unacceptable."

"Immoral to hold hands in public?" Jessica repeated incredulously.

"Yes. And certainly we know this is true by observing women in the West where public affection is casually acceptable and leads to all kinds of immoral acts."

"How can you say that? Have you ever been to America?"

"No. But I have seen some of your movies and your television programs. And I've read your books and magazines. Your women spend all their time talking of equality with men. They demand equal rights and then are expected by their husbands to work outside the home. They are rebellious in spirit, dress immodestly, and live in open immorality. Perhaps your parents are different, I don't know. And you're only a little girl. You would not know of such things. But you can't deny that what I say is true. I have seen it with my own eyes."

"But—" Jessica started to protest.

"Be quiet. I do not wish to talk of these matters any further with you."

She turned and walked away.

Jessica watched her pace back and forth, her eyes never leaving this woman of many contradictions. One moment she was warm and friendly, even caring. Then, suddenly, she could be cold and distant. Jessica felt disquieted by the conversation they had just had. She wanted to explain to Sultana that Hollywood was not the American norm, at least not the standard to which she aligned her lifestyle. But the woman had suddenly withdrawn into herself.

Sultana went to the door, opened it, and peered outside. For an instant, Jessica thought of screaming, then decided against it. It would do no good, and it would probably just get her into more trouble. That, she did not need.

The now familiar wave of hopelessness swept over her again. She bit her lip as she turned her head away. She felt like crying but was determined not to show any sign of weakness.

The next two hours dragged by slowly. For whatever reason, Sultana had shut off any further conversation. The humidity was oppressive. Jessica's body was soaked with perspiration and her arms itched under the tape. She was thirsty but refused to ask for something to drink. Something deep inside caused her to reject her obvious dependency on her captors.

A sudden knock on the door caused her to turn her head.

Sultana's husband and Amal walked in ahead of two more men. Strangers. Amal frowned as he looked over at Jessica and saw that the tape had been removed from her mouth. But he said nothing. The other men spoke in low tones. Sultana stood nearby, listening, but silent.

Jessica's arms ached from being kept immobile. She shifted to try to find a more tolerable position. Resentment. Anger. Frustration. Fear. They stirred within her like ingredients in one of her mother's mixing bowls.

One of the strangers handed an envelope to Sultana's husband. Without so much as a glance at Jessica, the two men with whom she had crossed the desert opened the door and disappeared into the hall. Sultana started to follow them out, then hesitated. She turned and walked over to where Jessica lay. For a brief moment their eyes met. A young girl full of questions and a woman with no answers. Sultana's hand brushed Jessica's face ever so lightly, a look of sadness in her eyes. Then, without a word, she turned and followed after the others.

The door closed.

Jessica was alone again—alone with two strangers.

Her emotional mixing bowl was ready for the oven!

32

FRIDAY, 28 OCTOBER, LOCAL TIME 0447
BAYTOWN, CALIFORNIA

The first ring sounded as if it came from somewhere far away. A distant place, perhaps. Esther started at first, then settled back. The second ring was insistent and shrill, jarring her into semiconsciousness. She struggled to open her eyes as she reached for the phone. But it was as if she was underwater and every movement was in slow motion. Once again it rang, demanding a response.

On the nightstand, the glowing red numbers on the digital clock were blinking 12:00—12:00—12:00. Esther brushed against her rings and a writing pen, left there from the night before. The rings clinked against the nightstand as they fell onto the floor. Finally, she managed to grasp it midway into the fourth ring.

"Hello?"

"Mom?"

"Jessica?"

"Mom?"

"Jessica, honey, I can hear you. Are you okay?"

"Mom?"

"Jessica, can you hear me?"

"Mom?"

"Jessica!"

"Esther. Esther. Wake up!" John was shaking her shoulder. "Honey, you're having a dream. Wake up."

She shook her head and tried to push him away. "No, John. It's Jessica. She's calling."

The dream faded, then dissolved altogether as Esther awoke, tears streaming down her face. Her voice cracked as she tried to tell the story to John.

"I dreamed that the phone rang and I was having a hard time getting to it; but when I answered, it was Jessica—but she couldn't hear me. I kept calling her name and she just kept saying, 'Mom? Mom?' It was awful!"

Esther turned over into a full embrace from John. They cried and prayed and held each other until their tears were spent. After a while, Esther dozed off into an exhausted, fitful sleep. John rolled out of bed and walked down the hallway to the kitchen.

An hour and a half later, Esther found John, chin in hands and elbows on the table, staring into a half-empty coffee cup. On the table was a yellow legal pad with notes scrawled all over it. Esther poured herself a cup from the nearly empty carafe and sat down across from him. It was John who finally broke the silence.

"I've got to do something."

Esther fixed her gaze on her husband. His face was strained, new lines furrowed deeply into his brow and around his eyes. Normally, at this time of year, he would still be looking fit and tan from an occasional game of golf or tennis. But not this morning. This morning he looked pale, almost ashen.

"What?" she asked finally. "What is there we can do that we haven't already done? We've contacted our congressman and senators. We've written to the Secretary of State. We've spoken to Charles Rodeway. We've sent letters to the White House, the FBI, the CIA, Homeland Security, and anyone else we could think of. We've encouraged others to do the same, and they have, by the hundreds and thousands. We've had her face and story featured in newspapers and magazines and on every major television network in the country and around the world. We've done everything but tack her picture on the light pole down at the corner. What else can we do?"

"Not we. *Me*."

"You? Don't leave me out of whatever it is you're thinking, John Cain. Okay?"

"I'm not leaving you out. But this is one time that I have to go it alone."

"What are you saying?"

John took a long sip from the coffee cup and leaned back in his chair, linking his hands behind his head, fingers intertwined, elbows splayed wide apart.

"I can't keep up with this 'business as usual' routine. I can't keep my mind on the church's needs, because our own needs seem so much greater right now. I'm losing it, sweetheart. I've got to focus on one thing, getting Jessica back. Everything else has to go. Our work, our plans, everything. There's no way to keep all the balls in the air until we get Jessica back."

"Translate that for me, John. I'm afraid that I don't have the gift of interpretation. What are you saying?"

"What am I saying?" John repeated the question slowly, each word rolling deliberately off his tongue. "What *am* I saying? I guess I'm saying that if no one else can do anything, then I've got to. I've at least got to try. We just can't keep living like this. I'm saying that . . . that I'm going to Iran to bring our daughter back myself!"

33

FRIDAY, 28 OCTOBER, LOCAL TIME 0815
HALIFAX, NOVA SCOTIA

"Thanks," the driver of the truck shouted. "I can handle it from here."

With one hand, he offered a friendly wave to the dock foreman, while stuffing his gloves into the pocket of his jacket with the other. He pulled a wool stocking cap down over his ears and swung the back doors shut, locking them with a heavy padlock.

A forklift roared past, headed toward a stack of wood crates still waiting to be loaded onto a flatbed. The dock crane had swung another pallet over to the *Grodno* and lowered it into position alongside the others.

The truck driver watched for a few seconds, then climbed up into the cab. The truck was unmarked, painted white, with a narrow sleeping space behind the seat for use on long hauls. He started the motor and released the brake. Satisfied that everything was in order, he shifted gears and let out the clutch, heading away from the noisy dock area and toward the city center of Halifax. Glancing at his watch, he grunted his approval. He had forty minutes before picking up his companion driver and the other two trucks, enough time to catch a bite before heading out on their long journey across Canada.

34

FRIDAY, 28 OCTOBER, LOCAL TIME 2000
BANDAR-É ABBÂS, IRAN

A small lamp and lampstand had been dragged over next to the door. On the lampstand was a tray filled with ashes and cigarette stubs, and an international English edition of *Newsweek*. A Daewoo DP-51 fast-action military pistol with a thirteen-round capacity lay on top of the magazine.

A soldier, or most law enforcement officers, would have immediately recognized the handgun as a NATO special, a standard issue of the Republic of South Korea armed forces. To the twelve-year-old girl peering through the smoky haze that filled the room, the steel blue weapon was simply another link in the fence that continued to separate her from those who truly loved her.

Jessica could not remember ever having seen a real gun in California. Only in movies and on television. These past few weeks, however, they seemed to be everywhere—dangling from the shoulders of Israeli soldiers on patrol, brandished by her terrorist captors, even worn or carried by men who didn't appear to have any official designation whatsoever. At first, all these weapons had frightened her. Now, they had become part of her life. She had not touched one yet, but her mind ran wild with thoughts of what she would do if she could. Too many movies and too much television added up to too many crazy ideas.

If only . . .

Blinking, she drove away the violent fantasies. With her hands and arms taped securely behind her back, how would she ever get a hold of the gun in the first place? Even if they cut her loose and handed her this one, what would she do with it? She knew enough to point it away from herself, but how do you hold a gun in order to fire accurately? She understood you had to pull the trigger in order for it to fire. But wasn't there a safety or something? Where was that, and how was it released?

And how many bullets are in that handgun? One? Five? Ten? Wait a minute. Get a grip, girl. Jessica attempted to rein in her thoughts. What difference would it make if she knew? It was better not to fantasize. Still, her mind wandered . . . *More than ten?*

The young guard was thumbing through a magazine. Something called *Tavoos Quarterly.* From where she was situated on the bed, it looked to be a magazine with articles in both Persian and English.

What do you suppose he's thinking about? This has to be as boring for him as it is for me.

She had already tried conversing with the two guards who took turns sitting just inside the door to her hotel cell.

"Do you speak English?"

The guard gave her a questioning look.

Jessica took that as a no. The best she could do was talk to herself. It was the only conversation she had until her bladder could no longer afford her to be silent. Many times during the past few weeks she had asked herself the question: How could a normal bodily function be such a constantly embarrassing problem to have to deal with?

"I need to go to the bathroom."

The guard looked up and then returned his gaze to his magazine.

"Hey. I need to go. Understand?"

He ignored her.

"*Taewaelit?* I need the toilet! Hey!" Her voice rose in urgency and volume. Finally, the young man stood up and nodded toward the bathroom. There was a questioning look on his face. He pointed to her and then to the room.

"Yes. Yes. The toilet. Please."

Glancing at his watch, he moved toward the chair. From his pocket, he pulled out a Swiss Army knife and flicked open the longest blade. He held it up in front of Jessica and began speaking.

"I don't understand what you are saying," Jessica interrupted, an edge of desperation in her voice. "If you are telling me not to try to run away, I won't. If you're asking me do I need my arms and legs free, the answer is yes. And if you're trying to say something to me in English, forget it. I'll have died from exploding kidneys long before I ever understand you!"

Having verbalized that embarrassing possibility aloud, Jessica inexplicably began to giggle. She couldn't resist the nervous release that had broken loose from deep inside. Here she was, talking to a guy who couldn't understand a word she said, and she was desperate to go to the bathroom. The personal nature of her problem simply added fuel to her giggle and pain to her abdomen. She closed her eyes in an effort to stop it.

Jessica shuddered involuntarily as the guard's hands rested on her shoulders. He rolled her over on her stomach. A moment later, she felt the knife blade against her arms. With a swift and very expert move, he cut through the tape and her arms fell free. Seconds later, her ankles were also released, but Jessica found herself unable to move. Her arms had been taped behind her back for so long that they would not function. She tried moving them, pushing herself up, only to fall back on her face again.

Suddenly, she felt herself being lifted and placed in a standing position. Blood rushed to her extremities. How many hours had it been? She swayed uncontrollably.

I'm going to faint!

The young man did not let her fall. Instead, he kept her balanced as she gingerly tried first one step, then another.

"One small step for man . . ." Jessica mumbled to herself with a chuckle, wondering all the while what it was that was so funny about all this. Finally, she was at the doorway.

What if he goes in with me?

Another involuntary giggle erupted at the thought.

"This is ridiculous," she said out loud, her voice breaking the sticky stillness that hung oppressively over the room.

At the sound of her voice, the young man let his hands fall away and he stepped back. Jessica swayed as she turned, the giggle still tickling her voice box.

"Thank you," she said.

"*Be shamâ khosh âmad miguyam,*" he said, still watching her.

"Whatever," Jessica said, and closed the door.

At least she had been spared that embarrassment. Eventually, feeling much better, she sat alone in the room and sighed with relief. Then tears filled her eyes.

What is this? First, I can't stop giggling and now I'm crying.

She buried her face in her hands, shoulders shaking spasmodically as each new wave of emotion rolled over her.

Oh, dear God, I am lost. I'm really lost. I don't have a clue where I am, and Daddy and Mom surely don't know either, or they would come and get me. What am I going to do?

Carefully, Jessica tore away the last remnants of tape from her arms and legs. There was a tin wastebasket near the sink. She put the pieces of tape into it. Next, she turned on the faucet in the sink and let her arms feel the soothing warmth of the water. They still were stinging from the tape removal.

Spying a bar of partially used soap, she took it and gingerly washed her arms, hands, ankles, and feet. She looked longingly at the shower, but was afraid that the guard might decide to come in if he heard her running the water.

In fact, at that very moment, there came a knock on the door and a voice on the other side.

"I'll be just a minute," she called out, wiping her hands and arms with a hotel towel. Hanging the towel back on the hook, she took a deep breath and opened the door. The guard was standing in the middle of the room, with the handgun that had been on the lampstand. He motioned to her with the gun, pointing toward the bed. Jessica was afraid that he would tie her up again, but he did not. When she was situated to the young man's satisfaction, he grinned at her and returned to his position by the door.

—∾—

For the next two days, Jessica remained free, but with no possibility of escape. The phone had been removed, though she knew she would not have much success in trying to use it, even if she got the chance. She had never made an international telephone call and didn't know the first thing about it. And then there was the language issue. In spite of her questions, the guards made no attempt to respond. If they understood any English at all, they were not going to let her know about it. They remained seated at the door, most of the time tipped back against the wall on the chair's rear legs, reading a book, magazine, or newspaper, or simply staring off into the distance.

An ancient-looking television on the opposite wall was never turned on. She had asked about it, pointing and making gestures in order to be understood, but had received only a shoulder shrug and a head shake in response. The TV stayed off.

By eight o'clock, on the evening of the second day, she was still wondering what would come next.

Five minutes later, the door opened, and she had her answer.

PART FIVE

These creations of terror are done not to achieve a strategic goal but to make a symbolic statement.

—Mark Juergensmeyer, *Terror in the Mind of God*
(Berkeley, Calif.: University of California Press, 2000)

The whole world lies under the power of the evil one.

—The Holy Bible
1 John 5:19 (NRSV)

"The thief comes only to steal and kill and destroy;
I have come that they may have life,
and have it to the full."

—Jesus in The Holy Bible
John 10:10

35

FRIDAY, 28 OCTOBER, LOCAL TIME 0655
BAYTOWN, CALIFORNIA

"You're going to do what?" Esther gripped the edge of the table, leaning forward, her countenance frozen in disbelief. "You can't be serious, John."

"I can be serious," John replied, steadily returning her gaze, "and I am."

"How on earth can you ever hope to do something like that?" Esther exclaimed, slumping back in her chair, her voice nettled with exasperation. "You're not James Bond, for goodness' sake. You're John Cain. You're a *pastor.* Do you think the Iranians are going to open their arms and welcome a Protestant pastor into their country? Especially one whose face has been all over the media for having thwarted a dream terrorist attack? They're probably using your picture for target practice.

"'Oh, yes, Pastor Cain, we're so pleased you have come. We're the people who funded the kidnapping of your little daughter so that we could thank you appropriately for spoiling our righteous attempt to assist the Palestinian Islamic Jihad in regaining their sovereignty and their homeland. Welcome, Pastor Cain. Now that you're here, we want to admit our wrongdoing, beg your forgiveness, and give your daughter back.' Is that what you think they're going to do?"

Esther was babbling and she knew it. She could feel herself sliding toward the edge of an emotional abyss. A sudden rush of resentment boiled to the surface. Banging her hands on the table, she stood up, rattling the cups and splashing coffee onto the tabletop in the process.

"Esther, listen—" John leaned forward and reached for Esther's hands across the table.

"No! No! No! No!" Esther was crying now, her hands shaking. "*You* listen! I've already lost Jenny. Jessica is somewhere out there, God only knows where. A few weeks ago, I thought I might lose you and Jeremy as well. John, I can't bear the thought of you leaving us . . . leaving *me* . . . and maybe . . . maybe never coming back. I know I'm being selfish, but I can't help it. There has got to be another way!"

John got to his feet, walked around the table and gently put his arms around Esther. She buried her face in his shoulder, feeling his arms encircle her as she tried in vain to control the sobs that wracked her body.

Eventually, the room grew quiet.

Esther did not want to move.

Let the world turn on its own for a while. I can't be responsible for it any longer. This is safe. This is where I want to be.

She caught her breath as John's strong hands moved to her shoulders. She forced herself to look up at him, ashamed now at the way her emotions had boiled over. His face was damp with tears as well.

"I'm sorry," she said simply.

John reached for a napkin and wiped her cheeks.

"It's okay. There's nothing for you to be sorry over. We're both living on the edge these days. It's impossible to stay on top all the time."

He ran the napkin over his own face then and dropped it on the table.

"Come on, love. Let's sit down and talk about this."

Arm in arm, they walked to the big chair in the corner of the family room near the fireplace. They sat down, pressing against each other, needing to feel each other's closeness. Esther's hand instinctively brushed beneath her eyes, to wipe away any leftover mascara run. Then she remembered she had not yet put on any makeup. She pushed her hair back from her forehead.

"Do I look as bad as I think I look?"

"Darling, you look fine."

"Be honest."

"Well, maybe a bit worse for wear, but you'll get over it."

Esther offered up a thin smile.

"Thanks. I needed that."

"No problem. Compliments are part of my extensive sensitivity training."

"Now I know you're lying," she came back with a half sob, half shudder. "But God will forgive you."

John chuckled.

They were silent for a few moments as the emotional hurricane blew itself out, replaced by a gradual calm.

"Okay, so what is this crazy idea about going off to Iran?"

"Actually, I've been thinking about it ever since we heard they might be taking her there. If those people have managed to get her into Iran, our government isn't going to do anything. That's what I think. Rodeway and the others in Washington will keep holding our hands and being sympathetic, but what will they do, really? What *can* they do?"

Esther remained silent, staring at the floor as John continued.

"You mentioned a minute ago about how the Iranians would feel if I showed up on their doorstep. But what we have to keep in mind is that this is not about a nation of people. Honey, there are probably a couple hundred thousand Iranians living right here in the Bay Area. Most of them are good people. They have children themselves and will regret what is happening to us once word gets out that Jessica may be held in their homeland. This whole madness is not about racism. It's about radicalism."

Esther leaned back against the chair, unaware of her fingers twisting the loose end of her blouse. She was looking at John with interest now.

"I've done some checking around this past week," John continued. "I spoke with Jerry Handover at our denominational headquarters."

"I don't know who he is," Esther said, feeling herself being drawn into what he was saying.

"He's one of the guys in the foreign missions department. I met him a couple of years ago when I spoke at our regional conference in L.A."

Esther nodded.

"He tells me that the church does exist in Iran. It is not very organized. In fact, it is mostly underground and the Christians stay pretty invisible because of persecution. But it's there, nonetheless. Maybe, if I can get to some of them . . ." his voice trailed off as he thought about the odds against anything meaningful happening in that arena.

"Does anybody even know who they are?"

"God does."

"But could we ever get in touch with these people? And even if that were possible, what can they do to help us get her out?"

John leaned forward, picked up the yellow legal pad from the floor at his feet where he had dropped it earlier, and began carefully explaining his plan. For the next two hours, he and Esther discussed, disputed, and defended their crisscross speculations. At last, they grew silent, studying the floor in front of them as if it were the womb of every deep thought they had ever conceived. Eventually, Esther slipped out of the chair and stood to her feet, looking down at John.

"This is absolutely the most ludicrous thing we have ever considered. It's too risky. What kind of a chance for success is there, really?" She looked away, then back again at John, her lips slowly forming into a half smile. "I guess if the Lord is with us, we're not supposed to fail. Isn't that the way it works?"

"That's the idea anyway," John agreed, getting up and walking over to the window that looked out onto the pool.

That's the idea. But will the idea really work in this case? It's a whole lot easier to preach to others about trusting the Lord than it is to live out that trust yourself. Especially with something like this, where so little is known and so much is at stake.

He took in the dance of the sun's rays on the water's surface. Then his gaze was drawn to the familiar object at the bottom of the "swimming hole," as Jeremy used to call it in those happier days when he and his sisters splashed and played there together.

The pool sweep rested quietly beneath the water, its reflection a dark shadow in an otherwise bluish-white world.

She's still there. Our beloved ghost. I miss you, Jenny. We both do. I know you can't come back, but now we've lost your sister, too. It's almost more than I can deal with, even though I know you're with Jesus. What do you understand up there in heaven, Jenny? You were so little when you left us. Do you have grown-up knowledge now? Do the angels ever give you "viewing privileges" so you can look down and see us? Do you know where Jessica is today? If you do, put in a good word for her, okay? And for us, too. We need to get her back.

John smiled. His understanding of Scripture and theology clearly ruled out any overt kind of spiritual contact with the dead. He knew that one should not try to converse with the departed. Still, once in a while, he felt extremely close to Jenny, almost as if she was physically near at hand. When it happened, the sensation of her nearness was a pleasant one. *Maybe Jesus has her in his arms during these moments when I feel especially close to her.*

"Where are you, sweetheart?" Esther's voice broke through his momentary reverie. She slipped her arm around his waist.

John looked down, flushing slightly with embarrassment.

"Sorry. Guess I was . . . out there . . . with the girls somewhere."

36

FRIDAY, 28 OCTOBER, LOCAL TIME 2005
BANDAR-É ABBÂS, IRAN

Jessica glanced up the moment she heard the knock on the door, expecting to witness another routine changing of the guard. When the guard unlocked the door this time, however, three women entered the room. The first was dressed in jeans and a loose-fitting shirt that reached almost to her knees. A plain, dark head scarf covered her hair and neck. Next came a woman dressed from top to toe in a black *châdor.* The third woman wore a full-length black skirt and a shirt with sleeves buttoned at the wrists. She, too, wore a dark-colored head scarf.

Two of the women remained near the door, on either side of the guard, while the one wearing jeans came forward until she stood at the edge of the bed. The first thing Jessica noticed was her skin. It was the color of ivory. Her face was also striking, a straight, narrow nose, high cheekbones, long lashes and dark, piercing eyes that remained fixed on the young girl in front of her. Jessica returned the stare, eyes not flickering. A few weeks ago, she would have been very uncomfortable, even fearful, in the presence of these women. The time spent with Sultana, however, had minimized her apprehension. Still, the longer the woman in jeans stood there, the more rapidly Jessica's heart beat.

"So, this is the daughter of the Great Satan's latest hollow hero, the cleric John Cain. Your name is Jessica, is that correct?" The woman's voice sounded low and harsh, as though conditioned by too many cigarettes, but her English was clear enough.

Jessica started at the sound of her father's name, but quickly regained her composure.

"Yes. Who are you?"

The woman ignored her question, turning her gaze to take in the rest of the room, as if she expected to see something out of the ordinary. Jessica could have assured her that there was nothing extraordinary about this room. In fact, she could tell her exactly how many tiles there were in the ceiling and how many dead flies there were on the room's solitary windowsill.

"For the time being, you are our prisoner," the woman said finally. "Gather up your things and come with us. Be sure to bring everything. You will not be back here again. Furthermore, once we have left the room, you will remain silent until I say that you may speak again. Is that clear?"

Jessica nodded.

The woman's eyes narrowed.

"In Iran, when addressing a stranger, especially one older than you, it is polite to begin your comments with *âghâ,* meaning 'sir,' or, *khânom,* meaning 'lady or madam.' We know, from experience, how ill-bred, illiterate, and impolite most Americans are. You, however, do not have that option as long as you are with us. Is that perfectly clear, Jessica?

"Yes."

"The word is *baleh.*"

Jessica stared at the woman.

"Say it."

"*Baleh,*" Jessica answered, her voice soft and uncertain.

"Speak up."

"*Baleh,*" Jessica repeated.

"*Baleh* what, Jessica?"

Jessica thought for a moment.

"*Baleh khânom,*" she said finally.

The woman nodded, pursing her lips.

"Now, get your things. We must hurry. Don't forget what you have just been taught. And remember to maintain absolute silence from this moment until I say otherwise. Understand?"

"*Baleh khânom,*" Jessica answered.

There was really nothing for Jessica to gather up. Her only possessions were the clothes she had been wearing ever since she was kidnapped in Israel, and the *châdor* she had been given in Jordan. She also had been given a toothbrush, a small tube of toothpaste, and a bar of hand soap. What remained of these items was all she had.

As she stuffed the toothbrush and toothpaste into her pocket, a mental flashback caused a brief smile.

"What do you find so humorous, Jessica Cain?" The woman in jeans glowered at her.

"I was just remembering how many times my mother has told me to gather up my things at home. There, it takes me five or ten minutes to get it all put away. At least that's not my problem here, is it?"

Out of the corner of her eye, as she gathered up the *châdor*, it appeared to Jessica that the woman's facial features changed for a split second, but it was hard to determine for sure. The beginning of a smile, perhaps? Or was she angry?

"Put it on."

Jessica looked at the woman quizzically.

"Hurry. Put it on."

Jessica wrapped the *châdor* over her own clothing. She knew it was going to be uncomfortable, but she took the woman's warning seriously and said nothing.

Hopefully, wherever we're going has air-conditioning.

The guard opened the door; without a word, the three women and the girl stepped through the doorway and started down the dimly lit hall.

37

FRIDAY, 28 OCTOBER, LOCAL TIME 1945
BAYTOWN, CALIFORNIA

The smell of fresh coffee lingered over the large mahogany table as pleasantries were exchanged between the men who had seated themselves in the worn, dark leather chairs. Cary Johnson, Calvary Church's business administrator, reached over each man's shoulder as he poured a fresh round into the mugs.

"Thanks, Cary," Harold Cawston acknowledged, reaching for the creamer. "You do this extremely well."

"Yes," agreed Jerry North, with a big grin. "I think you missed your calling. You should have been a waiter."

The others laughed and Cary chuckled with them. "Servant leadership, you know. That's what Pastor keeps reminding us."

He placed the coffeepot on a small table by the conference room door and pulled out a large plate loaded with fresh brownies, covered with chocolate frosting.

"All right!" exclaimed Mike Dewbar. "Now we're talking, Servant Leader. Pass those this way before Peping gets his hands on them, or they'll never make it around the table."

Scott Peping grinned, rubbing his hands together in mock anticipation. As longtime golfing buddies, he and Mike enjoyed kidding each other mercilessly about their game, their weight, their eating habits, and just about any other thing that might wander across their conversational agenda.

Just as the brownies reached Scott's place at the table, Dennis Lanier walked through the door, having rushed from a city planning staff meeting. As Baytown's city manager, his schedule often consisted of leaving one meeting a little early in order to arrive at another meeting a little late.

The others greeted him warmly as he scooted his chair in next to David Bolling and snared a brownie from off the serving plate.

At last, John Cain leaned forward in his chair, the conversation gradually decreased, and the room became quiet. All eyes were turned toward him expectantly, with the unspoken awareness that something unusual was about to transpire. For one thing, brownies were out of the ordinary. For another, there was no agenda in front of them, and the only thing in front of John was his Bible.

Normally, the board of Calvary Church included attorney Ken Ralsten; but he had not attended any of their meetings since the never-to-be-forgotten events of September 18 when, without warning, terrorists had attacked the church and held the congregation hostage. Ken and his son, Geoff, had managed to escape, but in so doing had placed the other hostages' lives in grave jeopardy.

Ken's subsequent depression over the events of that weekend had been devastating. John had spent considerable time with him, eventually referring him to a Christian psychologist skilled in post-traumatic stress therapy. Geoff was also in counseling, and John tried to stay in touch with the family by telephone or in person on a weekly basis. On Monday, the Ralstens had flown to Hawaii for a three-week vacation.

"Fellas, let's get started. Our meeting should not be long, but it is important. I appreciate some of you rearranging your lives in order to attend another meeting that was not originally on our schedule. We've had our share of these during the last few weeks, haven't we?" John smiled as he acknowledged the affirming nods around the table. "As we begin, let's remember Ken and his family. They have a couple of weeks in Hawaii, still. Let's ask the Lord to complete His work of healing there, as He has been doing for each of the rest of us. Okay? Any other needs you feel like mentioning?"

The room was silent.

There was something else, but no one needed to mention it. It was permanently imprinted on their hearts, a constant part of their lives that surfaced each time they bowed their heads in prayer at church or at home. Jessica's disappearance had become a sobering, never-ending ache in the hearts of every Calvary Church member.

"Okay, then. Jerry, will you lead us, please?" John said quietly.

38

When it came to meetings, Dennis Lanier was the expert. He had been in hundreds of them during his city government career, and he had a sixth sense about their importance, or lack of it. Most meetings were ordinary and often not really necessary; some were essential to the ongoing success of an organization. Then there were the occasional few that marked crucial moments of decision: success or failure, victory or defeat, life or death. Tonight, he sensed, was going to be one of those "occasional few."

It was in the air from the minute he entered the room.

A defining moment . . .

He had listened to the last bits of camaraderie, then leaned back and sipped on his coffee. When John finally brought the meeting to order, Dennis didn't just focus on John's words. He analyzed the tone of his voice. It was quiet and calm, but there were telltale signs of strain around his eyes.

I wonder what the personal pressure he's under right now must feel like? He's been doing a great job of shepherding the flock since returning from Israel. But his situation at home has to be unbelievably stressful. I can't imagine how Barbara and I would cope if it were one of our *children.*

Bowing his head, Dennis listened as Jerry led the group in prayer. A premonition gripped his spirit just before the "amen."

Something significant has happened. Have they found her? If they heard she was alive, John would be bouncing off the ceiling. If this is about Jessica, it can only mean one thing.

When Jerry finished, there was silence around the table.

John was the last to look up.

Dennis waited for him to open his Bible, but he didn't touch it. Instead, he sat back in his chair and let his eyes move slowly around the table, taking in each of the men gathered there. Then he shifted and leaned forward, until his elbows rested on the table and both hands fell across the Bible.

"Gentlemen, you're all wondering why I've called this special meeting. I'm not quite sure how to say what I'm about to say, so I'll just stumble along as best I can.

"After our September board meeting, just before leaving for Israel, I wrote a letter of resignation as senior pastor of this church."

Dennis shifted in his chair and noticed the worried glances cast between the others as John paused to take a deep breath.

"At the time, I was pretty discouraged, to say the least. Jenny's death and Esther's depression . . . well, it almost destroyed us. That, coupled with Jeremy and me not being able to talk to each other without becoming angry, was slowly sinking us as a family. Add to that, if you will, the pressures that go along with this business of pastoring, and the result was . . . actually still is, what the experts call 'clergy burnout.' It's not uncommon, as I'm sure you've read. You just get to a point of not having anything to give. You're used up, worn out, no more tread left. You can try to keep running on the rims, but eventually even the rims prove unsatisfactory for the job.

"At the time, I had decided I would step down when I got home from Israel and get out of the ministry altogether. The price for staying in was too high. My 'servant-leader account' was way overdrawn. My family needed me to focus on them. Even then, I wasn't sure we were going to make it. The only bright spot left in our lives was Jessica."

John paused and cleared his throat.

"Well, the events of the past few weeks have been something I could never have dreamed of. Not in my wildest nightmares. Honestly, the last couple of *years* are beyond my understanding. It's been like an out-of-control roller coaster.

"Anyway, there is some good news. Esther has experienced significant healing, both spiritually and emotionally. It has been a true 'God thing.' Jeremy and I are both different men than we used to be. We've been able to forgive old hurts and pull together as a family. My relationship with Esther has probably never been stronger than during these last few weeks. Jenny is not simply a source of grief any longer. She is our star in heaven."

John shifted and reached for his cup, picked it up, then set it back down without drinking. The silence was electric as each man listened to their pastor openly sharing his personal pain. Dennis had never thought about him quite like this before. Sure, he knew that John and Esther must experience some of the same marital and family problems as everyone else. But he'd always figured that a pastor would work things out differently than other people.

After all, he's our spiritual leader, our shepherd, isn't he?

Dennis watched John's body language. He had begun with his hands folded over his Bible, glancing down at it every once in a while, as if seeking some reassurance from it that wasn't there. In general, he had kept his eyes on the group as he spoke. That was a good sign. He spoke clearly, too, and when talking about his family, he opened his hands in an unconscious gesture that indicated he was hiding nothing.

"But of course, there is still Jessica," John said.

At the mention of his daughter's name, John looked down again. His shoulders and chest moved as he took a deep breath in an obvious effort to keep it together. Dennis braced himself for what would come next.

"This last Sunday, it became clear to me, fellas, that I can no longer carry on in the role of being your senior pastor. At least, not now. Not while Jessica is out there somewhere, waiting for me to come and get her."

Dennis heard one of the other men blowing his nose.

"So, I'm going to dig out that letter and give you a revised, updated version for the official minutes. I should have had it ready for this meeting, but I just didn't have the heart for it today. I'm sure you understand and will forgive me. Whatever it needs in order to be refreshed, the bottom line will still be the same."

John paused and smiled at the men. The smile was genuine, Dennis thought, but full of sadness.

He doesn't want to do this. But he's going to do it, and nothing is going to keep him from it.

No one moved.

No chair squeaked.

A group of monks could not have been more silent

At last, Dennis cleared his throat and spoke up. "John, I want you to know something up front. I personally do not want to hear that you are resigning."

There was an immediate chorus of affirmative voices, a shared emotional moment that released its intensity like the end of a boys' breath-holding contest. Chairs turned. There was coughing and clearing of throats. Mike Dewbar pushed his chair back and walked over to the window, turning his back on the others as he peered out at the darkness, wiping tears from his eyes.

"In fact, I'll go on record as saying that it's not a good idea," Dennis continued.

John immediately tensed up, as the other men again affirmed what Dennis was saying. Mike turned from the window and started to speak, but Dennis held up his hand. He was not finished.

"I don't believe it's a good idea for you or for the church."

John was leaning forward again, sitting up on the edge of his chair.

"Dennis," he began, "I appreciate what you are saying, but you have to understand that—"

"Excuse me, John," Dennis's voice was firm as he stood and moved away from the table. "Just let me finish."

"Please, Dennis, I—"

"John, you are my pastor, and I respect and love you more than you will ever know. You will always be one of my dearest friends, though there's never been enough time between us to spend on that relationship. However, more than being friends, you are my spiritual mentor. You're a shepherd to all of us in this room and in our church. You have been God's faithful servant among us since the day you arrived. You've taught us by word and by example. We're proud of you, John. Whatever else happens, we want you to know that. Right, fellas?"

"Yes."

"Absolutely."

"Couldn't say it any better."

"Without question."

"I agree one hundred percent, Dennis."

"There's got to be another way."

John dropped back in his chair and closed his eyes.

"I think there is." Dennis continued speaking as he walked around the table until he stood near where John was seated. "There is one thing you've never done before, John."

John looked up.

"And what might that be, Dennis?" he asked, with a good-natured sigh.

"You've never taken a sabbatical."

"A sabbatical?"

"Yes. An extended leave. Call it time off for good behavior."

The others laughed and even John chuckled as he backed the chair away from the table and stood up.

"Fellas, listen. I appreciate what you're saying and it is very tempting. I really don't want to leave Calvary. I love this church. I love the community. I know God called me here. But there are some things you don't understand. If I was only going to be away a few weeks or even months, that would be one thing. The fact is, I don't know how long I will need to be gone. I have to devote my energies, at least the energy I have left, to one task, and one task alone. I've got to find Jessica and bring her home. There's no way that I can promise I'll be back in a few weeks. Uncertainty is not healthy for a congregation. You'd better just let me cut myself loose."

Mike Dewbar walked back to the table. "John, everything Dennis is saying makes sense to me. For us to accept your resignation now, it's . . . well, it's too 'corporate' and not at all 'Christian.' Do you understand what I'm saying?" He looked around at the others. "It's the way big business does things. But we're not big business. We're God's business. We're the church. This is the time we all stick together.

"You are the example of Christ to us, in good times and in bad. It's not only what you teach us from the pulpit. We watch your life. For myself, I try to pattern my walk with Jesus like I see in you. We all need that, John, even if you can't show up in the pulpit or carry out the regular work of the church right now. We can bring extra help on board during this time. You have some close friends in the ministry. How about one of them, or maybe a pastor friend who has retired? Someone we can trust to serve both you and us in this crisis."

"But I can't—" John started to protest.

"Furthermore," Mike continued, looking around at the other men, "I believe we should continue John's full salary during this time. I know you've been drained with extra expenses while you try to find our girl. I don't see any other way. You've just got to let us do this. Jessica has become almost as much our little girl as she is yours."

Dennis had never heard Mike express himself so emotionally about anything in his life. Nor had he ever known him to cry in public, but tears were running down his face as he spoke.

John sat down and buried his face in his hands. Tears spilled onto his unopened Bible. Nobody said a word, but one of the men started a box of tissue around the table, and every man grabbed more than one.

"You guys are something else," John began, brushing at the tears on the cover of his Bible. "I really don't know what to say. Let me think about it. I need to talk to Esther."

John paused, and Dennis saw a look of concern, even dread, flash over his countenance.

"There is something else, though. . . . I don't know where my search for Jessica will lead me. I don't even know exactly what I may have to do in order to get her back. To be perfectly honest, I'm wrestling with my own conscience regarding what I might have to do, and whether it will even be morally acceptable at every turn. Things I don't feel free to talk about right now. But I don't want anything I do in the future to bring any discredit to God's reputation, or to Calvary Church. I just don't know . . ."

Every man was standing now and moving in around John. They seemed to understand what John was saying, what it was he was struggling with in his conscience.

Dennis knew exactly.

He had two children of his own.

He knew what he would do to protect them.

The men pressed in close together, laying hands on their troubled pastor. As Dennis thought about it, he realized that they had never done anything like this before as a board. It had taken a crisis to make them do what they should have been doing all along.

They waited, eyes closed, praying silently. Finally, Jerry North, led the men in prayer. His carefully chosen words united them in a heartfelt appeal to the Lord for their wounded shepherd.

And for Jessica.

39

TUESDAY, 01 NOVEMBER, LOCAL TIME 0935
CANADA-U.S. BORDER BETWEEN SASKATCHEWAN AND MONTANA

The three drivers stood away from their vehicles, smoking cigarettes, while the U.S. Border Patrol agent checked the various official papers, manifests, and bills of lading. Five thousand gallons of experimental bio-diesel fuel. Point of origin: Murmansk, Russia. Destination: Rad-Fuel Ltd., Reno, Nevada.

"You guys from Russia?" she queried pleasantly, eyes shifting to the three all-white trucks, each carrying a generous coat of mud from the journey and each emblazoned with a bright red Rad-Fuel Ltd. logo on the sides of the tanks.

"Are you kidding?" said the lead driver. "We're from Montreal. We picked this stuff up in Halifax, and we're just haulin' it down the road."

"Can I have a look?"

"You mean in the tanks?"

"Yeah. Can you open one of them for me?"

"Okay, lady. But be careful. I don't want to create an international incident with you fallin' into my truck. Swimmin' in diesel can't be a lot of fun."

"I think I can manage," she responded dryly. "And I'll need to check the other two trucks as well, so you guys get ready. Okay?"

"Sure. No problem."

Moments later the driver and the agent were on top of the lead tanker with the heavy-duty cap released and pulled away, permitting the woman to peer inside. There was nothing to see, but the strong odor of diesel fuel was unmistakable. She repeated the process with the other two.

"Okay, thanks," she said finally. "Seal 'em up, and you boys can be on your way. And don't spend all your money on the slots in Reno."

Backing down the steel ladder on the last tanker's side, the border agent dropped lightly to the ground, retrieving her clipboard from the bench where she had placed it moments before.

"Everything appears to be in order," she said to the drivers, impressing the entry stamps and scrawling her initials at the bottom of the various forms.

"Here you go. Welcome to the United States. Drive carefully and have a nice day."

"We will. And, thanks," the lead driver said as the men returned to their trucks. A moment later, they were moving slowly through the gears as they pulled out onto the highway and headed south.

40

TUESDAY, 01 NOVEMBER, LOCAL TIME 0930
BAYTOWN, CALIFORNIA

John turned through the yellow-page advertisements slowly, not completely certain where to look. Finally, he saw it.

> Gun Safety & Marksmanship Instruction.
> See Firearms Instruction:
> Schools-Gen Interest Guide
> Heading of Gun Safety & Marksmanship.

He proceeded back to *F*.

> Fingernail Salons, Fingerprinting, Fire Alarm Systems, Fire Department.

Not there.

Next, he went to the *S* section, and flipped through pages of various private schools. There was Calvary Christian Schools. He glanced approvingly at the attractive ad design.

> Business & Secretarial, Business & Vocational.

Here it is.

> Gun Safety & Marksmanship.

Only one place was listed: Sure Shot Firing Range. The address was across the bay in Santa Clara. He wrote down the phone number on a pad and replaced the directory in the drawer.

After dialing, he listened as the phone rang once, twice, three times.

Maybe they're not open.

Four times.

Maybe this is God's way of saying . . .

"Hello. Sure Shot. How can I help you?"

A woman's voice.

"Yes, I'm calling from Baytown. You seem to be the only firearms instruction center in the yellow pages. Can you tell me what you offer by way of classes?"

"Sure. We have a firearms safety class every Thursday. It's open to the public. Is that what you are looking for?"

"Not exactly," replied John, his voice hesitating for an instant. "I need an instructor to show me how to use a weapon correctly. I think that I'd like some private lessons. Do you have a teacher or someone who can help me?"

"Certainly. Any specific choice of weapon?"

John hesitated.

"I think probably a handgun."

"Are you primarily interested in self-defense?"

"Yes," he replied, thinking as he said it that his answer was only partially true. *Maybe I'm the aggressor, but I don't think you'd want to hear that.*

"We have one instructor available right now. Her name is Carla Chin. She's very good."

"Your instructor is a woman?" John was surprised.

"That's right. Is it a problem?"

"No, I guess not. Just seems kind of unusual."

"Would you like her phone number?" The woman ignored John's comment.

"Yes, please."

He wrote it down and repeated it back just to be sure. When he hung up the receiver, his hands felt damp.

Can you believe this? I'm acting like a kid making plans he knows his parents won't approve of. But the idea of firing a weapon at someone, maybe even killing another human being, is unreal. I just don't know. Can I really do this? Is it right for me to even be learning how to do this? Why am I so troubled? King David killed lots of people, didn't he? Still, if it comes right down to it, can I actually shoot someone? Even in self-defense? Even to get Jessica back? That's the bottom line, isn't it? And I don't honestly know the answer.

Anxious doubts continued to plague him. When he had talked to Esther about it a couple of days ago, she suddenly was silent and withdrawn. He could feel her retreating into her own private dread. Barely recovered from gunshot wounds that had almost taken her life, she wasn't ready for a dialogue on the moral implications of killing another person. So he had dropped the subject. He'd just have to work through it alone.

He dialed the number he'd been given. A woman's voice answered.

"Sorry I missed you. Leave your name, number, and a brief message. I'll call you back."

John left a message, then retreated to his desk and busied himself with unanswered correspondence. A virtual private network connection allowed him to work in his home study just as if he were at the church office. He logged on to the e-mail server and scrolled quickly through "New Mail" to see if there was anything from anyone he knew and should personally respond to. The rest could wait.

Next, he shuffled through a stack of cards and letters, some that hadn't even been opened yet. Over the past few weeks, a pattern had emerged, making one letter sound very similar to the next, even though they came from all over the United States and as far away as Asia and the Middle East. People wanted to express their encouragement and wish the Cains well. Some pledged to pray for them regularly, and every once in a while a check would be enclosed to help in the search for Jessica.

John and Esther were especially moved by the number of letters from Muslims around the world, expressing their regret over what they described as the actions of a minority group of radicals within their ranks. Many pledged to pray for Jessica's safe return and for a calming of the tensions that September's events had generated.

After almost two hours, the pile had diminished somewhat. John was reaching for another envelope when the phone rang.

"Hello?"

"Hello, is this Mr. Cain?"

"It is," John answered.

"My name is Carla Chin. You left a message."

"Oh, yes, Ms. Chin. Your name was given to me by the people at Sure Shot. They say you are a qualified firearms instructor?"

"That's right."

"Okay, Ms. Chin, here's my situation. Let's see if you can help."

For the next five minutes, they talked about guns. John spoke of his basic uncertainty and lack of knowledge. He told her that he had gone duck hunting with his father years ago—and once for pheasant and quail—but nothing in the past twenty years. He said nothing about his real motivation and was relieved when she did not seem to recognize his name. The more they talked, the more John began to relax.

Eventually, the instructor suggested a time and date, and John agreed to meet her at the range in Santa Clara. Replacing the receiver, he turned and walked away slowly, his hands in his pockets and his mind filled with a mixture of unsettling thoughts.

It's done. There's no turning back now.

41

Jeremy had been keeping a close eye on his parents. Something was up, he knew that for sure. He just didn't know what.

It was on his mind a lot, though.

Even now, standing just beyond the free-throw line, bouncing the ball on the newly resurfaced gym floor, he was thinking about it. In one fluid motion, his body left the floor and he released the ball, watching its familiar arc toward the basket, smiling with satisfaction as it went through, no rim, net only, with a satisfying swish. He was feeling good about his game, even this early in the preseason. His chances for retaining the position he had earned last year as Macarthur High's starting point guard looked a lot better than it had a few weeks ago.

Out of the corner of his eye, he saw the new kid practicing ballhandling techniques on the opposite side of the court. Jim Burnett was a junior transfer from a big school in Fresno, and he was good, no doubt about it. But Jeremy had the edge in experience. Then, last week at the first official team workout, the players had nominated Jeremy to be team captain.

He took another shot from twenty feet out that rattled the rim as it went through. Retrieving the ball, he paused to watch Jim working on his moves.

He's not only a good ball player; he's got discipline. Beyond that, he's a good guy, too.

Jeremy hadn't wanted to like him at first, because they were both competing for the same spot on the team. But Jim's big grin and unvarnished honesty had proven irresistible. He was too real to be fake, and too affable to dislike. The feeling had been mutual, and the two had quickly become good friends, pushing each other on the basketball court and in the weight room, where Jeremy was rapidly building his strength and conditioning.

All the publicity surrounding last month's events had spiked Jeremy's popularity around campus. A few months ago, the attention would have gone straight to his head. He knew that. But he had done a lot of growing up during this latest family crisis. He'd stopped drinking and fooling around with pot. He and his dad had bonded like never before, and his relationship with his mom was even more solid. Their mutual crises while his dad and Jessica were in the Middle East had served to bring them closer than he had ever dreamed possible.

On top of all this, there was Allison.

Thick brown hair that fell past her shoulders. Hazel eyes. Tall and slender. Nearly five-nine. The outdoor type. Excellent swimmer. Top student. A good chance to be valedictorian in May. Dr. Sydney and Helen Orwell's only daughter.

They were seeing each other regularly now. Daily at school, at youth group on Wednesday evenings, and in church on Sundays. Jeremy knew he had never cared for someone else the way he did for Allison. She was wonderful, the type who brings out the best in those around her. That had certainly been the case for Jeremy.

Jeremy liked the way their relationship was deepening. They had spent hours talking and really getting to know each other on the beach one day at Santa Cruz. During the annual Calvary Church high school outing to Disneyland, they'd sat together on the bus and talked about other years and trips and how this would be their last one before college. He loved talking with Allison. She was intelligent, fun to be around, and definitely up front with her Christian faith. Her friendship and unwavering commitment to Christ had been all the encouragement he'd needed to get serious about his own faith and values.

Jeremy took a few more shots, then tossed the ball toward the open door of the equipment room.

"See ya," he called out to Jim as he jogged off the court.

Jim waved back. "Later."

After a quick shower, Jeremy was out the side door of the gym and headed across campus toward the bike rack, schoolbooks in hand. It was usually somewhere between the gym and the bike rack that he dreamed about getting a car. It had been his top priority when he turned sixteen, but now he was glad he had waited. Biking was a great way to keep in shape, and even though borrowing his dad's car was not the same as owning his own, it was definitely cheaper.

Keeping a brisk pace, he could make it home in about fifteen minutes. His route took him past trees that were turning from summer green to varying shades of amber and gold. Jeremy loved this time of year. He thought that autumn would always be his favorite season.

He had been surprised when his parents talked to him about taking a sabbatical, as they called it. It sounded to him more like a leave of absence, but whatever. He'd always thought that a sabbatical was something someone took to go back to school or travel somewhere to strengthen their professional skills. He was sure that wasn't the reason in his father's case.

The light at the crossing turned red as he coasted up to the intersection. He stopped but his mind kept churning, trying to interpret the data in his family's puzzling circumstances.

For the past couple of weeks, he'd had a sense that his dad was holding something back, but he had decided not to press the matter, at least not yet. Their relationship was a complete turnaround from the past summer, but in spite of everything, it was fragile enough that Jeremy didn't want to put stress on it. There was still a lot of tension around the house, and there probably would be until Jessica came home.

Do you suppose they know something about Jessica? No, if they knew anything more, they would tell me. I'm sure of it. Still, what else could it be? Dad announced to the church that he had to spend more time working on the campaign to bring Jessica home. He and Mom have been making lots of calls and answering letters and stuff—but what if they're on to something that they're not telling anyone about? I'm sure they think she's still alive. . . . Maybe the time has come to start asking a few questions.

The light turned green and Jeremy pushed forward smoothly into the intersection. Five minutes later, he braked to a stop in the driveway, pushing his bicycle the rest of the way up onto the porch. Locking the wheel, he grabbed his books and headed for the front door.

—w—

Around the dinner table, it was quieter than usual. Esther had prepared tacos, everybody's favorite meal. Bowls of fresh lettuce, chopped onions, tomato slices, grated cheese, and spicy ground beef were arrayed on the table. Esther's special hot sauce was in a small container at the center. John and Jeremy built their tacos two at a time while Esther settled for one.

After the blessing, the conversation lagged. It seemed to Jeremy that everyone's mind was focused on something other than the people around the table.

"This is Jessica's favorite meal," Jeremy commented casually, his eyes darting from one parent to the other to catch their reaction. He noticed a slight quiver in his mother's hand, but she did not look up from her plate. John glanced his way, however, and nodded.

"Yes, it is," he replied, leaning over his plate as he took another bite. "I hope that wherever she is, they are feeding her well."

Jeremy decided to take the plunge and probe further.

"Dad, I've been doing some thinking since you and Mom started talking about taking this sabbatical. I'm really glad the church is letting you do it. I also agree with them that you shouldn't resign. The people need you right now, even if you're not directly in front of them every week. This way they won't feel abandoned. It's like they are a part of what you are doing, you know?"

John nodded, his eyes fastened on his son.

"Well, that's really important, you know. To feel like you're part of what's happening? Especially if it's really critical?" Jeremy paused, his statements sounding more like questions, which in fact they really were.

John swallowed and reached for his water glass.

"Go on, Son."

"Well, I was just wondering if there is . . . Is there . . ?"

"Is there something going on around here that you don't know about?" John finished the sentence.

"Well, yes, actually. You guys have been so quiet and so preoccupied the last few days. I know all of this is tough on you. But, it's also tough on me. She's—" Jeremy cleared his throat. "She's the only sister I've got now, and I want to help get her back, too."

"You've already been a great help, Son," Esther responded. "More than you'll ever know. But you're back in school; it's your senior year; basketball season is just around the corner; graduation will be here before you know it. We want . . . well, we want at least one of our kids to be able to live some kind of a normal life. I think Jessica would want that, too."

"But you're not getting it, Mom," Jeremy replied. "Life *can't* be normal as long as Jessica is missing. I'm in this as much as you guys are. I know that school is important, but if there's something going on that you aren't telling me about, then it's not fair. I want to know."

Jeremy looked intently across the table.

"I need to know!" he added emphatically.

Esther's face was lined with concern and she reached out to touch Jeremy's hand. John, however, was smiling as he finished off his glass of water.

"I hear what you're saying, Son," he began. "Let's see if I can rephrase it. You're saying that you think we're not being totally open about what we know, and you don't like it. You're reminding us that you'll soon be eighteen and ready for college and you need to be treated as an adult member of the family. You're telling us—in a very diplomatic way, I might add—that you can be trusted to keep confidential anything your mother and I know or are doing when it comes to getting Jessica back. Is that about it, Son?"

Jeremy grinned a little sheepishly and nodded.

John's gaze did not waver. He was not smiling now.

Jeremy's grin faded and his hands dropped to the table.

John pushed back his chair. With calculated deliberateness, he rose to his feet, glancing over at Esther at the same time. She nodded. He put out his hand to Jeremy.

"Okay, Son. You're in. You're in because you deserve to be. Because we need you to be. But what I'm about to tell you cannot go beyond the three of us. Understood?"

Jeremy nodded and grasped his father's hand, wondering what was coming next.

42

WEDNESDAY, 02 NOVEMBER, LOCAL TIME 2015
BANDAR-É ABBÂS, IRAN

Madeline Panay was used to the impersonal relationship that often exists between master and servant. She worked quietly and efficiently, spoke only when spoken to, and secretly counted the days until her contract was up and she could return to the Philippines to study nursing. Upon graduating, she intended to go to Saudi Arabia to work in one of the modern hospitals. She'd heard that other Filipino nurses were paid good salaries there, and she knew that she could support her entire family in the Philippines with such an income.

It was the dream that kept her going.

When she'd turned eighteen, she had sewn a dress from an old school coat and journeyed to Manila. There, she located an agency that employed Filipinos abroad and applied for a maid's position. The Lebanese owner of the agency had suggested that he could get her a job in Manila if she would agree to work in one of the brothels for a year. She would not have to leave her homeland and could earn a substantial amount of money, far beyond a maid's salary. Madeline was a devout Catholic and her indignation at the idea convinced the agency owner that she would not sell her body under any circumstance. With a disappointed sigh, he had told her how to fill out the application and that he would contact her if a maid's position became available.

A little over a month had passed before she was contacted. A contract had been negotiated to provide more than a thousand Filipino workers in the Persian Gulf region. The man told her she would do very well, because rich Arabs and Persians always requested pretty maids. Two weeks later, she learned that she would be going to work for a well-to-do Persian family in a place called Bandar-é Abbâs.

The night she'd arrived at the compound of Reza Fardusi, one week before her nineteenth birthday, she was frightened and completely overwhelmed by her new surroundings. She immediately attached herself to the eldest of ten Filipino maids that served the household. Her initial assignment had been to clean the rooms of the two youngest daughters. She worked quietly and efficiently and did her job well. It wasn't long before the other Filipino workers allowed her into their circle of friendship, providing her with an "insider's education" about her new employer and his family and her new surroundings.

She learned that before being deposed, the Shah had developed Bandar-é Abbâs's potential as a major Iranian port city. Parts of the surrounding desert had been irrigated and cultivated, turning the barren countryside into a lush, food-producing region. Much of the produce was exported from Bandar's updated port.

During the years of revitalization, Reza Fardusi had mastered the delicate art of keeping his hands near the reins of power, while at the same time giving the appearance of independent distance. The Shah had been more than willing to use him for his own grand purposes. Fardusi had used his ties to the Shah to further his wealth and position.

While the Shah sought to modernize and westernize the country's politics and culture, Fardusi remained firm in his commitment to traditional, conservative religious values. Because of his connections and his great wealth, Fardusi was always viewed with suspicion by whomever the country's leaders happened to be at the moment. But he had remained outwardly loyal to the government, and his influence had proven to be of great value. He had made powerful friends, in and out of Iran, and he was shrewd enough to keep his balance in the tricky, mysterious, and sometimes lethal world of Persian politics.

He was a vigorous, handsome man, medium in height, with a cleft chin, snow-white handlebar mustache, and hawklike eyes that were light green, an unusual color for an Iranian. He carried himself with the proud step of one who comes from a house of kings. At the time Madeline arrived on the scene, Reza Fardusi was nearing seventy years of age, the rare aging relic of a fallen dynasty. Although much of his power and influence had waned, he still ruled supreme within the walls of his own home, and on those rare occasions when Madeline caught sight of him, she was always in awe. He was like no man she had ever seen.

The Fardusi compound itself was a place of enchantment, tranquility, and striking beauty. At the center was a large, octagonal garden, filled with colorful flowers and surrounded by poplar trees. In the middle of the garden, a lovely blue-tiled pool and fountain sprayed thin plumes of silvery water, creating a respite from the discomfort of the city's long, hot season in which temperatures occasionally reached 140 degrees Fahrenheit.

A gravel road encircled the garden and its pool, with sufficient room to park the cars of several guests at one time. A ten-foot wall encompassing the entire complex could be entered from two directions only. An iron-studded, wooden gate served as the main entrance, and a service entrance at the opposite side, behind the garage, was always locked. Inside the walls were Reza's spacious home, the subcompounds of his four wives, a carpentry shop, and a sizable garage. On the opposite side of the compound was a large greenhouse, from which gardeners regularly replaced flowers and other growing things that had succumbed to the wilting desert heat.

In the women's quarters, gossip flowed with the same strength and muddy consistency of the Tigris River. Madeline heard all the stories about Fardusi's four wives and their children.

Sattareh was the eldest and the mother of three sons. Everyone knew the sons to be willful and spoiled. Rumors abounded about coerced sexual liaisons between the two older sons and some of the servants, and Madeline quickly learned to avoid the men when they were around.

Fardusi's second wife, Nefel, was a Kurdish woman who was bedridden with a serious illness. Rumor had it that she was not well mentally. Apart from the other wives, who visited her regularly, no one ever saw her except the servant who worked in her home.

Vrahsti and Mahnoosh were the other two wives. They each had children, among whom was Reza's favorite, Jabraiel. All the wives in the compound looked upon each other's children as their own and lived cooperatively as best friends.

During the four months following her arrival, Madeline had settled into her routine. Though the work was hard and the climate intolerable, she considered herself fortunate. She missed her mother and sister. She missed the lush green valley that had been her home in the islands. She missed going to Mass each Sunday. But she had comfortable quarters and was able to save money each month toward her schooling.

Near the end of her third month of employment, she had at last been given permission to go outside the compound with two of the other servants for a Sunday afternoon walk. They were careful to cover themselves to the ankles, and from wrist to neck, and they wore the customary head coverings required of women. For thirty minutes, they had meandered with no apparent destination in mind. Eventually, however, the other two turned down a narrow street and made their way to a doorway that was partially hidden behind a mazari palm tree. Madeline had followed, not knowing where they were going. When they knocked at the door, a young woman answered, motioning them in with a toss of her head.

To Madeline's surprise, fourteen others gathered in the small room, each with a Bible in hand, to listen to a young East Indian man teach from the Scriptures. After introductions were made, Madeline sat down with the others and began to listen. After a while, the young man finished his talk, and the group sang for several minutes. Madeline had never heard the songs before, but they were simple enough that soon she was singing along. Some of the others closed their eyes and lifted their hands as they sang. At first, Madeline was nervous, but after a bit it felt all right.

Another one of the members stood up and spoke from the Scriptures. Afterward, the people discussed what had been said, much as old friends or a family might. It was a different kind of church service than Madeline had ever attended in the Philippines, warm, sincere, and very personal. It felt to her as though God was especially near as they held hands and prayed for one another. Since that first Sunday, Madeline had been back to the tiny house church twice. It all depended on her supervisor's willingness to let her go outside the Fardusi compound.

Since her initial visit to the house church and with the encouragement of her two coworkers, Madeline had begun to read her tattered King James Version Bible, which her mother had received from a Christian missionary. She had insisted that Madeline pack it with her things. Now, just picking it up and feeling the worn leather that her mother's hands had so often touched made her feel close to the ones she loved. Each night, before turning out the light, she took the Bible from under her pillow, carefully opened its pages, and removed the bookmark. Psalms was her favorite portion of the Old Testament. In the New Testament, she was reading the Gospel of John.

Tonight, as she replaced the bookmark and set the Bible on the floor, where it would remain until morning, she experienced the usual deep pangs of loneliness. She wondered how her mother, and her little sister, Cora, were doing. She longed to see Cora now, but that was impossible. Anyway, tomorrow promised a fresh challenge that she hoped would take her mind off her homesickness. Just before she'd gone off duty, Mrs. Muños, her supervisor, had informed her that she was being assigned new duties at the main house. Beginning Friday, Reza Fardusi would be entertaining visitors in his private guest chambers. In the morning, Madeline would be shown the quarters where she was to clean, make beds, and provide for the personal needs of the guests as long as they remained. Âghâ Fardusi was not sure how long that might be.

One of the guests would be a twelve-year-old girl—the same age as Cora.

This should be fun, she thought as she settled her head back on the pillow.

43

THURSDAY, 03 NOVEMBER, LOCAL TIME 1740
NEAR RENO, NEVADA

Thirty miles east of Reno, the three white Rad-Fuel Ltd. tanker trucks turned off the highway and onto a dirt road. Half a mile down the road, they passed a horse corral surrounded by a wooden fence and turned into a rutted driveway. The trucks did not slow down as they churned past the ranch house, kicking up a flurry of dust. Moments later, all three had disappeared inside an old barn.

Early the next morning, well before dawn, three black trucks with the words *Potable Water* painted on the sides roared out of the barn, passed the house, and headed up the dirt road toward the highway. Upon reaching the highway, the trucks turned west.

They had been on the road for twelve hours by the time they drove past the Interstate 580 junction, heading south on 680. Traffic slowed as a wave of commuters merged onto the freeway. A beat-up looking brown Ford Pinto sped past on the shoulder, then cut in and braked abruptly in front of the lead truck. The driver slammed on his brakes and popped the air horn as he tried to avoid a collision. At the last moment, it appeared that the driver of the Pinto saw the truck coming up fast in his rearview mirror and sped up just enough to avoid being rear-ended.

"That was too close!" the lead driver swore as he muttered to himself. "I'm ready to park this stuff and get out of here. My nerves have had it."

He glanced at his sideview mirror. The others were still there. This had been a long, tension-filled haul, but the end was in sight. A mile farther south, he signaled to turn off the Interstate onto Highway 84, heading toward Livermore. Twenty minutes later, the three trucks turned left off the highway and onto a narrow, blacktop roadway, coasting to a stop in front of an iron gate where a man stood, waiting, next to a pickup truck.

The lead driver rolled down his window as the man approached.

"Everyone is here?" the guard asked without a greeting.

"This is it," the driver answered as he passed an envelope thick with hundred-dollar bills through the opening. The guard reached up and took it.

"Follow me."

The guard turned away and got into his pickup, leading the others along the road until they came to a large underground warehouse. The man motioned with his hand for them to proceed forward through the entrance. As soon as the last truck was inside, a large roll-up door came sliding down.

The lead driver shut off his truck's engine. Stepping down from the cab, he stretched his arms and legs and looked around. Even if a search was launched for the trucks with radiation detectors, no one would think to look in an empty underground storage unit at the Vallecitos atomic research center. Even if radiation detection helicopters were used to search for the trucks, the facility's dormant reactor was an established fact. Traces of low-level radiation would not be considered suspicious.

It had been a very long drive, but it was done.

He smiled as he watched the others clear their things out of the trucks, wiping off areas inside the cabs that might possibly have been touched with ungloved hands.

Tomorrow they would fly back to Canada.

It had gone so very easily.

44

FRIDAY, 04 NOVEMBER, LOCAL TIME 1915
SANTA CLARA, CALIFORNIA

John glanced at his watch as he pulled into the curbed parking area.

Fifteen minutes early.

He got out, locked the door and walked toward the entrance of the Sure Shot Firing Range. He wasn't certain what he had expected, but the building appeared to be just one more tilt-up concrete box.

As he entered, he looked past the heads and shoulders of three men whose backs were to him and caught sight of two women behind the reception counter. They appeared to be checking the men in for range practice. He dawdled for a moment, taking in the scene, then started past the desk toward the gun displays.

"Can I help you?" a short, heavyset woman with dark hair called out, her voice raspy with the telltale resonance of a heavy smoker.

"I have an appointment with Carla Chin."

The woman glanced down at an open calendar on the counter.

"Cain? It's at seven-thirty. You're early."

"Right. I'll just look around until she arrives."

He started to turn away.

"Do you have any firearms with you?"

John hesitated. "No. Nothing,"

He smiled to himself as he walked toward the displays. *Now* there's *a question no one has ever asked me before.*

Then he noticed a blue sign board with white letters tacked on the wall:

YOU MUST BE 21 TO RENT OR BUY A HANDGUN
OR AMMUNITION. FOR ADDITIONAL INFORMATION
PLEASE INQUIRE WITH THE MANAGEMENT.

Just beyond the retail area, through closed doors, he could hear the sounds of gunfire on an enclosed range. He peered through one of several spectator windows and saw a row of cubicles, each with a hand-operated target. The man closest was firing a pistol at a target that John estimated to be fifteen or twenty feet away.

All around the retail area were glass display cases filled with small firearms. John had never seen this many guns in one place before. Moving from case to case, he stopped to look at several larger semiautomatic rifles. Kneeling down, he read the hand-printed tag on the one nearest him:

SPRINGFIELD M-1A – $2950
SERIOUS INQUIRIES ONLY!

Wow! For that kind of money, it would have to be serious.

"Hello. Are you Mr. Cain?"

Engrossed in reading the tag, John was startled at hearing his name.

He looked up at a short Asian woman, her jet black hair clipped close to the neck and ears. She was stout and looked even more so, dressed as she was in jeans, a white pullover shirt, and a gray windbreaker open at the neck.

John stood up. Now he was looking down at her.

"That's me. And you're Ms. Chin."

"Carla, please." She motioned toward the case. "Find anything there that interests you?"

"To be honest, I don't know much about guns. That's why I called you. I decided it was time for me to learn."

"Any particular reason?"

"Well, you know how it is these days. Crime on the increase and all that. I've decided that I want to learn how to protect myself and my family." John thought his answer was acceptable and it wasn't a lie, even if it wasn't the whole truth.

The woman waited for a moment, as if expecting more. Then she turned and started walking toward the sound of guns firing. "Come along. Let's go back and acquaint you with the weapon you'll be using tonight."

John breathed a sigh of relief and followed her around the corner.

"You indicated on the phone that you were interested both in handguns and automatic weapons."

John nodded, looking at samples of each that Carla had laid out on a table.

"What's your profession, Mr. Cain?"

He hesitated for a moment, various answers racing through his mind. Finally, he sighed and said, "I'm the pastor of a church."

"A pastor?" Carla's eyes opened wide with surprise. "Isn't it a little unusual for a pastor to be interested in handguns and automatic weapons? Have you had some problems recently?"

"Some," John replied, noncommittally.

"Okay," Carla said, slowly. "I don't mean to pry, but it is important to me that I know a little about the person I'm training. That's why I ask. I don't want to be helping some psycho learn how to use a weapon."

"I can appreciate that. And I assure you that I'm no psycho. Now, shall we begin? You said on the phone that you charge thirty dollars an hour." John grinned. "I'm not a wealthy man."

Carla smiled for the first time and seemed to relax her attitude.

"All right, Mr. Cain. Sit down here and let me introduce you to these weapons."

John sat down.

Carla remained standing and reached for the handgun. "This is a Colt .45. You've probably seen some older versions of this gun in movies. It was adopted by the U.S. Army in 1911, as the standard-issue sidearm. Its appearance has changed a little over the years, but the basic components are the same." She turned the pistol over in her hand, as she continued.

"You can tell that this gun has been modified. Here, see? The edges have been beveled so that it will not get caught so easily in a person's clothing. It's called dehorning. And here. See the extra-large sights? This is called the notch and here, on the barrel end, is the post."

John listened carefully to the description of the Colt .45, as Carla went on with her explanation. "This is a beaver tail safety. When depressed it's in the off position and ready to fire. This is an extended thumb safety. It gives more leverage and is easier to operate. Okay? Any questions?"

He shook his head.

"See the trigger? It has been modified also. Most factory triggers require greater than necessary pressure. An average of about six to ten pounds makes the hammer fall. Four pounds is just right. When you pull the trigger, it should respond like breaking a glass rod or snapping an icicle. See?"

Carla pulled the trigger and John heard the hammer fall.

"This is the slide stop. Here, on the left side. You are right-handed? Good. Pull back the slide with your left hand after you insert a new magazine. Go ahead and try it."

John took the gun for the first time and awkwardly attempted to follow Carla's instructions. After a few tries, he began to get the hang of it.

"How many bullets in a clip?" he asked.

Carla frowned. "It's a magazine, Mr. Cain, not a clip."

"Sorry. How many in a magazine?"

"There are eight, plus one in the chamber, when the gun is loaded."

"And how much would a gun like this cost?"

"Modified like this?"

He nodded.

"About $1000 to $1500 for a combat-modified gun similar to this one. More if you include a tritium bar or three-dot night sight."

John let out a low whistle.

Carla showed him how she carried the weapon in an inside-the-belt holster. On the opposite side, she wore a small pouch that could contain two extra magazines.

"A pistol like this is a defensive weapon. It is underpowered and harder to be accurate. Up to fifteen yards is its primary operating range. If you want to be accurate at, say, twenty or twenty-five yards, then buckshot is a better way to go." Carla put the pistol down and picked up the assault rifle. "Of course, this is an entirely different animal."

"Is that yours?" John asked as he stared at the grim-looking, solid black rifle.

"Yes. It is a GH AR-15. You said you have an interest in automatic weapons. However, they are illegal, except for the military. This one is a semiautomatic and is the civilian version of the M-16. The fact of it being semiautomatic rather than fully automatic is the only difference. Here, hold it." She held it out to him.

"It feels heavy to me," John said, as he balanced it in his hands.

"No, it's not heavy. That's probably not more than six or seven pounds. Feel the butt stock? It's plastic. This over here is the ejection port, and here is the selective fire switch. By moving it, you go from single shot to semiautomatic. It fires twenty-round magazines like this," she said, holding one up for John to see. "If you had a fully automatic one of these and you wanted to be really bad, you could probably get off six to seven hundred rounds per minute."

John's mouth dropped. "Are you serious?"

"Very," she replied, without expression. "That's one reason the latest M-16s have been modified to three-round bursts. If you got excited with one of the earlier models, you could empty your weapon in a second. With the three-round burst, there is more time to go for accuracy.

"It might interest you to know that the first assault weapon in history was developed just prior to World War II. It was made by the Germans. Their original rifles had a range of about two hundred yards, but most of their battles were much closer than that. So they reduced the power of the cartridge and produced an assault weapon that is the grandfather of today's Russian AK-47 and the US M-16."

Carla dropped three wicked-looking bullets on the table in front of John. "These are called full metal jacket cartridges. No lead is exposed. See?" She held one up in the light.

"This one contains a hundred and fifty grains and has a range of twenty-seven hundred feet per second. Now, look at this. It's smaller. This one goes with the AK-47. It has one hundred and twenty-three grains and only travels twenty-three hundred feet per second."

John listened, trying to grasp the magnitude of weapons like this, firing away at hundreds of rounds per minute. He was beginning to feel overwhelmed.

"This smallest bullet is fired by the M-16. It only contains fifty-five grains. But it moves out at thirty-three hundred feet per second and has a kind of tumbling motion that produces more damage once it finds its target." Carla paused, taking the AR-15 from John and laying it on the table. "Any questions?"

John swallowed and wiped his hands on his pants. "I think I'd like to stay with the Colt for now, Carla. This one is a little too awesome."

"Good idea," she smiled again and then turned serious. "Mr. Cain. Your name and face are familiar, and I think now I know why. Are you the one whose church was taken hostage? And weren't you in Israel at the time?"

John hesitated, then nodded, wishing that she had not recognized him.

"And your little daughter is still missing?"

"Yes, that's true, Carla. Does that make any difference in your willingness to help me learn how to use a weapon?"

"Yes. It most definitely does, Mr. Cain." Her voice became quiet and restrained. John's spirits sank. "For one thing, you can forget the per-hour charge. I'll teach you for free."

John looked at her warily, not knowing quite what to say.

"And for another," she continued, her dark eyes flashing. "I don't know if you think these people will be back, or what your reason is for wanting to learn how to shoot. But if you will accept my instruction, I will personally work with you until you are good at this. Really good. Okay? And there will be no charge."

"But why. . . ," John stammered, all at once embarrassed by her sudden effusiveness.

"Because what these people are doing is wrong. Terribly wrong. There are better ways to right the ills of the world than to storm churches and kill innocent people and threaten to destroy whole cities and kidnap little girls. You may find this strange, Mr. Cain, but I sympathize with the plight of the Palestinian people. They are victims of wrongs that need to be made right, in my opinion. But engaging in further wrong is not the answer. There is a better way, a more humane way, than what they are doing. Besides," she hesitated before continuing, "I want to help you get your daughter back. That's what this is really all about, isn't it?"

John stared back into his instructor's searching eyes.

"Are you a Christian, Carla?" he asked.

Carla chuckled. "No, you're probably as close to 'Christian' as I've ever been. My family is Buddhist. Personally, I am not at all religious."

"Well, you are a very perceptive person, nonetheless. I can't say anything more, though. Hopefully, my reticence to talk about it won't offend you?"

"Not at all. I think I understand."

"Thank you. And I accept your offer."

"Good. Now, let's go get started. When we get out there, the first thing I want to show you is the Weaver stance for firing your weapon."

"The Weaver stance?"

"Yeah. It's named after the sheriff who made it popular. I'll show you the guard position, too. Come on, follow me."

"By the way," said John, as they walked toward the firing range, "what do you do in real life? I'm sure you can't make a living teaching guys like me how to shoot."

"You wouldn't believe me if I told you."

"What? Are you military? A police officer?"

Carla laughed. "Bad guess, Mr. Cain. Actually, I'm an RN, at South Peninsula Hospital. Pediatrics."

"No way. A gun-totin' gal like you is in pediatrics?" John exclaimed.

"I said you wouldn't believe me."

45

SATURDAY, 05 NOVEMBER, LOCAL TIME 0810
BANDAR-É ABBÂS, IRAN

It was still dark as the morning call to prayer resonated from minaret to minaret, urging the faithful to rise up for prayer.

Does anyone really get up to pray when that guy sounds off? What is it Sultana called him . . . oh, yeah, the muezzin. She taught me what the prayer meant. Let's see . . .

Allah u Akbar.

God is the greatest.

God is the greatest.

I witness that there is no god but God.

I witness that Muhammad is the prophet of God.

Rise to prayer.

Rise to . . . what was the word? . . . fell . . . felicity.

I wonder what that means? Well, anyway . . .

God is the greatest.

God is the greatest.

There is no god but God.

Sultana had told Jessica that when Islam was in its infancy, the Prophet's disciples used to gather around him for prayer. As their numbers increased, it became necessary to call them together. That's when Muhammad chose Bilal to be the first *muezzin,* or caller to prayer. Bilal was an African slave who had been freed after accepting the teachings of Islam. To accomplish his assignment, he climbed the roof of a house near the mosque that Muhammad had helped build and recited the *Adhan,* the call to prayer.

I wonder what Sultana is doing? Do you suppose she ever thinks of me?

Jessica pictured in her mind the bronze-skinned woman with the kind face. There had been something between them. Jessica had felt an unspoken bond. They had talked, really talked. Under other circumstances, Jessica thought the woman could probably have been a friend, like an aunt or an older cousin. Sultana had been a protector of sorts, even though she was one of Jessica's kidnappers.

Sultana, I wish you were here. . . . I wish we could talk some more. I wish . . . I wish I would have remembered to ask you what "felicity" means.

It was Friday, the Muslim holy day, and the normally bustling universe of Reza Fardusi's compound had slowed to a pace befitting this day of reflection.

By standing on the small cot, Jessica was able to see out of the room's only window. It wasn't very large, she guessed not more than eighteen inches wide and about two feet high. It was too high up to be able to look down at all, unless she stood on the bed. Otherwise, the only view through the window was blue sky. Besides, the glass was cracked and dirty. Last night, she had waited until no one else was in the room before pushing on the frame. At first, it stayed in place. Then, stretching as far as she could, and pushing with both hands, she discovered that it was not locked.

It moved!

A mistake, no doubt. Or maybe it can't be locked from the outside.

The sound of creaky hinges frightened her, and she stopped short of pushing it fully open. Instead, she carefully returned it to its original position and sat back down on the edge of the cot. For weeks, she had lived in a world of locked doors, guards, and social deprivation. To think that there was a window without bars that she could open at will was almost too much. Her heart beat with excitement.

Maybe it's a way out of here!

This morning, she took the chance to look out the window at first light. Her heart sank. To begin with, the opening looked even smaller in the light of day.

No wonder they aren't worried about it being unlocked. They probably wouldn't care, even if they knew.

Peeking out, she confirmed that she was on the second floor and there was no ledge really, only a narrow, decorative protrusion, about two or three inches wide, that ran along the full length of the building. There was nothing to keep her from falling, even if she did manage to crawl out the window. She pushed it open a few inches and let the powerful breath of roses from the garden below inveigle her sense of smell, tantalizing her with memories of her mother's roses on the patio back home.

Dropping onto the bed, Jessica sat with her back against the wall and stared at the door. After a while, she couldn't be sure how long, she heard the sound of voices, but not from the hall. They were coming from outside, beyond the cracked window. She had not closed it all the way.

Standing on the cot, she reached up to pull it shut. That's when she saw the people. A group of four small children were playfully running circles around one another and laughing. With them, three older boys and three women who acted very much like mothers made their way along the white gravel road toward the house where she was held prisoner.

I wonder who they are?

Just then, a door below her room opened.

Why are they coming here?

The children quieted, as if on cue, as one by one they disappeared inside. When the last person had entered and the door closed, all was quiet once more. The sounds of happy laughter and conversation that had drawn her to the small window had ceased.

Jessica pulled the window shut, dropped down on the cot, and cradled her face in her arms. After a minute, she rolled onto her back and stared at the ceiling. As depressed and homesick as she was, there were no tears this morning. She felt dried up. She wondered whether she would ever cry again. Was there a secret chamber of tears still hidden somewhere inside? Who could know? She pillowed her head in the palms of her hands, listening to the low, steady hum of the ceiling fan's electric motor, watching as it slowly turned. Her thoughts turned with it, looking to light on something pleasant.

She summoned up the cool, dampness of the Netherlands, contrasting its tiny green fields with the harsh desert region she had journeyed through these last weeks. She held her father's hand and walked through Amsterdam at night, with its magical, never-ending canals and flower vendors at the bus stops. Tiny shops were brightly lit for the tourists.

I wonder what ever happened to the things I bought for Mom and the kids in my class? Do you suppose that stuff ever got home? It was the first time she had considered this question since being taken hostage.

How long has it been now?

At first, she had kept track. But after moving from place to place, the days and nights had blurred. She had become confused about dates. After considerable thought, she decided it must be November and that Thanksgiving could not be all that far off. Then her mind returned to the cool streets and dark canals of Amsterdam.

She remembered getting lost with her dad and how embarrassed he had been when they arrived in the area where young prostitutes worked. She thought about the pretty young woman in the window. She could see her there, as if it were yesterday.

I promised to pray for her until I got back home.

Already depressed, Jessica now felt an added pang of guilt. Many days had come and gone since last she had prayed for the girl in the window. In her own stress-filled preoccupation with survival, she had forgotten. Silently, she let her lips move in prayer in behalf of the stranger. She wished she knew her name, but she was sure that God would know who that "pretty young girl in the window in Amsterdam" was.

She retraced the steps she and her father had taken the following morning, on their way to visit the Anne Frank Haus. Thoughtfully, reverently, Jessica let herself walk through Anne's secret home one more time. She touched a table, a lamp, a book. She was there again. With Anne.

What did she look like?

Jessica tried to remember.

The pictures had shown a young girl with dark hair and fair skin. Beyond that, she could not recall, so she began filling in Anne's features herself. A pretty girl. Her eyes are friendly, but there's sadness there, too. A firm chin. She looks pale, though, from being inside all the time. Anne was hidden for two years. No playmates, no school plays, no sports program, no sharing lunches, no laughing with friends, no waving good-bye with the assurance that she would see them again tomorrow.

Anne's daily companion was fear.

Only fear.

The fear of being discovered.

Jessica felt that same piercing fear herself, like a cold knife.

Only here, in Iran, it was different.

For Jessica, it was the fear of *never* being discovered.

Or being discovered too late!

46

Saturday, 05 November, local time 1000
Santa Clara, California

John met Carla at ten o'clock on the range at Sure Shot. During their initial meeting, they had agreed that the Colt .45 ACP would be the weapon of choice. This semiautomatic pistol appeared to John to combine the most accuracy and penetration potential, yet it was light to carry and relatively easy to handle.

Before going onto the firing line, Carla went over the fundamentals of firearm safety rules.

"Mr. Cain . . ."

"Please, Carla. The name is John."

Carla smiled politely.

"John." She repeated his name softly. Placing the handgun on the table, she turned to face him directly. "For me to call you by your first name, Mr. Cain, will take some getting used to. I must tell you that after our initial meeting, I went to the library near where I work and read through several news accounts of your experience in Israel back in September. I am somewhat in awe of you as a result."

John looked surprised. "Carla, you can't be serious. I'm the one who's in awe. I'm standing here with a female firearms instructor, who in real life is a pediatric nurse. Besides what she knows about children, she is more knowledgeable and proficient with guns than I will ever be. What you handle so easily and professionally scares the living daylights out of me. Believe me, you have no reason to be in awe. God is the one who gets the credit for what happened in Israel. I was just the instrument that he decided to use."

"I'm not sure about God deserving the credit; but if you say so, I will accept it. What I read about does seem to have been a bit miraculous, to say the very least. Anyway, enough of this. Let's get to work. I am honored to be your teacher . . . *John*."

Carla picked up the .45 and turned it over in her hand.

"There are four things you must always remember with any gun. First, every gun is loaded. At least, that must be your assumption until you have personally inspected the weapon to be sure that it is empty. Don't accept as fact what anyone else says about it. Always check for yourself. Too many people have been killed or injured with 'unloaded' guns.

"Second, never point the muzzle at anything or anyone you are not willing to destroy."

She paused and looked up.

John let out his breath and nodded for her to continue.

"Third, keep your finger *off* the trigger until your sight is on the target. Finally, be absolutely sure of your target. Don't shoot at shadows or sounds. Okay?"

"Okay."

"So, let's go out and fire a few rounds—but first, put these in." She handed him a pair of earplugs.

They opened the door and walked to the nearest vacant shooting booth. Handguns were being fired in four other locations, forcing Carla to speak up in order to be heard.

"When you grip the weapon, be consistent. Learn the right way and then use that same method each time. Your right forearm should always be an extension of the barrel itself. Like this. See?" She demonstrated while John watched.

"Now, you do it," she said, handing him the gun.

"Put your hand directly behind the weapon . . . that's right. A little higher. Grip it as high as possible and you'll minimize the recoil. Okay, there's the target. It's at five yards. Take a couple of shots. Safety off. . . . Take your time."

John fired once. Twice.

"Safety on?" Carla reached to take the gun from John's hand. "Let's see how you did."

She hand-reeled the target in until it hung directly in front of them. There were no bullet holes.

"I guess I failed Shooting 101, huh?" John said sheepishly.

"There is a great difference between failing and being a failure, Mr. . . . John," Carla rejoined. "But we obviously have a little work ahead of us. Would you agree?"

"I would agree," he answered.

"You will now learn to use the proper stance," she continued authoritatively. "There are several, but the one I prefer is the Weaver stance. It's preferred by law enforcement and competition shooters. Here, take the gun."

She handed the .45 back to John, who decided upon taking it that it felt more natural in his hand than it had the first time he'd prepared to fire it. He was starting to relax.

"Left elbow down slightly. Feet approximately even. Flex your right arm a little. Now, put your left hand over your right hand . . . no, it must be vertical. Yes, like that. Hold the thumb high. Now, advance the left shoulder . . . that's right. Are you comfortable? It feels okay?"

"It feels pretty good, considering I've never done this before," John answered.

"Your left hand is going to help keep the pistol down when it is fired. It absorbs the recoil and provides you with more accuracy. Now, try a couple of shots again."

This time, John had two marks, one in the second ring and the other at the outer edge of the third ring.

"Good job," Carla shouted enthusiastically. "We'll make a marksman out of you yet."

For the next thirty minutes, they practiced proper technique. When Carla announced that it was time to quit for the day, John was surprised. He looked at his watch. Sure enough, she was right.

"I can meet you again on Tuesday evening, if that works for you," she said, flipping the pages of a small pocket calendar. "Of course, you can come in on your own at any time and practice. I think working on your own will be more valuable after a couple of additional lessons. But suit yourself."

"Tuesday will be fine," John replied. "How long do you think it will take before I can at least hit the side of a barn with this thing?"

"In a few weeks we'll have you shooting like a Texas Ranger," Carla beamed. Then, the glow of enthusiasm suddenly disappeared and she lowered her eyes. "Do you have a time limitation, John?"

John put his hands on the shelf in front of him and stared at the paper bull's-eye, ten yards out. "I don't know for sure. I just need to be ready as soon as possible."

"How do you feel about it now that you've had your first lesson?"

"What do you mean?"

"I mean I noticed your tentativeness. You obviously are not afraid to deal with things that are dangerous. So, I assume it has something to do with your feelings about guns. You'll have to work that out, you know. Whatever convictions you carry about shooting someone need to be dealt with early on. Otherwise, having a handgun in your possession will only be a danger to you, not a deterrent to others."

John turned his gaze from the target and looked down at Carla.

"I understand."

Carla nodded, then turned toward the exit.

"Next Tuesday, then. Seven o'clock?"

"I'll be here."

He followed her out into the cool autumn air, his mind swirling with thoughts about the moral implications of what he was preparing to do.

47

SUNDAY, 06 NOVEMBER, LOCAL TIME 1810
BANDAR-É ABBÂS, IRAN

Reza Fardusi peered at his house guest over the remains of a large dish of steamed *chelo* rice. At the beginning of the meal, the *chelo* had been covered with a crunchy egg yolk crust, broken up and served on top. Nearby was a side dish of *mâst*—yogurt mixed with diced cucumber, fresh herbs, and spices. Fardusi's guest had declined an offer of prawns, opting instead for fresh vegetables and *barbari,* a crisp and salty Iranian bread. A pitcher of boiled drinking water was off to one side, near a tray of assorted almonds, pistachios, and hazelnuts.

Typical of an Iranian meal, there was not much conversation during the meal. At just the right moment, a servant mysteriously appeared, carrying a bowl filled with fresh pomegranates, bananas, and rosy-fleshed grapefruit, to be served in place of dessert. A moment later, she returned with two small glass cups, each with a detachable metal holder, and proceeded to fill them with scalding hot black tea. At a nod from Fardusi, the servant quickly cleared the table until only the fruit and tea remained.

"*Mersi, khosh maze bud,*" the guest said, smiling as she looked across the table at her host. "Thank you, it was delicious."

"*Ghâbel nabud,*" Reza Fardusi nodded politely. "Don't mention it."

"It is an honor for me to sit at your table," she continued.

"The privilege is mine," he responded.

The pleasantries continued for a few minutes as they savored the fruit, drank the tea, and sized each other up.

"My apologies for not being able to greet you earlier," said Fardusi. "Of necessity, I had to attend to matters in Kermân Province."

"I understand. How did you find it there?"

"Things are not so good, as you might well imagine. The economy continues to suffer severe regression. I have many friends in that area from the days when Bandar was the major trade outlet for their crops. I'm sure you understand just how dependent they have become on the *ghanâtas*—the underground water channels—for their irrigation. The drought has been insufferable. To make life even more difficult, the water table is decreasing, and some say it has become contaminated. At any rate, problems continue to loom over that region of our homeland. But enough of this. Tell me, please, the nature of your unexpected visit. I understand that you have brought a young guest to my house."

He watched Leila Azari push back a wisp of hair that had slipped from under her head covering. In some circles, that slight indiscretion alone would be enough to land her in jail. Personally, as a Muslim, Fardusi thought such things to be unimportant. It was just one item, on a growing list of things that discouraged his respect for the mullahs who spent their time enforcing such foolishness. Leila reached for the teapot, a classic piece of British porcelain, and refilled her glass cup. Looking across the table, her eyes asked if her host wished more tea, without words being spoken.

"Yes, please," he responded, holding up his cup as she poured.

"You know of Marwan Dosha?" she began, returning the teapot to the table.

"Of course," the old man answered. His eyes fluttered slightly at the mention of the name, then quickly regained their cryptic appearance.

"And you have read about the failure of recent Islamic jihad operations in America and Israel?"

Fardusi waited silently, never taking his eyes off Leila's.

"Dosha was the overseer of that mission," she continued. "He also led the attack in the U.S., on the city of Boston. It was a triple-pronged attack and the Palestinian Islamic Jihad's most sophisticated operation to date. Dosha was the architect, working at the behest of Hafez Tabatai and Mahmoud Assad in Lebanon. I know Tabatai from the training camps in southern Lebanon."

Leila paused to sip her tea.

"As you have read, an American cleric named John Cain was instrumental in foiling the mission. He and his American followers were taken hostage—"

"And ultimately escaped, if, at my age, my memory still serves me correctly," Fardusi interrupted, a thin smile on his weathered face.

"That's correct. All escaped, but one."

"The daughter?"

"Yes."

"And this is the little girl who is a guest in my house?"

"Yes."

Fardusi shifted his body with a suddenness that surprised Leila, causing her to clutch nervously at her cup of tea. Leaning forward, he rested his hands loosely on the table, eyes snapping like emeralds in the sun, as he spoke with deliberate slowness. "And why, may I ask, is she here? What purpose is being served by holding this American child? What is the reason for her being kept here, in my house? And can you tell me please why I was not first asked if this would be acceptable?"

Fardusi had already decided that Leila Azari was not one to be easily intimidated. Without a doubt, she relied on her beauty and charm, edged with a hint of steel. But Fardusi was unconcerned. Though far past the age of being physically formidable, over the years he had honed his skills at mental and emotional intimidation to a sharp and very effective point. He saw no reason not to establish the upper hand at the outset of his acquaintance with Leila Azari.

"I am only a servant of the cause, Âghâ. I follow orders." There was an edge to her voice and her eyes flashed as she spoke. "A short time ago, my superior called me in from the field to entrust me with the child's welfare. She was brought to Bandar by the PIJ at Marwan Dosha's specific instruction. I was informed that your home would be ideal. It is private, well provided for, and secure. I'm certain your full cooperation was assumed without question by our leaders."

"Our leaders assume a great deal these days," remarked Fardusi, the fingers of his right hand impatiently rapping on the table's surface. "Are you telling me that you have no knowledge about the purpose of your mission?"

He felt her hesitation. She obviously was not used to being interrogated by anyone, especially an old man. She had expected him to be more acquiescent. He saw that she was put off by his questions. It was exactly what he wanted.

His fingers ceased their drumroll on the table. Relaxing his body, he leaned back, resting his hands with fingers intertwined, on the table. He looked across at the woman and smiled so warmly that the distance between them suddenly seemed to shrink.

"Mrs. Azari."

Leila started.

"I am not married," she blurted out, without thinking.

"Ah, but you were. Your husband was killed at the front in the war with Iraq. It is regrettable. I am very sorry."

Leila eyed him guardedly now, yet he gave no hint of anything but genuine sympathy. How long had it been since any of the people she worked with had expressed compassion over the loss of her husband in the war? It suddenly hit her—no one until now had said a word.

"How did you know?" she asked.

"I know many things. An old man has little else to do but to listen and to know things. I would like to see the girl. Theresa!"

The servant reappeared at the door.

"There is a young child upstairs in the first room on the right, just beyond the landing. I want you to bring her to me."

Theresa turned and started toward the staircase that curved upward from the great room toward the second-floor hall.

"Wait," Leila called out. Theresa stopped. "The room is locked and she is guarded."

"She is guarded in a locked room?" Fardusi was twisting the pointed end of his mustache, an amused look on his face. "How old is this woman who is so dangerous that she needs to be both locked up and guarded?"

"She is twelve," Leila said sharply, "but my instructions are to keep her secure." She stood and moved toward the hall. "I will need to bring her to you."

"Very well," Fardusi responded, tilting his head slightly forward, an amused twinkle in his eyes. "It will be a pleasure to meet our little guest. Oh, and, Mrs. Azari, if you would be so kind to remember, my servants answer to my bidding, not yours."

Smiling beneficently, Fardusi pushed back his chair and stood. Pain shot through his foot as he limped to a nearby lounging chair and sat down once again. From here, he could command a view of the entire room, as well as the small garden just outside the double French doors. He liked this spot. It was his favorite place in the house. It also provided an excellent view of the staircase leading up to the next floor landing. Sitting back in the chair, he waited.

48

Jessica heard the key turning in the lock, and watched as the door swung open. The woman who entered was unquestionably the leader of the guards. Just as unquestionably, she was now angry. Her face appeared flushed and her dark eyes flashed as she entered.

"Get up!" she ordered.

Jessica sat up on the edge of the cot.

"Come with me. There is someone who wants to see you."

"Who?"

"Do not speak unless spoken to."

"I thought you were speaking to me."

The woman's hand lashed across Jessica's face.

"Do not try to act smart with me. It will get you nothing but pain."

"Hey, what did I do?" For an instant, Jessica's vision blurred as her cheek began to redden from the force of the blow.

"Cover your head and come with me."

Jessica scooped the scarf from off her bed and wrapped it around her head the way Sultana had taught her, until only her face could be seen. The woman walked ahead of her into the hall as they retraced the steps Jessica had taken the night she arrived. The one who had been sitting in the hall, guarding the door, followed closely behind.

At the landing, Jessica noticed an elegant chandelier hanging over the center of the great room. Hundreds of exquisitely cut crystal pieces caught the late afternoon sun, reflecting prisms of golden light that danced across both floor and ceiling. She slowed her pace for a moment until the guard pushed her from behind. She reached the edge of the steps and began her descent behind the first woman.

As she reached for the handrail she caught sight of someone sitting in a chair in the room below. A man with a white mustache, with one foot wrapped in a bandage and propped up. He looked to be about the age of her grandfathers. Her heart pounded with apprehension as she reached the main floor and walked across the room until she was standing close enough to touch the man's foot.

She decided that touching the old man's foot was probably not in her best interest.

She felt a hand on her shoulder, pushing her forward.

"This is the girl," Leila Azari said.

Jessica stood still, waiting. *Who is this? What does he want from me?*

"What is your name, child?" The man's voice was deep, his English clear, with a light British accent. He lowered his bandaged foot to the floor and leaned forward to listen.

"Jessica."

"Jessica," he repeated. "That's a very nice name. Jessica what?"

"Jessica Cain."

"Where are you from, Jessica Cain?"

"My home is in California. Baytown, California—in the United States."

"I believe you are from near San Francisco, is that not correct?"

"Yes. What is your name?" Jessica looked directly at the man now, taking in all his features. She decided that he reminded her more of Papa Cain than Papa Stevens—not so much in looks, but in the sound of his voice. Papa Cain had a deep voice like this man's.

"Jessica, you are not to ask questions!" The woman's hand pressed tightly on her shoulder. Jessica twisted away from her grip and glared up at her captor.

Reza Fardusi lifted his hand. "Stop it."

The woman halted abruptly, and Jessica straightened up, turning back once more to the elderly man.

"I understand that this girl is your prisoner, Mrs. Azari." He spoke sternly, looking past Jessica to the others. "However, as long as you make my home her prison, I am quite certain that you wish to respect the fact that this truly is *my* home?"

Leila did not answer.

His voice quieted. "She most assuredly is your prisoner, but as long as she remains in my home, she is my responsibility, as are all of my guests, including each of you. And, as always, I intend for my guests to be treated in the best manner possible.

"You will be in no danger here," he said, looking directly at Jessica. "It would seem we have not been properly introduced. This woman who brought you here is Leila Azari. And my name is Reza Fardusi."

Jessica could feel tension slicing through the atmosphere in the room. *What this man is saying about me not being in danger and what I am feeling right now are two entirely different things.*

"Come closer, child." Fardusi reached out his hand. Jessica took a half step, then another. Then she did something that surprised even her.

She reached out and placed her hand in the man's hand.

It was a big hand, compared to hers. Hard, not soft. A workingman's hand. *He looks too old to be an ordinary worker. Besides, check this place out. This room is huge.*

"How did you get such a beautiful house like this?" asked Jessica. "I thought everyone in this part of the world was poor."

Fardusi laughed. It was a hearty sounding laugh. Then, his hand closed over Jessica's and drew her closer.

She started to pull back just as he released her.

"Do you know why you are my guest, Jessica Cain?"

"No, sir, and I am not your *guest*," Jessica's eyes flashed as she spit out the words. "I'm being held hostage here against my will. There's a big difference."

"Right you are, young lady," Fardusi replied calmly. "A big difference indeed."

"I want to go home. That's all."

"I'm sure that in due time, you will get to go home. But for now you are here with us. And as for this humble abode, I have worked hard to provide for my family a suitable place. This has been my home for many years."

"You have a family? Are your children grown up?"

Fardusi chuckled once again, pleased at how the young girl handled herself. "My family was here a short while ago."

Jessica flashed back to the women and children she had seen earlier. Could some of those have been his family? She started to say that she had seen them along the roadway, but checked herself. *Wait. Don't say anything. They'll know I looked through the window and they won't like that. If they check it out, they will discover that it's not locked.*

Fardusi saw her mouth open, then close. "You wished to say something, child?"

"I . . . I was wondering. . . . How many children do you have?"

Fardusi folded his hands against his chest and leaned back in the chair. He tried to reposition the foot that had begun to ache with renewed gusto.

"My wife, Sattareh, is the mother of my three sons. Nefal and Mahnoosh have each provided me with two daughters. Mahnoosh is also the mother of my youngest son, Jabreiel."

"You have three wives?" Jessica blurted out.

Fardusi laughed uproariously.

"Yes, indeed," he answered, and then, just as suddenly as the laughter had come, his countenance changed. "Actually, I have four wives. Allah permits us to have up to four wives, provided that we can care for each of them equally well."

Jessica tried to grasp the reality of the idea. "I cannot imagine my daddy having four wives. That would be against our religion. In fact, it would be illegal in my country. In America, you can only have one wife."

". . . at a time," Fardusi corrected with a smile. "Your males can only marry one woman at a time. But your divorce rate is such that many men in America have more than one wife in their lifetime. So, what is the difference, do you think?"

Jessica was at a loss to answer the question. It was true. A number of her friends' parents, both at church and school, had divorced. It hurt her to even think about the possibility with her own parents. She chose to leave the thought alone, though she had sensed her parents' struggles and secretly wondered if the terrible ogre of divorce would tear her own family apart.

"You said you have four wives," she countered, deciding not to answer the elderly man's question.

"That is correct."

"But you mentioned only three by name."

Fardusi hesitated. A shadow seemed to cross his face.

"My fourth wife is Nefel. She is ill."

"Does she have children?"

The somber shadow remained. He looked away.

"There were two. They are both dead."

The mood in the room was suddenly subdued.

At last, Fardusi sighed heavily, breaking the silence. "Mashti would be twenty this year. His sister, Korsum, would be eighteen."

"I'm sorry." Without thinking, Jessica reached out and touched the man's hand again. "I have a little sister who died. Her name is Jenny. It really hurts, doesn't it?" All at once, the man looked very old and haggard. Clearly, the memory was distressing to him. At her touch, his eyes found hers and looked into them steadily. There was sadness, but there was something more, as well. Jessica sensed that something had just passed between them, but she couldn't put her finger on it.

"Were they sick?" she asked.

He dropped his gaze and moved his hand away from hers.

"They died six years ago. In the war."

Jessica remained silent. She didn't know what else to say. She wanted to ask, *What war?* But this was neither the time nor the place. Besides, this man was the enemy. She was being held hostage in his home. She tried to stir up the embers of anger and resentment that had burned a hole into her heart during these past weeks. But the glow was faint at the moment.

The fire was almost out.

Only the ashes remained.

In its place, something else was beginning to take shape.

A determination.

A resilience fueled by an ever-increasing will to live.

Survival.

Endurance.

Jessica gritted her teeth and silently whispered to herself.

I want to go home!

Fardusi studied the girl intently. For a long moment, the pain inside seemed deeper and more intense than at any time since the day he had been notified of the martyrdom of his two children—killed on the Iraqi front by a land mine. Mashti had been fourteen at the time, Korsum only twelve.

"Do you have any more questions of the girl?" Leila Azari finally broke the long silence.

Fardusi shifted in the chair and looked up.

"No," he replied. "Not at the present moment. *Ruz be kheyr*, Jessica. Good day."

Jessica hesitated for just a moment, then felt the hand of the Azari woman come down on her shoulder. Without a word, she turned and headed back toward the stairs.

—w—

As Fardusi watched her climb the stairs between the two women, there came to him the words of an anonymous Iranian poet, who had written during the war:

That black smoke that rose from the roof—
that was our black smoke. It came from us.
That burning fire that swayed left and right—

that was our fire. It came from us.
Do not denounce the foreigner, or lament anyone but us.
This is the heart of the matter—
our affliction came from us.

His gaze followed the girl until she disappeared from sight.
Amazing.
Her eyes, so green.
Like two flashing emeralds.
Like Korsum's.

49

Outside the open doorway to the second room on Madeline's duty list, she heard footsteps in the hall. There were voices, too, conversing in low, angry tones. Across the hall, she heard the door open and close. A moment later, a woman entered the room where Madeline continued her cleaning chores. Without so much as a word acknowledging the maid's presence, she pulled the dark-colored scarf away from her hair and threw it onto the bed. Madeline glanced up. The woman was unusually attractive—and visibly upset.

I've not seen her here before.

Madeline busied herself with the feather duster, attempting to brush away particles of dust that seemed bent on coming together and resettling in the same area. The room had no closet, only an open nook with wall hooks and a bar stretched across containing several wooden hangers. Clothes had been flung carelessly over a few hangers. In the corner of the nook, half-hidden under the clothes, a black semiautomatic rifle stood propped against the wall.

Madeline made short work out of smartening up the disheveled covers on the bed. Quietly, she gathered up her things to carry across the hall to the last room. The woman ignored her as she walked past.

Stepping outside, she was surprised to see one of the other women sitting directly in front of the door.

"I beg your pardon," Madeline said to the woman, mentally noting the handgun strapped to her waist. She was reading a copy of *Mahjubah,* a popular Islamic family magazine published in Tehran. Madeline had seen it before at a newsstand. The guard looked up.

"Please, I need to go inside and take care of the room."

The woman's gaze dropped to the cloths, towels, feather duster, damp mop, and pail on the pushcart, then back to Madeline. Madeline decided to try one of the few conversational phrases she had so far learned in Farsi.

"*Bebakhshid: Fârsi ballad ni stam.* I'm sorry, I don't speak Persian. *Shomâ Engelisi baladid*? Do you know English?"

"I speak it well enough to understand what you are saying and far better than you speak my language. Who are you?"

"My name is Madeline. I have been assigned by my supervisor to care for these three rooms during your stay here. I understand that one of your group will have her meals served in the room. Is it this room?"

The female guard nodded.

"Is your associate ill?"

"She is not our 'associate,'" the guard replied. "She is our prisoner. You will need to bring her meals because she cannot be released to eat with others."

Madeline felt her skin crawl.

"Is she dangerous? Will I be safe inside?"

The guard's face broke into a gradual smile. "Yes, I assure you that you are safe. But while you are inside, you must not speak with her. She is to talk to no one. That includes you."

Madeline nodded. "I understand," she replied.

The guard got up from the chair, turned the key in the door, and stepped aside.

Madeline knocked and waited. There was no response from behind the door. She knocked again. Nothing.

"Go on. Go inside and do your work. Be quick about it."

Madeline nervously opened the door. She was not prepared for what she saw.

—w—

Having ignored the knock, Jessica listened disconsolately to the sound of the door latch. She glanced up from her cot, the only piece of furniture in the room, situated against the wall beneath the window.

She watched a young, dark-skinned woman enter the room, leaving the door open behind her. A metal pushcart filled with cleaning supplies had been pulled halfway through the doorway. The woman wore the uniform of a maid, brown pants and smock, high to the neck and buttoned at the wrists. Jessica thought she looked Asian, but she wasn't sure. The woman stepped into the room, glancing around hesitantly, as if she expected to find something or someone else.

"Hello," said Jessica, pushing herself to a sitting position on the edge of the cot.

The maid stared at her for a long moment but said nothing.

"My name is Jessica. Jessica Cain."

The young servant dipped her mop into the pail of brownish water and began mopping the tiled surface of the floor.

"I am an American. Do you speak English? Do you understand me?"

The servant continued mopping, push and pull, back and forth, but Jessica noticed an almost imperceptible nod of the head. Just then, the guard's face appeared in the doorway.

"Be quiet. You must not speak unless spoken to."

"It can't hurt to be a little sociable."

"If you refuse to be quiet, I will tape your mouth."

Jessica thought about that possibility, a feeling of anger rising inside her. She remembered the panicky discomfort of being bound and gagged, however, and decided not to chance it.

Back and forth.

The maid came nearer, stooping over her dreary task. Jessica lifted her feet as she watched the mop make wet designs on the surface of the tiles by the side of the cot.

"Madeline."

Jessica's heart stopped for an instant. Had she heard correctly? Had the woman just spoken her name? The maid kept pushing the mop back and forth, under the edge of her cot. Her back was toward the guard.

"My name is Madeline," she whispered again.

Jessica strained to hear more, but that was all. As soon as Madeline finished, she moved away from that corner of the room, without looking again at Jessica. Minutes later, she was at the door, putting her cleaning tools on the cart. She did not look back, and the guard closed the door.

Jessica heard the lock turn.

Once again she was alone.

But a new player had just been introduced into her game of survival.

Madeline.

She speaks English.

She works for them, but apparently she is not one of them.

Jessica stared at the door for a long time.

50

Sunset was Reza Fardusi's favorite time of the day in the enclosed garden—the *pairidaeza.* It was the Farsi word from which the English word *paradise* derived. Warm breezes moving in off the Gulf were beginning to temper the extreme heat. The shadows were growing longer under the olive and fig palms. The silence was disturbed only by one of the three gardeners who lived and worked at the compound, who just now was carefully raking up weeds and leaves around an area of green shrubbery.

Fardusi's white shirt was open at the collar. Sweat beads lined his forehead and perspiration formed damp circles underneath his arms. Today had been unusually warm for this time of year. Swatting at a pesky fly, he hoped that tomorrow would be cooler.

With the help of a crutch, he walked slowly to the end of the path and turned to face the great house. His heart swelled with pride as he surveyed the surrounding compound. Persian and foreign guests still came to visit on occasion to discuss matters in the shipping industry. Even though he was now retired, Fardusi's counsel and connections were still sought after by those who had succeeded him. He remained powerful, respected both for his honesty and shrewdness, although his dominating influence had diminished significantly during the past decade—a fact that he, more than anyone else, was mindful of. The election of former minister of culture Mohammad Khatami—a modern clergyman and intellectual—as president had come with the promise of greater openness and less meddling from the die-hard defenders of the Islamic regime. However, change had been slow, and the people were tired of waiting.

The fanatical determination of the mullahs to turn Iran into a religious state, scrupulously adhering to the ancient codes and beliefs of Islam, had diverted the spotlight from the nation's desperate economy. By the time the spotlight had refocused, it was almost too late. There had been some improvements in recent years—paved roads, water, and electricity in most rural areas and access to higher education for women. But Fardusi thought that those now in leadership were woefully lacking in the art of governing and almost totally ignorant in the ways of commerce and enterprise. World distrust of the new leaders had sharply affected the availability of much-needed investment capital, both foreign and domestic.

Trade embargoes, a falling petroleum output, a slump in world prices, the punitive cost of the eight-year war with Iraq, and subsequent years of official indifference to the state of the economy had all left their heavy marks. Perhaps a dozen business leaders remained in the country because their connections were crucial to maintaining Iran's position in the world marketplace. Eventually, the new political leaders had come to the realization that, without those businessmen, the economic viability of the country could disintegrate overnight. Thus, although the Iranian officials neither trusted nor approved of such people, they were tolerated out of sheer necessity.

And imposed upon at will, Fardusi thought as he looked up at the second floor of the great house and stared at the window of one of the rooms where Leila Azari and her associates were residing. He thought of the young American hostage, alone in her room across the hall. He did not like it. Not at all. Having these women in his house ran against the grain with him. He was of the old school. Iran's new women of war were not at all to his liking. Such a change in culture was a sign of the nation's weakening status, both at home and abroad. Of this, he was certain. These new female warriors were fanatical, thoroughly committed to the concept of jihad. And undoubtedly they were connected in some way with al-Qaeda, a movement he personally despised.

Fardusi considered himself a dedicated Muslim. He was also well-educated, an avid reader with a special fondness for Persian poetry, and a serious student of Islamic art and history. It was from this latter discipline that questions had surfaced in his mind regarding the matter of jihad. Sooner or later, the Muslim community would have to deal with these issues. Of this, he was also certain.

Jihad. It never seems to be enough. Jihad has become a way of life . . . and death . . . for millions. For my own children. Surely this is not the way in which the Prophet intended for us to walk. And now it has entered my house. When will it end?

Dusk was turning to darkness as Reza Fardusi limped slowly, painfully, back to the house. The garden was quiet. Beyond the *pairidaeza* wall, a truck could be heard making its way up the hill. Reza opened the door and went inside. His thoughts turned once again to the unwelcome women upstairs, and to the American child named Jessica.

He called for a cup of hot tea and settled into his favorite chair. When the tea arrived, he dismissed the servant and leaned back, clenching a chunk of *ghand,* a crudely broken sugar, between his front teeth while sipping the brew through it. It was the traditional Persian way of drinking tea, and tonight Fardusi was feeling very traditional. Not until the cup of tea was finished did the last of the sugar lump disappear.

By that time, he had decided what he would do about his little guest with the green eyes.

51

Madeline checked her watch. It was later than usual when she took the Bible from under her pillow. She ran her fingers over its worn cover, while at the same time her eyes were drawn to the small photograph of her mother and Cora that she kept on the lamp table. Her thoughts were jumbled together tonight, a mix of mother and little sister, dreams of becoming a nurse, her beloved homeland that she missed so very much . . . *and the girl.*

It had been impossible to get the pathetic little waif out of her mind. She had been taken by surprise, expecting to find a menacing adult on the other side of the locked and guarded door. Instead, she had found a little girl. It had to be the same one she had heard about earlier when she was told that three women and a girl were guests of Reza Fardusi.

But this girl is not a guest. She is a prisoner. Apparently, these three women have been assigned to guard her. What could a child like that have possibly done? She said she was an American. And she sounded like one.

Madeline was quite familiar with the American accent, having lived only a few miles from a U.S. air base in the Philippines until the Americans had closed the facility and gone away.

She had spoken about the new guests with one of the women who had introduced her to the house church, only to discover that the matter was already an item of great speculation among the other servants. Madeline's contact with the American girl simply added fuel to hallway gossip in the servants' quarters.

One rumor had it that Reza Fardusi was adopting a young girl who was the same age that Korsum had been when she died. Another rumor was that he had chosen her as a child bride. Still another said that she was to be wed to Sattareh's oldest son, Aghajun. Madeline pitied the girl if *that* was to be her fate. She did not like Aghajun at all. None of the rumors rang true to Madeline, however. She could not forget the female guard outside the door and the other two not far away.

Yes, the girl definitely sounded like an American, and her face was so pale. But it doesn't make sense. Who is she? Why is she here?

Madeline opened her Bible, took out the bookmark, and began reading where she had left off the night before. Just barely into Psalm 82, she stopped and stared at verses three and four. Then, she read them again.

> Defend the poor and fatherless:
> do justice to the afflicted and needy.
> Deliver the poor and needy:
> rid them out of the hand of the wicked. [KJV]

Madeline stared at the wall, the Bible open on her lap. At last, giving in to weariness, she replaced the bookmark and laid the Bible on the floor. Turning out the light, she settled back onto her pillow and looked up at the darkness. Her lips moved in the now familiar whispered prayer for her mother and Cora back home in the Philippines.

She started to say "Amen," then hesitated.

The American girl.

She said her name was Jessica.

Jessica Cain.

When she looked at me, I had the feeling she thought I might know her.

But how could that be?

I've never seen her before.

Madeline scooted further down under the lightweight cover and closed her eyes.

"Do justice to the afflicted and needy, Madeline; rid them out of the hand of the wicked."

What?

Madeline bolted straight, her hands gripping the sides of her bed.

"Hello?"

She turned on the light and looked around. Throwing back the cover, she got out of bed and went to the door. It was still shut tightly. Opening it, she looked both ways up and down the hall. No one was about. Puzzled, she closed the door again and returned to bed. Turning the light out, she slipped between the covers again. It was getting late and she had to be up early in the morning. Her eyes closed and at last she felt herself drifting off to sleep.

"Do justice to the afflicted and needy, Madeline; rid them out of the hand of the wicked."

This time, she did not move. Her body tingled as she stared wide-eyed into the darkness. It was a voice all right. At least it was like a voice, but different than any voice she had ever heard. Was it coming from somewhere in the room? Or was it only in her mind?

Is that you, God?

Silence.

Nothing else.

Only the face.

The face of the little prisoner locked away in the *biruni.*

Is this about that little girl?

More silence.

God, are you trying to say something to me about her?

I've heard other people say that you talk to them.

Even my mother used to say that you did.

But I've never heard you.

Have I?

"Is that really you, God?" she said aloud to the darkness.

Madeline lay awake for a long time, listening to the stillness that somehow felt incredibly soothing . . . gentle . . . before she finally drifted off to sleep, not at all afraid.

52

Sunday, 13 November, local time 0825
Baytown, California

John dropped the comics on the floor and thumbed idly through the sports pages. The "Niners" were playing in Kansas City today. The Golden State Warriors were at the Coliseum for an evening game against the Suns. And San Jose's Sharks didn't seem to be anywhere, as far as he could tell. He tossed the section on top of the comics and stood up.

What difference does it make, anyway? Who actually cares?

There had been a time, a few months ago, when John would have taped the San Francisco Forty Niners' game to watch after church.

How his world had changed.

Months? It feels more like years ago!

He picked up his coffee cup and walked to the window. This was his second Sunday out of the pulpit. The sky was overcast, matching his mood. The weather report offered a 60 percent chance of rain in the East Bay, with possible afternoon clearing.

Esther entered the room from the back of the house, pushing back a renegade lock of hair with her hand. "Some days it just doesn't pay to have hair," she stated emphatically, kissing John and reaching for the steaming cup he had set on the counter, all in the same move.

A tentative sip was followed by a smile and a satisfied sigh. "You are such a coffee maker, love," she said.

"I know," John answered. "It's a gift."

"The gift of coffee making? Now that's one that I've never heard of before. Did Paul discover that after preaching to the Gentiles?"

"No, it was found in ancient manuscripts rolled up in an old coffee can near the site of the Dead Sea Scrolls."

Esther laughed and they hugged and kissed again.

"You're silly. Anything in the newspaper?"

"Well, the Niners are facing the Kansas City Chiefs this morning. The

Warriors are playing Phoenix tonight. The price of housing is up—again. So are interest rates. The stock market was down last week—again. So was the dollar. Snoopy went to sleep while typing the great American novel. Fell off his dog-house. Took a nosedive right into the old dog food dish."

"Did he hurt himself?"

"Guess not. He just can't smell to write anything."

"Oh, that's bad, John!"

"What do you expect for Sunday morning without a pulpit?"

Esther walked over to the sofa and sat down. "It does seem strange to not be at the church. Especially when we're right here in town."

"You can say that again."

"It does seem strange—"

"Okay, okay. Enough already."

Esther leaned back, never taking her eyes off of John. She watched him tap his foot to some internal beat. He touched the tips of his fingers together, released, then touched again, over and over.

"Want to talk about it?" Her voice had a warm lilt and a half smile that suggested curiosity. "Feeling guilty about being at home instead of in church?"

John stopped his foot tapping and grinned sheepishly.

"Kind of, in a way. No, nothing like that, actually," he answered. "But you're right about one thing. I want to talk about it. Do you want to listen?"

"I'm here for you."

"Just like always. You know how much I love you?"

"How much?"

"About this much." John held up his fingers, a small fraction of an inch apart in measurement. It was something they had done with each other all their married lives.

"That much? I'm so impressed." Esther smiled and swallowed another sip of coffee. "It sounds like this could take awhile. How about if I pour you another cup?"

A moment later, she returned and handed John a fresh cup as she sat down. "Okay, friend and lover and father of my kids, fire on in here. Tell me what's going on in that head of yours."

There was a long silence, while John wrestled with how to begin.

"Okay. It has to do with Jessica."

Esther waited, tracing the rim of her cup with a finger.

"Actually, I guess it has to do mostly with me. I'm wondering about . . .

about whether or not what I'm doing is morally right. I'm learning how to fire a gun so that I can go to wherever she is and get her back. Carla says that I should never point the muzzle of a gun at something or someone that I am not ready to destroy. Honey, sometimes there is so much anger inside me at the people who have taken her that I could kill them all. But when I get a gun in my hands on the firing range, and I actually think about doing it—I don't know if I could. Is it right for a Christian to kill someone?"

Esther did not answer. She held back, sensing he wasn't through yet.

"I guess it goes deeper than that. Is it right for a pastor, a shepherd of God's flock, to kill someone? To actually be the aggressor and shoot someone, if it's necessary to get Jessica back? Part of me says, why do I even ask the question? Of course I have both the right and the duty. Do whatever it takes. Lie, cheat, steal, kill. Just get her back! But another part of me asks, what sort of example am I supposed to be to the family of God? I tell them that God answers prayer. Do I really believe that? I think my answer is yes. But if that's true, why doesn't God tell us where she is? Why doesn't he just deposit her on our doorstep? Or on *any* doorstep for that matter, where someone will have compassion and take care of her and see to it that she gets home?"

John paused and took a deep breath, before letting it out.

"And what if all this is just a big internal ruse? What if I'm simply too scared to do it? A coward. Too frightened to face whatever odds are out there between Jessica and us."

Esther put her cup down and moved closer to John. She took his hand and began weaving her fingers together with his.

"Look at me," she said. He hesitated at first, before allowing his troubled eyes to be caught in her steady gaze. "First of all, get this straight. One thing you are not is a coward. Trust me on that one. You have proven that beyond all shadow of a doubt. Are you frightened? I hope so. If you have a lick of sense left in you, after these last few weeks, you should be scared. I know I am. I'm scared half to death. But you can use that fear to hone your senses. It can either rob you of your courage or put the final edge on your survival skills.

"I know a little about how you feel regarding firing a weapon at another human being. I've never liked guns. And anymore, I'm frightened to death of them. But if it was a life or death matter where *you* were concerned, and a gun was at my disposal, I would use it to save your life. You can count on that, John. I really mean it."

His eyes never left her.

"If a burglar came into our home, entered our bedroom and started to stab me and you had a gun on the nightstand, would you use it to defend me?"

"Of course, but that is different. In that situation, the burglar is the aggressor."

"And doesn't the biblical ideal dictate that you are to be my protector?"

"Of course."

"Then what is the difference in this circumstance? You are Jessica's father. She's counting on you being her protector, just like I am."

John sat absolutely still, pondering. Finally, he looked up.

"Remember what David wrote in Psalm 20? 'Some trust in chariots and some in horses, but we trust in the name of the LORD our God.' Am I putting my trust in man's ability instead of God's?"

"I'll answer you with another Psalm. It's Psalm 147. Do you remember it? 'His pleasure is not in the strength of the horse, nor his delight in the legs of a man; the LORD delights in those who fear him, who put their hope in his unfailing love.' Let me ask you, darling, do you 'fear him'? Is your hope in 'his unfailing love'?"

"You already know the answer to that."

"I know I do; but say it anyway."

"Yes. I fear God with reverence and great awe. I don't want to do anything that will displease him. And I do hope in his unfailing love. What else do I have to hope in?"

"Then, my dear, relax. His good pleasure is upon you. He sees your . . . *our* situation. The very fact that you wrestle over this issue, when both God and I know that you want Jessica back more than life itself, is proof enough that you are not relying on your strength or ability. Even if you learn to shoot like the Lone Ranger, how will you ever know where to go to find her or what to do when you get there? We have a situation that is so impossible that, unless God intervenes, we will most certainly fail. Agreed?"

John nodded, finding it hard to believe that Esther was talking like this, with such confident and outspoken faith.

She squeezed his hand in hers. "Besides, how well do you shoot?"

"Carla considers me lucky that I haven't seriously wounded myself yet."

"See what I mean?"

John reached out, pulled Esther over onto his chest and wrapped his arms around her. They remained that way for a long time.

In the distance, they could hear the bells at St. Mark's Lutheran Church, releasing the faithful to another week.

"Come on, dear," said Esther, pulling loose from John's embrace at last. "Let's get some breakfast and smell the roses and think about how nice it is that you don't have to preach this morning."

53

Sunday, 13 November, local time 0840
Bandar-é Abbâs, Iran

Reza Fardusi was at his dining table spreading goat's cheese on a piece of *lavâsh*, a thin type of bread, folded twice into a square. The servant had also placed yogurt, jam, and honey on the table in case the master of the house desired them. Occasionally, he liked a bowl of corn flakes for breakfast, even though such luxuries were very expensive. But not this morning. He had other things on his mind today.

He paused to scribble a message on a piece of paper, folded it once, and called for his servant. He handed the message to her, with instructions to deliver it to the person occupying the first room on the left, at the head of the stairs. The servant curtsied, stepped back, and turned to leave.

"Wait."

She stopped in midstride.

"You are new here, aren't you? I've not seen you serving in this house before."

"I have been in the *biruni,* for one week, Âghâ," she answered, a touch of nervousness in her voice, "but my work has been on the second floor only. My name is Madeline. I have been in your employ for four months now."

"Where is Theresa?"

"She is sick today, Âghâ. It's nothing serious, but Madame thought she should stay in bed. She may be well by tomorrow."

"Where were you yesterday? I did not see you here."

"My assignment is to clean the guest rooms on the second floor. I am also to provide them food and any other needs they may have. My reason for serving you this morning is Theresa's illness. I hope I have not displeased you."

"You've done quite well, thank you . . . Madeline. You are serving all three people upstairs?"

"Four actually, Âghâ. There is a young girl in the room opposite the others."

"You have seen her?"

"*Baleh*. Yes." Madeline was becoming accustomed to using her fledgling Farsi vocabulary, though she continued speaking in English with Fardusi.

"Have you spoken to her?"

Madeline hesitated. Was she about to get into trouble with her employer? She decided to heed her mother's advice: *Tell the truth always. Then you never have to remember what you said.*

"She spoke to me first. When I started to respond, one of the women told me not to say anything. If I did, she promised that I would be in trouble."

"What did the girl say?"

"She told me her name."

"And does she know yours?"

Again, Madeline paused before she confessed.

"I whispered it to her when my back was turned to the woman, but nothing more since then. It makes the guards angry. But, she seems so . . ."

"Yes, go on."

" . . . so lonely. I am sorry if it makes you unhappy, Âghâ."

Fardusi smiled and motioned with his hand. "You did well, Madeline, just what I would have done in your place. You will be serving lunch today?"

"*Baleh,* Âghâ."

"I am inviting *khânom* Azari to join me. Ask the cook to prepare a light lunch."

"*Baleh*. At once."

"But before you do anything else, please deliver the message. First door on the left. And be careful . . ."

She shot a questioning look over her shoulder.

". . . of the stairs, Madeline. Be careful of the stairs."

She started up the steps, still shaking inside from having actually carried on a conversation with the great Reza Fardusi, paying little attention to the stairs as she went up. They were wide, well constructed, and not at all dangerous. As she ascended, however, it slowly dawned on her that the old man's warning had been given with something else in mind.

54

"What you are proposing is entirely out of the question. It is simply not acceptable. It's impossible."

Eyeing her host warily, Leila pushed back from the table, while pouring the last bit of Coca Cola from a bottle into her glass.

"Why is such a thing impossible? Where will she go? She is a little girl, thousands of miles from her home."

"No, I am sorry. It cannot be permitted." Her tone was adamant. So was the scowl on her face.

"When is Marwan Dosha scheduled to arrive?" Fardusi continued to press.

"We do not know. It could be tomorrow."

"And it could be a month from tomorrow. Or even longer. When was the last time anyone heard from him?"

Leila was silent. The truth was, she didn't know.

"Do you consider it wise to keep the child locked up indefinitely?"

"Those are my orders."

"To keep her under lock and key?"

"To keep her secure here in this compound."

"It is no problem, then. You can release her into the compound. Keep a guard with her if you like, though I seriously doubt that she can climb these ten-foot walls with her bare hands.

"See it from this point of view. The girl needs socialization. Look at her. She is too thin. I'm told she hardly eats. She's been locked up in one room or another since mid-September. She has been upstairs here for nearly two weeks. Soon it will be December. She needs to play with other children. She can continue her training here. It will break up the monotony for her. She is not dangerous. But keeping her in that room cut off from any social contact is cruel. Don't you think it a rather unusual form of punishment for a child? And for what reason? What has she done? She was born to an American father who has embarrassed Marwan Dosha, who is supposedly one of the world's elite terrorists."

"Her father did not simply embarrass Marwan Dosha," Leila shot back. "This man aligned himself against our cause. He foiled a critical part of the Holy

War effort to recover the land of Palestine for its rightful citizens. A cause every sincere follower of Islam adheres to. He must be punished and the work we have started must go on."

"But the girl did nothing, did she? Don't you see? She is an innocent. Perhaps you are right. Perhaps the incident originally planned for Jerusalem would have been a benchmark victory that is still needed in order to show the world just how serious our people are. On the other hand, we could be enmeshed right now in a deadly all-out war with Israel if Dosha's scheme had been successful, a war that surely would have drawn in the Americans—a war our nation would be sorely pressed to carry out successfully. It is not for me to say."

"Perhaps the girl is needed as a pawn in some larger scheme that will move our cause forward," Leila countered lamely.

Fardusi folded his arms over his chest. "That still is no reason to deprive her of the basic rights deserved by any child. It is not the Iranian way."

Leila stood and began pacing back and forth.

"It is not the Iranian way? What right do you have to judge whether or not this or that is the Iranian way?" she snapped back in indignation. "You were obviously born to a privileged class, under the Shah. Otherwise you would not exist in all this . . . this opulence. If you had grown up on the streets in Tehran, you would see things differently."

She pulled out a pack of cigarettes, shook one out, and placed it between her lips. She was reaching into her pocket for a book of matches when Fardusi spoke up. "Please, do not light that here in the house. I am one of the few left in our country who does not smoke. I apologize for inconveniencing you, but if you must smoke, do it outside. And please remind your two friends to do the same. I will die soon enough as it is, and I intend to do so without your help or anyone else's."

Irritated, Leila replaced the cigarette and dropped the pack into her shirt pocket. "Why are you so interested in this girl?"

Fardusi shrugged. "Why not? I believe she is the focus of a worldwide search, is she not? And now I find that you have brought her to me for safekeeping—without first asking, I remind you again. If our roles were reversed, would you not find that an interesting circumstance?"

"You want her to be taught by a private tutor here in the compound?"

"Yes. It will be easy. I have such people in my employ for the benefit of my own children."

"And you want to allow her to mingle with your children as well? I find that very strange. Aren't you at all concerned about her influence and the immoral ideas she might foist off on your children? What about her 'Christian' ideals?"

"What about them?"

"Well, what if she draws one of your children away from the faith?"

"*Bebakh-shid, khânom.* Excuse me, Madame. I thank you for your great concern over the spiritual welfare of my children. But I do not believe you are worried about a twelve-year-old American girl making my children apostates and inciting them to renounce their faith. You can't be serious."

Leila did not respond. She moved slowly across to the far side of the room and then turned to face him.

"I have thought about it and my answer is still no. It would be a violation of my orders. Furthermore, it smacks of giving privilege to the enemy that is unwarranted and undeserved. They did not give my mother and baby brother any special consideration," she added vehemently. "Nor my father. They shot them down in cold blood. My only other brother died at the front for all the people, not for the privileged class alone!"

Fardusi was standing now, facing Leila. He smiled thinly, but his face was hard and cold, like chiseled steel, his eyes passionless and restrained.

"Forgive me if I have been presumptuous in all this. You have suffered much, of course, and your family has given the ultimate gift of devotion to our cause. I apologize for not adequately appreciating your feelings in this matter.

"There is something I wish to make clear, however," he continued, the tone of his voice matter-of-fact. "I was born into a family of seven children, in the poorest section of Sir Jân. I, too, grew up on the streets. I polished shoes, sold cheap socks and T-shirts. I toted a samovar on my back around the marketplace each day, in order to sell hot tea and make a few rials to help support our family. I was not born into privilege. Nor should you think of me as just an old, aberrant leftover of the Shah's fallen regime. That would be a grave mistake on your part. Though I may not see things to be quite as black and white as you seem to do, I assure you that I am a devoted Muslim and my love for Iran is unconditional."

"I, too, apologize if my words or their tone have been offensive in any way to you, Âghâ Fardusi," Leila responded in a belated attempt to diminish the growing confrontation between her and the old man. Then she quickly turned toward the staircase. "We are grateful for your cooperation in the use of your compound and for your kind hospitality."

"You are most welcome," responded Fardusi, with a slight bow. *No sense in upsetting you more, Leila Azari, at least not for now. Even though you and your kind are eating away the very core of our nation's pride and heritage by your attitudes and actions.*

55

LOCAL TIME 1750

Madeline and her friend, Alisha, arrived at the house church about ten minutes early. Several of the other regulars were there already. Madeline excused herself while Alisha talked with two of her Filipino friends, who were employed by another family, not far from the Fardusi compound. She waited while the leader, Arun, a slim, gentle, former Hindu from Calcutta, finished talking to another of the group's young members.

"Excuse me," she began, with nervous politeness. "We have not spoken before, but my name is Madeline."

"I know. I have seen you here, off and on, over the last couple of months. What can I do for you?"

Glancing at her wristwatch, and aware that the service was to begin in a matter of minutes, Madeline spoke quickly and in low tones. Arun's eyes narrowed as he listened to her story of the American girl in the upstairs room at Reza Fardusi's residence. Partway through, he stopped her and motioned to another young man to join them. She continued as they both listened intently.

"You're sure the name was Jessica? Jessica Cain?"

"Yes," she replied. "I am sure."

The rest of the group had seated themselves in a semicircle on the floor and in the few chairs that were part of the room's furnishings.

"It is time to begin the service," Arun said finally. "But when we have finished, I want to talk with you further. Okay?"

Madeline nodded and quickly stepped back to join the others.

Ninety minutes later, the meeting broke up. In twos or threes, the participants visited for a while before departing for their respective homes. Alisha stayed behind with Madeline, but kept checking her watch, worried that they might be late returning to their rooms. At last, Arun and the other young man came over to where they were sitting and immediately started talking as if there had been no interruption of their earlier conversation.

"Can you describe what the girl looks like?"

Madeline nodded, while Alisha listened with ever-increasing curiosity, as her friend gave a detailed description. When Madeline had finished, Arun went over to a corner in which old newspapers were stacked at least three feet high. His hands shuffled through the pile, occasionally pulling a section out, then dropping it to one side. Finally, he stopped and turned, with a section of the *Emirates News*, a small English daily published in the UAE, in his hands.

"Here. I bought this in Abu Dhabi two weeks ago," he stated, handing Madeline the paper. "Is this the girl?"

Madeline stared at Jessica's picture, underneath the headline caption:

AMERICAN GIRL STILL MISSING

The article briefly restated the story of Jessica's disappearance. It highlighted that the authorities believed she was being held as a hostage somewhere in the Middle East, possibly in Saudi Arabia, the UAE, or Iran. The governments of all three countries denied any involvement in her abduction or any knowledge of her whereabouts, and all pledged to do everything in their power to assist in her recovery. A telephone and telex number of the American Embassy in Abu Dhabi, UAE, was included at the end of the article.

"It's her." Madeline looked incredulously at Arun. "It's the same girl."

"You are certain of this?"

"There's no question. This is the girl! She is at the Fardusi compound, where I am employed. I take care of her room and bring her food. She is under twenty-four-hour guard."

Alisha was reading the article now, looking at the picture, her eyes wide with excitement.

Arun introduced Madeline to his best friend, Rashad, a fellow believer. Rashad was an Arab, a five-year convert to Christianity, and an official representative of the phosphate mining industry at Wadi al-Hesa in Jordan. His English was as good as Arun's. They had met three years before, introduced by a mutual friend while drinking tea at a sidewalk café. Once they discovered their common faith in Jesus Christ, they had become inseparable in fellowship.

Arun explained that Rashad came to Iran every month or so, always managing to include an extra New Testament, a paperback Christian book, or a Bible commentary, among his personal things. If the book or a magazine looked too obviously Christian, he simply removed the cover and glued another in its place, in order to make certain that it would not be confiscated when entering

Iran. So far, he had been one hundred percent successful in his efforts at increasing his friend Arun's Christian library resources.

"We must do something," Arun exclaimed, looking at Rashad.

Rashad nodded in agreement. "But what?"

Ten minutes of animated discussion passed by, until Alisha pulled on Madeline's sleeve. "We've got to go. If we are late, it will mean trouble."

Madeline nodded and started walking to the door with the others.

"All right," Arun rehearsed the plan. "Rashad is leaving for Jordan on Tuesday. As soon as he arrives there, he will contact the American embassy."

"Will they believe me?" asked Rashad. "And even if they do, will they do anything? You know how the Americans are. Most of them are well-intentioned, but sometimes I think they don't have any idea how to deal with us Middle Easterners."

"Just a minute," the excitement was electric in Arun's voice. "Madeline, we'll need something from the girl as proof that she is here."

"Like what? I can't walk in with a camera and take her picture. Anything that I do will be very dangerous, both for her and for me."

"But she is one of us, don't you see?" said Arun. "Her father is the pastor of a church in California. This girl must be a Christian, too, and in great trouble because of what her father has done. Now that we know where she is, we have to do everything we can to help her."

Madeline nervously traced an invisible pattern on the floor with the toe of her sandal. Finally, she looked up at Arun. "You are right, of course, but I am frightened. If something happens, those women who are guarding her are not above killing us both."

The others were silent in the knowledge that what Madeline said was undoubtedly true.

"Will you pray for me?" she whispered.

They formed a tiny circle and joined their hands together. Arun led in prayer, asking for God's wisdom and protection to be with each of them.

As soon as he said "Amen," the girls rushed through the doorway and ran toward the Fardusi compound.

56

MONDAY, 14 NOVEMBER, LOCAL TIME 0800
BANDAR-É ABBÂS, IRAN

How long had it been since she had slept through the *Adhan?* Maybe the tape broke and there wasn't any call to prayer this morning.

Jessica smiled mischievously at the thought of slipping into the minaret and cutting up the magnetically taped prayer with a pair of scissors. She tried to stretch. It was a halfhearted try, at best. She knew that she was getting weaker from lack of exercise and her recent refusal to eat. She was too depressed to eat—and, besides, the food she was given tasted bland and unappetizing

Since her arrival, she had mostly lain on the cot and stared at the ceiling. The feeling of despondency was so very deep, like a pain in her belly. How long had it been now? Weeks, she knew for sure. Months? It had to be. She had lost track, but thought it had to be sometime in November. Even the realization that she couldn't remember the exact date was depressing to her.

Thanksgiving! It's probably getting close. Turkey and all the trimmings. The whole family together. I wonder if Papa and Gramma Stevens and Papa and Gramma Cain will come to California this year for the holiday? Jeremy. Wouldn't it be great to wrestle with Jeremy on the living room floor until Mother yelled at us to stop it? Mom and Dad. We would all be holding hands around our beautiful dining room table. It would be loaded down with corn on the cob, turkey stuffing, a fruit salad. Cranberries. Sparkling cider. And pumpkin pie with whipped cream.

Jessica turned onto her side and faced the wall. She stretched out her arm and with the other hand began moving the tips of her fingers back and forth, barely touching the skin, creating a pleasant, tingling sensation. *Daddy used to do this all the time when I was little. I would sit on his lap and he would read or watch cartoons with me and I'd stretch out my arm like this . . . and he would . . .*

She closed her eyes to shut out that memory. It was way too painful to think about home and family and Thanksgiving this year.

This would be a good time to pray—that is, if I thought God really cared. But I've been praying for an awfully long time and . . . zippo . . . nothing has happened.

Jessica started at the sound of the door being unlocked.

She rubbed her eyes with the realization that she had dozed off again. Her arm was asleep from the circulation being cut off by the position she had been lying in. She moved it slowly, dreading the moment that the blood would return in full force.

It was the servant again, the one named Madeline.

The guard stood in the doorway, watching as the servant placed Jessica's food tray on the cot. There was no other place for it, except the floor. Jessica looked up in time to see her wink one eye and then look down at the tray. Reaching over, she took the pillow from under Jessica's head and proceeded to fluff it up. She bent down and lifted Jessica's head, placing the pillow underneath her once again.

"Write something to your father."

Jessica stiffened with surprise, as she looked up at the young woman serving her. *Did she just whisper to me? Or am I starting to lose my mind?*

Again the servant winked and smiled.

Then she turned, walked across the room and disappeared through the doorway without another word. The door closed after her and Jessica heard the familiar sound of the lock tumblers falling into place.

What was that all about?

Jessica lifted her feet and legs over the food tray and sat up on the edge of the cot. In her weakened condition, the room started to swirl. Her stomach growled. She closed her eyes until things began to settle down, then, slowly opened them again.

The tray was still there.

Bread. Cucumbers. Tomatoes. Yogurt. *Yuckurt!* And some kind of mush in a bowl. Jessica put the tip of her finger into the mush to see if it was warm. Surprise. It was. She picked up the spoon and lifted the bowl from the tray.

What's this?

Underneath was a small piece of white paper, folded.

She sat the bowl down again and picked up the paper. As she opened the fold, another paper fell out. This one had something printed on it . . . she picked it up, disbelieving.

The Gospel According to St. Mark!

Jessica stared at the words.

It was a page from the Bible.

Chapter 1.

"The beginning of the gospel of Jesus Christ, the Son of God; As it is written in the prophets, Behold, I send my messenger before thy face, which shall prepare thy way before thee."

And, on and on and on!

She turned it over.

There was more on the back. It went all the way to verse 43 of the first chapter of Mark. *Unbelievable!* She ran her fingers over the paper, turning it over again. Something dropped onto its surface. A tear.

She must be a Christian, too!

The realization was almost too wonderful to comprehend.

Jessica put the leaf from the Bible down on the bed and looked at the door.

The guard could come in at any moment.

That thought caused her to roll up the page and secure it between the mattress and the metal frame, under her pillow. She could hardly wait to read it. It had been weeks since she had read anything at all. Now, to have a page out of the Bible . . . *Oh, thank you, God!*

Picking up the bread, she took a bite. It was fresh and tasted good. She bit into it again. Next, she took the spoon and dipped into the mush.

What's this?

There was something in her mush!

Yuk! Wouldn't you know it?

Gingerly, she reached into the pastelike substance and pulled it out.

Hey!

It was a small pencil.

She licked it with her tongue and wiped it dry on the thin, lumpy mattress. The piece of blank paper she had dropped in her excitement caught her eye again.

"*Write something to your father.*"

Jessica's hand shook as fear and exhilaration ran together inside her mind.

What is this? Could it be some kind of trick? No. Surely not. This isn't the sort of thing these goofballs would do. The girl is telling me she's a Christian. That's why she put the Scripture here under the bowl. And she must know who I am. She's read about what Daddy did in Israel and knows that I've been kidnapped. She's trying to help me!

Suddenly she was hungry. She began eating the mush with fresh enthusiasm. It didn't taste as bad as it looked, though she wondered in passing how much lead might be left in it from the pencil.

Oh, well. A small price to pay. Isn't there something in the Bible about "eating any deadly thing and it will not hurt you"? I've probably tested that verse out several times in the last few weeks anyway.

She dabbled her spoon in the small side dish filled with creamy white *yuckurt* before putting it down and moving the tray to one side.

No sense in pushing my luck on those "deadly things" if I don't have to.

Jessica gathered up the pencil and paper, checking the door at the same time to be certain it was still closed. For a while, she thought about what to write. Then, setting the bowl and the yogurt on the floor, she put a carrot stick in her mouth and used the food tray as a writing table.

The piece of paper was very small.

What can I put down that will let them know it's me? That I'm here? Here? Where is here? I can't tell them where I am, because I don't know myself. But that girl knows, doesn't she? She can tell them. Okay, then. "Write something to your father." Put something down on paper that will let him know that it's really you writing.

For a long moment, she pondered.

Then, carefully, in her best handwriting, she wrote three words and a capital letter.

Underneath, she signed her name.

Jessica.

Painstakingly, she folded the tiny missal and placed it on the tray. She put the empty bowl over it, checking to be sure that nothing was sticking out from under the edges. She added the container of uneaten yogurt to the bowl, for extra weight, to keep it from slipping off the hidden miniature message that would assure the world that Jessica Cain was *somewhere*—and that she was still alive.

Finally, she stuffed the last of the bread in her mouth and sat back with carrot stick in hand.

And waited.

Waiting was something she was getting good at.

—~—

Madeline placed the guard's food tray on top of the others before opening the door. She carried them into the room, placed them on the edge of the girl's cot, and began rearranging the dishes to make them easier to carry. She could feel the guard watching her every move.

Be careful.

That's what Reza Fardusi had said yesterday as she prepared to go upstairs and attend to the three female warriors and their child hostage.

If he only knew the half of it.

She desperately wanted to see if the girl had hidden a message. But she was afraid to look now. Her hand shook as she placed Jessica's tray on top of the others. As she turned toward the door, all at once her ankle gave way and she stumbled.

Jessica's tray slid forward.

Madeline tried to regain her balance, dropping to her knees.

She was able to keep all of the trays together.

Except for one.

From her kneeling position, Madeline watched in horror as the contents of Jessica's tray scattered across the tile floor.

57

The large bowl pitched over the tray's edge, sending the container of yogurt flying toward the guard, who at that moment had stepped into the doorway. She tried to avoid being hit, but it was too late.

"Watch what you are doing!" she yelled as the upside-down container landed on her foot. Soft yogurt spilled out over her toes and onto the floor.

Madeline let out an involuntary groan as she put the remaining trays down. She saw the small piece of paper, directly in front of her, halfway between herself and the guard. But the guard's attention was focused on her foot, from which she was angrily wiping the spilled yogurt. Still crouched on both knees, Madeline reached for the bowl and scooped in the piece of paper with the same motion.

Getting to her feet, she dropped the paper into the bodice of her uniform and quickly began gathering up the wayward utensils.

"I'm so very sorry, *khânom*," she pleaded, with a look that gave the impression of being suitably penitent. "It was an accident."

"You should have been more careful. I need a towel."

"*Baleh, khânom*. Wait just a moment. I'll get one for you."

"Be quick about it!" the guard snapped, now facing Madeline with yogurt dripping off her fingers as well as on her foot.

Madeline gathered up the contents of the trays and hurried down the stairs to the kitchen. Moments later, she returned with a damp towel. The guard wiped her hands and feet with the cloth and then handed it to Madeline. Without a word of thanks, she closed and locked the door to Jessica's room and slouched down on the nearby chair.

"I am truly sorry for the inconvenience, *khânom*," apologized Madeline. "Can I get you anything else before I go?"

"No. Just get away from me." The woman shook her head and picked up a section of the *Tehran Times* from the floor.

Madeline retraced her steps down the staircase and across the great room. Alone in the kitchen, she quickly washed the dishes and trays, putting them in the storage area. Looking around to be sure no one had slipped in without her knowing, she released the top two buttons of her uniform and felt for the paper. Thankfully, it was still there. She was glad to see that it had escaped any damage from the yogurt. Madeline could not keep from smiling as she thought about what had happened. It could have been a disaster. Instead, it had turned out to be rather humorous.

Anxiously, she opened the tiny missive and read the message.

She frowned in puzzlement. It was definitely written and signed by Jessica. But what could it mean?

Shaking her head, she refolded the paper and slipped out the back door.

58

Tuesday, 15 November, local time 1710
Amman, Jordan

A few minutes after five o'clock, Rashad Raufbar's flight descended into Queen Alia International Airport, thirty-five kilometers south of Jordan's capital city. His frustration had been building for the past three hours. Equipment problems had delayed takeoff, and now he wondered if the American embassy would be closed by the time he got there.

Clearing customs was fairly swift. Rashad had only his carry-on luggage. He was used to traveling light and had no purchases to declare. No one noticed that he was arriving lighter by one Bible, two New Testaments, and a commentary on the Gospel of Mark. Pausing at a public phone near the main exit of the ultra-modern terminal, he looked through the phone book. Finally, he found what he wanted and dialed the six digit number. Once, twice, three times the phone rang.

Four, five, six.

Great. I've missed them. They're gone for the day. Now what . . .

"Hello," the male voice was low and clear. "You've reached the American embassy. Our offices are closed. We are open Monday through Friday, from 0900 to 1600 hours. If this is an emergency, and you are at a touch-tone phone, press 0 and then #. Someone will answer your call as quickly as possible. Thank you and have a good day."

Rashad hesitated for just a moment before pressing 0 and #. It was ringing, but the sounds of people moving in all directions through the terminal made hearing difficult. He was about to hang up when a voice said, "Hello, how may I help you?"

"Hello," Rashad shouted into the telephone. "My name is Raufbar. Rashad Raufbar. I would like to speak to someone concerning a missing person."

"A missing person?" repeated the voice.

"Yes, thank you."

"All personnel who can assist you have gone home for the day. If you will call again tomorrow after nine o'clock—"

"Please. I have information concerning the whereabouts of an American child named Jessica Cain. She has been missing for several weeks. I know where she is."

"I am sorry, sir. I am unable to help you. You will need to call again in the morning, after nine o'clock."

"But it is very important that I speak with someone now. My plane was late getting in or I would have contacted you sooner."

"I am sorry, sir. There is no one here to help you."

"Thank you," said Rashad, by this time thoroughly exasperated by the bureaucratic apparatchik on the other end of the line. "May I have your name, please?"

His only response was the sound of the phone disconnecting.

Frowning, Rashad gathered up his carry-on and pushed through the terminal door. People were jostling one another for taxis in the usual confusion outside Amman's airport. Seeing a city bus pulling up to the curb across from him, Rashad made his decision. He would call his office tonight and leave word that he would not be in for work until after noon. That would give him time to go to the embassy and talk with someone in person in the morning. Tonight, he would stay with friends in the city.

59

Wednesday, 16 November, local time 0900
Amman, Jordan

The following morning, Rashad's friend dropped him at the American embassy, between the second and third circles. Rashad walked up to the security barricade and explained the nature of his visit to one of the men in military uniform who stood guarding the entrance. He waited while the soldier spoke with someone inside. After a cursory body search, the guard motioned for Rashad to go in.

Walking quickly across the open area, he arrived at the door, where yet another soldier stood guard. Inside the building, he was immediately confronted by a woman who motioned him through a metal detector. He emptied his pockets of keys and coins, removed his shoes, and passed through successfully the first time. A male member of the embassy's security staff did a cursory body search, then stepped back, nodding to the woman.

"Put your shoes on and come with me," she said, with a smile. "Over here. Please fill out this form and specify the nature of your visit. When you are finished, I'll be at that desk over there. Bring it to me."

"Thank you," said Rashad, not knowing whether he was simply impressed by the security measures or grateful at the feeling of finally getting somewhere. For the next few minutes, he busied himself filling out the form. When he was done, he walked to where the woman sat talking with someone on the telephone, and handed her the paper. She glanced over it quickly, with a practiced eye, then looked up at him as she put down the receiver.

"You say here that you have knowledge of an American citizen who has been declared a missing person? May I have the name, please?"

"Her name is Jessica Cain."

The woman started to write the name and then looked up again, this time quizzically. "Did you say Jessica Cain?"

"Yes, that's correct."

"One moment, please."

The woman reached for her phone. "There is a gentleman here, a Mr. Rashad Raufbar, who says he knows the whereabouts of Jessica Cain. . . . Yes. That is correct. . . . No, I'm not certain of that. He says he called after hours yesterday. He has taken off work this morning in order to speak with someone personally. Yes, I'll tell him. Thank you, sir."

She put the phone down and turned to Rashad.

"Mr. Johnson will see you in a few minutes, Mr. Raufbar."

"What is his position here in the embassy?"

"He is an assistant to the ambassador."

Rashad checked his watch. "I need to be in my office before noon."

"He'll only be a few minutes. May I get you some tea or coffee?"

"No, thank you."

"Have a seat over there then. I'll call you when he's free."

Rashad sat down and began thumbing through a recent *National Geographic*. There was also an international edition of *Time* and a copy of the latest *New Yorker* on the table. By the time thirty-five minutes had passed, he had thumbed his way through all three. Just as he put the *Time* back on the table, he saw the woman at the desk wave to him. He walked over to where she was seated.

"Mr. Johnson is ready to see you now. This gentleman will show you to his office."

A man in a lightweight business suit smiled and held out his hand. "My name is Ryker. Ken Ryker. Please come this way."

Rashad followed the man along a corridor, past open doorways of rooms where people were working in cluttered cubicles. Ryker stopped at one of the doorways and motioned for him to enter. The office was small and the furnishings were plain and functional. By the looks of things, Rashad knew he still had a ways to go to get to the top man.

"Mr. Johnson, this is Mr. Raufbar. He wishes to talk to you about a missing person named Jessica Cain."

Roy Johnson, assistant to the ambassador, stood to his feet and came around the corner of his desk.

"Mornin'," Johnson drawled, giving away his southeastern Texas heritage. He grasped Rashad's hand in a firm handshake. "How ya doin'? Here. Sit down and make yourself at home. It's a little close in here, but we're tight on space. Worse yet, I'm long on paper but short on secretary. Can I offer you some coffee? Maybe some tea?"

At least he's not a pretentious bore.

"No, thank you."

"Will that be all, Roy?"

"You got a minute, Ken? Why don't you stick around?"

Ryker nodded. He pulled back one of the vinyl chairs and motioned for Rashad to sit down. He then claimed the other chair for himself, stretching his legs out full length and folding his hands over his stomach. Johnson pushed back some papers and sat on the edge of the desk.

"Now, tell us what it is you think you have for us, Mr. Raufbar. Mr. Ryker here says you've got some news about one of our many missin' citizens."

Rashad noticed that Johnson had not taken his eyes off him since he stepped into the room. His first impression of the man had been one of mayhem and low-ladder status. Now he wondered if he might have misjudged. There was more to this man than was at first apparent. Tall and lanky, leathery face with high cheekbones. Tie, loose at the neck, top collar button undone. Suit jacket pushed back by a hand that was casually tucked into a pants pocket. He looked like a cowboy dressed in city clothes, but Rashad guessed the man knew his way around. Maybe even CIA.

"Yes sir," said Rashad. "I know where Jessica Cain is located."

Johnson's eyes never flickered as they bored into the Jordanian sitting before him. "Jessica Cain?" he repeated slowly.

"Yes, sir, the young girl who was kidnapped in Israel back in September. She's the daughter of the pastor who's group was held hostage and who—"

"I know who she is, Mr. Raufbar. And I know that there have been hundreds of 'Jessica sightings' around the world these last two months. None of them panned out. What makes you think you've seen her?" Johnson got to his feet and walked toward the window.

"Well, actually, sir, I haven't seen her—"

Johnson whirled around, his long, bony finger suddenly inches away from Rashad. "Now, you look here, son. I've got a ton of things to get done today. I personally have handled a dozen of these blasted sightings, and I'm actually gettin' mighty tired of 'em. If you haven't seen her, then what are you doin' here sayin' that you *have* seen her?"

Rashad remained outwardly calm, but his heart had kicked into high gear.

"I understand your concern about the authenticity of my report of her whereabouts, Mr. Johnson, but please hear me out. While it is true that I have not seen her, I am acquainted with a maid who works in the home where she is being held prisoner."

"What's her name?"

"Madeline."

"Madeline what?"

"I'm sorry. I was introduced to her on Sunday evening and didn't think to ask her last name. I met her at a house church gathering that a friend of mine leads."

"How do you know that she has found Jessica Cain?"

"She identified her from a picture in the *Emirates News*."

"The *Emirates News*? Just where *is* this maid who thinks she knows Jessica Cain? Are you sayin' she's in the UAE?"

"No sir, she is not."

"Well, then, where is she?"

"In Iran."

Johnson stared at Rashad, then looked over at Ryker.

"In Iran," he repeated, his voice suddenly flat. "And just where in Iran is she supposed to be?"

"She is being held in the house of a man whose name is Reza Fardusi, a well-to-do businessman who lives in Bandar-é Abbâs. She has been there, under twenty-four-hour guard, for several days."

Johnson glanced at Ryker again. Ryker was writing on a yellow pad he had picked up from Johnson's desk. Johnson walked back around the desk and dropped into his chair. He cupped his hands behind his neck and looked hard at Rashad.

"You sayin' you're just comin' in from Iran?"

"Yes, I do business there on a regular basis. I work for this company." Rashad laid his business card on the desk. "We're located at Wadi al-Hesa. Phosphate mining. We also have offices here in Amman."

"How do you know the maid is tellin' you the truth?" asked Johnson, looking at the card, then tossing it onto the desktop. "Maybe she's just makin' this up. Maybe she's a plant or somethin'. Could be she wants some fame and fortune. Or maybe she's hopin' to lead us on another wild goose chase."

"Goose chase?" asked Rashad, puzzled. "What is goose chase?"

"Never mind," Johnson brushed his question aside with a wave of his hand. "You got the address of this place?"

"Yes, and I have something more."

"Something more? What?"

"This." Rashad reached into his wallet, withdrew a small piece of paper, and handed it to Johnson.

"What's this supposed to be?" asked Johnson, taking it from Rashad.

"It is a note by Jessica's own hand. See? She signed it."

Johnson stared at the crudely penciled message.

"What's it supposed to mean?" he asked, handing it to Ryker.

"We do not know. The maid asked her to write something to her father. We wanted her to give us something that would clearly identify her beyond any doubt. That is what she wrote, three words and the letter *F*, and her name."

"You got no idea what it means?"

"None," answered Rashad.

Ryker shrugged. "Could be some kind of coded message. The maid asked her to write something specifically to her father?"

"Yes."

"Well, then," Johnson said, reaching for the phone, "Ken, let's get a copy of this off to Washington for a handwriting check. They can contact the father and find out if he makes any sense out of this message. Mr. Raufbar, I'd like for you to meet the ambassador before you leave. I'm sure he'll want to thank you for your help."

Ryker scooped up Rashad's business card, the yellow pad, and the piece of white paper with its mysterious penciled message and disappeared through the doorway.

Johnson dialed the ambassador's extension and sat back in his chair, listening as it rang.

Rashad glanced at his watch. He was happy for the chance to meet the United States ambassador, but he was also anxious about the time. He needed to get to work.

Johnson noticed Rashad's nervous glance and read between the lines. "I'd like to provide you with a letter of appreciation, on embassy stationery, to your employer for what you have done here. I can't give him the details, of course. In fact, if this turns out to be Jessica Cain, it will be critical to this young girl's safety that you keep quiet about this. I'm sure you understand?"

Rashad nodded.

"Good. Now, can you give me a name?"

Rashad wrote down the name of his supervisor and handed it to the cowboy in a business suit.

No doubt about it, thought Rashad, *I missed totally on my first impression. Mr. Johnson is very sharp indeed.*

60

Thursday, 17 November, local time 1014
Baytown, California

When the phone rang, Esther breathed a sigh of relief and politely excused herself from the two young men in white shirts and dark ties at her front door, explaining that she was not able to spend any more time today discussing their ideas and contrasting them with orthodox Christianity. She closed the door and hurried to pick up the phone.

"Hello?"

"Hello. Is this Mrs. Cain?" The feminine voice at the other end of the line sounded familiar.

"Yes."

"Mrs. Cain, I'm calling from the State Department, in Washington, D.C., on behalf of Mr. Charles Rodeway. He would like to speak with you and your husband."

"John is not here right now."

"Mrs. Cain, I apologize for this, but I must have verification of your identity. We've been through this routine before."

"Yes, I know. All right."

After the routine questions had been asked and answered, the woman said, "Thank you for your patience, Mrs. Cain. I'll transfer you to Mr. Rodeway now."

Esther's heart was pounding as she waited and wondered what had prompted this latest call from the State Department.

"Hello, Mrs. Cain. Charles Rodeway, here at the State Department."

"Good morning, Mr. Rodeway."

"You husband is not available?"

"No, I'm sorry. He's away at the moment making hospital calls, and I don't expect him back for at least an hour. I might be able to reach him on his cell phone, but he often shuts it off when he's inside the hospital."

"Okay if we talk for a few minutes?"

"Yes, of course. Have you some new word about our daughter?"

"Actually, that's why I'm calling. We do have something and need your help in determining just how authentic this might be. You're well aware of all the 'Jessica sightings' these last few weeks. She's been seen all over the globe and, of course, all the follow-up has come up empty. This one, however, appears to have some possibilities. I hesitate to get your hopes up unduly, Mrs. Cain, but this is something that only you or your husband can verify."

"Okay." Esther's heart was pounding. Her mouth was dry. Her legs felt suddenly weak and she looked around for a chair to sit on.

"Well, it seems that a young businessman visited our embassy in Amman, Jordan, yesterday. He had been to some sort of house church meeting where he was introduced to a maid by his friend, who is the leader of the group."

"A Christian church group?" Esther interrupted.

"Yes, I believe so. It seems the maid is working at the home of a well-to-do businessman and thinks that your daughter is being held there against her will."

Esther's head was pounding now. She clenched her fists, resisting the temptation to break down and cry over the news that someone might actually have seen Jessica alive.

"Are you sure that it's Jessica?" asked Esther, her voice quivering.

"No, we're not sure, not absolutely. The maid apparently identified your daughter from a newspaper picture. This Jordanian businessman, the church leader, and the maid decided to try to get something from the girl that would verify to us that it is really your daughter. The maid managed to slip her some paper and a pencil, hidden in a bowl of breakfast food. Supposedly, she asked the girl to write something to her father. What they got back is a small piece of paper with three words and the letter *F* written with a pencil."

"What words?"

"The words are, 'I remember Anne F.' That's A-n-n-e. Do they mean anything to you?"

I remember . . .

Esther's mind suddenly froze on the memory of a conversation she'd had with John one evening out by the pool.

"Mrs. Cain, are you still there? Do those words mean something?"

"Yes. Yes, they mean something. When John and Jessica were in Amsterdam, they visited the Anne Frank Haus. That has never been in any of the media coverage. It was unimportant. But John told me about their visit and how much it moved Jessica to be there where that poor little girl. . . ." Her voice broke.

"I understand, Mrs. Cain. That's terrific. Anne Frank. Isn't that something? That daughter of yours is quite a girl to have so much presence of mind that she could come up with an item she knew only her father would remember. That's what we needed to be certain that this person really is your daughter. I'd also like a handwriting comparison check to be done. Do you have something there that you could fax to me?"

Esther thought for a moment. "There are some papers in her desk from the opening of school this year."

"Good. Send me a couple of sheets that have a good sample of her handwriting. Even though we don't have much here, I think there is enough to be able to corroborate that this is your daughter. And we have her signature. That was written out, not printed. Our experts will be able to tell."

"If she is in Jordan will their government help us get her back?"

There was a pause on the other end of the line. Esther heard Rodeway clear his throat.

"Mrs. Cain, I'm sorry if I've misled you. What I said was that a Jordanian businessman reported this to our embassy in that country. But this man had been traveling. Your daughter is not in Jordan."

Esther's throat began to constrict as she tried pushing back the sudden apprehension. "Then where is she?"

"This man was on a trip to a city called Bandar-é Abbâs when this encounter took place."

"Bandar-é Abbâs? Where in the world is that?"

"Iran, Mrs. Cain. It would appear that your daughter is in Iran."

—∾—

An hour and a half later, John came in from the garage.

"Honey?" he called out.

"In here."

John followed the sound of Esther's voice until he stood in the doorway to Jessica's room. Esther was sitting on the bed, legs folded yoga-style, a family album of pictures opened up on her lap. He could tell that she had been crying.

"What's up?" he asked, his senses spiking with sudden alarm.

"They think they've found Jessica."

"Is she . . ."

"She's alive, and I'm almost certain it's her."

"Fantastic!" John clapped his hands together. "So, what are the tears about? What else do you know?"

John hastily pulled the chair out from the desk where Jessica most often did her homework. For the next hour they talked back and forth, their emotions running alternately hot and cold, reflecting excitement, dismay, and relief. John laughed, wiping his eyes as he heard about the message.

"'I remember Anne F.' Can you believe that?" His voice choked with emotion. "She knew that we would recognize it was her. At least she's still alert. I wonder if they're treating her okay?"

"It sounds as though she's in some wealthy Iranian's home. The maid that brings her food said she is in a locked room, under twenty-four-hour guard. Why didn't they just let her go, John? What do they want with a little twelve-year-old girl?"

John did not answer. He did not want to say what had been in the back of his mind during this whole ordeal.

"Does Rodeway know the exact location where she's being held?"

"I'm not sure. I didn't have enough presence of mind to ask. But he must. He also wants a sample of Jessica's handwriting. He said that would definitely confirm whether it's her."

"I'll give him a call, hon. Don't worry about it. We'll find out. Have you located something she's written?"

Esther nodded. "It's on the desk, behind you. Oh, I just know that this is her. What will they do to get her back?"

"I'm not sure. That's something else we'll ask. Where is Rodeway's number?"

"On the counter in the kitchen, by the phone."

61

Friday, 18 November, local time 1130
Washington, D.C.

Charles Rodeway tapped his fingers on the arm of the chair. The two men with whom he'd been speaking for the last fifteen minutes sat directly across the desk from him.

Donald Furlong was a Washington fixture, though his soft, pudgy, features were out of keeping with his gray three-piece suit and burgundy colored tie. Wire-rimmed glasses sat perched on the end of his nose, the thick lenses reinforcing his waning eyesight. He had spent his entire career in the State Department. There was no finer handwriting analyst in the country. Bar none, he was the best.

Frank Galinger was also a career man at State. An old-timer. Thirty-two years. He'd seen it all at posts in Saudi Arabia, Egypt, Jordan, and Iran—before the Revolution. He was thin, about six feet tall, with a face that his friends said could make him Clint Eastwood's brother. In addition to other assignments with the Department, he had, for most of his diplomatic career, done undercover work for the CIA.

"That's it then. It really is the girl?" Rodeway looked across the desk at Furlong. "There's no doubt about it?"

"Absolutely none," Furlong answered. "I'm 99.9 percent sure on this one. It would have helped to have a little more from the subject to compare with the samples her parents sent, but I'm positive as it is. It's the girl."

Rodeway pressed his fingers together, back and forth, like a spider doing push-ups on a mirror. "What's to be done, then?"

Galinger popped some gum in his mouth. He hated the no-smoking rule that had been adopted throughout the building. He was an inveterate smoker, with a habit that was longer in tenure than his diplomatic career. He supposed all the warnings were accurate, but life was too intense not to have some form of nervous release. At least that's the way he justified the habit to himself. His wife smoked, too, so he considered reform a lost cause.

"Well, Charlie, we've got no diplomatic relations. No embassy. Everything we do in there has to go through the Swiss or the Australians. We don't know the exact relationship that exists between 'official' Iran and these misbegotten malcontents, but we have to assume some sort of connection. The group that took her claims to be the Palestinian Islamic Jihad. We know they've got financial aid coming in from Hezbollah sources. Al-Qaeda's in there, too. They've been trained in terrorist tactics by the Iranian Revolutionary Guards up in the Bekaa Valley in Lebanon. The whole thing is a rat's nest and has been for years. No, it's worse than that. It's a hive of killer bees, and if we get involved, our chances of getting stung really bad are higher than the boss is going to want to take."

"You don't think he's going to want to take action here?" asked Rodeway.

"Oh, sure, he'll *want* to take action. But will he approve our sending in Special Forces to get her out? Come on, Charlie. I know it's been a big deal in the media and all, but what we've got here is somebody's kid. One little kid. Do you think he's going to risk an international showdown for one little kid? You've seen the polls. So has the boss. We may have picked off Saddam and a few hundred insurgents in Iraq, but let's face it—we're still stuck there. In Afghanistan, the Taliban are coming back up north.

"Africa's coming apart at the seams. There's trouble spiking again in Croatia. Things are heating up in Indonesia. And that's just for starters. You think he's going to stir things up again in the Gulf—over one kid? Forget it."

"Then what?"

"You've got two choices. One, send in a team of our best players to pull her out. That is, if you're really sure you know where she is. It'll take a chunk of money to pull it off, of course, but we could drop the boys in from one of our carriers. I don't know who's out there in that department, but it's easy enough to find out. When you're ready, put them in small craft; run them up to shore; arrange transportation to get them from the beach to the target; be willing to take out all opposition; get the girl and drive back to the beach; hope the boats haven't been discovered and scuttled; jump in and run back out to sea; and get picked up by the navy. A simple life-and-death operation, with little or no chance of success, and only a dozen or so of our best men at risk.

"Or, two, you do the prudent thing and quietly walk away."

"Walk away? You can't be serious."

"I can be, and I am. Do you for one minute believe the boss is ready to put his whole administration on the line for this kid? I'm telling you, I don't think so."

"But we can't just leave her there."

"You've heard my ideas. Do you have a better one?"

The room grew heavy with silence.

Galinger pushed himself up out of the chair and moved to the door. "All right then. You've got my recommendations, and you know the one I favor. You can quote me on that."

Rodeway did not respond.

Galinger opened the door and disappeared down the hall.

Furlong sighed and got to his feet.

"If there's nothing else, Charlie, I'll be going."

Rodeway waved him off with a hand motion.

"Thanks, Don. As usual, you've been a big help."

Furlong paused at the door and looked back.

"Sorry, man. Hate to leave you with it looking like it does."

"Goes with the turf," Rodeway smiled briefly. "See you around."

Furlong stepped into the hall and went in the opposite direction from Galinger.

Alone again, Rodeway turned his chair around so that he could look out the window. He could feel a little girl's future slipping through his fingers. Galinger was right. Sending the kind of team into Iran that would be needed to rescue her was a political football with way too much risk attached to it. The administration already had forces spread too thin in hot spots around the world and was still trying to get Iraq into a fully self-governing, self-supporting status. Politics aside, the international community would erupt in protest if the president approved such a raid in the Middle East. The options would be presented to the Secretary, but he already knew the answer that would be forthcoming.

Rodeway began laying out in his mind a strategy for handling the Cain family, as well as anyone else that might become involved. You never knew when some reporter would stick his nose in and second-guess the Department. These days, you had to be ready for a hit from any direction. Rodeway recognized what the decision would be. It was predestined. He just had to develop a way to cover that decision with the appearance that "We're doing everything possible here in Washington to find and rescue Jessica Cain from her captors."

It wouldn't be easy, but it had been done before.

62

FRIDAY, 18 NOVEMBER, LOCAL TIME 1343
BAYTOWN, CALIFORNIA

"It's nice to be able to share some good news with you. Y'all have been through such a great deal this last couple of months." Charles Rodeway's voice carried an obvious mollifying tone. John sensed there was more here than was being said. Rodeway was giving himself away; he was trying to soothe a delicate situation. "The handwriting on the note definitely matches the samples that you sent to us. I'm sorry it has taken so long to get back to you, but we wanted to be sure."

"Thank you," John answered. "We were already positive that Jessica wrote that note, but we're very grateful for this extra confirmation."

John could hear muffled sounds over the extension phone in their bedroom. He knew it was Esther, crying. His own eyes were moist at the realization that Jessica really was out there somewhere, trying to communicate to her parents that she was still alive, pleading with them to find her.

"So what happens now?" he asked.

"Well, Reverend Cain, it's Friday. Some of the key people that we need to confer with are outside the Beltway for the weekend. Once they get back, we'll need to bring them up-to-date and go from there. It's possible we won't know what option is best until sometime later next week."

An alarm went off inside John's head.

"Wait a minute, Mr. Rodeway. Are you saying that no one is going to work on this until next week? This is our daughter we're talking about. This is a helpless twelve-year-old American citizen, who's being held against her will by some international terrorist thugs. Who knows what's going on with her right now?"

"Of course, of course," Rodeway's appeasing tone continued. "You are absolutely right. I didn't mean to infer that we would not be working on this every single day. I've already been in touch with some of our people in the Department, and beyond. The Secretary has also been informed. But we need some time to determine the proper course of action."

"How much time?" John persisted.

"As I said a moment ago, it may take a few days. But we should have a strategy in place, I would think, by next Friday, if not before."

"Will you be in touch with the Iranian government before then?"

John noticed the slight pause.

"That's one of the problems in this case," Rodeway answered. "We're unsure at this point as to whether there is a direct connection between your daughter's abduction and 'official' Iran."

"What do you mean?" John pressed. "I don't know what you're saying. Are you indicating that Iran's leaders may be behind this?"

"I'm saying we don't know at the moment," Rodeway answered. "The Iranians are a difficult crowd to deal with on a good day, and we certainly don't want to do anything to jeopardize your daughter's situation. If the government *is* involved, as soon as they realize we know her whereabouts, they'll deny any knowledge, quietly move her, and we'll be back to square one."

A chill gripped John. What Rodeway was saying made sense. It would be devastating to know where she was, only to have her disappear again.

"Okay," he said, finally. "Honey, do you have any questions to ask Mr. Rodeway?"

"No." Esther's voice was husky, "We appreciate all that you're doing. It's just this feeling of helplessness, Mr. Rodeway. I want my baby back."

"We're working very hard to make that happen, Mrs. Cain. I'll be back to you next week, as soon as I have something further to report. In the meantime, it is imperative that this be kept confidential. If the media gets hold of what we know or think we know, all bets are off."

"We understand," replied John.

"Well, that's it for now, folks. I'll be in touch."

Rodeway punched the speaker button on the desk phone. It was suddenly very quiet in his office. Leaning back in his chair, he looked at the picture of his wife and son on the corner of his desk and tried to imagine how the Cains must be feeling right now. He rubbed the back of his neck to relieve some of the tension as he closed Jessica's file, slipped it into the cabinet drawer, and locked it.

63

Esther dabbed at her eyes with a tissue as she came out of the bedroom. John put his arms around her and held her close, gathering strength from feeling her there, pressed against him. His thoughts were leap-frogging over dirt paths, stone walls, rooftops, and walls with chains attached.

What has our little girl been through? What is happening to her right now? Is it anything like I went through in Jerusalem? He looked down at Esther, her head buried against his chest. *These people are killers. They will stop at nothing to reach their objectives. They must have taken her on the spur of the moment, so why are they going to such great lengths to keep her with them? Why didn't they just get rid of her? They've had plenty of chances.*

"What, honey?"

"What?" John looked down again at Esther.

"What did you say?"

John had been so deep in thought that he suddenly realized he must have spoken out loud. "I guess I was just . . . wondering about Jessica. I can't figure out what these people hope to gain by holding her hostage."

Esther was silent as she slipped out of John's arms and walked over to the window. He was surprised to hear her ask the same question that he was thinking that very moment. "Do you think those people in Washington are really going to do anything to help get her back? Or was Rodeway just pacifying us?"

Now it was John's turn to be silent. He stood next to Esther, his arm over her shoulder.

"I don't know," he said after a prolonged pause. "I wish I could be sure, but I don't know. Rodeway did sound kind of evasive, didn't he? I guess you picked up on the tone in his voice, as I did. I felt as though he was trying to give us hope, without committing to anything. Did he come across to you that way?"

Esther nodded her head and then turned to look up at John.

"We've got to do something," she exclaimed, the strain of her emotions seeping through the spoken words.

The phone started ringing again.

John went to answer it, thinking that perhaps Rodeway was calling back.

"Hello."

"Hello there, Pastor Cain. I know you told me to call you John, and I'm workin' on that. Maybe I could call you Father John, for starters, and work my way down from there."

"Why, hello, Jim," John responded warmly, recognizing Jim Brainard's distinct "down east" accent. "Where in the world are you?"

"The only place in the world that anyone should ever be, of course. It's just a shame everyone can't be. I'm here in God's country, listenin' to the wind blow and watchin' the clouds roll in over the bay. I tell you, the whitecaps are sittin' up on top of a deep blue sea, and the sky is dark and ominous lookin'. Course, as long as I can watch it all from my window, without havin' to venture outdoors too much, it's as cozy as a corner of heaven."

Esther looked at John, questioningly. John mouthed the words *Jim Brainard, Booth Bay.*

"So anyway, I got to thinkin' 'bout you folks out there in sunny California, and thought I'd give you a call." John listened as the tone of Jim's voice changed to one of concern. "Any word on Jessica yet?"

"Well, nothing I can say over the phone, Jim, but we're still trying to be optimistic."

There was a long pause and John could sense that Jim was trying to interpret what had been said as well as what was being left unspoken.

"Well . . . that's good, Pastor."

"The name is John, and, if you don't start using it, I'm going to quit thinking of you as my favorite Roman Catholic friend."

"All right, *John,* I can probably get used to callin' you by your first name 'bout as quick as I'm gettin' used to bein' around my first Protestant preacher. Although, if it wasn't for that beautiful young thing you married, I don't know if I'd waste my time on you."

After the hostage crisis in Baytown back in September, and his own encounter with the terrorist team that had attacked Boston, Jim Brainard had flown cross-country to California, "followin' a leadin' of the Lord," he had said, in order to be with Jeremy and Esther while John was still in Israel. The family had quickly grown fond of the crusty, warmhearted innkeeper from Booth Bay, Maine, and had stayed in contact with him after he'd returned home.

"Well, I'm looking at Esther right now, Jim, and I can tell you that she's just as pretty as ever. Before I forget it, thanks for the card and letter, too. It was good to hear from you and I apologize for not writing. I've been sending out lots of letters lately, but not so many to my friends, I guess."

"I understand perfectly. I see Jessica's picture on TV all the way back here. I know that this thing is runnin' you both ragged. That's part of the reason I felt led to call."

"Okay, I guess I don't quite follow," answered John.

"What I mean is that, in a few days, Thanksgiving's comin' around again. Have you thought of that? No. I didn't think so. Look, how's about you and the family jumpin' on a plane and flyin' back to Boston? I'll come get you and we can spend Thanksgivin' at my place in Booth Bay. The inn's empty—it'd just be you folks and me. What do you say?"

"I'd say that was a very kind offer, Jim. To be honest, we haven't given Thanksgiving a lot of thought. Just a minute." John put his hand over the phone.

"Jim Brainard wants to know if we'll spend Thanksgiving at his guest house in Booth Bay."

"What? Oh, goodness, John, how can we possibly . . . I mean . . . there's so many loose ends. . . ."

"Listen, Jim, as you can imagine, we're standing here in total shock over the idea. We'd be honored to spend Thanksgiving with you, but we've been so focused on getting Jessica back that we've thought of little else."

"All the more reason for you to come. You need a respite. It ain't Florida, mind you. But there's somethin' about walkin' in a coastal Maine breeze that clears the mind and soul of a man. Just sorta gets in under your jacket and makes you glad to be alive. You folks need a few days of that kind of livin' so's you can get on with whatever you're doin' and get that little gal of yours back home."

John stood silent, not knowing exactly what to say.

"I take that silence to be a resounding yes to my invitation." Jim went on. "I knew you'd want to do this, so I've already made reservations on United, from San Francisco to Boston. You know, Thanksgiving is the busiest time of the year for travel, so I didn't think we could wait for you to make up your mind. I've got the seats, three of 'em. You can pick your electronic tickets up at SFO. They're faxin' copies to your church office. They're all paid for. Room and board is on me, of course."

"No, Jim, wait. You can't possibly do that."

"Don't need no Protestant preacher tellin' me what I can or can't do, now, do I? I've already gone and done it anyway, so pack your bags and I'll see you on Wednesday evening, in Boston. Your plane leaves at ten-thirty that morning."

"Jim, I don't know what to say. . . ."

"Good. It's nice to know a preacher who's at a loss for words. Aren't many of those around anymore. Well, I can't sit jawin' with you all day, so I'll see you next week."

"Okay, Jim. I guess we'll see you then. And . . . thanks," John said, belatedly, as he heard the phone line go dead.

John hung up the phone and turned to Esther.

"How can we just up and leave?" Esther questioned, arms folded across her chest. "What if there is further word about Jessica?"

"We'll give Rodeway the number. The church, too. Hon, I think maybe it's a good idea. It's awfully spur-of-the-moment, but we've been at this nonstop since the day I got home from Israel. Here's an opportunity for our first break. Jim's already bought the tickets and is planning to meet us in Boston."

"When will we come back?"

"I didn't think to ask, but we can probably come back on Sunday or Monday, depending on traffic. Maybe he's already taken care of that, too."

Esther let her arms fall to her sides and she smiled weakly. "I guess I'm outnumbered. Actually, it does sound pretty good. I've never been to Maine. It sounds sort of 'lobster and clam bake-ish,' doesn't it?"

"It does, and that makes two of us who've not been to Maine. No, three of us. Jeremy hasn't been there either. Besides," he added, his voice pensive, "we'll be that much closer to Jessica—five or six hours in fact."

Esther nodded and turned her attention to what they would need to pack for the trip.

Closer is better.

PART SIX

We can say that [the Islamists] took over 80 percent of the mosques in the United States. There are more than three thousand. . . . This means that the ideology of extremism has been spread to 80 percent of the Muslim population, mostly the youth and the new generation.

—Sheikh Kabbani of the Islamic Council of America, January 1999

Fight them until there is no persecution and the religion is Allah's.

—The Qur'an
Surah 2: Baqarah:193

My grace is sufficient for you, for my power is made perfect in weakness. . . . That is why, for Christ's sake, I delight in weaknesses, in insults, in hardships, in persecutions, in difficulties. For when I am weak, then I am strong.

—The Holy Bible
2 Corinthians 12:9–10

64

Monday, 21 November, local time 0835
Bandar-é Abbâs, Iran

The silence was becoming intolerable.

Several days had come and gone since anyone had spoken to Jessica, and she had not been permitted to talk to anyone.

Not since that old man talked with me. The guards don't say anything. They won't let me talk to the maid. I can't leave the room except to go down the hall to the bathroom. I have nothing to read . . . except this.

Jessica reached under the top edge of the mattress and pulled out the tiny roll of paper containing the first forty-three verses of Mark's Gospel. These verses had become a pathway to the familiar for her. She had read them over and over so many times that she could quote large sections by heart.

The ministry of John the Baptist. The first eight verses. She tried to imagine what he must have looked and sounded like. *I'll bet the people back home would have a hard time relating to this guy if he showed up to preach on Sunday.*

The baptism of Jesus. Verses nine through eleven. Jessica didn't really understand why Jesus had been baptized. *I was baptized to show my faith in Jesus and that he had forgiven my sins. So, why baptize the Son of God? I remember Daddy saying that he wanted to be an example for all his followers, and as Christians, we're supposed to do the same thing. Okay, I guess I can buy that, but it still seems a little strange.*

Jessica thought about her baptism. It had taken place at church, during a Sunday service. She remembered being both nervous and excited as she donned the obligatory white robe worn by all baptism candidates at Calvary Church. When she walked down the steps and into the tepid water, there was her dad, waiting for her. He had this really big smile on his face. There was something comforting, reassuring, about having her father there. He was someone she looked up to in many ways, but mostly, he was just her dad. She could always count on his being there.

That is, until now.

Now, there was no way for him to be there for her. Unless . . .

Unless that maid managed to get my note out. Do you suppose, through some miracle, that she did?

Jessica did not know. She had not seen the maid named Madeline since the yogurt incident, and the woman who brought her meals lately barely looked at her, let alone spoke.

Jessica turned the Bible page over and ran her finger over verse 37, the verse that she clung to for hope. "*And when they had found him, they said unto him, 'All men seek for thee.'*" Madeline had underlined the last five words.

After that, a leper had been healed. Verses forty through forty-three. That's where her precious page ended . . . at verse forty-three. "*And he straitly charged him, and forthwith sent him away. . . .*" *I wonder what the "charge" was all about?*

She felt a growing skepticism about whether she would ever find out. Those verses were on the next page. She didn't have the next page. Her mysterious friend had not been back. *Where is she? I wish I could see her . . . talk to her. . . . Oh, God, I wish I could talk to her.*

Suddenly furious with the whole circumstance, she picked up her shoe and threw it at the door. It hit with a thud.

A moment later, the door was opened, and the guard poked her head through the opening. Seeing the shoe, she grinned and shut the door again.

Jessica was certain that the woman believed they were finally getting to her.

Well, the woman was right!

65

WEDNESDAY, 23 NOVEMBER, LOCAL TIME 1927
LOGAN INTERNATIONAL AIRPORT, BOSTON, MASSACHUSETTS

Rows of lights danced with seductive brilliance against the dark backdrop, preparing the way for the star of the show as it appeared from out of the sky. Moments later, the sound of rubber crushing against concrete marked the grand finale of another mystery tale of human beings in flight. After a brief interlude on the way to the gate, the lights would go up, the doors would open, and the audience would leave, scattering into a rain-swept Boston night.

The morning fog had shrouded San Francisco in a gossamer fantasy, so that only the tips of the tallest buildings and the twin towers of the Golden Gate Bridge had been able to poke their way through to sunlight. This evening, however, the rain that fell on Boston, from clouds made invisible by the darkness, was no fantasy. It was a cold and soggy reality.

Inside the terminal, John shook hands with Jim Brainard, and Jeremy hugged him, as they waited for Esther near the restroom door. When she reappeared, Jim greeted her with polite tenderness.

"How are you, Mrs. Cain?" he asked, taking her gently by the hand.

"I'm fine, Jim," she smiled and stepped up to him with a warm hug.

"Your wounds are all healed?" he asked, concern in his voice. There was a twinkle in his eye as he stood back to look at her.

"Completely."

"Oh, that's wonderful. You really do look ravishing."

"Well, thank you," Esther responded, laughing. "I feel like anything but ravishing after flying for the last five hours, but your compliment is removing my travel creases even as we speak."

"Splendid," said Jim, putting his arm around Jeremy's shoulder. "Come on, Jeremy. Let's go gather up the luggage and get on the road. We've got about two and a half hours of driving ahead, maybe a little longer in this weather, and then we'll be home."

"Great," Jeremy said enthusiastically.

"Ever been down east before?"

"No, it's my first time."

"Well, this is God's country, son. Not like that swarming gaggle of surfers and freeway fanatics you put up with in California."

"Wait a minute," Jeremy laughed, as he protested. "California's not so bad."

"Ah, you've been brainwashed, son. You've got sand between your toes and your ears. Right here is the best place for livin' in the whole world. Just wait'll you see it tomorrow. You won't want to go home. Fact is, I been thinkin' 'bout you, after you get out of school next spring. If you don't have a job, I could use some help durin' tourist season."

"Really?"

"Yup. Ever painted much? And I don't mean pictures."

"I helped Dad do our house the summer before last. I've painted my room, too."

"Great. With that kind of experience and a couple of good references, I might be able to keep you busy. That is, if your mom and dad approved."

Jeremy glanced back at John, a sudden look of boyish enthusiasm filling his face. The unexpected possibility of spending an entire summer working in New England, before starting his first year in college, was a pleasurable idea. New people. New places. New opportunities. It appealed to the adventurous spirit of an eighteen-year-old.

"That's a nice prospect, Son," John said, winking at Esther. "Let's give it some thought."

Twenty minutes later, luggage stored safely in the trunk of Jim's Buick, they drove out of the parking area and made their way toward Interstate 95.

Once on I-95, Jim drove at the speed limit most of the time, though a sudden heavy downpour caused him to slow considerably as they crossed from Massachusetts into New Hampshire.

"Welcome to winter's eve in New England, folks," Jim chuckled, as he turned the windshield wipers to full speed. "Just be thankful that this is rain and not snow."

Another severe squall hammered their car between Portland and Freeport. Eventually, they left the turnpike and crossed over the Kennebec River. Turning onto U.S. 1, they made their way through Wiscasset and the dark countryside beyond.

In the backseat, Esther's head rested on John's shoulder. Small talk had lapsed while Jim concentrated on the road, and the others dozed, weary from the day's travel. At last, leaving Highway 1, they turned onto Route 27 for the final leg.

Two hours and twenty minutes after leaving Logan Airport, Jim eased the Buick along Booth Bay's dark, narrow streets. There were few lights in the windows at this hour, and even fewer traffic lights. His passengers were awake and peering out the side windows, trying to glimpse some of the character of this historic fishing village. The darkness held its secrets well, however, revealing little of its mystical seaside charm.

Five minutes later, collars up and shoulders hunched over, the three men lifted luggage from the car's trunk while Esther ran for the cover of a front porch, made visible by a solitary light. The others followed after her, Jim fumbling for the key, then pressing it into the lock. As the door opened, wind chimes signaled their entrance. Jim flipped on a light switch, and the four pushed their way inside, eager to get out of the chilly wind and rain.

Slipping out of her coat, Esther looked around the room appreciatively. They were standing in a spacious parlor, with wall-to-wall hardwood floors partially covered by a large oriental rug. At the near side, a tall grandfather clock, finished in rosewood, stood like a sentinel at the bottom of the staircase. Across the room, a large cherrywood desk served as the place for registering guests during the tourist season.

A fireplace lay in between, together with two high-back leather chairs and a coffee table covered with assorted magazines. A lamp and breakfast table surrounded with padded straight-back chairs occupied a place in front of the double windows, while a solitary straight-back chair standing against the opposite wall gave an impression of detached aloofness, so far as the rest of the room was concerned. Elaborately framed pictures of fishing boats and quaint villages, reflecting life along the Maine coast, tastefully accented the walls of the old house.

"What a lovely home, Jim," exclaimed Esther, an enthralled look of delight on her face. "It is truly exquisite."

Jim smiled as he moved across the room to the kitchen. "The credit goes to Middie. I've just tried to keep it pretty well like she left it. Added a couple of pictures, but that's about it."

John and Jeremy expressed their approval as well, after setting the suitcases down on the entry floor near the door.

Jim called out from the kitchen. "Let me put on some tea water, and then I'll show you to your rooms. We're the only ones here, so you've got the run of the place. A cup of hot tea, then a good night's rest. Sleep in tomorrow, if you like. I'll set a few things out and make some coffee in the mornin'. You can get up when you want to."

"Please, Jim," Esther replied, "there's no need for you to wait on us. It's enough that we're here to enjoy this weekend with you."

"It's what I do, my dear," Jim said, walking across to the stairs. "Come on now, let me show you where you'll be makin' your beds for the next few nights."

66

THURSDAY, 24 NOVEMBER
BOOTH BAY, MAINE

Esther was the first to awaken. The comforter had been a welcome sight the night before, and it had made the large bed cozy and warm. Rising up far enough to see out the window, she realized that the dawning of a new day had already come and gone. She had slept soundly and felt amazingly rested.

New England must agree with me.

Outside the window, the rain had stopped and low, dark clouds moved swiftly across the horizon. Quietly, so as not to disturb John, who was still asleep, Esther got out of bed, pulled an emerald-green silk robe over her pajamas, and went to the window. She could hear the wind whistling through the eaves. The view was even more picturesque than she had expected. It was breathtaking.

Several boats were tied up at the docks near the bottom of the hill. A lone figure could be seen walking across the deck of a single-masted sailboat, evidently making last preparations for winter. Straight ahead, a deep blue sea wearing hundreds of whitecaps stretched toward the horizon. On either side of the harbor, the rocky, tree-lined coastal rim furnished a protective barrier from the open sea.

Minutes passed as Esther stood quietly, her thoughts suspended somewhere beyond the clouds. Hearing a sound behind her, she turned to see that John was awake. Hands behind his head, he was looking across to where she stood at the window.

"It's beautiful, John," she announced with relish. "Come and see."

"You're beautiful," he answered with a sleepy smile, "and I can see from here just fine."

"You've got a one-track mind."

"And you've got the cutest caboose on the track."

Esther moved around to the opposite side of the bed, picked up a pillow and threw it at him.

"You're bad," she said, with a flirtatious air.

John stopped the pillow's flight in midair with one hand; with the other he reached out and pulled Esther down on the bed. They wrestled playfully, laughing as the bedcovers flew. John ducked as Esther flung a pillow at him again. An instant later, he was pinned on his back, with Esther extended above him, looking down. The sounds of their laughter quieted. Her expression was one of confident assurance, a tempting brew of coyness and innocence, seductiveness and desire. Slowly, she lowered herself toward him.

Their lips brushed lightly, then again, more deeply, passionately.

"I love you, my darling."

"I love you, too."

Even the room's early morning chill felt provocative. Breathlessly, they kissed again.

Jim Brainard was busy preparing vegetables in the kitchen sink when Esther appeared in the doorway.

"Good mornin'," he called out, observing the pleasing blush on her cheeks. "You're lookin' mighty pert and healthy this mornin,' dear lady."

Esther felt her face warm as she thought back over the last hour, but Jim's attention was already back at the sink with the vegetables.

"Sleep well?"

"Like a stone," she replied. "That bed is so comfortable and the room is absolutely marvelous. Middie's decorating flair, I presume?"

"Naturally. You don't think an old codger like me could fix up a room like that, do you? My Middie made it an art form."

"She must have been quite a woman."

"Yup, that she was. A lot like you, I imagine. She was a beauty. Brains, too. Everybody who knew her loved her," he said, a bit wistfully, as he looked up from his task. "Especially me."

He returned once again to his task, and Esther watched silently for a few minutes.

At first glance, she thought Jim appeared gruff and distant. His silver-gray hair, uncombed, poked unruly strands in all directions. His big, well-scrubbed hands made the carrots he was peeling look tiny by comparison. His face, like the trunk of a tree, had been lined by the years, and his brown eyes were the sleepy, sad eyes of an old dog. But she loved it when he smiled. In those moments, she knew instantly why she liked this man. Everything about him lit up. His gruffness was a big ruse. And Middie had no doubt brought out the best in him.

"I wish I could have known her," Esther said at last.

Jim moved the carrots to one side and looked up.

"She would have liked you."

Esther walked over next to the sink.

"I'll bet that if she were here, she'd be telling me what to do next to help get dinner going."

Jim smiled. "Right you are. Well, how good are you at turkey stuffing?"

"If you've got the stuff, I'm great at it."

"Good, because the first and last time I tried it, it tasted an awful lot like wet sawdust."

67

The table normally used for guests of the inn at breakfast had been opened up and extra leaves put in place. The beautiful tablecloth with matching napkins had come from Jim and Middie's one trip to Europe. Plates, glasses, cups, forks. A perfectly browned turkey presented at the center of the table, surrounded by mashed potatoes, brown gravy, carrots and beans, cranberries, and apple cider.

Pumpkin pie cooling on the cherrywood desk.

The smell of wood burning in the fireplace.

Curtains pulled back to present a yard that was still green and a glorious seascape stretching to the horizon.

More than enough. The perfect Thanksgiving dinner.

Jim helped Esther with her chair. When she was seated, the men sat down, John to her right and Jeremy opposite.

"Let's hold hands and pray," said Jim, reaching out to Esther and Jeremy. "I know it's usually your job to do the prayin', John, but I guess I'd like to do it today, if that's all right?"

"It's not just all right. I was hoping you would lead us."

The others bowed their heads, while Jim tilted his slightly upward and closed his eyes. "God, we're mighty grateful that you've let us be here today, thanks to those good pilgrim folk that got this whole great country of ours goin'. We're mighty appreciative of their sacrifices, and we're askin' for your help in keepin' this good land strong.

"I'd have to say, too, that it feels awfully good havin' my new friends here with me. Lord, you know these folks have been through a lot lately. We admire 'em for it, but it's got to take its toll, and so my prayer is that you will bless this good family. Refresh their spirits. And, wherever their precious little daughter Jessica is right now, I want you to watch over her. Keep her safe, and make some plans for gettin' her home soon.

"We're thinkin' 'bout little Jenny and my Middie today, too. 'Course we know they're up there with you, but we'd still appreciate you're checkin' in on 'em, this bein' Thanksgivin' and all. And we'll thank you for that favor in advance. Now, please, bless this food to the nourishment of our bodies. Amen."

Jim opened his eyes and glanced around the table. Esther had produced a tissue to wipe the tears running freely down her cheeks. John continued to stare at his plate, apparently not trusting himself to speak. Even Jeremy appeared to be swallowing back a wave of emotion that kept trying to break out.

"Now, I want to make somethin' clear," Jim said, waiting until the others were looking his way. "You all have every right to shed tears while you're here. I hope you can cry out all the bitterness and the anger you must be feelin'. In fact, I may do a little cryin' once in a while, myself. We've all suffered some powerful blows lately. You lost your little Jenny in the accident. Now your other girl is bein' held captive somewhere. You've been through a lot.

"My Middie's gone. I've got no family close by. We couldn't have any children of our own, which means no grandchildren. So, I've just up and adopted whoever looked like they needed a grandpa. Actually, it works pretty well for the most part. Still, it seems like my lonely times get to be pretty long stretches. God is good, though. That's one thing I'm findin' out for sure here, lately. It may not look like he's workin' much, but he is. So, lets be thankful for all the good things we have goin' for us and stop dwellin' on the bad."

"A good idea," John agreed.

Esther smiled and patted Jim's big hand. "You're not just good to us, Jim. You are good *for* us."

Jim's face lit up at that notion as he cleared his throat.

"Jeremy!"

Jim Brainard glowered at him, his countenance full of mock sternness. "Are you goin' to start passin' somethin' before it freezes over? Or are you just plannin' to sit there and starve us all to death?"

Laughter filled the air as food began circling the table.

Esther's gaze went to the window.

It was starting to rain.

—∾—

Thousands of miles east of Booth Bay, the darkness of night had settled outside a window with a cracked pane. A bowl and a spoon rested on a tray, on the floor beside a cot. Thanksgiving Day's dinner had consisted of *âbgusht,* a thick brew of potato chunks, fatty meat, and lentils mashed in a bowl, served with some thick, oval-shaped and pulpy *sangak* bread, and a glass of strong tea. It had barely been touched.

There was no laughter in this room.
Its sole occupant lay curled in fetal fashion, facing a blank wall.
No pumpkin pie cooled nearby.
Such unachievable delicacies were too painful to even think about.
This room was drenched in emptiness.
It saturated the motionless form huddled on the bed beneath the window.
No cheery smell of logs burning in a fireplace.
Nothing to be thankful for.
Nothing at all.
The last flicker of hope had gone out.
Jessica Cain had finally given up.

68

LOCAL TIME 1700

The grandfather clock had just finished striking five when the last dish was put away. Excess food was stored in containers that made the refrigerator look as full as Esther felt. While clearing away the dishes, she had discovered an espresso maker in the kitchen. Her offer to make lattés all around had received resounding affirmation from the male contingent now seated contentedly in front of the fireplace.

After serving the hot drinks, she dropped onto the rug in front of the fire and leaned back against John's legs. She felt a chill and thought about running upstairs for an extra sweater, but the fire's warm glow on her face quickly dispelled that notion.

A low-pitched moan reverberated through the house as nature's forces tugged unremittingly at the eaves, rain pelting against the large window directly behind them. Esther turned far enough around to see tiny transparent pearls of water, aglow in the window's reflection of the fireplace.

"What did you say, hon?" John asked.

"What? Oh, I must have been thinking out loud. I was listening to the storm and mesmerized by the fire at the same time." Esther sipped at the latté before setting it on the stone hearth. "I was thinking, 'A shelter in the time of storm.' That's what this place reminds me of."

She looked over at Jim.

Sitting back in his chair, he had stretched his shoeless feet toward the fire. Heavy gray socks, dark pants held up by navy blue suspenders over a red and black plaid shirt open at the neck. Esther thought he was a living, breathing stereotype of the Maine woodsman. And there was more. The flicker of firelight had softened the old man's face, releasing the vestiges of a little boy, long hidden by the disguise of aging.

"You're borin' holes through me, young lady," Jim growled good-naturedly. "You got somethin' on your mind? Out with it."

Esther laughed as she reached for her cup. "I'm seeing in you a mischievous lad who is not yet done playing, and I'll bet he comes out in all sorts of situations. He's the part of you that children love so much. I bet a lot of the kids in this town call you 'Grandpa.' It just fits who you are so much better."

"Humph," Jim snorted, as a twinkle appeared in his eyes. "You see the 'kid' in me, and it makes you want to call me 'Grandpa.' Here I was hopin' I reminded you of Robert Redford or maybe Harrison Ford. Instead, I'll bet you look at me and think of oatmeal!"

For a moment, Esther couldn't imagine what he was talking about.

"You know," he went on, "the old geezer in the commercial? That's the guy I remind you of. Right?"

Everyone laughed.

"I hope you don't mind what I just said, Jim. I guess it was a bit personal."

"Of course I don't mind. 'Grandpa' it is. I kinda feel like family anyway."

"Jim," said John, putting a hand on the older man's arm, "considering you a part of our family would be an honor. It seems as though, in the midst of our personal crises, God has indeed brought us together. I think, truth be known, we need each other, don't you?"

"There's no doubt about it." Jim's voice sounded husky as he placed his big hand over John's. His eyes grew moist. "I think we need each other very much."

"I just wish Jessica could . . ." Jeremy blurted out, then paused, his features alight with the reddish glow of the fire. ". . . I just wish she was here with us. Right here, right now. Wouldn't she love this?"

Everyone stared straight ahead, alone with their thoughts, the moment far too fragile for words. A small pocket of wood pitch broke the silence, sputtering and sending a shower of sparks upward into the chimney. Jim Brainard shifted his position in the chair, throwing one leg up over the other.

"Has the government made any headway toward findin' out where she is?" he asked at last.

He glanced around when there was no immediate response and saw his house guests looking at each other.

It was John who finally spoke up.

"Jim, since you're a member of our family now, I guess that makes Jessica another one of your adopted grandchildren. You have a right to know what we know. In fact, in the back of my mind, I intended to talk this over with you anyway, because I remember you telling me that you served in the military some years ago."

"In Korea," Jim confirmed, "I was there in the final months and for a while after the truce." Esther saw his eyes take on the distant look of someone who was remembering.

I suppose the thoughts of war are never far from those who've been there.

Her attention drifted as John shared the familiar "Jessica sightings" that had followed her out of Israel to Jordan, then to Saudi Arabia and the United Arab Emirates.

How did we ever become involved in this madness? We are ordinary people living ordinary lives, at least until Jenny died, . . . and then the terrorists came.

Of course we knew they were out there . . . somewhere far away, . . . but for us to suddenly be thrust into the middle of it all. It seems so unreal to me even yet. It seems like a lifetime ago. But it isn't. It's been exactly sixty-eight days since that weekend. Sixty-eight days since the world was held hostage by those terrible people. Sixty-eight days since they took you from us, Jessica. Oh, sweetheart, I pray that God is watching over you right now!

Esther came back to the conversation as John was sharing what had been learned recently, confirming Jessica's present location in a city in Iran called Bandar-é Abbâs.

Jim got up from his chair and went to a small bookcase near the grandfather clock. He ran his hand over the book spines on the top row, then pulled out a large, hardbound volume and returned to his chair. "This atlas is three or four years old, but maybe we can locate this city on the map."

"I know exactly where it is," John said. "We plotted it at home the first day we found out. We've also been checking it out on the Internet."

Jim flipped through the pages, finally coming to a stop.

"Here's Iran."

They circled in close together to look.

"And there is Bandar-é Abbâs," John said, putting his index finger on the tiny spot. "I found out that Bandar means 'port' in Farsi. It's a city of about two hundred thousand. Do you know anything about it?"

"I don't know much about Iran, period. Nothing at all about this Bandar place."

"I don't think any of us knew much about Iran before the hostage crisis back in '79 and '80," John said. "And there hasn't been a lot of news out of there in the years since, either. At least not much that I ever paid any real attention to. But I've been reading up on Iran these last couple of weeks, and it isn't a pretty picture."

"Fill me in," Jim said.

"Well, over the years, various Iranian-backed terrorist groups have been responsible for taking hostages in Lebanon, killing our U.S. Marines in that truck bombing in Beirut, and scores of other actions. They sponsor an Iranian Revolutionary Guard training camp for terrorists in Lebanon's Bekaa Valley. No doubt there are other camps around, as well. They've been backing fresh incursions into Iraq since the Americans, the Brits, and the coalition forces toppled Saddam."

"Not the kind of people you want to see move into the neighborhood," commented Jeremy.

"In the most recent conflict, they have limited themselves to backing terrorist infiltration in an attempt to continue Iraq's destabilization. President Khatami is a moderate and seems to want normalcy and progress, but it's hard going. Especially when the Islamic fundamentalists are still the real power base."

"Do you think this has anything to do with Jessica?" asked Esther, repeating a question she had asked herself hundreds of times already. "I simply can't figure it."

John leaned forward.

"Authorities have confirmed that last September's events in Baytown and Boston and at the Wall in Jerusalem were carried out under the banner of the Palestinian Islamic Jihad. The PIJ is a radical core group that works under the umbrella of Hamas. Hamas is far to the right of the PLO, if that gives you any perspective at all. Hamas rejects the idea of permitting Jews to remain in what they consider to be their land. They reject the nation of Israel outright; and now that the PNA is trying to settle its differences with Israel by carving out the beginnings of a new Palestinian state, Hamas opposes them as well. I think Israel's prime minister, Soreka Wallach, and Barika Al-Kassem for the PNA are still talking, but things have really gone downhill since September."

"I still don't get the connection," Jim muttered.

"The Palestinian Islamic Jihad is a terrorist group that receives much of its financial backing and tactical training from the Iranians. They must be planning to do something with Jessica. I'm sure she's only a pawn, but this Marwan Dosha character has got something up his sleeve for using her. You can count on it. The guy is evil personified."

Esther shivered involuntarily, a silent reminder flashing through her mind that two months ago, Marwan Dosha and three other terrorists had actually lived in secret for a week in this very house.

"He's gotten his people to move her to Iran," John concluded, "because it's safer to hold her there."

"Okay," Jim mused, rubbing his chin, "it's starting to make some sense. That could be the thread that ties it up all right. So, back to my original question. What's the government doin' to get her back?"

John reached for the poker and prodded the logs, causing another shower of sparks to fly upward as he revived the low-burning flame. Then he settled back in his chair.

"That's the question of the hour, Jim. At first, the State Department told us they were working around the clock. Then, when this sighting of Jessica was finally confirmed, they told us they were thinking about the best way to approach the problem. They said they needed a few more days. We expected to hear from them every day—but there was nothing. I finally called Rodeway, our contact there, to see what was happening. He tells me some behind-the-scenes contacts are being made, but they have to be careful in that no one knows for sure what level of involvement the Iranian government may have in this."

"Hmm, makes sense," Jim said thoughtfully. "But it could also be a stalling tactic by a bunch of bureaucrats who don't want to admit they're afraid of another Jimmy Carter scenario."

"That's exactly what we've been thinking. It's been two weeks now and nothing has happened. It's the reason I want to talk about Korea."

"What's Korea got to do with this?"

"What I need right now is someone who is retired from Special Forces. Somebody experienced in covert military tactics."

"Well, I was just a grunt back in those days. And guys that I knew then are too old now, if you're thinkin' what I think you're thinkin'."

"But their sons aren't. And if not their sons, then maybe some other connections they've maintained through the years. There's got to be somebody out there who can help me. I . . . *we* made a decision this past week."

"And what might that be?"

"I'm not waiting any longer for something to happen. If these terrorists get wind that we know where she's being held, they'll move her. When was the last time our government carried out a successful hostage exchange? She could be there for years. Worse, they might decide they have no further use for her. I'm going in to get her, Jim. I'm going to bring her home."

Jim Brainard was silent, his eyes fixed steadily on John's determined face.

Esther looked away, anxiously twisting the corner of her blouse.

Jeremy watched his father with a look of admiration.

"You ever had any military duty?" Jim's question broke the stillness.

"No, unfortunately not, as it now turns out. I know that would stand me in good stead. It's another reason why I need someone to go with me. I have been learning how to fire a handgun, though," he added.

"Think you could shoot somebody?"

"That's been the big question. I've been wrestling with it ever since taking my first lesson. The conclusion I've come to is that I could do it to protect my family. I'll fire only in defense, but I will do it, if necessary."

"Hmm," Jim mumbled, as if he was not at all convinced. "Are you good?"

"Good?"

"Yes, at shootin' your handgun."

"Not the greatest, but good enough. I've worked hard and I've had a good instructor."

"Does he know what you're up to?"

"He's a 'she,' and, yes, she guessed it."

"Does she think you're a good enough shot?"

John paused before answering. For some reason, he was uncomfortable talking about his shooting prowess in front of Esther and Jeremy. Especially Jeremy.

"You know, Jim," he said, finally, "I'm not the least bit comfortable with any of this. I'm not a warrior. I'm a peacemaker. But the handwriting is on the wall. These people have kidnapped my own flesh and blood. Now that I know where Jessica is being held, I could never live with myself if I didn't try to go in after her. I hope that I don't have to point my gun at anyone, but in order to protect and recover my daughter, yes, I will shoot."

Once again, Jim was silent. His mood seemed to take him out of the intimate circle that they had become.

Where is he? Esther watched to see his response to her husband's audacious proposal. *What is he thinking?*

Jim scooted to the edge of his chair, reached down, and picked up another piece of firewood. Pulling back the screen that covered the fireplace, he tossed the log expertly onto the embers. Then he turned to John and smiled.

"I've got to hand it to you, Rev," he said, placing his hand on John's arm. "You've got more guts than I ever thought a preacher could muster up. I'm concerned about the brains department, but maybe you'll surprise me there, too. When I think of you sneakin' into Iran, rescuin' our girl, and gettin' back out again successfully, well, it's about as far-fetched an idea as the virgin birth. But somehow God managed to pull that one off, so I reckon he can do the same with you."

He looked again at the map.

"You sure about this? That she's really at this Bandar place?"

"I know she was a week ago. No doubt about it. How much longer she'll be there is another question. Maybe the fellow who gave the information to our embassy in Jordan will be able to confirm that she is still at the same location. We can see if State will give us his name. I could say that I want to thank him for what he has done."

"Well, then, I guess we'd better get goin' on this. It's too late tonight; but first thing in the mornin', I'm callin' a friend that I've kept in touch with over the years. We served in Korea together. He's not the one you want, 'cause he's been missin' a leg ever since the war. He was in the marine invasion at Inchon. Got a medal for it, too. Not the best kind of exchange, but several of his buddies are still livin' today on account of that leg. You're lookin' at one of 'em. This here fella's got a son that retired from the U.S. Navy SEALs about three years ago. I believe he's workin' for some kind of private security organization now. If anybody can give us a hand here, he may be the one. Let's just hope we can reach him okay."

"Thanks, Jim." John let out a heavy sigh. "Thanks for helping, instead of knocking my plan. I know it's a long shot, but it's all we've got."

"Don't thank me," snorted Jim. "I think you're nuts. I think you should have your head examined. I also think that it wouldn't do any good to say so, because you're gonna do it anyway. I just need to find someone who's crazy enough to go in with you and get you back safely to your family."

Jim paused for a moment. His countenance was serious. "For what it's worth, though, I'll tell you this much: If the situation involved my family, I expect I'd be doin' exactly what you're doin'!"

"Maybe if we pray about this together, it will go smoothly." It was Esther who spoke up now, a worried look on her face. "Truth is, I'm scared. I'm scared to death."

She glanced up at John, and then at Jeremy and Jim.

"My insides are in knots just listening to us talk about this. I don't know whether I'm supposed to fall apart or suck it up and be the brave warrior's wife. The thought of losing one more member of my family is . . . well, it's too much. It's just too much. I can't chance losing the man I love. We've suffered more than enough already, without that. But I want my Jessica back, too, and I can't fault John for wanting to go after her. There doesn't seem to be any other way. We can't simply abandon her. She's our baby. Have we missed something, Jim? Is there an alternative?"

"The only alternative seems to be to wait and see if the State Department can work things out," answered Jim. "From the sound of things, they may be shinin' you on to cover their bureaucratic buns. Could be they've already decided that she's expendable. I guess it boils down to who you trust. You know what they say . . . the Lord works in mysterious ways."

Jim looked at Jeremy.

"You've got one great dad here, young fella. Here's somethin' else to put under your hat. If you were out there, instead of Jessica, just think about it. He'd be layin' plans to come and get *you*."

Jeremy blinked back a sudden rush of tears.

"Same is true for you, Esther. I guess the question you have to answer is would you want him to act any other way if things were different, and you were the hostage?"

Esther got to her feet, walked to the window, and stared out into the stormy darkness. Then she turned to face the others.

"No," she said quietly, her voice full of passion. "John, do what you have to do. Go get her and bring her home where she belongs."

She came back to where the others were standing and put her face in John's chest, circling his waist with her arms. She held him tightly, while the others watched. Then she looked up, her eyes moist and filled with concern.

"And if you don't come back alive, I am going to kill you myself!"

Everyone broke into laughter. After a moment, John turned to Jeremy.

"How about leading us in prayer, Son. Jim is right. I would be coming for you. And, if your mom and I were there, you'd be figuring out some way to do the same. Hey, we're family. We're responsible for each other. Whether we succeed or fail, all we have left is to do all we can and trust the Lord for the rest."

Jeremy swallowed back his emotions and held out his hands. A circle of prayer formed for the second time that day, as Mom, Dad, and Jim listened to Jeremy pray for his sister's safe return.

69

Friday, 25 November, local time 0915
Booth Bay, Maine

Jim hung up the phone and looked up at John.

"Well, that's it. Harry tells me that his boy is out in the Seattle area. Lives someplace called Bellevue."

"That's my old stomping grounds," John said. "I pastored my first church near there before going to Baytown. My parents still live in Kirkland."

"Never been out that way, but I hear it's beautiful. Anyhow, he's workin' for a big computer software company. Name is Herschel Towner. Widower already, and he's only thirty-five. Wife was killed by a drunk driver. No kids. From what Harry said, I don't think his boy has gotten over losin' her."

He paused for a second, shook his head as if fending off cobwebs, then continued. "Happened two years ago. He's been headin' up the security for the whole enterprise and particularly for their top-level people. Harry said he'd give him a call and get back to us. Maybe today, if we're lucky. You heard me tell him that we're in a bit of a hurry, so let's just sit tight. Interested in some breakfast?"

"Sure," said John as he headed for the kitchen. "We'll let Esther and Jeremy make their own when they get back." The two of them had been gone nearly an hour now. Jeremy wanted to get out of the house and look around, now that the rain had stopped. He had talked a reluctant Esther into bundling up against the low 30s temperature and going with him.

John and Jim sat at the table that had been the scene of their Thanksgiving dinner the afternoon before. They ate toast with peanut butter and jam made by a neighbor and drank fresh ground Costa Rican coffee.

"I pay a great price for this jam, so eat hearty, lad," Jim said, waving his hand toward the homes located immediately behind Hill House. "Been a widow for 'bout five years and thinks I ought to be a bit more attentive. She comes over every other day or so. Says she wants to make sure everything is okay."

"I see," John grinned as he reached for his cup. "All this time you've been holding out on us, eh?"

"Get out. Nice lady, but not my type."

"Is that so? And just what is your type?"

"I like 'em svelte, more like your Esther. Although you really do need to feed that woman, lad, 'cause she's too thin, don't you know?"

"Too thin?" echoed John questioningly. "Hey, I've got news for you. I like her just the way she is . . . slender, sleek, and sexy."

"She is all of that, for sure. I thought preachers' wives were supposed to be plain and dowdy. That is, unless they're on TV. Then they can be super-stylish and have hairdos that look like mattress factory explosions. Your wife's got nothin' to worry about from any of them, and that's the truth."

"She's special, all right," John said with a smile.

"And don't you forget it, either," Jim agreed. "Anyway, you know the old sayin', 'Once you've been to Paris, there ain't no goin' back to the farm,' right?"

John chuckled as he guided the hot coffee over his lips.

"I've been there with Middie," Jim continued. "She was everything a woman oughta be. The way I see it, a woman needs to be able to talk 'bout somethin' besides roses, weather, and jam. Alice there has spent her whole life livin' on this hill. Took over the home from her parents when they died. She's a fine person and has done well, too, but doesn't seem to care much about anything beyond the city limits. I'm used to somebody that's interested in the world; know what I mean?"

John nodded.

"I'm adjustin' to Middie not bein' here, and I'm happy enough, at least most of the time. Probably too old and too set in my ways to include anybody else in my life now, anyhow. Middie and I, we knew each other the way . . . well, you know, the way you and Esther seem to. When you've been lucky enough to have had a person like that in your life, anything else is bound to be second best."

John nodded again.

"I get lonely," Jim said wistfully. "It's mighty quiet here in the wintertime. But I'm still doin' okay."

"I can see that you are, Jim. Of course, now that we've agreed to adopt each other, you're going to have to come and spend part of these winters with us."

"In California?"

"That's where we live."

"Oh, I don't know. Too many freeways, a jillion people, and . . ."

"Don't give me excuses, Jim. Just make up your mind. We aren't going to take no for an answer."

"Now you're startin' to sound like a stubborn Mainer and you've barely been here twenty-four hours," Jim retorted good-naturedly. "Here, have some more coffee."

70

It was ten after three when the call came.

Jim took the phone.

"Hello." He listened for a moment, then motioned to John. "Just a minute. He's right here. I'll let you talk to him."

"Hello, this is John Cain."

"Hello, Reverend." The voice was brusque, sounding just a little ill-tempered and detached. "I got a call from my dad saying you've got some cockamamy idea about going to Iran to rescue your kidnapped daughter."

"Yes sir, that's it in a nutshell," John replied.

"You've gotta be certified nuts, Preacher!" The voice boomed into John's ear.

"You'll get little argument from anyone on that score."

"It's a crazy idea. Insane. Forget it, Reverend. It'll never work."

"I can't forget it, Mr. Towner. They've got my daughter."

"Let the diplomats work it out."

"I don't have any confidence that they will be able, or even willing, to put our country at risk to achieve my daughter's release."

There was silence on the other end of the line, broken only by the sound of breathing.

"Well, that's the first sensible thing I've heard since my dad hung up the phone. You're right on that. There is very little they can do, short of starting a war—maybe nothing. And there's nothing you can do, either."

"They tell me that they are working on all the different options," John continued, ignoring the man's last comment.

Towner swore into the phone. "Sorry, Reverend. But that's what it is. Just a big crock of—"

"I get the picture," John broke in, "and I agree with you. That's why I've decided to go get her myself. We know where she is."

"That's what Dad said. You're absolutely sure about her location?"

"Ninety-nine percent. Unless they move her before we get there." John casually threw the "we" pronoun into the conversation. He desperately needed to hook Towner and reel him in. "But I can't do it by myself."

"You can't do it at all," bellowed Towner. "There's no way! Who do you think you are? You can't just walk in and say, 'Come on, sweetheart. Daddy's here, so get your things and let's go home.' Surely you understand that."

John paused, pushing down the feeling of anger that was rapidly overtaking his emotions. *Careful, careful. You need this guy. Or someone like him.*

"You know, Mr. Towner, you are right on all points. I'm crazy for even thinking about this mission. I can't just walk in and take her out. I know that. But I can't simply sit here and do nothing, either. Forgive me for tossing your own words back, but surely *you* understand *that*. I'm told that you can help us; that if anyone has the skills needed for getting in and out safely, it's you. It has even been suggested to me that you may have been inside Iran at one time or another in the not-so-distant past. The truth is, I don't believe we're going to get my daughter out of there by conventional means. So, here I am, asking. Are you willing to help me? If it's money, I'll do my best to make it worth your while."

John could hear the man breathing. Then Herschel Towner swore into the phone again, this time softly.

"I must be crazy. Dad explained your situation to me. Actually, I followed your escapades in the media back in September. Pretty impressive stuff." His tone had taken on a grudging respect. "You may not have any sense, but you've got guts."

"So I've been hearing. I'll accept that as a compliment, coming from someone like you. Now, what do you say, Mr. Towner?"

"The name is Hersch. Give me a day to transfer my duties over to my assistant. If I can find him, that is. It's a holiday, you know."

"I know," John broke into a grin, nodding affirmatively to Jim. Jim smiled and gave him a thumbs-up.

"Can you be out here Monday morning?"

"I can try. It's the highest air traffic weekend of the year. We've got tickets back to San Francisco for Monday morning. I'll see if I can do a destination change."

"Okay. Get out here, and meanwhile I'll see what I can do. Let me know your ETA and I'll pick you up at SeaTac Airport."

"Thanks, Mr. . . . Hersch. And my name is John."

"The last name is spelled with a *C*, right?"

"That's right."

"Okay. Just make sure the undertaker can spell it right. I'll not kid you, sir.

We stand a good chance of getting ourselves killed." Towner's voice sounded flat, empty of emotion.

"I know," John replied.

71

Friday, 25 November, local time 1225
Bellevue, Washington

Herschel Winslow Towner III put down the telephone, pushed away from the huge oak desk, and walked across plush carpet to the window. His steel-gray eyes stared out over the huge employee parking lot. Usually every space was filled with cars of all colors and descriptions, but the long holiday weekend had left it as empty as the limbs of a tree in winter. He brushed at the top of his shaved head while rocking his muscular six-foot frame back and forth on the balls of his feet.

The parking area nearest his building was reserved for executives, his bread and butter. Usually, a quick glance at the rows of Mercedes and BMWs was enough to remind him of the megabucks that flowed like water through this place. There were probably more millionaires per capita here than in any other comparable business on the West Coast. His own six-figure salary and benefits would have him on easy street in a few years. Having little interest in money per se, however, he plowed most of his earnings back into the corporation's stock plan for employees because it was the easiest thing to do.

A lot of his friends thought he had it made.

He knew better.

Money could never compensate for what he had lost.

His life was as empty as the parking lot outside his window.

He still lived in the small two-bedroom condominium that Sharon had picked out the first week after they arrived in Bellevue. They had been married by one of the base chaplains in San Diego. A week later, he signed his final release papers and concluded a twelve-year stint as a member of the elite U.S. Navy special forces unit, the SEALs.

Until Sharon came along, the SEALs had been his whole life. Nothing else could quite measure up. But everything changed the day he spoke at the San Diego Downtown Rotary Club. Until then, he had lumped all Rotarians together as well-to-do, bald-headed, and overweight. To his surprise, he had seen

Sharon talking with two other female Rotarians during the lunch hour. Afterward, she came forward and shook his hand, thanking him for his talk. That had been the beginning.

In that rarest of human occurrences, they found themselves instantly smitten by the other's presence. He had invited her to dinner on the following Saturday. She accepted. Four months later, he watched as she approached him in a simple light-beige dress, edged with lace. Ten minutes later, they were husband and wife.

He'd left the SEALs without a second thought. Life had suddenly blossomed with a love he had never dreamed possible. Sharon Parker-Towner had become his new life. His job as director of security for OCEANS, an upstart software manufacturing company that was rapidly overtaking a highly competitive marketplace with the latest innovations in voice-activated word processing, had brought them to the attractive mini-metropolis of Bellevue, spreading out along the east side of Lake Washington.

Sharon had chosen a condominium that faced west across the lake toward Seattle. She liked the view along the water's edge, where tall evergreens reached for the sky, their ample trunks framed by generous expanses of green grass. Each grassy blade stood at attention, wearing a jaunty cap of fresh morning dew, while rhododendrons in full bloom framed their new home. They both had agreed. This must be the last stop before heaven. By nightfall, papers had been signed and the sixteen-hundred-square-foot unit that would soon be their home was in escrow.

Four months later, Sharon announced that she was pregnant. He was ecstatic.

Then, before the child was born, it was all over. Sharon and the baby were killed by a drunk driver who ran a red light and plowed into the driver's side of her vehicle at sixty miles per hour. Rescue workers had worked for nearly an hour to extricate her broken body from the twisted remains of her car. They rushed her to Overlake Hospital, where she and their son—he would have been Herschel Winslow Towner IV—were pronounced dead on arrival. The drunk driver had no license, no insurance, and no injuries beyond a few cuts and bruises.

It had been two years since two policemen had stepped into his office and informed him of the "accident." He didn't see it as accidental. To Hersch, it was out-and-out murder. And in that very moment, the shocking reality of their deaths killed something inside him, too. He still lived in the same condo and worked in the same office for the same company, but he was not the same man. He was hollow, except for the anger. All reason for living had vanished at that across-town intersection.

At first, he had been totally consumed with hatred toward the man whose irresponsible act had taken Sharon and their unborn child from him. He wanted to kill him—slowly, with his own hands. Instead, the judge had given the man five to seven years for manslaughter. Hersch was resigned to the fact that the man would be out on the road again and would probably end up killing someone else. Meanwhile, Sharon was gone forever. The scales of justice were pitifully unbalanced.

He'd thought of ways to kill himself, but every option seemed cowardly. Still, as time went on, he had found it increasingly hard to think of reasons to go on living.

The only thing that kept him from "the deed," as he called it, was his one unspoken fear.

The fear of the unknown.

Neither he nor Sharon had been regular churchgoers. During their first month in Bellevue, however, a neighbor had invited Sharon to join her and a small group of friends in a weekly Bible study. Sharon was reluctant, but Hersch encouraged her to go and make some friends. She had returned home with a glowing report after her first meeting. The women were all about her age, and they attended the same church. They had invited her and Hersch to join them some Sunday for services. He quickly declined the offer, but Sharon had gone one Sunday when he was called in to the office to deal with a break-in, and she never missed a week of the Bible study.

During the last month of her life, she had begun to talk more and more about God and about who Jesus was. Looking back, Hersch was certain that a definite change had overtaken her. One that he'd liked, actually. Her eyes sparkled more than ever. Her laughter lit up the room. The ardor of her love for him continued to soften his military bearing.

Then suddenly it was over.

She was gone.

The object of his worship was no more.

Heaven had turned out to be hell after all.

As he stood now, staring out at the bleak, wet stretch of asphalt outside his window, he thought back over the call from John Cain.

Who knows? Maybe I've finally found my way out.

Heroic.

Violent.

It fits.

Slowly, he walked back to his desk, reached for the phone, and dialed his assistant.

72

Monday, 28 November, local time 1317
Seattle, Washington

The terminal was crowded, but still not as wall-to-wall as John had expected. His flight from Boston had been uneventful, despite the fact he could never quite put out of his mind the thought that every commercial airliner was shaped and powered by two hundred and eighty thousand moving parts, each one manufactured by the lowest bidder. He hoped that Esther and Jeremy's flight into San Francisco had gone as smoothly as his.

He was still rehearsing all the reasons why he hated to fly when he saw the man he was looking for.

Self-assured and relaxed in jeans and a solid-black sport shirt open at the collar under a gray tweed jacket, a bald man stood holding a small sign with *J. Cain* scrawled across it. John approached him, shifting his carry-on to his left hand and offering his right hand in greeting.

"Hello. I'm John Cain."

"Herschel Towner." The man's grip was firm and his gaze unwavering. Clearly, the military veteran was taking measure of this preacher with the cockamamy mission. "You check anything?"

"No. This is it."

"Good. My car is this way."

They moved into the steady flow of people headed toward the exits.

"Busy place," John noted, in an effort to strike up conversation.

Towner nodded.

"I appreciate you meeting me."

"No problem," Towner answered, matter-of-factly.

Moments later, they were in the multilevel parking lot. As they stepped out of the elevator on the third level, Towner pointed toward a dark green 1992 Mercedes.

"That's it," he said. "Hop in, and let's get out of here."

As they sped away from the parking lot toll booth, John noticed that the roadway was wet, though at the moment it was not raining.

"You hungry?" asked Towner, looking John over as if still sizing up the stranger beside him.

"I had breakfast on the plane, but I could eat something light," John replied.

"Good. There's a restaurant in the Marriott that's pretty good. We'll go there."

The Marriott proved to be not far from the airport and soon they were inside ordering.

John expected Towner to say, *"Okay, I'm running this show so listen up and do what I say. Here's the plan."* Instead, he began by asking questions and listened attentively as John spoke. He wanted to know about Jessica, her age, physical condition, emotional maturity, everything. How did John think she might be holding up? Was there any word as to whether she had been abused or otherwise mistreated? John responded with what he knew, increasingly aware as he spoke that he really knew precious little. It was mostly conjecture.

What did John know about Bandar-é Abbâs? Where else in the Middle East had he traveled? Had he been told anything about the place where Jessica was being held? The traffic, what the buildings were made of, the number of people in the streets, how many policemen or guards, how were they armed? Before long, John realized how ill-prepared he really was.

"I'm afraid there's little else I can contribute," he said, finally. "Now that I'm sitting here with someone who knows the score in matters like this, I appreciate what we're up against more than ever."

"Good," said Towner. "I'd hate to think that, in addition to being completely unprepared for what's ahead, you are also stupid. For what it's worth, just sitting here listening, I've been able to discern that much."

"That much what?"

"Whatever else you may be, Reverend, you're not stupid. Touched, balmy, but not stupid." Towner smiled for the first time, as John laughed out loud in response.

"Okay, then. Assuming you're right, let's get a couple of other things squared away. My name is not 'Reverend.' It's John." Towner half-smiled again, nodding as John continued. "And, since I'm asking for the privilege of putting my life and the life of my daughter into your hands, I'd like to know up front why you don't like me very much."

Towner's eyes lifted in surprise. "What makes you think I don't like you?"

"Look, I've been in the people business all my life. I know when I'm being accepted and when I'm being put off. So far, you've put me in the latter category. Now, I'm not suggesting that we have to be bosom buddies, but I need to know where I stand and just how much you can be counted on when things get a bit rougher than they are right now. So, the question stands."

Towner stared into his cup while the waitress delivered their food. As she moved on to the next table, John looked across at Towner. "Mind if I ask a blessing?"

He caught another flicker of surprise in Towner's eyes. Then Towner motioned with his hand, as if to say, "*Be my guest.*"

John bowed his head. "Thanks, Lord, for bringing us here safely. Thanks for the food that has been prepared for us. And thanks for Mr. Towner. Help our relationship be good and our efforts successful. Continue to watch over Jessica until we can bring her home again. Amen."

John opened his eyes in time to see Towner still staring into his cup. Slowly, he looked up.

"The name is Hersch, not Mr. Towner," he began, leaning forward until both elbows rested on the table and his hands were folded in fistlike fashion under his chin. "Although I'm not sure that God remembers either name. I haven't been in church since I was a kid, and I don't know what I think about God. I guess I think that if he really exists, he's doing a mighty poor job of things, what with my wife and son being dead and your daughter being where she is. On top of that, I've never liked preachers much, not since being harangued to death in church as a kid. Now does that answer your question?"

"How many preachers have you known, Hersch?"

Hersch blinked. "I've watched some of those TV preachers."

"Do you know any of them?"

"No, not personally. Actually, I've only known one preacher personally. When I was a kid."

"And?"

"And I didn't like him. Too much hellfire for my tastes."

"So, on the basis of some preachers you've clicked your way past on television and what you remember about a preacher you knew when you were a kid, you've wiped out the whole category. Is that about it?"

Hersch went on eating without responding.

"Come on, Hersch," John continued, "I hate to start an argument before we even get to know each other, but you can't put us all in the same box with one person you remember that you didn't like. I'm sorry your experience with religion has been so negative, but you need to lighten up a little. There's a lot of good stuff about God and the way he works in our lives. Don't blame God because some of us preachers mess the picture up. Cut him some slack. You've had a few losers working for you, too, haven't you?"

John smiled and waited. Hersch looked at him for a long moment, then glanced way.

"You are a lot different than I pictured," he finally admitted.

"Thanks . . . I think," John smiled back. "If I wasn't a preacher, I just might be the kind of guy you could learn to like, right?"

"Okay, okay." Hersch put down his fork and extended his hand across the table. "Truce. I hear you and I accept you. You're the second preacher I've known personally. You don't seem all that bad, so *maybe* we'll get along. I said *maybe.* What I've read about you in the papers makes me think you're more of a man than I might have given you credit for being. Besides, you're right. If we're going to pull this off, we've got to trust each other with our lives."

John reached out and gripped Hersch's hand firmly.

"Are you prepared to die doing this?" asked Hersch.

"No."

"Good. I wouldn't take anyone with me who is planning on dying. Let's go out by the pool and get started. We can sit out there the rest of the day without being bothered by anybody. You can see through the window from here that the whole area is covered by a sunroof so the rain can't get us." He shrugged and chuckled at the juxtaposition of those two concepts. "It's Seattle. I've done a little research and made a few phone calls since we talked last. I'm going to give you my thoughts on this operation. You jump in any time with questions or ideas. Okay?"

John nodded his agreement.

—ꟺ—

By the end of the day, John had developed a healthy admiration for Herschel Winslow Towner III. He knew his stuff. His attention to detail was impressive. His matter-of-fact attitude toward the whole project was actually a bit intimidating.

Together they hammered out a plan. It was predicated on ample amounts of courage, surprise, and sheer audacity. Hersch drove John back to the airport and they shook hands a final time.

"It's been . . . *interesting* is the word, I guess . . . getting to know you, John. I'll see you on Wednesday at JFK in New York. We'll meet at the British Airways ticket counter at two o'clock to join up with the others. Then, on to London and Tehran. Once we're inside Iran, we'll put the next phase of the plan in motion. Twenty-four hours later, we'll be toasting our success in Dubai."

John's excitement was growing. Impulsively, he grabbed Hersch's hand with both of his and shook it vigorously.

"One more thing," said John, releasing his grip. "We've talked about the money needed for expenses, but we've not discussed your fee. I've been so focused about the tactical side of things that I forgot to ask about that. I apologize. Will you give me an idea so that I can start getting ready?"

Hersch was quiet as he stared into John's eyes.

"Tell you what, partner. Before I met you, I had something in mind. Since I've spent the day with you, I think I'll need to revise it somewhat. From what I gather, it doesn't make any difference to you, does it? We're going to get your girl and bring her out of there, whatever the cost. Right?"

"That's right."

"Okay, then. Let's not worry about it. To be honest, you can't afford me anyhow. Not on a preacher's salary. Besides, I've got my own reasons for taking on this mission—and I could use a little break from the regular grind."

He waved as he turned to walk back to the car.

"Wednesday at two," John repeated, shaking his head in amazement. *He could use a little break . . . ?*

73

WEDNESDAY, 30 NOVEMBER
IN TRANSIT TO TEHRAN, IRAN

The flight from New York to London to Tehran was uneventful. Long, boring hours. Modest meals. Bad movies. Crowded seats and aisles. The usual tourist? class experience. John was certain that Hersch was used to flying business or first class, but he had settled into his seat without a word and had fallen asleep within ten minutes of takeoff.

After returning home from Seattle, John had emptied the special bank account that had been set up to collect funds to help find Jessica. It totaled $33,479, which he and Hersch had strapped to their left legs and around their waists in currency pouches. In addition, John carried a telephone credit card and his ticket from SFO to JFK. The thought of carrying all that cash made him nervous, though he knew it was small change in the underworld of international terrorism and counterterrorism. But it was all he had. And the people he might be dealing with didn't accept MasterCard, VISA, or American Express.

At JFK International, John and Hersch met up with Ms. Azadeh Nabavi, the group leader for Blue Planet tours. She had two married couples and four other singles in tow. A few hours from now, this all-American contingent would meet a group of twelve additional British citizens, rounding out another exotic, out-of-the-ordinary tour group, just the sort of thing for which Blue Planet was famous.

One of Hersch's former SEAL team members was a founding partner of Blue Planet. The two of them had served together in the Gulf region. After Hersch's initial telephone conversation with John, he had contacted his friend on the chance that he might want to join the rescue team. When the situation was described, his friend told him about the Blue Planet tour already scheduled for Iran right after the holiday. It was a relatively easy matter to add the two men to the list of travelers.

The visas were the biggest hurdle, on such late notice. Technically, anyone applying for a tourist visa had to wait for the forms to be sent to the Ministry of Foreign Affairs in Tehran for approval. This could sometimes mean two or three months. But Iranians are not great lovers of rules, and several well-placed phone calls, numerous forms, two new passports that didn't look new, and a palm-greasing stack of John's U.S. dollars resulted in two transit visas valid for up to two weeks.

Hersch had slipped the new passport to John in New York.

"You are now Dr. John Castle, professor of religious studies at Union Seminary, Berkeley. I am Harold Trent, a dealer in oriental rugs. I have a business in Seattle. We're two bachelors who've known one another since college days. You okay with that? No problems masquerading as someone else?"

Did he have a problem with carrying a passport that was not his own—in effect, lying about his identity? Yes, actually, he did. He was uncomfortable with the deception. He just couldn't come up with a better solution.

"I'll manage," he said.

During the layover in London, the two men exchanged small talk with their fellow tour members, careful to keep their true identities hidden. John felt foolish at first, but eventually slipped into his new role like an actor on stage.

Early on, a couple of the single ladies appeared interested in the two bachelors. Once aboard the plane, John was relieved to see that their seats were several rows apart. He and Hersch reviewed the plan while they ate their meal, then settled back to watch the in-flight movie. Exhausted by this time, John dozed through most of it.

Hours later, the plane began its final descent into Tehran. This was no ordinary, white-knuckle approach for John, however. This was the real thing. It was time to really step onstage and take on the leading role. He looked at Hersch, who smiled and nodded. A moment later, John began experiencing "pain" in his left ear. As they dropped lower in altitude, John's "agony" increased.

Ms. Nabavi, the tour leader, was eventually summoned by one of the other tour group members. From the look on John's face, she could see that the pain was intense. He said that he felt like throwing up and reached for a sick bag, just to emphasize the point. He chewed gum, yawned, moved his head back and forth, all to no avail.

By the time they landed at Mehrabad airport, John was "one sick dude," in the words of a sympathetic fellow passenger. Hersch managed to get him through customs after convincing the not-so-friendly agent that John was not a worthy candidate for quarantine. It was simply the case of an ear that needed to pop open in order to give an American professor on an educational tour some relief.

It was clear to John just by looking at the airport decor that they were in a different world. Even after the passing of years, the walls still framed large photographs of Ayatollah Ruhollah Khomeini, along with ones of his successor, Ayatollah Ali Khamenei, and the president of Iran, Mohammad Khatami. After waiting at length in the baggage claim area, Ms. Nabavi returned to inform the group that their bus was not going to be available until the next day. This was not a problem, however. They would simply take taxis to their hotel.

John, Hersch, and a married couple from Tennessee made the long ride into Tehran's central district in a dilapidated Iranian-made Peykan. It coughed and sputtered the entire distance. The combination of an ancient engine and low-grade fuel made a worthy contribution to the city's reputation for having the third-highest level of airborne sulfur dioxide of any city in the world. Hersch informed them that, on many days during the year, the pollution levels were so high that the government warned the elderly and others with respiratory problems not to leave their homes.

"Kind of like L.A., only more so," he noted dryly.

On this day, however, the air was clear and snow could be seen on the Elburz mountain range at the city's northern edge. Hersch went on to explain that in the foothills were private villas with high walls, barred windows, and swimming pools, renting for at least $2000 U.S., and sometimes much more, a month. Homes here could easily cost over $2 million. Iran's highest peak, Mount Demavend, towered into the sky at 18,300 feet, northeast of Tehran. The mountain range was obviously the glory of an otherwise dilapidated and depressingly grimy urban sprawl.

As they came closer to the city center, the wife of the couple finally asked the question that had been teasing John's mind as well.

"What do you suppose this decal is about?" she asked of no one in particular. On the inside of the taxi's passenger door, where one might expect to find a No Smoking sign in America, a decal was affixed showing the silhouette of a woman's covered head and the words, "For the respect of Islam, *hejab* is mandatory."

"It means that they will not serve you unless you wear a proper *hejab*," Hersch said. "I saw a decal just like this back in the airport, only it said, 'Bad *hejab* is prostitution.' That's really kind of funny since Iran's prostitutes tend to keep themselves more covered than ordinary women. They even veil their faces."

The woman looked curiously at Hersch.

"You seem to know a great deal about this place, Mr. Trent. Have you been here before?"

"Once or twice," he replied. "I have a business that sells Persian rugs."

The group eventually arrived at Hotel-é Bozorg-é Ferdosî, the area's only good, three-star hotel. Owing to John's evident discomfort, he and Hersch were assigned their room first and quickly disappeared into the elevator.

Later at dinner, Hersch reported that John was too sick to come down, but he promised to take some food up to the room in case his roommate felt up to eating later.

74

THURSDAY, 01 DECEMBER, LOCAL TIME 1830
BANDAR-É ABBÂS, IRAN

The taxi stopped directly in front of the compound entrance. Rolling down the rear window, a lone passenger handed the requisite identification papers to the armed guard. The man looked at the picture and then at the occupant before nodding imperceptibly.

"You are expected at the main house, the second building on the right, straight ahead." He motioned the car forward.

Marwan Dosha did not respond as the car moved slowly into the compound. A servant was standing at the door to the main house as they drove up. He opened the passenger door and stood back as Dosha got out, paid the fare, and handed the driver several two-thousand-rial notes as a tip.

"*Kheilî mamnûnam*," the man smiled, taking the money. "Thank you very much."

Dosha turned away from the taxi.

"*Salâm aleikom, Âghâ-ye. In taraf.*" The servant greeted him with a slight bow as the taxi pulled away. "Peace be upon you, sir. This way."

Dosha followed him inside the house until they stood in the entry area.

"Wait here, please." The servant disappeared through a doorway. A moment later, he was back.

"Âghâ Reza will see you now."

As Dosha entered the room, he was greeted by an old man with a well-trimmed mustache and striking green eyes that were unyielding in their intensity.

"We've been waiting for you for some time," Reza Fardusi said as they greeted one another. "At last, you are here. I am honored." He motioned toward a dark leather chair, partially covered with a multicolored woolen Afghan. "Please, make yourself at home."

"It is good to finally be here. I had hoped to arrive a couple of weeks ago, but other matters detained me." Dosha reached into his pocket and pulled out a cigarette. "May I offer you one?"

"Thank you, no. If it is not too much to ask of my guest, I will join you in the garden, while you smoke. It is not permitted in the *biruni.*" Fardusi raised his palms in an open-handed signal of apology.

"That's all right. I'll wait until later," responded Dosha.

At that moment, a young Filipino woman appeared, bearing a pot of tea and several glass cups, which she placed between them on a small table.

"Thank you, Madeline," acknowledged Fardusi.

"You are most welcome, Âghâ," she replied. Taking a step back, she turned and left the room.

For the next few minutes, the men exchanged pleasantries, sounding for all purposes like two partners preparing to close a business deal. Then came a lull in the conversation. Dosha shifted in the chair.

"You have the girl?" he asked.

"Of course."

"Is she in this house?"

"On the second floor."

"I would like to see her."

"I assumed as much. First, let me introduce you to the individual selected by our friends in Tehran to be the girl's official guardian."

Fardusi called out, "Madeline?" The maid reappeared from the kitchen.

"Would you ask khânom Leila to join us?"

"*Baleh, Âghâ-yé.* Yes sir."

Even though he spoke to her in English, Madeline always tried to answer in Farsi whenever possible, from the growing number of words and phrases she had been learning since her arrival. Fardusi liked that. She walked rapidly across the room and up the stairs. A minute later, she reappeared, followed by Leila Azari.

Leila was dressed in denim jeans, a long white shirt, buttoned at the wrists, her head covered with an embroidered scarf. As Madeline returned to the kitchen, Leila moved easily and confidently across the room on bare feet to where the two men rose to greet her.

"Leila Azari, please. This is Marwan Dosha," Fardusi said in English, politely accommodating the differences in his two guests' native languages.

"I have heard your name many times," Leila said diffidently. "It is a pleasure to have the privilege of this meeting."

"And I have heard of your exploits, as well," Dosha responded. "You have a well-deserved reputation for the work you have done in Lebanon and Germany."

"Will you join us in some tea?" invited Fardusi.

"Thank you," Leila said, waiting while Dosha moved a third chair over from the dining table and Fardusi attended to the tea. The three of them sat down.

"I have inquired about the girl and Âghâ Fardusi has informed me that you have been overseeing her stay. Is she well?"

"Yes. However, she is weaker than at the beginning. The last several days, she eats very little. Her despondency is increasing. I do not think she will last another month unless something is done."

"Fortunately, that will be unnecessary," said Dosha. "Everything will be finished, as far as she is concerned, by tomorrow night."

"Oh?" queried Fardusi, eyebrows lifted. "Will you be moving her to a new location?"

"No. May I see her?"

"Of course," answered Leila, standing quickly to her feet. "I will take you to her at once."

"Please," Fardusi interjected, as he and Dosha stood. "If you do not plan to move her, then what?"

Leila was impatient to guide Dosha away from Fardusi's questions. Her dislike for this testy old man had increased with each passing week, and she would be glad when this assignment was finally over. She hated the way he held his ground with her, refusing to yield to her right to be in charge. Besides, this was a moment in which to look important in the eyes of a man whose reputation she admired. And now that she had seen Marwan Dosha, her pulse rose at the thought of being alone with him, even for a short while.

Dosha paused, turning back to address Fardusi.

"Tomorrow night, the members of the Council will join us, is that not true?"

"It is as you say. I have arranged it as was requested."

"You have a camera and an operator?"

"Yes. This, too, has been arranged."

"Good. When everyone has arrived, we will enjoy dinner together, as planned. Then we shall film the girl reading a prepared statement outlining our demands. Afterward, thanks to your kind hospitality, we shall enjoy some dessert."

"It will all be the finest cuisine. My chef is most accomplished. Will there be anything else?"

"That is all we will need. After dessert, we will return to her room and film the girl one last time, as she is executed."

The cold, matter-of-factness of the man's tone fell like a sledgehammer. Fardusi stopped in midstride to stare at him. Even Leila looked stunned.

"It is a small but essential part of a much larger and more important plan," Dosha assured them with a thin smile. "A symbolic sacrifice is needed to back up our threats, so the world will know that they cannot push aside our demands. There can be no better sacrifice than Jessica Cain. Her face has been made commonplace by the media. She is known around the world. Her demise will assure people everywhere that we are not to be denied. Now, may we continue? I want to see her before I go on to my hotel."

Leila Azari silently ascended the stairs, followed closely by Marwan Dosha. Reza Fardusi turned away and walked to the glass door opening out onto the illuminated garden. Its low-lit beauty did not give him the normal infusion of pleasure. Not tonight. Not after what he had just heard.

—∾—

In the kitchen, Madeline stepped back from pressing her ear to the door. Her mouth was dry, her heart pounding twice as fast as usual. What she had just heard twisted like a sharp knife in her stomach. Rushing to the sink, she retched, then reached for a glass of water to rinse out the awful taste.

That poor girl. Oh, dear God, that poor little girl. She could be my sister! Madeline closed her eyes and leaned against the counter, struggling to rein in her emotions. *Lord, how could I ever bear it if something like this were to happen to Cora? It would be too terrible. But little Jessica is your child, too, Lord. Something must be done. This cannot be permitted to happen. But what? What can I do? What can anyone do to help her?*

75

FRIDAY, 02 DECEMBER, LOCAL TIME 0800
TEHRAN, IRAN

The morning following John's "illness," Hersch reported to Ms. Nabavi that Dr. Castle had spent a restless night. He was feeling somewhat better, but had decided to remain in the room in order to be ready for the next day's tour of the countryside. Mr. Trent had decided to stay with his friend, though he regretted that he would miss the day tour of Tehran. Ms. Nabavi offered to request the services of a physician through the hotel management, but Hersch declined. Dr. Castle looked better, he said, and with rest, ought to be fine for the next day's travel plans.

Hersch stood in the hotel entry, waving good-bye to the group as they boarded a bus for what promised to be a smog-choked day in Tehran. As the bus rounded the corner and disappeared from sight, he waited for a moment, watching the flow of foot-traffic moving by. It looked too much like a funeral, he decided, with all the black *châdors*. Some of the younger people were dressed in more Western-style clothing, but all the women were required by law to observe the *hejab,* the Islamic dress code, by covering their hair and concealing the curves of their bodies. He noticed a few who, in silent protest, were wearing makeup and showing tufts of hair from under their scarves.

The only vivid colors he noticed were the dresses of little girls, with bare arms and legs, a symbol of freedom soon to be lost. Hersch knew that legally they would be required to don the *châdor* by the age of nine—the age at which Ayatollah Khomeini had declared girls mature enough to be married.

He walked back into the lobby and waited for the elevator to take him to the fifth floor. When the elevator door opened, a dour-looking man stepped out, glaring at Hersch as he brushed past. Behind him were two women completely covered with black *châdors*. A third woman stepped out in an ankle-length coat that Tehran residents called by the French word *manteau.* It was dark green in color and buttoned up the front, much too warm for today's temperature, but less likely to fall open and expose the wearer, a crime that fundamentalists still held punishable by flogging or even imprisonment.

He shook his head.

Khomeini was right. There is no joy in Mudville.

Hersch was alone in the elevator when the door closed behind him. He looked forward to a few hours of relaxation before the mission's next phase would commence.

—∞—

At three o'clock, an hour before their group was scheduled to return from sightseeing, Mr. Harold Trent and Dr. John Castle stepped out of the elevator and made their way across the hotel lobby.

The desk clerk, aware of his sick American guest, nodded at them both. Dr. Castle looked much better.

The two Americans paused long enough to leave their key at the desk and a message in Ms. Nabavi's box. Dr. Castle was feeling so much better that the two of them had decided to see what they could of Tehran on their own. They might not be back in time for dinner, but would be ready to rejoin the group tomorrow morning. The clerk watched, through the hotel's glass doors, as the men climbed into an orange and white Peugeot taxi and quickly became lost in the never-ending river of old metal, treadless rubber, and carbon monoxide fumes.

At Mehrabad Airport, Trent and Castle presented their tickets for the 5:30 *Havâpeimâ'î-yé Jomhürî-yé Esâmî-yé Irân* flight to Bandar-é Abbâs. Its full Persian name was a mouthful, even for locals, so, most referred to it simply as Homâ, after the mythical bird used as the airline's symbol. The rest of the world knew it as Iran Air.

There had been no problem getting domestic tickets through a downtown agency, even though Iran Air's own ticketing personnel had pronounced the flight completely booked. A friend back home, who had spent considerable time in Iran on behalf of the State Department, had informed Hersch that the airline usually reserved a certain number of seats on every flight for "special customers" until a few hours before boarding time. Foreigners often counted as special customers, especially if they could offer the agent a handsome number of rials above the regular ticket purchase price. This had proven to be the case for Mr. Trent and Dr. Castle.

A few minutes before six o'clock, the Boeing 737 lifted off the runway and began its journey, banking toward the southeast, away from the teeming metropolis below. Two uneventful hours later, the plane touched down a few miles east of Bandar-é Abbâs.

As Mr. Trent and Dr. Castle disembarked with the other passengers, they immediately sensed the difference in weather conditions. The air felt much warmer and muggier here than in Tehran. They carried no luggage, nor had they checked any. It was all still in a closet at the hotel in Tehran. If anyone looked in on them this evening, they would be reassured that the men had simply not yet come back from being out on the town.

They had no return tickets. There were no flights out until the next day anyway. By that time, if everything had gone as planned, they would be knocking on the doors of the U.S. Embassy in Dubai, slapping one another on the back, and holding tightly onto the twelve-year-old package they had come halfway around the world to claim.

76

FRIDAY, 02 DECEMBER, LOCAL TIME 0030
EAST OF SAN FRANCISCO, CALIFORNIA

"Are we ready?" Paul Heilbrun called out to the eleven other men.

"You bet."

"Yeah."

"Ready, boss."

The response was enthusiastic in spite of the fact that, at twelve-thirty at night, it was a chilly forty-two degrees and falling.

"Okay, Buddy, let's ride."

Lights on, the truck moved slowly forward into the tunnel.

"I get a kick out of this run every time we do it," Buddy Ryan said to his boss as he guided the battery-powered, electric industrial truck along the tunnel floor.

"You always were a bit of a mole," Heilbrun replied.

"It's an amazing piece of work, though, you know? I can't help it."

"How many times have you been through?"

"This makes five . . . no, six for me. And you?"

"I've lost track, maybe ten or eleven. I'm not sure."

As the men talked, their eyes never left their appointed task, that of inspecting the Coast Range Tunnel superstructure, between the Tesla and Irvington Portals. Though no structural problems were anticipated, the vehicle carried enough tools and supplies to take care of any minor difficulty that might be encountered in the pipeline that carried the Bay Area's primary water supply.

To ensure its integrity, the water was periodically shut off and a crew sent through for an official check of the twenty-nine-mile tunnel beneath the rolling hills south of the burgeoning suburban towns of Pleasanton and Livermore. It was a bumpy ride, with lots of dampness and chill, but it was essential to keeping the promise that had been made to the people of California eighty years ago.

The Coast Range Tunnel served as an important link in the aqueduct system that delivered precious water from the Hetch Hetchy Reservoir, nestled high in the Sierra range, to residents living in the San Francisco Bay Area.

Out of the reservoir at the O'Shaughnessy Dam, water flowed along an eleven-mile stretch of the Tuolumne River, as far as Early Intake Dam. At Early Intake, the water began its enclosed descent through a nineteen-mile tunnel to an artificial lake at Priest Dam. From there it continued through a mile-long bore, connecting the reservoir to the Moccasin Hydroelectric Powerhouse, then dropped steadily westward through a sixteen-mile shaft under the foothills east of the San Joaquin Valley.

At Oakdale Portal, just south of Knight's Ferry, the water entered a forty-seven-mile underground pressure pipe stretching across the valley and connecting with the twenty-nine-mile Coast Range Tunnel. At Irvington Portal it flowed from the Tunnel into the Bay Pipe Line, crossed the San Francisco Bay beneath the Dumbarton Bridge, and on through additional pipelines routed around the southern end of the Bay. This precious resource then poured through the one-and-one-half-mile Pulgas Tunnel, finally spilling out from under the Pulgas Water Temple and into the Peninsula's Spring Valley Reservoirs. This vast network, one hundred and forty-nine miles long, brought pure, sparkling mountain water every day to the citizens of San Francisco, Santa Clara, Alameda, and San Mateo counties.

Paul Heilbrun looked at his watch. *One-ten.* The trip, at an average speed of approximately six miles per hour, could be accomplished in five or six hours. With the occasional stop to check and repair any suspicious-looking area, the inspection was normally an all-night assignment.

Heilbrun felt a sudden chill run up his back. He buttoned the top of his coat and slipped his hands into a pair of waterproof gloves. Buddy glanced over at his boss and smiled.

—⁓—

Less than a mile behind the inspection crew, four dark-clad figures moved swiftly and silently, headlamps their only source of light. Two of the intruders attached small waterproof packages at intervals along the sides of the tunnel. The other two followed, connecting each package with a small insulated wire. Once in place, they were concealed well enough that they would not be noticed unless someone were to carefully inspect the hidden crevices for suspicious material. That was highly unlikely. The inspection crew had already passed by. And once the water was running again, it would be too late.

They worked without conversation for almost an hour before pausing over the nearly completed task.

"This place looks very solid," one of the dark-clad figures commented. "Do you think this will actually work?"

The lead man patted the most recently installed package.

"With this material, there will be no problem. It is small, but powerful. It will work, so long as you have wired it correctly."

"No problem. When the button is pushed . . . boom!"

They laughed.

"Come on, let's finish and get out of here. I'm dying for a cigarette."

77

Friday, 02 December, local time 2000
Bandar-é Abbâs, Iran

The Council members arrived precisely at the predetermined hour. They waited at the main gate of the Fardusi compound while the guard checked their identification and called ahead to announce their arrival.

Shadows of evening fell across the gravel drive as the two cars proceeded toward the main house, past gardens and fountains and still more gardens. The architectural symmetry of the scene was accented by low lights flickering along the gracefully curving drive. The setting was a reminder of a grand and glorious Persian past.

A servant stepped out from the entry to the main house and made his way toward them. He paused and bowed his head politely, waiting for the men to exit from their cars. Gathering together, they shuffled forward, following the servant into the main house, engrossed in conversation as they had been before arriving at the gate.

Just before eight-thirty, the last guest arrived at the security gate in a taxi. Rolling down the rear window, he showed his face to the guard, but offered no papers.

"*Shab bekheir, Âghâ-yé.*" The guard was respectfully cordial as he gave instructions to the driver. A moment later, the car moved slowly up the driveway to the main house.

Marwan Dosha opened the car door and presented the driver with a generous tip before stepping out. As the taxi pulled away, he stood for a moment taking in the surroundings.

This is, indeed, a place of beauty. And beautiful things will happen here tonight.

This would be the young infidel's last night on earth. The very thought of the helplessness of the girl and the powerlessness of her father to intervene brought a rush of satisfaction. And then there was Leila Azari. After the tasks of the evening were over, perhaps . . . well, there would be time for that later. He followed the servant to the door.

Once inside, he was ushered into the dining room, where the others were already busily helping themselves to generous portions of *chelo kabâb* and *jüjé kabâb,* long thin strips of lamb and chicken, that had been marinated overnight in seasoned yogurt. Just before serving, it had been grilled and was now presented with mounds of *chelo* rice. The main dish was accompanied by a raw onion, a large pat of butter, and a bowl of yogurt to stir into each portion of rice.

Reza Fardusi rose to greet his last guest. Kissing first one cheek and then the other in the Middle Eastern custom, he was again conscious of the scar that ran across Dosha's otherwise flawless face, disappearing into his beard. Yet in spite of the formality, there was a coolness in the greeting that did not escape the notice of either man.

"*Khosh âmadîd.* Welcome."

"*Motashakkeram. Salâm.* Thank you. Hello."

"Allow me to introduce you."

Fardusi proceeded with the formalities, and Dosha took note that only one man stood when introduced. It was evident that not everyone was pleased at his presence.

He was mindful that his most recent failure had evoked strong criticism within Hezbollah circles, and there were subtle, effective ways to express these feelings without saying a word. He had used them advantageously on others himself. Now he was on the receiving end and the subtlety was not lost on him. His jaw tightened as he moved around the table and took his seat.

The meal commenced in relative quiet, with little conversation. Marwan Dosha, with his penchant for details, observed in passing that it was the same Filipino servant who had been on duty the previous evening. He dismissed the detail as unimportant.

When she had finished serving the table, Madeline nodded politely to Reza Fardusi and backed several steps away from the men before turning to disappear into the kitchen.

78

It was Madeline's second day in the main house since her banishment after "The Great Spill," as she had dubbed it in her mind. Her friend Alisha had taken her place serving Âghâ Fardusi and attending to the guest rooms, working an alternating schedule with Theresa, who was still not completely recovered from her recent illness. At first, Madeline thought it might be God's way of setting her aside for her clumsiness. She viewed Alisha as a far more mature Christian anyway, and maybe God knew that Alisha would be more trustworthy. When it became clear to Madeline that she was now *persona non grata* in the guest quarters, she decided that she had better confide in Alisha about the little girl named Jessica.

At first, Alisha appeared stunned, so much so that Madeline wondered whether sharing this secret with her had been wise. She had done it, however, and there was no turning back.

To Madeline's chagrin, Alisha refused to serve as a go-between. She would carry no messages or do anything else that might jeopardize her job—or her life. She was sympathetic to the little girl's plight but inflexible about any involvement that might help her. Alisha was too frightened to be a reliable ally.

Two days ago, Alisha had gone to bed with a virus similar to that which had stricken Theresa. When this was reported to Reza Fardusi, he specifically asked for Madeline to replace her. Mrs. Muños had warned her to be on her best behavior tonight, especially while serving the important officials who were coming for dinner.

Unable to shake the apprehension she felt, Madeline stacked the dirty dishes to one side of the stainless steel kitchen sink. The only other person present was the chef, who was busily concluding her cleanup of the food preparation area by depositing fruit peelings in a garbage container.

"Make sure the dishes are washed and put away before you leave tonight," the chef said, without looking up.

"Of course."

"I'll be going in a few minutes. You can handle the rest of the evening?" It was more of an order than a question.

"*Motashakkeram.* I will be fine," Madeline replied.

The older woman sniffed as she continued putting the last of her cooking utensils in the sink. It sounded to Madeline more like a note of skepticism than a runny nose, but she didn't let it bother her. The sooner the woman left, the better. She was desperate to know more about what the men in the next room were up to. She still could think of no way to help the young American. It all seemed so impossible.

While serving the men this evening, Madeline had overheard little. Typical of an Iranian dinner, the conversation was limited, and most of the men were speaking in Farsi. Madeline understood enough to know that she wasn't missing anything important. However, one brief exchange in English had startled her into paying closer attention to what was being said.

It was the man who had casually declared the night before that he was going to kill the girl. Tonight, he was seated next to Reza Fardusi. As Madeline was pouring hot tea into a glass cup near his plate, the man turned to Fardusi and asked, "Where is the girl?"

Fardusi motioned toward the staircase as he bit into a generous portion of *chelo kabâb.* "Up there. The women are guarding her."

"I would like to see her again."

"And you will, of course," said Fardusi, wiping his mouth with the back of his hand. "But first you must have some *pâlüdé.* It is delicious. Madeline? *Lotfan.* Please."

Madeline set the teapot to one side, moving gracefully and efficiently, as she placed a small bowl of *pâlüdé* in front of the stranger. He did not look up or acknowledge her presence. His mind was obviously on other things.

Those things undoubtedly include the helpless hostage upstairs. Madeline was sure of it. She was sick with apprehension.

All these men are here about Jessica Cain!

Her mind was racing now as she busied herself at the sink. The frightening suspicion that this evil man's threat of murder would soon be carried out set off an inner panic that bordered on desperation.

At the opposite end of the counter, the chef gathered up a small basket of fruit and left the kitchen. The door had barely closed behind her when Madeline rushed to the other door, the one leading into the great room where the men were finishing their dessert. She tried pressing her ear against the wood panel, but all that resulted was an unintelligible jumble of voices.

Bravely deciding on a more direct approach, she opened the door and stepped unobtrusively into the room. She waited quietly, as if prepared to respond to any command, while in reality she was straining to listen to the conversations. She gathered that Farsi was not the first language of the man with the scar. For that reason, they spoke in English, with only occasional lapses into Farsi.

". . . it is extremely dangerous," one of the men was arguing, shaking his head vehemently.

"I agree," affirmed his table companion. "Once the world realizes that we have her, the outcry will be great."

"The world will never know where she is," said the man with the scar. "They know that the Palestinian Islamic Jihad is responsible for taking her. That is enough. Only a chosen few know exactly where she is. We will remain silent as to her whereabouts."

Madeline noted the discontented murmur that followed as the men debated the proposed plan back and forth. She did not always understand what they were saying; nevertheless, she had the distinct feeling that it really didn't matter in the long run what the others thought. The man with the scar had already decided what was to happen.

Reza Fardusi appeared to have been listening more as an observer than a participant. When he noticed Madeline standing near the doorway to the kitchen, he lifted his eyes questioningly. Responding to Fardusi's expression, the other men quickly quieted and looked in her direction.

Madeline stepped forward.

"May I bring you anything else?" she asked, making a conscious effort to keep her voice calm, free of the terror she felt roiling inside.

Fardusi waved her off. "No, Madeline. But please stay nearby. We may wish to have some refreshments later."

Madeline backed away, then turned and fled into the kitchen. Once again by herself, she leaned against the counter and released a deep breath. Fortunately, her presence had not been questioned. Unfortunately, she had learned very little other than to confirm what she already knew, that something terrible was about to happen to the girl upstairs.

Her mind raced, but she could think of nothing else to do. Just then, she heard a female voice and the sound of chairs scraping on the tile floor in the dining room.

Madeline pressed her ear against the door once again. She could barely make out what was being said. Reza Fardusi was introducing Leila Azari. The voices faded as the men began moving to the opposite side of the room, toward the staircase. Madeline reached down, carefully turning the doorknob until it released from the catch. She pushed it forward until a small crack permitted her to see and hear.

What she saw caused her to catch her breath.

The men were following the Azari woman up the staircase. One carried a video camera and tripod. She saw them pause at the head of the stairs while the woman unlocked the door to Jessica's room. One by one they disappeared inside.

Madeline's heart sank.

Poor Jessica. Oh, God, please help that little girl. We've done all we can, but it is not enough. Surely you are watching over her. Do something. There are bad people in this house.

Madeline's eyes filled with tears as she stared up at the ceiling in desperation.

What else can I do?

79

LOCAL TIME 2030

Hersch and John stood cloaked in darkness on the street corner opposite the Fardusi compound. John's hands were damp with nervous perspiration. Who would have believed a couple of weeks ago that he would be this close to taking Jessica home? He could hardly imagine they had come this far so easily. True, the most difficult part of their mission lay ahead, but still . . .

He glanced over at Hersch. The man's eyes were riveted on the complex across the way. His nostrils flared slightly with each breath, his concentration total. John could see that the hound was close to the quarry.

"I checked on this Fardusi fella, before we left the States," Hersch said at last. He spoke quietly, his gaze never leaving the compound gate, where a guard walked back and forth surreptitiously smoking a cigarette. "He's somewhat of a maverick, even for these parts. Survived the Shah and still manages to ingratiate himself with the powers that be. Nobody knows how he does it, but it has to be one delicate dance, that's for sure. He's envied, but not liked; feared, but not trusted. Most say he survived by working both sides of the street. That's probably an understatement. The fundamentalists generally see him as not fully committed to the cause, whatever that means. He is pretty much retired now, but obviously still keeps his hand in this holy war business."

"What do you think is going on in there?" asked John. Two dark-colored Mercedes had entered the gate a short while ago, and a taxi was being waved through now.

"Hard to say. Wish we could see through that wall."

Just then, another taxi rolled past the guardhouse.

"A party, maybe?" John said, almost to himself.

"Doubtful." Hersch's response was tinged with cynicism. "These boys aren't the partying kind. Their idea of fun is to see how many people like us they can shoot at the beginning of the day with one bullet."

John chuckled nervously. "Remind me to be on that boat when dawn rolls around."

"Right. By the way, now that we're here, how are you doing?"

"I'm shaking in my boots, amazed that we've pulled it off so far."

"Ah, we've been doing the easy part. That's over now. This is the moment of truth. Getting in, getting your daughter, and getting out. Remember, once we get her out of there, the next hurdle is meeting up with the boat and leaving Iran in our wake. We show up in the UAE, and take a taxi to the American embassy and throw ourselves on the mercy of the country that loves us. By the way, did you remember to bring cab fare?"

"No problem," John grinned, checking the time on his watch and thinking of the remaining cash still strapped to his body. "It all sounds like a piece of cake."

"Just don't forget."

"Forget what?"

"Cake has a way of crumbling when you least expect it. Come on, let's fall back a few doors. We can still see what's happening. Hopefully, whoever's been gathered in there this evening will be gone soon. We can wait until one-thirty. Two at the latest. Then, whatever the status, we hit the compound. If there's resistance, we take it out."

Hersch glanced over at John. "We go in, grab your little girl, and get out. Not a minute longer than necessary. We know the room she's supposed to be in, so it should be easy. The boat is set to pick us up at four."

John nodded. They had rehearsed the plan several times.

"You mind if we pray?" he asked.

"Pray?"

"Yes, you know. Ask God to enable us for what is ahead."

Hersch was quiet.

"Sure," he said at last. "Go ahead. I'm not sure he knows who I am, but you're probably no stranger."

"Trust me, Hersch," John whispered hoarsely in the darkness. "God knows who you are. He knows when the sparrow falls. He counts the number of hairs on your head. He sees us standing here right now."

"Okay, Rev, okay. I get the point. So, pray already—and while you're at it, put in for a couple of angels long on courage and short on brains."

John smiled. It grew quiet, with only the occasional sound of an automobile on a nearby street. He put his hand on Hersch's shoulder and asked God to watch over them.

80

LOCAL TIME 2130

Jessica was dozing fitfully on the cot, two of her fingers moving back and forth, lightly touching her upper lip—a habitual motion she had used to comfort herself since early childhood. At the sound of approaching voices and footsteps, she rolled over and stared blankly at the door. When the key entered the lock, she struggled to sit up. At some point the room had grown dark and she surmised that night had fallen. When the door opened, several shadowy figures stood in the entrance. One of the shadows reached out and turned on the light, forcing Jessica to shield her eyes with a hand while squinting to see who was entering.

She anticipated one of the guards or a servant, the only persons who had entered her prison in weeks, except for the man who had stood in the doorway yesterday with the Azari woman and stared at her for a while, saying nothing. She was startled to see Leila Azari come through the open doorway, followed by several men. As her eyes grew accustomed to the light, she recognized one of them. It was the old man who was the owner of the house. He was the last one to enter.

"This is the girl," Azari indicated, motioning toward Jessica with a wave of her hand. The men quieted, spreading themselves around the room, gazing at her curiously. One of them stepped forward until he was directly in front of her.

What is going on? She shrank back, suddenly recognizing the stranger who had stood in the doorway staring at her yesterday.

The man was unsmiling, his hard look accentuated by a scar on his cheek. Jessica licked her lips in an effort to counter the sudden dryness in her mouth. Fear clutched at her heart as she stared up into the stranger's eyes. These were not the eyes of a kind man. She ran her tongue across her lips again.

"Who are you?" asked Jessica, her voice small and quivering.

Before she could move, the man reached out and grasped her chin, his fingers digging cruelly into the sides of her jaw. She tried pulling away, but he held her face like a steel vise gripping clay. Any sudden movement on her part and she might break.

"Don't move," he said quietly, confirming her fear. "I can easily snap your neck with this one hand."

Jessica clutched at the edge of the cot with both hands, the man's face now only inches away from her own. Their eyes met. He turned her head slightly to the left, then back to the right, before releasing his hold and stepping back, his fingers leaving reddish marks on her jaw. His eyes never left her face.

"You resemble your father, Jessica Cain, but perhaps your mother even more."

"You know my parents?" Jessica gasped in disbelief, rubbing the sides of her face with her hands.

A slight smile could be seen on the man's face, though his eyes never relinquished their hardness.

"I know them all too well," he replied. He abruptly turned and spoke to one of the other men. "Set the camera up facing that wall over there."

For the first time, Jessica noticed the camera.

"You say you know my parents, and you know my name. What's yours?" asked Jessica, recovering from her initial shock. The man turned to her once again.

"My name is Marwan Dosha."

He paused, as if expecting that his name would mean something to her.

"I don't know you," she answered.

The man with the video camera said something to Dosha that Jessica couldn't understand. Dosha nodded and then took hold of Jessica's shoulder. She winced as he dragged her roughly from the bed and pushed her up against the wall, facing the camera. She was shaking now, her legs wobbly, partly from having eaten very little the last several days, but mostly out of sheer terror. The others in the room came around the cameraman now, stretching to see her image through the viewing lens. Unsmiling, they watched Jessica standing alone in front of them, bravely trying not to shake but quivering uncontrollably all the while.

"Take this and read it," Dosha said, handing her several pieces of paper.

"What is it?"

"It's a message to your parents. Read it. Don't add anything to it, and don't leave anything out. Read exactly what is written."

Jessica looked down at the script and swallowed as she tried to hold it steady.

"Read! The camera is rolling."

Jessica glanced up into the round lens, a few short feet away. She saw the red light come on, indicating that she was now being recorded. Brushing at her matted hair, she looked back at the paper and began to read.

"My name is Jessica Cain. It is Friday, December 2." She paused and looked over at Dosha. *Is it really December? I've lost track of the days.* She wanted to ask if this was the actual date, but he motioned for her to continue, and the grim look he gave cautioned her about further questioning.

She focused her attention on the papers again and continued reading in a thin, wavering voice.

"I am a prisoner of war, held by the righteous freedom fighters of Hamas and the Palestinian Islamic Jihad. I have learned of the terrible plight of the Palestinian people since I was taken captive in Israel. They have been grossly abused and mistreated by the Jews and by the United Nations. The world has robbed them of their land and given it to the Jews, who, in turn, have raped their wives and daughters, killed their fathers and sons, and destroyed their homes. Allah has called these righteous freedom fighters to strike back. It will be a war to the death, if necessary. Their fighters are prepared to die. There is no other alternative until the Jews and their chief collaborators, the Americans and their allies, agree to their terms.

"I, Jessica Cain, am the first of many children of the world who must pay for the sins of their parents. Unless the following terms are agreed to, others will follow me in death. They will be taken from the streets of their towns and cities. For every Palestinian home that has been destroyed by Jews, ten homes will be destroyed in occupied Palestine and ten more in the United States, that Great Satan, who together with her wicked allies, fills the cruel hands of the Palestinian Islamic Jihad's sworn enemies.

"These are the hands of the Jews who, with weapons and money provided by the Great Satan, are able to continue their oppression of the Palestinian peoples. Your schools will be blown up. Your synagogues and churches will be burned down. Unless the following terms are met, another of America's cities will feel the noose of persecution that the Palestinian people feel every day. It will tighten and cut off their very source of life. The sentence already carried out in New York City will seem like child's play if you do not come to terms with us.

"First, those under the judgment of Allah must at once agree to sit at the table of surrender and negotiate a just peace.

"Second, the United Nations must agree to rescind its 1948 decision that destroyed the future of the Palestinian people by taking from them their God-given right to the land of their father's fathers.

"Third, a new nation of Palestine must be at once recognized by the world community of nations, and it must encompass all of the territory now falsely known as the land of Israel.

"Be reminded of the recent deaths of the children in the city of Boston. Their martyrdom was necessary to demonstrate how easily the things that I have mentioned can be carried out within the borders of the United States. Israel is even more vulnerable.

"Be reminded of the most recent martyrdom bombings carried out in cities around the world. The true Palestinian people will not be denied their rightful inheritance. It has been promised to them by Allah himself. Nothing you can do will change his divine will in this matter.

"As a symbol of your positive response to their demands, my release has been pledged, upon receipt of one hundred million dollars, or, approximately one dollar for every boy and girl in Israel and the United States.

"This must be accomplished by the end of this month. If you are sincere, it will be easy for every man, woman, and child to give up one dollar of their Christmas shopping money for the righteous cause of Islam's true followers. However, if the money is not deposited in a designated bank account by December 31, I will be killed. Please help me come home. I forgive my father for abandoning me in Israel in order to do harm to the Palestinians. He . . . he did not know what he was doing. I want to come home safely. Please do everything they say."

Jessica looked up at the camera.

It clearly recorded the fear in her eyes.

And something else.

The red light went off.

Dosha stepped forward and took the script from her hand. As he did, Jessica's knees gave way and she crumpled to the floor. No one offered to help her.

The cameraman folded up his gear while the others stood about questioning Dosha regarding the message that had been read.

"How do you propose to carry out these attacks against churches, schools, and synagogues?"

"Our freedom fighters are already in place and prepared to act when the order comes," Dosha answered. "We have many cells ready to awaken in the United States and Canada, as well as Great Britain and Europe. We will begin this month and continue unabated until the enemy says, 'Enough.'"

"They are in place already?"

"Yes."

"The targets have all been chosen?"

"They have. But we need additional financial backing. The weapons and explosives needed are very expensive. So also is the establishing and maintaining of our commandos in places where they can strike terror into the hearts of Allah's enemies."

"How have you done this?"

"Some are in America under the guise of political asylum. A few are well entrenched in corporations in major cities. A number of them are students on college campuses."

"And so you have come to ask us for additional funds beyond what is already allocated to Hamas and the Jihad? Exactly how much will you need?"

"We need ten million dollars immediately to complete funding of the preemptive attacks."

A murmur of surprise rippled among the men. Finally, the head of the Council spoke to Marwan Dosha.

"Before we can agree to such a large sum as you are asking, you must tell us what you intend to do in the city of which you speak? What is meant exactly by the 'tightening of the noose'? We know you have been dealing with scientists in Tripoli and Moscow. Have you acquired the bomb?"

"No, not the bomb," Dosha replied, "not yet. But I have something akin to its devastating power. All I am prepared to say now is that a major city in America has been chosen, and our people are in place. Our weapon of choice, which for now must remain secret, will be placed in their hands in the days to come. It is silent. It is simple. And it is deadly. That which flows from under the Temple will poison the earth. Tens of thousands will die, and the world will finally understand that they can resist us no longer."

The video operator had collapsed the tripod and put the camera back in its case. He was standing with the others now, listening solemnly to Dosha's discourse on death.

"But let us enjoy our dessert now, and we can talk further," Dosha suggested, looking at Reza Fardusi. Fardusi nodded, his countenance grim. The other men shuffled out first, followed by Fardusi and Dosha. Leila Azari was the last to leave. She paused at the door and looked back at Jessica's wilted figure lying crumpled along the wall. Then she flicked off the light switch and entered the hall, closing the door behind her.

81

LOCAL TIME 2200

Madeline stood in the kitchen doorway as the parade of men made their way down the stairs. Reza Fardusi kept a hand on the railing as he descended, a look of serious displeasure on his face. As he reached the main floor, he glanced up and saw her standing there.

"Madeline." His voice was stern, eyes snapping in anger. Madeline started, fearing that he was upset at seeing her there again.

"Madeline," he said again, "take some bread and water up to the girl. She is not feeling well. And stay with her until she is better."

"Would it not be better to serve dessert before occupying your servant with other matters?" Azari's voice had an edge to it. Fardusi glared at her.

"You and I will do the honors of serving dessert, khânom Azari. It will be a privilege, don't you think?"

Leila's eyes flashed resentment at being relegated to a servant's task, but she knew she had been trapped by the wily old man. "Of course," she replied smoothly.

Madeline's eyes moved rapidly across the faces of the others, but she saw nothing that would indicate concern. The person with the camera equipment was talking to another man standing nearby, and the man with the scar was smiling as he paused near the bottom of the stairs.

Quickly, she ran back into the kitchen. There had been a note of urgency in Reza Fardusi's voice.

Something is definitely wrong.

She withdrew a pitcher of water from the refrigerator and gathered up a half-loaf of bread left over from the evening dinner table.

She reentered the main room. Some of the men had seated themselves; others stood around talking noisily. Leila Azari moved among them with a tray of glass cups, filled with hot tea taken from the serving bar. She paused briefly to talk to the man with the scar. As unobtrusively as possible, Madeline made her way past them and started up the stairs.

One of the female guards was standing at the head of the staircase, watching events unfold below. Madeline groaned inwardly. It was the woman who had demanded that she be taken off second-floor duty in the first place. She braced herself for a confrontation, but the woman merely scowled and moved back into the hallway to unlock the door.

She must have overheard Âghâ Reza's orders, Madeline thought as she moved past, vowing not to allow another incident to occur.

Turning on the light upon entering the room, she was shocked to see Jessica sprawled on the floor opposite the doorway. The door closed behind her. Madeline glanced over her shoulder to be sure the guard had remained outside. There was no table in the room, so she put the pitcher on the floor and balanced the bread loaf on top of it. Then she knelt by Jessica.

The girl's eyes were open, but she did not move.

"Jessica."

No response.

"Jessica!"

Jessica's eyes flickered, as she tried to concentrate on where the voice was coming from. Madeline could not believe it. The girl must have passed out in front of the people who were now downstairs. They had walked away, leaving her alone in this condition.

"Here, Jessica. Take some water." In her haste, Madeline had forgotten to bring a glass. She knelt down on the floor and cradled Jessica with one arm while putting the pitcher to the girl's lips with her free hand. Water ran down her face and neck, spilling onto her blouse. The blouse was dirty and Madeline wondered when it had last been washed. Jessica was focusing now. She pushed the pitcher away.

"Thank you," she said, weakly, squinting as she sought to identify her newfound benefactor. "You're the one. . . . the message . . . Madeline?"

"Shhh," Madeline warned, placing her fingers lightly on Jessica's lips. "Walls sometimes have ears. It is best to whisper, okay?"

Jessica nodded and offered a slight smile.

"Yes, I am Madeline," she said softly. "The message that you gave me was sent to your father. We have heard nothing, but we know that he has received it."

Jessica attempted to get up.

"Here, let me help," Madeline spoke, pushing herself up awkwardly, while half-holding on to the girl. Once on their feet, Madeline held onto Jessica until they reached the bed.

"Lie down and rest," she admonished, kneeling beside her again. "Here, eat some of this. It is fresh bread."

"I'm not hungry."

"Eat." Madeline's voice was low, but firm. "You need some food for strength. What happened in here?"

"They . . . they put me in front of . . . a camera. A man said it was a message to my dad and made me . . . read from some pieces of paper." Jessica stopped and looked up. A tear spilled onto her cheek. Madeline reached over and brushed it away with the tip of her finger.

"What did it say?"

"I don't remember everything. It was long. Something about the Palestinians demanding their rights and stuff."

Madeline nodded. "What else?"

"If they don't get what they want, they will kill me. And a lot of other kids, too. They . . . they want money before they will let me go home."

"How much?"

"A hundred million dollars."

"Are you sure? You can't be serious."

"That's what they made me say. It's supposed to represent a dollar from every boy and girl in Israel and America. They said that they had to get it by the end of December. If they don't, they will kill me. And a lot of other children will die, too, and keep on dying until they get what they want."

They fell silent as the impact of the message sank in. Jessica took another bite of bread. Madeline could not fathom the heartless reality of what was happening, nor could she comprehend what sort of evil mind would declare war on the children of the world.

"Wait here," she said, getting to her feet.

"Please, don't go," Jessica pleaded.

"No. It's okay. I'm not going to leave you."

Madeline went to the door. She had not remembered hearing the lock set after she came in. Turning the knob slowly, testing it, she was careful not to make a sound. It opened. She paused, half expecting the guard to pull it open all the way and confront her. There was nothing. She cracked it further until she could see the guard, leaning on the rail at the landing, watching the people below in the main room. Turning, she touched her lips with a finger, urging Jessica to remain silent. Then mouthing the words, "I'll be right back," she stepped through the doorway.

Madeline crept, unnoticed, to within a few feet of the guard, who remained engrossed in the proceedings below. Madeline was not close enough to see what was happening, but she could hear the voices, and they were conversing in English again. She was struck by the tone of disbelief she heard in Reza Fardusi's voice.

"Surely you do not seriously believe that the Jews and the Americans will give you this amount of money for the child."

"Perhaps. Perhaps not. If they do, it will go a long way toward underwriting our goals. If they do not, we will continue with the plan anyway. It is a roll of the dice in either case. Not that I would ever roll the dice literally, you understand. I, too, am a Muslim. It's against my religion to gamble," Dosha concluded with a smile.

"Humph," Fardusi grunted in disdain. "It appears to me as though this whole operation is a gamble. And you seem to think you hold all the cards."

"Not all the cards," replied Dosha, his smile now turning to a look of hard determination. "Just the trump card."

The others had grown silent, listening as one of the most feared terrorists in the world stood toe to toe with one of Iran's most feared and well-known citizens.

"You wager the future of your people and ours," accused Fardusi. "This plan of yours has too many pitfalls. How can we be expected to believe that it will succeed when your most recent efforts have ended with such failure?"

No one moved. All eyes were on the defiant old Iranian and the younger man with the scar. Fardusi's words hung between them like autumn leaves, tinged with flaming brilliance, yet so fragile that a thoughtless whisper might cause them to fall, leaving the old branch vulnerable to winter's final chill.

"I am your guest, Âghâ Fardusi. As such, I will not to respond to your indelicate words, though, under different circumstances and in a different place, you may be certain that I would be at ease in doing so. My world is filled with dangerous tangles. The only order is that which I impose on it myself. With the help of Allah, of course."

"Of course," murmured Fardusi, appearing not the least bit intimidated by the outlaw standing in front of him. "My apologies, as your host, for drawing attention to such recent unpleasant memories. However, you have used my house for these past weeks as a prison for a child. Now you want to ransom her in front of the world for an amount that you cannot hope to collect. Are you sure that it is the good of our Holy War that you envision? Do you have the Palestinian people and their future clearly in mind with this plan?

"Or, is it possible—forgive me for even mentioning it, but still I must—is it possible that you have your own, personal agenda to which you wish to commit us? After all, the girl upstairs is an insignificant child. A pawn. But her father is the one who thwarted your assault on Jerusalem, is he not? How can we be assured that you are not merely meting out revenge on the father through his child?"

Fardusi looked around. He saw that the other men were processing what he had just suggested. Score one.

Dosha felt it, too. He wished that he and the old man were alone. He would make short work of him. A quick twist of the neck and Reza Fardusi would be a piece of Iranian history not worth mentioning. Violence could always overwhelm logic when given the opportunity. But such an act was impossible here.

"I think the plan is ingenious."

The standoff between the two men was broken by a strong, feminine voice. Leila Azari stood confidently at the center of the great room, a woman obviously comfortable with expressing her own views in a male-dominated world.

"The message recorded tonight will strike fear and trembling into the hearts of every Jewish and American family," she continued, hands on hips, feet spread apart. She was smiling, but a space opened around her as Fardusi's guests became aware of the authority in her voice. "A few synagogues, churches, and schools blown to bits will let them know that no one is safe. We must drive them out, one way or another. You all know that. We must bring the oppressors to their knees."

Her voice rose slightly, carrying with it an edge of excitement.

"It is the only way our Holy War can be waged successfully against the Great Satan. These agents of hell are responsible for the deaths of my mother and father and brothers. Am I not correct in assuming that they have killed some of your family members, too? An eye for an eye. That is what the Prophet Muhammad, may the blessings and peace of Allah be upon him, has commanded."

Two of the men nodded their heads in agreement.

"And if the world does not acquiesce to your demands?" roared Fardusi, his countenance flushed, his green eyes flashing in anger.

"It will not matter," interjected Dosha. "A church, a school, a synagogue. Each will serve as a graphic example. We will blow the infidels into bits and pieces and present them to the world as Happy Hanukkah and Merry Christmas gifts. We will celebrate their New Year's Eve parties with them. They will feel such terror as never before in their hearts and in their homelands. Then, on the Christian holiday known as Good Friday, we will launch the ultimate weapon against the Great Satan. Tens of thousands will die. Millions will be scattered from their homes. We will break America's pride and glory. They will beg for a seat at the negotiation table.

"This time," he concluded grimly, staring coldly at Fardusi, "we will succeed."

82

Madeline remained mesmerized in the shadows. The guard, completely engrossed in what was happening below, still had not detected her presence by the time she slipped back through the door into Jessica's room.

Jessica was sitting on the edge of the cot, with a desolate stare, watching the door. Madeline saw her countenance quickly change from despair to one that grasped for a strand of hope. Any strand would do.

"Did you find out anything?" Jessica asked, her voice a mere whisper.

Madeline vacillated, not wanting to add anything to Jessica's emotional overload.

"What is it?" Jessica's sensors were on a high pitch, picking up the least little hesitation. "What's happening?"

"It is not good," Madeline answered, measuring her words. "These people are very evil. They are talking about the message that you read. What you said is apparently true."

"They said that they would kill me."

"I know."

"Would they really do that?" Jessica's plaintive tone caused Madeline to sit beside her and put her arm around her reassuringly. Then she answered her own question. "They would, wouldn't they?"

"I wish I could say otherwise, Jessica, but I honestly believe that they might. Last night, I overheard them talking about you. The man with the scar, his name is Dosha . . ." Madeline's voice broke. ". . . he said. . . ."

"He said what?" Jessica demanded.

"He said that . . . he will kill you tonight, after the others have gone."

Jessica swallowed hard in disbelief.

"But why? Why does he want to do this?"

"I don't know, but we have to get you out of here, and we have to do it now."

"How? Those women out there guard me twenty-four hours a day."

"I know," Madeline admitted. She scanned the familiar simplicity of the room, from the door to the hall, to the pictureless walls, to the small window. Her gaze lingered for an instant on the window, before continuing on in a hopeless perusal.

Jessica's eyes followed Madeline's.

"It's not locked." Her tone was subdued, matter-of-fact.

"What's not locked?" Madeline stared at her.

"The window. It's not locked. I can open it, but there is no balcony outside. I've looked before."

Madeline went to the door and cracked it open. The voices had quieted and the guard had returned to her place, occupied with another magazine. An M-16 was propped against the doorjamb. It would be impossible for Jessica to slip out this way now. She closed the door again and moved to the cot. Standing on the cot, Madeline pushed on the window. It moved outward.

Jessica was right.

She looked down and smiled.

"Turn out the light."

Jessica did as she was told and the room settled into darkness, except for moonlight and the diffused glow emanating from lighted windows in other buildings in the compound. Madeline pushed the cracked window open and hoisted herself up with her elbows on the sill. She could see out and, looking down, caught a glimpse of a narrow protrusion, maybe three inches wide at the very most. Then she looked to her left. A few feet away, the window into the next room was open.

Praise God!

"There's a place about three feet or so below the windowsill, Jessica," Madeline whispered. "You've seen it. It is very narrow, but it runs past an open window in the room next door. That's where the guards sleep, but it is empty now. One of them is outside guarding the door, and I overheard the Azari woman send the other one on an errand."

Madeline dropped back onto the cot and took Jessica's shoulders into her hands. They felt frail. For a moment, she wondered if the girl had the strength left to do it, or if it was even possible on such a narrow ledge. But there was no other way. They had to act now. Otherwise it would be too late.

"I'll run downstairs to the kitchen, go outside, and come around to the back of the house. Do you understand, Jessica? Are you listening to me?"

Jessica nodded, her eyes staring down at the floor.

"When I leave, I'll tell the guard you have gone to sleep. Stay in bed until you're sure she's not going to look in on you anymore. But don't wait long. The men are still downstairs, but they could come back at any time. As soon as you know the guard has settled down, go through that window. You can make it to the next room. It's only a few feet away, Jessica. Your only chance is to go out this window and back through the other one. I've been in there. It's a corner room with a second door that opens onto an outside staircase. You can slip out without being seen. All you have to do is get into that room."

"It sounds scary. I don't think I can do it."

"You can do it. You must. It's your only chance. Do you understand that? You have no other choice. You've got to make your move as soon as possible after I go. I know it's scary, but it's the only way. I'll meet you at the bottom of the stairs. I can help you over the wall. We'll get you to friends of mine who are Christians. They're the ones who took the message to your father. I'm certain they will hide you until we can get you out of the country."

Jessica nervously cracked her fingers. "I don't know. . . ."

Madeline stood to her feet. "I have to go now. You can do it. You must!"

Jessica remained hunched on the edge of the cot, looking up at this stranger who had become her friend. Her *only* friend. "I'm scared, Madeline."

"I know." Madeline drew Jessica to her and hugged her tightly. "So am I. Wait. Let's pray and ask God to help us. Okay?"

"Yes," she whispered. Madeline grasped her hands.

"Lord," Madeline began, "we are holding hands with each other, and we need you to hold our hands, too. We will do our best, but you must help us. Without your help, we cannot do it, but with you, we can do all things. We are your children. Go with Jessica as she leaves this terrible room. Give her courage and strength. In Jesus' name, amen."

"Amen," whispered Jessica.

"In a few minutes then?"

Jessica nodded slowly. "I guess."

83

LOCAL TIME 2225

Madeline opened the door and stepped into the hallway. The guard leaned forward in her chair and looked into the room as Madeline reached for the light switch. Jessica lay curled up on the bed, in a fetal position, her face to the wall. The leftover bread and water was on the floor nearby. Madeline waited until the guard nodded, then turned out the light. The guard then closed the door and locked it.

As Madeline walked down the staircase, she saw that the men were standing up, preparing to leave. Leila Azari was saying something to the man with the scar. They both broke into laughter over whatever it was. Leila's eye caught Madeline's as she reached the bottom of the stairs, then she quickly returned to her conversation. Madeline noticed Fardusi looking her way, but she passed to one side without a word and went into the kitchen.

As soon as the door closed behind her, she ran to the outside exit, pausing for a moment to catch her breath and steady her nerves. Then she turned the knob and rushed out into the darkness, hurried around to the side of the house facing the driveway, and looked up along the wall. The darkness partially hid the view, but not altogether. Madeline caught her breath and her hand involuntarily went to her mouth.

Jessica was partway out the window!

Madeline glanced around. The men inside would soon be coming out. To her dismay, she saw the security guard standing at the entrance to the compound. Her eyes darted back to Jessica, then to the guard. She would be easy to spot if he turned in that direction and there was no way to draw his attention away. But there was no turning back, either. Madeline's heart pounded madly. They were committed now. The young girl either made it, or she didn't.

84

Jessica had remained on the cot only as long as it took for the light to go out and the door to shut. Then she was up, reaching under the cot to retrieve her shoes. Fortunately, her captors had never thought to take them away from her. No doubt they had not considered the possibility of escape.

Clambering up onto the bed, she pushed at the window until it swung open. She felt weak, but by placing her elbows on the sill, as Madeline had done, she was able to pull herself up until her head and shoulders poked through the opening. Looking down, she saw the narrow ledge. She felt dizzy. It was not really a ledge at all. It wasn't even the width of her foot.

"Oh, God, I can't do this," she said out loud as her body sagged against the sill.

You must!

Jessica could hear Madeline's warning ringing in her ears.

It's your only chance!

Carefully, she worked herself through the open window until she was finally able to turn around to a sitting position on the sill. The narrowness of the opening and the need to be quiet made movement difficult. But by twisting and pulling, she finally managed to lift one leg across the sill and out along the wall, feeling with her foot to find the ledge. Then she drew the other leg through. Though unable to look down, she slid her foot along the wall until it touched the ledge. Now all the way outside, she hung precariously against the wall, holding onto the sill with both hands. The muscles in her legs were tight as bow strings as she clung to the side of the wall with the toes of her shoes.

Jessica looked to her right once again. The open window appeared to be about six or eight feet away. Too far to hang on to the one she had just climbed out of while reaching for the other. There was a span of two or three feet where she would have to let go.

Can I do it?

Her breath came in short gasps now, and she realized again just how weak she was.

It's your only chance!

Slowly, she edged along, ducking under the open frame that held the cracked glass. She straightened up, her body hugging the wall and one hand still on the window she had just come through. To move farther, she had to let go.

I can't keep my balance. I'm going to fall for sure. No! You've got to do it, Jessica. There's no other option.

Gingerly, Jessica slid her foot to the side, at the same time flattening every part of her body against the wall. She closed her eyes.

Think tightrope. You're balancing on a tightrope. Stay perfectly upright. There's a net below to catch you, but you're not going to fall. The band is playing. The crowd is watching. Stay tight to the wall.

Both hands were flat, sliding against the stucco exterior, both feet jammed against the wall, heels hanging well over the edge.

A little farther. Come on, you're almost there. Easy . . . easy.

Her fingers felt the outer edge of the window casing. Her heart was banging away inside her chest. Another inch. And another.

One more step to the right.

Jessica's right hand reached over the windowsill. She opened her eyes.

Careful. Don't panic now.

Tension was so much in control of her body that it was hard to release enough air to make room for more. She pressed against the wall, inching her way over until both hands were on the windowsill. She hung there for a moment, forcing herself to breathe normally. Then she tried heaving herself up, but missed getting all the way through the opening.

She could feel herself sliding back. Her toe missed the ledge.

No!

She fought with her fingers to hold onto the sill. All her strength was focused now as her feet felt for the ledge. There! Once more, totally out of breath, she heaved her body up and through the opening. This time, her stomach landed on the windowsill. With one final push, she propelled herself through the window and fell to the floor inside the darkened room.

—∞—

All at once aware that she wasn't breathing, Madeline drew in a deep breath and whispered, "Yes! You did it, Jessica. I can't believe it, but you did it!"

Turning, she looked in the direction of the guardhouse. The guard was still there but appeared to be occupied with a magazine. Obviously, he had not seen anything. She hurried past the front entrance to the main house and slipped silently around the corner. Here she waited, her fingers drumming the railing impatiently as she watched for the door at the top of the stairs to open.

Come on, Jessica. Hurry. There isn't much time.

85

Inside the room, Jessica moved her hands along the tile floor. The shadow of a bed loomed nearby. On the opposite wall, she made out the silhouette of a dresser, along with a table and chair. Her heartbeat was almost back to normal when a voice in the distance called out something in Farsi. She heard the doorknob turn and caught her breath as the voice that answered back came from right outside the door.

In the same instant that the door opened, Jessica rolled under the bed. She heard the click of the switch and froze as the room suddenly filled with light. She could see bare feet walking across the floor to the desk. She wanted to push farther back against the wall but didn't dare move, for fear of making a noise. She recognized both voices now: two of her guards, but not the Azari woman. The one who had called out to the guard at the door entered the room and sat down on the edge of the bed, her feet only inches from Jessica's face.

Both of them are in the room. I'm dead.

Their conversation, all in Farsi, continued for several minutes, until finally the woman sitting on the bed rose and moved away. Jessica's eyes followed her feet to the door, where they turned back into the room again as the other woman said something. Then the second guard walked to the door, flipping off the light as she went out. Jessica heard the door close and released a huge sigh of relief. She was soaked with sweat as she rolled out from under the bed and stood up.

In the dark, the outline of the second door could barely be seen, but Jessica made her way to it quickly. Carefully, she pushed it open and peered out. It opened onto an outside landing that led to a kind of fire escape with wooden steps. These were the stairs that Madeline had promised would be there. Jessica slipped through the door and shut it tightly behind her. Slinking across the landing, she hurried down the steps, catching her breath for an instant as a dark form emerged from the shadows.

"Oh, you scared me."

"Jessica! Oh, my goodness, you made it. You actually did it! You are *so* brave and I am so relieved and so proud of you. I can hardly believe it!"

They hugged each other tightly, exorcising the tension that clutched at their throats.

"What do we do now?" Jessica asked.

"Come with me. We've got to get you over that wall. Beyond is a dirt walkway that leads to the street. It's too high to get over without help. I'll boost you up and you can drop over on the other side. It's about ten feet at the top."

"Then what?"

"Then you must go in that direction." Madeline pointed off to the right. "You will cross four streets. When you have crossed over to the opposite side of the fourth street, turn left and go two more blocks. There is a house there. I know you can't read the street signs, but you will find it. It is brown and has a blue door. You can knock. If it is locked and no one answers, hide across the street until morning. When you get inside the house, ask for Arun. He is Indian."

"Indian?" Jessica repeated, with surprise.

"Not like an American Indian," Madeline explained. "Arun is from India. He is the leader of the church that meets there. Tell him your name. He will know what to do. And remember, you are a fugitive. You must think like one until you are safely back to your family again. That means you can't trust anybody except Arun. When you reach him, do whatever he says. Trust no one else."

"What about you, Madeline? What will you do now?"

"I must hurry back to the main house before I am missed. Now, do you remember your instructions?"

"Go that way. Cross four streets. Turn left two more blocks. Brown house. Blue door. The man's name is Arun."

"Right. Now, hurry. Up you go."

"Wait! How can I just leave you like this? You've risked your life to save mine? Why?"

"We are sisters because of Jesus, Jessica. We will see each other again someday." Madeline put her arms around Jessica's frail body and kissed her on the forehead. Jessica held on tightly.

"Come, now. Up and over."

Jessica turned and stretched against the wall. Madeline cupped her hands together into a stirrup and Jessica stepped up into it.

Just then, they heard shouts coming from the main house, followed by the fearsome sound of an automatic weapon being fired from the opposite side of the building. Jessica looked at Madeline with alarm.

"Hurry," Madeline hissed.

Jessica felt herself propelled upward and fell hard against the top of the wall, momentarily knocking her breath away. There were pebbles and bird droppings along the ten-inch-wide surface, but thankfully, no wire or broken glass to protect against intruders. Out of the corner of her eye, she saw Madeline hurry off into the darkness. Then, without looking, she lowered herself down the other side and dropped onto the dirt path.

86

"She's what?" bellowed Marwan Dosha. He pushed Leila Azari to one side and rushed past her toward the stairs, taking them two at a time to the top. One of the female guards was at the open door. The other was inside, standing on the cot in bare feet, looking out the window. She had fired an M-16 into the air to alert the staff that something was wrong.

"Where is she?" he screamed, his face livid with rage. "How could she have gotten away?"

The woman on the bed turned back and stared helplessly.

"We don't know, Âghâ," said the one at the door. "We have both been here ever since the maid left the room. I saw her lying on the bed before the light was turned out. The door was locked. She could not have come out this way. There is only the window. . . ."

"Why was the window not locked?"

"It was," lied the one with bare feet, not wanting to admit that they had failed to check it. "Besides, it is at least seven meters to the pavement below. There was nothing she could have used to lower herself down, and it is too far to jump."

"Do you expect me to believe that she simply evaporated into thin air? That she just vanished?"

"Perhaps the maid?" Leila Azari had pushed her way into the room as others crowded in to see for themselves the now empty space. "She was the last one to be with her. Get her at once."

The guard at the door rushed down the stairs.

"I saw her go into the kitchen," Leila shouted after her.

The guard bounded across the dining room and burst into the kitchen, sliding to a stop in front of the serving counter. Madeline looked up from where she was seated.

"What is happening? I heard gunfire, and I was afraid to go out."

"Come with me!"

The guard pushed Madeline roughly out into the dining room. Leila and the other guard were hurrying down the stairs, on the heels of Marwan Dosha. Dosha came forward and grabbed Madeline by the arm.

"What do you know about this?" he shouted, his eyes aflame with anger.

"I am sorry, Âghâ," Madeline answered, looking anxiously up at him. "I was in the kitchen and was afraid to come out. I heard gunfire and people shouting. I do not know what you are asking?"

"You were the last to see the girl!"

"The girl? I left her in her room. The guard looked in on her when I left. Âghâ Reza asked me to take her bread and water. She was very weak and upset when I went to her."

"Did she speak to you?"

"Yes. She said that she had read a message to her father and that those of you who were there had filmed it for her."

"Anything else? Did she say anything at all?"

"Not that I remember, Âghâ. She was very upset."

Dosha swore and turned to Leila. "You let her escape. Get out there and find her! Where can she go? An American girl in this town can't go far without being noticed, can she? Do it now and don't return until she is found."

Leila stood her ground. "How do you know this girl did not help her escape? What if she is not telling the truth?"

Dosha turned back to Madeline. He reached out and gripped her face in his hand. She flinched with pain, but did not move.

"If you are not telling everything you know, you had—"

"Stop it! Release her now!" Reza Fardusi moved in and put his hand on Dosha's wrist. "Now!"

Dosha let her go and stepped back, bristling with rage as he turned to face Fardusi.

"She is *my* servant, not yours," Fardusi declared emphatically. "If a servant of mine deserves punishment, I will see to it that it is done without any help from you. In fact, Madeline has obeyed everything that I have ever asked her to do. She is completely trustworthy, I assure you. She has worked so well for me that she sometimes responds to my wishes before I have had opportunity to ask."

Most of the others were outside by this time and lights were on everywhere as the entire compound waited and wondered about the evening's events. Madeline's only thought now was to get back to her room safely. She desperately did not want to be the center of Marwan Dosha's attention, and therefore was totally unprepared for what came next.

"Besides," Fardusi continued, "I stepped into the kitchen a short while ago, and I can assure you that Madeline was there, busy as usual, working at cleaning up the remains of this evening's meal."

Madeline looked at the old man with a start. If he had been in the kitchen, then he knew that she had not been there. If he had not come into the kitchen, why would he lie about it to his guest?

"You may go to your room, Madeline," he said. "If there is further need, I will send for you later."

"As you wish, Âghâ. Good night."

"Good night, Madeline. And thank you for everything you did for us tonight. You served us all very well."

"You are most welcome," she whispered, backing away and then disappearing through the kitchen door. For a few moments, she leaned against the serving counter, her knees shaking and her heart beating at twice the normal pace. As she gathered herself together, the puzzling encounter with Reza Fardusi gradually became clear.

"She sometimes responds to my wishes before I have had opportunity to ask. . . . Madeline was there . . . cleaning up . . . this evening's meal. . . . Thank you for everything you did for us tonight. You served us all very well."

Madeline clapped her hands together, stifling a sudden desire to laugh out loud. She had done exactly what Reza Fardusi wanted but could not have accomplished without her help.

He had wanted Jessica to escape!

Madeline ran toward the servants' quarters, certain that she had seen a twinkle in the old man's green eyes.

87

LOCAL TIME 2247

At the first sound of gunfire, Hersch and John recoiled, looked at one another, then scrambled to their feet and began running toward the compound.

"Wait a second." Hersch grabbed John's arm.

"But something's happening in there," John exclaimed, twisting away.

"Hold it, man. Use your head. We can't just go running in there and say, 'Hey, what's happening?'"

They watched anxiously as the security guard ran into the street. He had in hand what looked like an M-16 or an AK-47. It was too dark for Hersch to tell which. Another man came running through the compound gate. The two were shouting to each other, pointing first in one direction, then the other, obviously in a state of confusion.

"This is the time I wish I understood Farsi," Hersch growled under his breath. They were crouched between a garbage can and some bushes, three houses down the street from the compound gate. "Okay, get ready. It looks like God does answer prayer."

"What do you mean?" John said.

"We need a weapon. Here it comes now."

A man in civilian clothes, carrying an automatic rifle, was jogging in their direction. Two houses away, he stopped abruptly and turned as someone shouted something. Then he began running in the opposite direction.

Hersch swore, banging a fist against his leg.

"Sorry, Rev," he apologized.

"Me, too," John said as he watched the man disappear around a corner.

"I meant . . . never mind."

A car roared out of the compound gate. Then another. The first car swung to the right, the second to the left. The sound of their engines faded as their taillights disappeared into the night.

"What do you suppose happened?" John's voice was filled with anxiety.

"We'll find out soon enough."

"We will? How do you propose to do that?"

"Look, I know you want to run out there and grab someone and demand your daughter back. But there's nothing we can do while everyone is running around pointing guns. Good grief, it's a wonder they don't kill each other. We wait until it calms down. There's nothing we can do until things settle a bit."

"But Jessica—"

"No buts," Hersch whispered harshly, grabbing John by the shoulders, their faces inches apart. "We agreed before we left that I was in charge all the way. If something has happened to your daughter, there's not a thing we can do about it. Get that through your head. Chances are she's still okay. Whatever just happened in there may not even be about her. We'll cool it for a bit until things settle. Then we go in, just like we planned. Only maybe instead of over the wall . . . we'll just walk in through the front gate and knock on the door."

"Are you serious?"

"The element of surprise, my good man." Hersch's attempt to mimic an Englishman's accent wasn't half bad. "It's unlikely they're expecting Jessica's father to drop in for a social visit, don't you think? Besides, there's been no more gunfire. Maybe someone accidentally shot his toe off or something. Who knows with this gang of thugs? We'll just sit back here in the shadows for a while and wait our turn at Mr. Fardusi and his crowd."

John glanced at his watch. *Five after eleven.* They moved back from the street into the shadows of a house that appeared to be unoccupied and settled down to wait.

It was after one o'clock before the lights in the compound began to dim. One by one, the windows that could be seen through the main gate darkened. One of the cars that had left earlier returned, then left again. Two taxis entered and a few minutes later drove away. Whoever the "extras" were, they were leaving. That was good. The fewer the better. By ten minutes to two, it had been quiet for nearly an hour.

"Okay," Hersch said, getting up from the concrete block he had been using for a chair. "It's time. Let's go. I'll lead the way. You stay out of the way. All right?"

John nodded.

"Don't mess me up now," Hersch cautioned. "Don't try to be a 'hero dad' or you'll get us both killed. They've got real bullets in those guns."

They moved out from the shadows and started toward the gate.

88

Inside the main house, Reza Fardusi turned out the light in Jessica's room and walked down the stairs to the dining area. For the first night in weeks, he was able to move through his house without Leila Azari and her female warriors being somewhere about. They were history at last. They had left the compound together in a taxi, without so much as a word of thanks to their host.

A flick of another switch and the lights in the dining room were dimmed, except for two small lamps at either end. Fardusi's gaze went to the kitchen door and his thoughts to the maid named Madeline.

"How did she do it?" He spoke the words out loud, his emerald eyes emitting flashes of excitement at the thought of what had just occurred. A small victory perhaps, but one carried off under the very noses of those who had been determined to defile his house with an innocent child's blood.

Fardusi was weary of the turmoil and terror of the times. Whatever happened to "peace on earth"? The "holy war" had given the world a generation that only knew how to hate, not love. Even his own people spied on each other, brother conspiring against brother. He stared through the glass door at the softly lit patio garden.

Pairidaeza.

The beauty of what our land once was has been reduced to postage-stamp gardens like this. Must the children of the world now be slaughtered to fertilize what is left? When will enough blood have been spilled around the world to satisfy the anger of Allah? Was the price we paid in the conflict with Iraq not sufficient? Surely, Allah cannot be pleased with what is happening in our land today. The people are poorer. The times are harder. And defective souls like Leila Azari and Marwan Dosha run rampant, killing the innocent with no remorse. Are we participating in our destiny or our punishment?

89

John winced as the security guard fell. He had watched from the shadows as Hersch moved closer to the entrance. His slow, stealthy movement was capped by a sudden, surprising swiftness. The guard fell, without a sound, under a hard chop to the back of his neck.

John helped drag the man inside the small guard shelter and Hersch commandeered the M-16 that leaned against the wall. John lifted a handgun from a small leather holster on the guard's belt. Hersch motioned for John to hand it to him for inspection.

"A Taurus PT-145," Hersch said, gripping the weapon expertly. "Company started years ago in South America. Moved to the States in the sixties. It carries ten, plus one in the chamber." He handed it back to John. "It'll get the job done, but be careful with it. Come on, let's get out of here."

Hersch began jogging through the shadows toward the largest of the buildings. John followed on his heels.

"This looks like the main house, where the guy said your daughter was being held."

Just then, a light went out on the second floor. They waited in the shadows and watched. Moments later, the main lights on the lower floor subsided as well. Now all was dark except for the low outdoor lighting and what looked to be a small source of light on the first floor.

They walked up the steps to the front door. Hersch looked at John. "This is it," he said softly and proceeded to knock.

John didn't know whether to laugh or gag. He could not believe they were standing at the enemy's front door, knocking.

Hersch knocked again, louder this time, the M-16 held loosely in his right hand. After seeing his swift dispatch of the security guard, John had no doubt that the gun could be at ready status in a flash.

Suddenly the door opened.

"Yes, what is—"

Hersch pushed his way into the house, the gun now pointed at the old man who had answered the knock. John followed him in and closed the door, checking cautiously to see if others were about. The man saw him looking.

"No one else is here, please. I do not know you, but you may put your gun down. I'm an old man as you can see, and quite harmless. You do not look like robbers, but this is a night of surprises. What is it that you wish from me?"

"Are you Reza Fardusi?" asked Hersch.

"I am," the man replied.

John stepped forward.

"Where is my daughter?"

The old man started, his eyes blinking.

"You have been holding my daughter here as a hostage. We've come to get her and take her home."

"I must say that I am surprised beyond words. You are the cleric from America? The Reverend John Cain?"

John said nothing.

"And you?" the man asked, his hand nervously smoothing his mustache.

"Who I am is unimportant, and we haven't all day to visit." Hersch poked the barrel of the gun at the man's chest. "We want the girl. Where is she?"

"Ah, my friends, I regret to tell you that you are too late. She is not here."

John started forward, ready to pounce in outrage. Hersch pushed him back.

"She was here then? Where has she gone?"

"That, gentlemen, is something many people would like to know. She left us a few hours ago, under her own power, for a destination known only to her." Fardusi smiled, carefully pushing the gun barrel to one side.

"What happened?" John said. "How could she have gotten away? How much do you know?"

Fardusi proceeded to tell what had happened in the earlier hours of the evening. John could hardly stand still as the story unfolded. The old man spoke softly, yet with authority. He was undoubtedly accustomed to having people answer his beck and call, not the other way around.

It was difficult for John to contain his emotions when the name Marwan Dosha was mentioned. He had been here, intent on killing Jessica this very night, coming and going in one of the cars they had seen earlier. Fardusi sounded like a bystander, like someone he might have heard on television describing what happened at an accident scene.

This man had held his daughter hostage in his home for more than a month. Yet here he was, sounding for all purposes like a concerned father himself, relieved that Jessica had escaped. Admiring her courage and ingenuity. Gradually, John got the feeling that the man had been a hostage of sorts himself. He wanted to hate him; but he didn't. It was crazy. It was the Middle East.

"A moment ago, you said there might be one person who would know where Jessica has gone," John said, finally.

"Yes, permit me to make a call. She can be here in minutes."

"No funny stuff, Fardusi," Hersch growled.

"I assure you, there will be none. You have the upper hand, my friend."

Fardusi picked up the phone and dialed.

"Mrs. Muños. My apologies for the lateness of the hour, but would you please send Madeline to the main house at once. It is urgent. Tell her not to waste time dressing, just hurry. . . . No, there is not a problem. . . . Yes, I am fine. Attend to this quickly. *Baleh, moteshakkeram. Shab be kheyr.* "Yes, thank you. Good night." Fardusi put down the receiver.

"The young lady who most surely knows will be here in a moment."

"Who is she?"

"One of my staff, a young Filipino lady named Madeline. I believe she helped your daughter leave the premises."

"How did she do this?"

"We will ask her when she arrives. I will be most interested to know myself. If it is as I suspect, it was an act of great courage and valor. I hope it has been arranged for the girl to meet someone on the outside. We will see. Meanwhile, may I offer you some tea?"

90

Madeline threw a housecoat over her nightgown and hurried to the house, barefoot. Her heart was in her throat. Being called out by Âghâ Reza at this hour, on this night, could only mean one of two things. Either she was in serious trouble, or Jessica had been recaptured, or both.

She entered through the servant's door, turned on the light, and ran across the kitchen. She stopped at the door to catch her breath before entering the great room.

Reza was there, alone, waiting by two small lamps that illuminated the room. Madeline was taken aback as two other persons appeared from the shadows, one on either side of her, each with a gun in his hand.

"It's all right, Madeline," Fardusi's voice sounded reassuring. "These men have come for Jessica."

Madeline went to Fardusi and stood beside him, facing the two strangers.

"Let me introduce you. I don't know this one's name, but this gentleman," Fardusi pointed to John, "is Jessica's father."

Madeline felt her heart skip a beat as she stared at John. She stepped forward slowly.

"You are the Reverend John Cain? Jessica's father?" she asked incredulously.

"Yes. I am Jessica's father. I understand you may know where she is."

Madeline glanced over at Reza Fardusi. He smiled and nodded.

"It's all right, Madeline. I have the idea that you were instrumental in Jessica's timely disappearance tonight. You did the right thing, whatever it was. If you had not, she would have been dead before these men could have rescued her. We are all very curious, though. How did you do it? And where is the girl now?"

Madeline was at a loss for words. This meeting with Âghâ Reza could not possibly be happening. Add to it that Jessica's own father was standing here in the great room. She stared back and forth at them both. Finally, she began.

For the next few minutes she spoke quietly, connecting the sequence of events surrounding Jessica's escape.

"Where is she now?" asked John, finally, impatient to find her.

"I gave her directions to the house of my spiritual leader," she answered. Glancing at Fardusi, she continued. "A small group of Christians meet in the house of Arun. He is from India, a former Hindu. I worship with them when I can."

"Will you show us how to get there?" asked Hersch.

"Of course. If Âghâ Reza permits."

"Certainly. In fact, I will take you there in my car," said Fardusi, smiling at Hersch. "I imagine that you will want to keep an eye on me until you leave our country, in any event, to be certain that I do not give away your presence here. You are planning to leave soon, I trust?"

Hersch smiled thinly. "Right you are, Mr. Fardusi. Right you are."

John looked at his watch. "It's nearly two-thirty."

"I am not dressed appropriately to be out in the city, Âghâ Reza," Madeline said, hesitating.

"It is all right, my dear," Fardusi said reassuringly. "There is no time for you to change. Allah will forgive us a small indiscretion."

They went outside together to where a cream-color, four-door Mercedes was parked on one side of the driveway.

"I will drive," said Fardusi, flourishing a set of keys he had brought with him from the *biruni*, "though I will admit to it having been awhile. We'll not bother my driver for this little excursion. He would not understand Madeline's attire."

Fardusi proved surprisingly adept behind the wheel and seemed to be taking genuine delight in the turn of events. They drove the short distance, directed by Madeline. Four streets. Turn left. Two more blocks.

"There it is." The brown house with the blue door. Fardusi parked two houses away, while John and Madeline ran back to the brown house and up the steps to knock on the door.

No response.

John pounded harder this time.

A light came on inside.

A moment later the door opened.

"Arun, it is Madeline. Is Jessica here?"

Arun rubbed the sleep from his eyes and stared at the woman in the housecoat and the man beside her.

"This is Reverend John Cain. He is Jessica's father. We've come so that he can take her home."

"Come in, please," Arun invited, stepping back.

"I'm sorry," John responded. "There is no time. We are leaving the country in a matter of minutes. Where is she?"

"I'm sorry, too," Arun answered, glancing first at Madeline, then back at John. "I do not know where your daughter is. I have not seen her. She has not come here."

91

Back in the car, the mood was clouded over with disappointment.

So close. We were so close! Where is she? Has she been recaptured?

The most terrible thought of all: *Did they find her and kill her, disposing of her body only God knows where?*

So many questions and no answers.

The Mercedes moved slowly through the poorly lit streets as they retraced their path, discussing what to do now, glancing both ways as they crossed intersections, hoping for some sign of Jessica. There was nothing. Thankfully, at this hour, the streets were empty of police as well.

John stared out the side window, desolate.

He heard Hersch outlining the next step to their newfound chauffeur, Reza Fardusi. Their way out of the country—a speedboat—was coming in from offshore at four o'clock. They were to meet the boat at the beach exactly one mile north of the Hotel-é Naghsh-é Jahân. If they were late, and if the boatman's arrival was undetected, he was committed to waiting an extra ten minutes. No longer.

John looked at his watch for the tenth time in the past half hour. *Three-thirty-five!* His stomach felt hollow, empty. He felt a hand on his arm and turned to look into the eyes of Fardusi's maid. They were brimming with tears.

"I am sorry, Reverend Cain. I don't know what happened to her, but Jessica has a very strong spirit, full of courage. I believe she got away—and, if so, she will be all right. Perhaps she has to hide out for now and will come to Arun later. I wish I could do more."

"I'm sorry, too, Mad—Madeline, is that your name?"

She nodded and smiled, looking down.

"Madeline," John began, "if it were not for you, Jessica would be dead. You saved her life and did it at your own peril. How can I ever thank you?"

She looked up shyly as a single tear splashed onto her check.

"It was my privilege and duty as her Christian sister," she said simply.

"Uh oh."

Fardusi's hands tightened on the steering wheel, his eyes focused on the rearview mirror.

"What?" demanded Hersch.

"The car that just passed. They are turning around."

"So?"

"It is the Guard."

"Are you sure?"

"There is no question. They love driving around the city in their favorite brand of vehicles, the Nissan Patrol. I saw two of them for sure. There may be others. We recognize them easily. Their symbol is an arm with a bandaged hand clutching a rifle—and their emblem is also on the license plate. I saw it as they went by."

"What Guard?" John asked. "What is the Guard?"

"It's the Revolutionary Guard," Hersch explained. "They're kind of a cross between the Spanish Inquisitors and the Gestapo. They monitor internal security and enforce Islamic law. Not the kind of people you want to run into in the middle of the night with a woman in your car."

Twisting around to take a better look at the car that was now directly behind them and closing the gap, Hersch resumed his conversation with Reza Fardusi. "Do they have radio contact with their little friends?"

"Most likely, yes."

"So what's the normal procedure?"

"They will follow us until they decide what to do. Perhaps they will leave us alone. Or they might pull alongside for a better look. Wait. Here they come now."

The Nissan pulled up alongside and kept pace while the men inside checked out the passengers in the Mercedes. John could see three men now, all young and very serious. The driver was in plainclothes; the other two sported short stubbly beards and black collarless shirts. They were obviously curious about the car, its passengers, and the reason for them being out at this hour.

Again, John checked his watch. *Three-forty-five!*

The Nissan dropped back and swung in behind them.

"What are they doing now?" asked Hersch.

"They are likely calling ahead for help. They have seen a foreign woman in the car, her head uncovered, together with three men. We are probably going to be arrested."

"I have an idea. How far are we from your compound?"

"Five minutes at the most."

"Go quickly. And give John instructions for getting down to the road headed north. We've got a boat to catch."

"No! I left Israel without Jessica. I can't leave without her again!" John fairly shouted as he leaned forward, grasping Hersch's shoulder.

"You have no choice, buddy boy. We stay here, best case is we'll be tossed into the slammer. Worst case, they'll stand us up against a wall at dawn. Hey, if they've got her, then that's it. If they don't have her, she's obviously got friends who can hide her until we can do something else. But we've got to stay alive if we're going to do that girl of yours any good. And remember, you're with me. I give the orders."

"He's right, Reverend Cain." Madeline's hand touched his once again. "You cannot help her tonight. If she has not been caught, she will be all right. We prayed, Jessica and I, before she escaped. I believe God has heard us and is watching out for her."

They could see the entrance to Fardusi's compound about a block away now. Hersch was giving instructions.

"When we get close, sir, slam on the brakes. Open the door. I'll push you out. John, you shove Madeline out the other door and jump in behind the wheel. Madeline, fall on the pavement. Sorry if you get skinned up, but stay low. I'll fire over your heads and we'll drive off. Make up a story about being kidnapped. You should be pretty good at that by now. You can pick up your car at the beach."

Fardusi nodded. Moments later, he stepped hard on the brakes and skidded to a stop. His door flew open and he fell to the pavement. John leaned over Madeline and pushed the door open, virtually throwing her from the backseat. He followed her through the opening and slid in behind the steering wheel. Meanwhile, Hersch fired two rounds over their heads and then leaned out the window, getting off two additional rounds aimed at the Nissan, which was sliding to a stop behind them.

The Mercedes peeled away with a force that slammed the open doors shut as they roared off into the night. In the mirror, John saw three confused and rattled Revolutionary Guard members stumble out of their vehicle. The Guardsmen stopped first to stare at the two bullet holes in their windshield, then ran over to where Fardusi was helping Madeline to her feet.

John skidded around a corner and the scene disappeared from view.

"They'll be okay," Hersch announced, as if this sort of thing happened every day.

"I hope so."

"Do you remember the directions?"

"I hope so," John repeated. "What time is it?"

"Almost four o'clock. Don't stop for red lights."

Their route ran directly through downtown. No time to go around. John pushed the speedometer to eighty kilometers. Buildings flashed by. Thankfully, there was little traffic—but there was some! John braked suddenly, the car skidding to one side as he barely avoided hitting a car that was entering the intersection from the right. A block further down, he swung to the left to avoid a garbage truck that was parked in the street. The surprised collectors gaped openly at the car speeding past.

"Company," John called out, checking the mirror again.

Hersch looked over his shoulder.

Several blocks back, one vehicle was being joined by another in pursuit of the Mercedes. John weaved in and out, narrowly missing a street maintenance crew, as they set up for the day's work. Past the NIOC building on the right. The Mosâferkhüné-yé Iran on the left. John kept his foot on the gas pedal as they sped by the Iran Air and Valfajre-8 Shipping headquarters building. He slowed slightly, skidding, as the road made a sharp left bend, then a short way ahead another hard right.

"That's the ferry landing," Hersch said. "You're doing great, Rev. You'll make a good living racing Indy cars if we survive this and you ever decide to change careers."

Another hard right, then a left. The Mercedes' tires squealed their protest while trying to maintain their grip on the blacktop. The road straightened out and John ran the speedometer up to 170 kilometers per hour.

"That's the hotel off to the left. Mark the odometer. We don't want to overrun the gangplank."

John glanced down, checking the numbers as they rolled by.

"Almost there," he said, peering out into the darkness. "I don't see anything."

"Well, it's showtime, one way or the other. Either our ride is there or it isn't. Wait. Over there. There it is. See it?"

The dark outline of a small craft could be seen, lying in the water, a few feet offshore.

"Yes," John felt relief and excitement at the same time.

He put the car into a slow slide, peeling away from the road and onto a stony stretch of hardpan that fell off toward the water. The car came to a stop, lights out, about fifty feet from where the speedboat rocked gently in the shallows.

"Run for it!" shouted Hersch as he scrambled from the car and dropped to his knees. The two pursuing vehicles had stopped at the edge of the roadway. At least five or six men could be seen getting out and running toward them. Hersch fired off a couple of quick bursts. Two men fell and the others scrambled for cover.

Hersch began backing down the beach, firing sporadic rounds as he went. John was almost to the water's edge when the Guardsmen began returning fire.

The sound of automatic weapons and the thump of bullets in the sand and ricocheting off rocks was high motivation for John to run as fast as he had ever run in his life. He heard the motor start up in the launch and saw it maneuvering away from the shore. At first, he thought they were being left behind, then realized that the boatman was simply turning around for a fast getaway.

Can't be fast enough for me, he thought.

Just then, he heard a sudden cry of pain. He stopped and turned to see Hersch rolling on the ground about twenty-five feet away.

For a brief instant, John hesitated; then he started back toward his fallen partner.

"No, man, keep going," Hersch grunted.

"Not without you!"

"Keep going. That's an order."

"Shut up and give me that gun."

John grabbed up the M-16.

"Is this the switch for fully automatic?"

"Yes."

He flipped it, pulled it up to his shoulders and sprayed bullets back and forth at will. In a matter of seconds the magazine was empty.

"Here." Hersch handed him another one. John remembered his training from the Santa Clara shooting range. In his mind, he could hear Carla Chin's voice. "*Fully automatic you will probably not hit anything. But you might scare somebody to death.*" Right now, that was all John wanted to do. The full magazine went in smoothly. Hersch was trying to crawl, with one leg dangling helplessly and bleeding profusely.

Another bullet whizzed past.

John flipped the switch to bursts of three rounds each. The sporadic burp of the weapon terrified him as he fired in the general direction of their pursuers. He hoped they felt the same way.

Then the gun was empty again. He threw it to one side and grabbed Hersch.

"Get out of here, man," Hersch grunted through clenched teeth.

"Not without you. So shut up."

Okay, God. I need your help. Otherwise, we're dead right here.

From somewhere a surge of strength came that surprised even John. Maybe it was the adrenaline pumping through his system from the excitement and danger. Maybe it was sheer desperation and fright. But it felt to John like someone had come alongside and helped him lift Hersch to his feet. Half carrying, half dragging, they staggered into the water.

"Here," a man's voice called out. "Let me have him."

The boatman dragged and John pushed as Hersch fell into the bottom of the boat. John scrambled over the side just as another hail of bullets came from somewhere back near the Mercedes. It was then that John remembered the handgun. Miraculously, it was still tucked in his belt. Pulling it out, he cocked and fired.

Never point the muzzle at anything or anyone you're not willing to destroy. John pointed in the direction of the gun flashes, steadying his one hand with the other as he crouched in the boat. He fired.

Bam!

That's for Hersch.

Bam!

This is for Jessica.

Bam!

Here's one from me.

The boat continued moving back into deeper water, then suddenly roared to life and raced out to sea.

Away from the deadly hail of bullets.

Away from the Guardsmen who had shot Hersch.

Away from enemies he did not know, who were determined to take his life.

Away from Madeline and Reza Fardusi.

Away from Jessica.

John's face was wet with tears of frustration, the pistol still pointed at the shore, his finger pressing the trigger again and again, though the magazine had long since been spent.

Hersch reached up and pried it from his hand.

John shook as he leaned back and wept for Jessica.

PART SEVEN

Jihad, bullets, and martyrdom operations are the only way to destroy the degradation and disbelief which have spread in the Muslim lands.

—from an al-Qaeda recruiting video
seized by London police soon after the
September 11, 2001, attacks

And slay them wherever you catch them, and turn them out from where they have turned you out, for tumult and oppression are worse than slaughter.

—The Qur'an
Surah 2: Baqarah:191

From the LORD comes deliverance.

—The Holy Bible
Psalm 3:8a

92

Friday, 02 December, local time 2247
Bandar-é Abbâs, Iran

Dropping from the wall to the ground, Jessica lost her footing and fell backward onto the hard surface, stifling a cry of pain as her shoulder struck a loose rock. Rolling over and getting to her feet, she looked around frantically. She could hear shouts coming from the other side of the wall.

She ran to the corner nearest the street. Just then, someone dashed out of the compound, waving a gun in the air and shouting at someone behind him. Another man emerged and ran in her direction. Jessica ducked behind the corner.

I've got to get out of here! The directions that Madeline had given her were not going to work.

Running back along the wall, Jessica passed the place where she had fallen, and she sprinted into a narrow alleyway that stretched between two rows of single-story, cinder-block houses. She stumbled over a garbage can and fell forward, scrambling to her feet as it careened noisily across the alley. Gathering herself up, she ran on. Something dark scurried across her path. She hoped it was a cat, but her skin crawled with the realization that it was probably a rat and there were certain to be more wherever it had come from.

Sprinting across an empty street, she entered another dark alley. At the far end, she stopped to catch her breath and look around. It took only an instant for Jessica to realize that she was totally lost.

Which way did Madeline say?

The landmarks were unfamiliar. In her fright, she had lost all sense of direction. Should she go to the right or the left? Maybe it would be better to retrace and start over.

No. Not that. I can't go back to that place. I've got to keep going.

Jessica looked around frantically, trying to get her bearings. The street to the right sloped downward. She started walking slowly, uncertainly, and then picked up her pace. Down was easier than up, and by now her lack of nutrition and exercise was becoming apparent. Her breathing was raspy and her lungs felt as if they were on fire. Soon she was stopping at every street corner, partly to see that the way was clear, partly to catch her breath.

A cream-colored car went by. Jessica shrank back into the shadows in order not to be seen. Then she ran on. After what she guessed was a half mile or more, she dropped to the ground when another car approached. As it drew closer, it looked like a police car, but she could not be sure.

The police! Maybe they will help me.

She started to get up and call out.

No!

She froze.

No. You can't trust anyone. Everyone here is your enemy. Everyone except Madeline. I still can't believe she risked her life to get me out of there. But now I can't trust anyone. No one. If you're going to get out of here alive, Jessica Cain, you've got to do it on your own. Don't ask anyone for help.

She stood to her feet and watched as the taillights disappeared around a corner.

Okay, think, Jessica. Just how you are you going to do it?

She continued jogging down the street, her lungs still burning for relief.

Lord, please help me find the house that Madeline told me about. It's the only thing I can think of that sounds safe.

The landscape was leveling out now, and Jessica could smell salt water. Coming to another cross street, she looked to the left. In the distance, she made out the silhouette of a ship. Hesitating, she glanced around quickly. She was surrounded by three- and four-story buildings. They were old and dilapidated, generally in need of repair. About a block away, two men were walking toward her. A car approached along the road from the opposite direction.

Do something.

Jessica dodged down the narrow street to her left, running toward the docks. As she came closer, she saw the distinct outlines of three large ships.

Maybe if I could get on a ferry like the one they brought me over on . . . no, that would be too dangerous . . . and I'd need a ticket. Besides, this doesn't even look like the same dock. It's a different place than before.

She ran out to the edge of the dock and looked down. Water was lapping against the concrete wall. It was dark and smelly. To her right, a short distance away, a giant crane stood out in the moonlight, resting on tracks that permitted it to move from one ship to another. Along the tracks the dock was covered with a thick, black dust.

Just then, she spotted a man walking in her direction. Instinctively, she ducked beneath a smaller, nearby crane, crouching down behind one of the wheels. The man continued to approach until he was no more than fifteen or twenty feet away. He was dressed in dark, baggy trousers and wore a jacket pulled over a collarless shirt. In his hand was a flashlight.

Jessica held her breath as he stopped and snapped on the beam, shining it back and forth in her direction.

He's seen me! What should I do?

After what seemed an eternity, he turned off the light and continued on past.

Jessica let out a sigh of relief.

That time, I was lucky; but I need to get somewhere safe.

She started walking again, careful to stay in the shadows as much as possible. A little farther along, she paused alongside the biggest ship she had ever seen up close. From somewhere deep inside the massive hull, Jessica could hear the engine idling steadily. Triple strand mooring lines kept the vessel secure at the dock. She also noticed a series of numbers running vertically up the side of the vessel.

12 M
8
6
4
2
11 M
8

The vessel was painted black just below the 12 M number and a greenish-blue above. Signs of rust were apparent here and there and it looked as if someone had simply splashed paint over the worst rust spots without any thought as to how it might appear. Jessica was fascinated by seeing the numbers—or anything else that she could read, for that matter—after weeks of mental deprivation. She decided the M might stand for "meters," but she wasn't sure. She had never been this close to such a large ship. It was not a passenger liner. That much she knew. It had to be a cargo vessel of some kind. Stepping forward, Jessica was able to make out the ship's name.

M/V Evvoia.

And then she saw it.

A ladder!

She drew back and looked at the long set of steel steps leading up to the ship's lower deck.

The motors are running. Maybe that means it's getting ready to leave. Where do you suppose it is going? Does it matter? If I stay here, sooner or later I'll be caught and taken back to that house. Or worse. If this ship is headed out to sea, wherever it is going has to be better than this place.

She glanced over her shoulder. The man she had seen earlier must have been a watchman. He had disappeared, though, and no one else seemed to be about. She looked up the ladder again. It appeared there was no one around to stop her; but there was only one way to find out. Jessica took a deep breath and stepped over the chain someone had stretched across the first step.

The ladder swayed slightly as she climbed, but a safety net had been tied to one handrail, pulled underneath, and secured to the railing on the opposite side. If she fell, at least she wouldn't go very far.

Jessica looked back one last time. There was still no sign of anyone. As quickly as possible, she reached the level of the first deck and poked her head above for a look around. All clear.

Hurry!

Quickly, she climbed the last few steps until she stood on the nonskid decking. All at once, she heard voices off to her left.

Hide! But where?

Ducking into a nearby doorway, she pressed herself against the wall as two men walked by. They were smoking cigarettes and speaking a language she did not recognize. But she knew it was different from anything she had heard in recent months.

Once the men were past, she stepped out onto the deck again and continued looking for a good hiding place. Each doorway she came to looked foreboding. The walkways were narrow and she could not tell where most of them went.

I'll be found for sure if I stay out here. There must be a place to hide where they put the cargo. Or maybe the engine room?

If only she knew how to get there. She was thankful to be wearing the shoes she had worn every day while walking with her father in Israel. They enabled her to move quietly. Being careful to stay away from the ship's rail, where someone below might see her more easily, she edged along the superstructure until she came to a wooden ladder. She looked up.

A lifeboat.

At that moment, voices rang out in laughter. She couldn't see them, but they sounded near enough and getting closer. Quickly, she started up the ladder. Iron pegs imbedded into a crude wood frame.

. . . three, four, five, six rungs!

Jessica scrambled over the side and dropped noiselessly into the lifeboat just as two men passed beneath her. A moment later, they were gone. Letting out another sigh of relief—how many times had she done that tonight?—she stretched out, exhausted.

And cold.

Now she knew why the watchman had been wearing a jacket. For the first time, she noticed that the temperature had dropped considerably in these hours just before dawn. Her desperation to escape had forced every other thought from her mind. She shivered now, wishing for the *châdor* she had left behind. All she had were warm-weather underclothes, a pair of pants that reached her ankles, and a loose-fitting, once-upon-a-time-white shirt. She hugged herself, briskly rubbing her arms, as she looked around for anything that might help.

The lifeboat was large, with space for several persons. There were bench-like seats, wrapping all the way around the outer edge, with oars lashed to one side, and four bench seats spanning the width of the boat. It looked as if it had been refurbished fairly recently, too, in a dark red color. The faint odor of paint was still present.

Several bundles were stored in the bottom of the boat, bound together and wrapped in waterproof plastic-coated canvas. Jessica's fingers were stiff with cold and clumsy as she worked at untying the knots. Finally, one of the bundles broke open. Inside, she found a blanket, which she quickly pulled out and threw over her shoulders. To her surprise, she also discovered some crackers, protected with waterproof wrap, along with several tins of food. She managed to get the crackers open and ate a handful of them, suddenly aware of how hungry she had become.

And how exhausted.

She was thirsty, too, but didn't see anything to drink. With a sigh, she folded the canvas back over the food tins and laid her head on the pack. Pulling the blanket tightly around her shoulders, she looked up at the sky. The stars had disappeared as the blackness of night gave way to the slate gray of early dawn. The warmth of the blanket eased her soreness and exhaustion. She closed her eyes and soon fell into a dreamless sleep.

93

Saturday, 03 December, early morning
Bandar-É Abbâs, Iran

Reza Fardusi stood at the door of the main house, watching as a parade of official vehicles slowly wound its way around the fountain and out the compound gate, two cars carrying Bandar policemen, and three more with Revolutionary Guardsmen.

"Do you think they really believed us?" asked Madeline, nursing the dark bruise and a cut on her knee with a damp cloth. She was sitting on one of the dining table chairs, her left leg protruding stiffly from beneath Fardusi's afghan, which had been given her to wrap around her shoulders for the sake of modesty and to ease the morning chill.

Fardusi glanced in her direction, then let his gaze return to the last car as it bumped its way out onto the street and disappeared. Then he closed the door.

"Of course they did. I think we were very convincing, don't you?"

Madeline smiled. "I think *you* were convincing, Âghâ. As for me, I am not sure. I was shaking too badly."

"It was your fright that gave a stamp of authenticity to your testimony. Those *Komîté* members are too dull to distinguish whether your fear was from being questioned or from being kidnapped. If they were more discerning, they would be doing something worthwhile with their time, instead of merely intimidating the populace."

He still marveled at the quick thinking that had saved them. Seeing him thrown unceremoniously from his own car in front of the compound had momentarily confused their pursuers. He remembered hearing shots fired, and later had been shown two bullet holes in the windshield of the Guardsmen's Nissan. Unfortunately, none of the Guardsmen had been hit, but they had been sufficiently frightened.

At first, Fardusi had been suitably upset and profusely thanked the Guardsmen for saving his life and the life of his employee. The men had stared disapprovingly at Madeline, even as she tried to cover herself with her torn housecoat and the nightgown that did not quite reach to her knees. Her face and hair were inappropriately uncovered as well. At first, they had taken her for a prostitute—or worse, some Persian man's wife or daughter caught in an act of immorality with three men. But Fardusi soon set the matter straight by concocting an elaborate kidnapping story. That shots had been fired as the "kidnappers" commandeered the car and sped away lent credence to the old man's story.

"Are you all right now, Madeline?" Fardusi's voice was gentle and full of concern.

"Yes, Âghâ," she replied. "I am starting to feel a few bruises and sore muscles, but they will soon go away."

"I will have one of my sons help you to your room and send for a doctor to look at your knee."

"Please," Madeline protested, not wanting to be near Reza's sons, especially the way she was dressed, "Mrs. Muños can help me to my room. And you must get some rest yourself. It has been a long night."

Fardusi walked over to the glass door facing the inner garden. His thoughts ran back over the extraordinary events of the night, pausing finally to ponder the frightened green eyes of the young American girl who had been held hostage in his home during these past weeks. As Madeline stood to her feet, preparing to leave, he turned and smiled. "I am still amazed by what you did this evening."

Madeline paused and looked at her employer, embarrassed that the subject of her clandestine activities was being raised. "I meant no disrespect for you, Âghâ. I know you must have your reasons for having kept her here. But as a Christian, I could not stand by and let one of my sisters in Christ be executed for no good reason. I . . . I had to do something."

"No disrespect has been received, Madeline, only shame on my part for not having had the courage to do the same as you. To begin with, I was not asked if I would permit her to be held here. I was told. It seemed a little thing at first, one of the Guardsmen's many inconsequential games. Still, I was troubled when I saw how young she was. Such an attractive little girl, too. And so bright. Then, of course, there was that woman, Azari, and her female warriors. Never again."

The old man shook his head sadly. "Do I understand you to say that you did this because you are a Christian?"

Madeline nodded and smiled.

"I wish that I could say the same as a Muslim, without feeling shamed," he responded wistfully, his eyes still resting on the young woman standing before him. "We must speak further sometime about this God we serve. He has provided me with much sorrow and little peace in this life. You seem to have found a side to him that I have missed."

"I have found Jesus Christ."

"Ah, yes, Jesus. He was a great prophet."

"He is more than a prophet, Âghâ. He is the Son of God." Madeline spoke gently. Fardusi's piercing green eyes met hers, at first flint-hard, then slowly softening.

"The Son of God, eh?" he repeated thoughtfully. "That is where we differ when it comes to the prophet Jesus."

"I know."

"Then we must talk further. Perhaps I can straighten out your understanding on this matter," Fardusi said, smiling.

"Perhaps, Âghâ, but I doubt it." Madeline said. "I know too well just how much change Jesus Christ has brought to my life."

"I am certainly impressed with your 'life,' as you call it, Madeline. And curious about how your faith has changed you. We will speak of this again. As for now, you must go and rest. I will ask Mrs. Muños to have something brought for you to eat. You will remain off duty until she assures me that you are sufficiently recovered. Understood?"

"Thank you, Âghâ, for your kindness."

"Mrs. Muños?" Fardusi called out.

A moment later, the housekeeping supervisor entered the room from the kitchen.

"Take this young woman to her room, please, and see that she gets what she needs in order to be comfortable. I will send a physician to look at her knee. You can be very proud of Madeline, Mrs. Muños. She is a courageous young woman."

Mrs. Muños smiled proudly at Reza Fardusi as Madeline put an arm over her shoulder. She wasn't quite sure why her employer praised Madeline so, but she was nonetheless grateful to know he was pleased.

Fardusi watched them disappear into the kitchen, then made his way through the house to his own quarters. On the way, his mind wandered back to the green-eyed American girl and her father, who had come too late to rescue her.

What do you suppose has happened to them?

94

Saturday, 03 December, early morning
Straits of Hormuz, off United Arab Emirates

While dawn was still breaking, the speedboat raced through open waters, dodging cargo ships and offshore supertanker loading facilities, dhows, and fishing boats, finally slowing to move through shallow seas dotted with offshore islands and coral reefs.

The sun lay low in the east but was already driving the chill from the night air. It would be warm again today, as it was every day. Thankfully, however, it was the time of year when the normally sweltering humidity would remain mercifully endurable.

The coastline was directly ahead now, outlined clearly by the sun rising at their backs. The coastline of the seven United Arab Emirates extended for nearly four hundred miles, from the frontier of the Sultanate of Oman to Khor al-Odaid, on the Qatar peninsula in the Persian Gulf. Six of the seven emirates were located along the Persian Gulf coast. The seventh, Fujairah, lay on the eastern coast of the peninsula, with direct access to the Gulf of Oman.

The boatman painstakingly steered through the shallows off Fujairah, all the while keeping an eye on the intricate pattern of sand banks and small gulfs that shaped the shoreline. He finally saw what he was looking for and pointed, looking over his shoulder at John, who was seated just behind him. John nodded and glanced down at the other passenger, checking him for the fiftieth time on their early morning journey.

Herschel Towner rested on some flotation gear, propped against the side of the boat with one leg stretched out. The leg was bare where his trousers had been cut away. A crude tourniquet fashioned from an anchor rope had been tied around his upper thigh to minimize blood loss. It was neither comfortable nor sanitary, but it was the best they could do under the circumstances. Fortunately, the bullet had gone completely through the leg, though it had left a gaping, bloody wound in its path.

The boat handler maneuvered expertly as they came near the sandy beach, cutting the engine at the last second. Their onshore contact had parked along the highway above the beach and was waiting at the water's edge. He waded in, reaching for the side of the small craft to hold it steady.

"We've got one wounded," the boatman said.

"So I see. How bad is he?"

"He needs medical attention as quick as possible. He's lost quite a bit of blood. My guess is that he's in shock."

"Help me get him up and over the side." It was John who spoke up, impatient to get Hersch to a hospital.

"Be careful, Rev. Don't get blood on your shirt. That stuff's hard to get out." Hersch tried to joke, even though his words were slurred through gritted teeth, each syllable shaped by pain.

"Shut up, Hersch," John said gruffly, patting his arm at the same time, grateful that the man who had become his friend under fire was talking, even if he wasn't making any sense.

Dragging the boat up onto the beach, the three men worked to lift Hersch over the side and onto the sand. With one at each end and the third placing his hands under Hersch's waist and thighs, they kept him as rigid as possible while making their way up to the car. Once they had laid him in the backseat, the boatman shook John's hand.

"See you around, buddy," he said with a smile. Looking toward the car, he added, "Take care of ol' Hersch. I owed him one, so this makes us even. I've got to get out of here now, but I'll check on you guys later."

"Thanks so much for everything," John exclaimed. "We would be dead men back there if it weren't for you."

"Well, one thing's for sure, if you want to live long, you gotta learn to stay away from this guy," he said, pointing toward the backseat. "He can get in and out of more trouble than any five people I know. Actually, things have been pretty slow around here lately, so I guess a little excitement makes living in this place tolerable. Besides, some guys will do anything to get out of Iran."

"Isn't that the truth," John responded, with a grim smile.

"You know that you'll probably have a little explaining to do once the powers-that-be catch up to you guys?"

"I know."

"Okay. Take care of our friend now, y'hear?"

"I promise."

John sat across from the driver, looking over his shoulder to check on Hersch again, as the car set out along the highway.

"If I'd known you guys were starting a war over there," the driver remarked, "I'd have brought an ambulance instead of this car. The first word we had on this operation was when Hersch called from London and said you needed some backup. I don't suppose you've got anybody at home who's authorized this little escapade?"

John shook his head.

"Passports? Visas? Wait. Do I even want to hear your answer?"

"Probably not."

"Figures. I guess that's why the boss was treating this with kid gloves. You two were trying to get somebody's daughter out of there, is that it?"

"Mine," John answered, staring out across the open sea.

"Sorry. Obviously no luck?"

"No luck. I'm sorry, too."

"Couldn't find her?"

"Not soon enough. She escaped from where they were holding her a couple of hours before we hit the place." Lines of worry furrowed deeply into John's face. "She's out there, though, and she's alive."

"She get busted for drugs or something?"

"She's twelve."

"Twelve," exclaimed the driver, looking at John in disbelief. "Are you serious? A twelve-year-old?"

"Yeah."

"Wait a minute. Are we talking about that the girl who was kidnapped in Israel a couple of months ago?"

"The same."

"I heard Hersch call you 'Rev' back there. Are you really the preacher?"

"In another life, my friend. In another life."

95

SATURDAY, 03 DECEMBER, EARLY MORNING
BANDAR-É ABBÂS, IRAN

Jessica awoke to the sound of shouting and the footfalls of someone running nearby.

The noise forced her eyes open, as she struggled to awaken from an exhausted stupor. She lay still, afraid to move a muscle, trying to gather herself together.

What is happening? Where am I?

Her eyes slowly focused on a blue ceiling . . . no, it wasn't a ceiling. It was something else. There was the distinct odor of new paint. Like the time she woke up that first morning after she and her mother painted her bedroom.

Finally, another shout jolted her, causing the unbalanced images floating in and out of her mind to vanish abruptly. She caught her breath at the cry of a seagull, and smiled as it swooped across her line of vision. The familiar gray and white scavenger bird looked as glorious as an eagle.

Sky. It's not a ceiling at all. I'm looking at the sky!

Jessica turned her head to one side on the water-repellent package-turned-into-a-pillow. Her movement released another odor, this one of canvas and something else she did not recognize, mingling with the smell of paint . . . and fresh air. *Fresh air.*

Oh, dear Lord Jesus. I'm free. I really made it! I'm out of that horrible place at last!

For a moment, the full force of freedom actually took her breath away. Her excitement continued to build as she started to replay the events of the night before. Then another shout broke her reverie and Jessica struggled to her knees, lifting her head until she could see over the edge of the lifeboat.

Below, on the dock, two men were looking up at the ship. One called something out to a man who was standing on deck a short distance from Jessica's lifeboat and leaning over the side. Further forward, more men were moving about, releasing mooring lines as thick as a man's wrist.

The engines were louder now and Jessica could feel their vibration all the way to where she was hidden. Smoke was rising from the ship's stacks, and she heard the sound of a loud horn. A narrow strip of dirty water became visible between the bow and the pier. Gradually, the ship was moving away from its moorings.

Yes!

Jessica's heart was pounding. She had guessed right.

We're moving. We're actually leaving this place.

She wanted to stand up and shout.

Don't trust anybody, Jessica. These people may be just as bad as the others.

Her sudden rush of feeling free deflated rapidly, replaced by mixed emotions of foreboding and reprieve.

It's not over yet.

Jessica peered cautiously over the outer edge of the lifeboat, watching as the huge dock crane and waterfront buildings slowly receded from view.

96

On the way to the United States embassy in Abu Dhabi's Safarat District, wherever John looked there seemed to be suntanned female flesh on display out from under backless T-shirts, spaghetti-strap minidresses, even shorts. In Palm Springs, no one would have looked twice, but when compared with the streets in Iran, it was, to say the least, different. He had been informed by his driver that these women were all foreigners, but still, they set the pace for the rest of the principality.

The traffic was heavy, just as in Tehran. The difference here was that it appeared to consist wholly of BMWs, Ferraris, and Mercedes, sprinkled with a healthy number of Jeeps and Landcruisers. He noticed an entire fleet of Toyota Cressida taxis in operation, as well.

After arriving at the embassy, he was led to a small sitting room. The ambassador, he was informed, had someone in his office at the moment. Since John had no appointment, he would have to wait. Meanwhile, an aide provided what surprisingly enough proved to be an excellent cup of coffee.

After waiting for half an hour, John was ushered into Ambassador Geoffrey Carson's office. The ambassador was standing behind his desk, a sheaf of papers in his hand. He waved John into a chair and tossed the papers onto the desktop in the same motion. When John was seated, the ambassador fixed him with a steely glare.

"Let me get this straight, Reverend Cain." The ambassador's voice was stern and measured as he glanced at the notes on his desk and shaped his mouth around each word. "You and this Herschel Winslow Towner *the Third* decided to take on the whole Hezbollah terrorist crowd and the rest of the radical Muslim world all by yourselves.

"You entered the sovereign nation of Iran, using forged passports and counterfeit visas. Next, you feigned illness and left your tour group and its leader wondering what in the name of peace happened to their two missing male members. You flew to Bandar-é Abbâs; broke into the home of an Iranian citizen named Reza Fardusi; shot up a contingent of Revolutionary Guardsmen and then fled in a speedboat driven by somebody whose name I do *not* want to hear; entered the UAE illegally, without passports or any genuine identification papers whatsoever; and this morning . . . Herschel Winslow Towner *the Third* was admitted into a local hospital to receive treatment for a bullet wound—a gift, I gather, from the Iranian 'Welcome Wagon.' And now, here you are, sitting in my office requesting assistance in getting temporary passports so that you can return home. Is that about it, Reverend Cain? Are there any details of which I am still unaware?"

John shook his head. "No, that pretty well covers it, sir."

The ambassador swore just as a secretary walked into the office and handed him a fax. He scanned it briefly and walked around the edge of his desk.

"Excuse me. Just stay seated, Reverend Cain. Don't go *anywhere.* Don't even move a muscle."

Ambassador Carson disappeared into the next room.

In defiance of the ambassador's parting directive, John drummed his fingers impatiently on the arm of the chair while staring straight ahead, still trying to come to terms with the disappointment of the night before. At the same time, he reflected in amazement at where he was now.

Ten minutes came and went before the ambassador returned, a handsomely carved pipe cupped in his hand. He sat on the edge of his desk and resumed his look of stern disapproval.

"Reverend Cain, there's something I'd like to be certain that you understand. During my tenure here, I have never heard of such audacity. You and your friend have broken most of the laws that anyone could be guilty of breaking in a forty-eight-hour period. Do you realize that?"

"Yes sir." John was beginning to feel like a student in the principal's office.

"For goodness sake, man, do you think that your conduct is in keeping with the way someone from your calling and persuasion should be acting?"

"No sir."

"Good, because you're right!"

Ambassador Carson bit down on the pipe stem and stood to his feet. "If we provide you with sanctuary and assistance toward your safe return to the States, you have to promise me that you will cease and desist from any future shenanigans of this nature. I can appreciate your parental motivation, but you've got to let your government handle this matter through normal channels. Agreed?"

"I'm sorry, sir," John said at last, "but no, I cannot agree to that."

Carson glared at John, stood up, and walked around to the other side of his desk. "And why not, Reverend Cain? Why do you, of all people, find it so difficult to submit to the authority of your government and follow the rules?"

"With all due respect, Mr. Ambassador, I *have* submitted to that authority. I have followed the rules and pressed the appropriate buttons for weeks. All to no avail."

"But State informs me that they are working on this case."

"State has given up on this case, Mr. Ambassador. They've been stringing us along, sure, but there's really nothing that they've been able—or willing—to do. It came down to me trying to do something, or the death of my daughter. What would you do, sir, if you were in my position?"

Carson fingered the bowl on his pipe. John did not move, but kept his eyes steadily focused on the ambassador, waiting for an answer.

"You and your friend Towner are a real pain, Cain." The ambassador chuckled at his own inadvertent rhyme, but John's expression remained unchanged.

"Okay, you've made your point, Reverend," Carson said, as he sat on the edge of the desk. "On an official level, I find your actions both foolish and reprehensible. You just *cannot* keep on going around doing what you have been doing."

He shifted his body and leaned forward. John was surprised to see traces of a slight smile crack the otherwise solemn facial veneer.

"On a personal level," he went on, "I admire your guts."

Carson stood and smacked a fist into his hand. "I still can't believe you actually did it. You just got on a plane, flew in, and kicked butt the way we all wish we could. It's incredible."

Carson burst out laughing. "Just incredible," he said again.

"Begging your pardon, Mr. Ambassador," John interrupted. "I have to say that I'm not really proud of what we did. Breaking laws, like Hersch and I have done these past two days, is wrong. I know that. But standing up against evil for the rights of oppressed people, in this case, my daughter . . . well, I think that is right. It's just hard to always know where the line runs and at what point a person should cross over. In my business, we have a saying that may sum up my being here in your office this morning. Sometimes it's a lot easier to get forgiveness than it is permission."

Carson laughed again. "When it comes to governmental red tape, I'm afraid you're right."

"My concern now is that I don't know where Jessica has gone. She must still be somewhere in Bandar. One of Fardusi's maids directed her to a small group of Christians who promised to keep an eye out for her. That's really my only hope now. I'm concerned, too, about Fardusi and his maid. Believe it or not, they were the key to us getting out of there. Our escape may have left them in a dangerous position, though."

"My guess is that Fardusi will work his way out of it," responded Carson. "We know a little about that fellow. He's a wily one, that's for sure. Actually, I had my staff check the foreign news services in Iran, this morning, to see if there was anything of interest. There was."

"What?" John's voice was anxious as he sat up straight.

"Jacques Kandau is a correspondent with *Agence France-Presse* who works out of Tehran. Yesterday he reported two missing Americans. Their personal effects were found in the hotel room in which they were registered. A rug merchant named Trent, and a religion professor." Carson picked up one of the documents lying on the desk and flipped it open. "Dr. Castle, I presume?"

John smothered a grin and brushed at his rumpled suit trousers.

"Yes, well, it seems that we may have solved the mystery of the missing Americans," continued Carson, unfolding a piece of paper from his shirt pocket. "Now, about an hour ago, another story came over the wire from the TASS news agency. They report that bandits entered the Bandar-é Abbâs home of the highly respected Reza Fardusi, apparently with the intent of kidnapping him for ransom. A maid was also forced into Fardusi's stolen vehicle—good grief, did you guys actually kidnap these people and steal a car along with everything else?—and the two hostages were being driven away when a Revolutionary Guard patrol became suspicious and stopped them.

"A furious gun battle ensued, leaving two wounded Guardsmen. It is believed that one of the bandits was also wounded. Both of the criminals escaped in a powerboat and remain at large, though an area-wide search is under way right now. Authorities in neighboring countries are being requested to be on the lookout for the kidnappers.

"Fortunately for you, from the descriptions, both appear to be from the Middle East, most likely Iranian—given that both men spoke fluent Farsi." Carson looked up. "Would you like to regale me with some of your 'fluent Farsi,' Reverend?"

John shook his head in wonder, as he rose from the chair. "I can't believe it. The man holds my daughter for over a month as a hostage in his house. Then he helps us escape and bids us well in finding her."

"It sounds as though you helped him escape some local retribution as well. He was just being grateful by returning the favor."

The two men looked at each other for a long moment. Then Ambassador Carson reached out and shook John's hand.

"That's life," he said, smiling. "And this is the Middle East."

He escorted John to the doorway.

"I'll have our staff work on arranging things for you and Mr. Towner. We'll get passport replacements for the ones you seem to have misplaced. You'll have tickets home. One way, I might add. I can't promise you anything, but I'll do what I can to get State to become more motivated in locating your daughter. Especially now that we know she's on the run somewhere. Take heart, Reverend Cain. It sounds as though your Jessica is made of the same stuff as her old man."

"I really do appreciate whatever you can do, Ambassador. I know I can't ask you for miracles, but I can ask him," said John, glancing upward. "And I will."

"Remember, you're heading for home, now, understand?" Carson admonished. "Just as soon as your friend is ready to travel. From what I'm told, though, that may be a few more days. Do you have a place to stay?"

"Not yet," John answered, "but I'll find something."

"I'll have Susan make a reservation for you. Come with me. She's at the front desk."

"Thank you. I'm sorry to have put you to this much trouble."

"Well, you have livened up my day, Reverend, that's for sure. We'll be in touch. I think we can take care of you and your friend without any trouble. Then, as soon as he is able to travel, we'll arrange for you to head home."

"Thank you again, Mr. Ambassador," John said, adding to himself, *but I'm not going home without Jessica. No matter what. Not on your life.*

97

SATURDAY, 03 DECEMBER, LOCAL TIME 1130
GULF OF OMAN

Captain George Callimachus strolled across the bridge, his dark eyes routinely checking instruments and gauges. The *M/V Evvoia* was steaming steadily toward the imaginary line known as the Tropic of Cancer, approximately twenty-three and one-half degrees north of the equator, the northernmost latitude reached by the overhead sun. In Bandar-é Abbâs, the vessel had taken on a load of wheat and rice for delivery to the port city of Split, Croatia.

The *Evvoia*'s bridge was twenty-five feet wide and ten feet deep. It was crammed with radar consoles, helm, engine-order telegraph, and a plotting table. Two leather chairs were perched on pedestals to the left and right. Immediately above the instrument panel were large windows, permitting the captain a panoramic view of the forward section of the ship as well as the seas ahead. Glancing at the overhead clock, he estimated they would reach the invisible parallel sometime after nightfall.

Captain Callimachus dressed casually when in his normal shipboard routine, and the crew followed his example. He could most often be found roaming the decks in blue jeans and a white dress shirt, always with an open collar. Fair skinned, with a large, bulbous nose and dark hair solidly streaked with gray, George Callimachus was likable but resolute. Strong and sure of himself but quiet.

The rest of the ship's crew, including First Mate Paulo Morales, was Filipino, ranging in age from eighteen to thirty-five. Each man had contracted to serve aboard the *Evvoia* for a specific time, with duties that ranged from the most menial to engineer status. They lived aboard in private cabins, sparsely outfitted with a bed, chair, writing table, and sea trunk for personal items. All meals were taken in the crew's mess.

The captain brushed an imaginary fleck from his white shirt. A refreshing breeze was coming through the open doors at each end of the bridge. The steady vibration from the engine room tickled the soles of his feet. His hand rested briefly on the polished brass handrail that ran the full length of the instrument panel.

First Mate Morales was bent over the radarscope at the far side of the bridge, evaluating the distance between the *Evvoia* and other nearby ships in the Gulf. Due to the amount of time required for their vessel to take evasive action or stop altogether, that information was essential while working in this heavily trafficked region.

Captain Callimachus took a pitcher of water from the counter and poured himself a glass. He drank slowly, savoring both the taste and the feel. In the summer, the Gulf was invariably frying-pan hot, with temperatures regularly soaring to 45°C or even 50°C, and with an oppressive humidity. "If you don't believe in hell," he often said to his seafaring counterparts, "wait until you sail the Gulf in summer." Late November to early March, however, was generally pleasant, though today seemed a bit warmer than usual. It felt good to be inside and away from the sun's relentless rays.

—∞—

Slightly above and about a hundred feet back of the bridge, on the side of the ship facing east, Jessica was stretched out in the bottom of the lifeboat. The blending of the sun's heat and the clear blue skies, the throbbing of the engine and the languid roll of the ship, had soothed her spirit with a tranquility she had not known in months. As the day moved on into the afternoon, she occasionally sipped from the water bottle she had found sealed in another package.

Don't let yourself get dehydrated, sweetheart.

It was her father's voice again, there in her mind. How long had it been since she had heard it? They were the last words she remembered him saying to her.

I wonder what he's doing. How is Mother handling this? Jeremy, I miss our wrestling matches. I even miss your teasing.

There appeared to be a sufficient supply of food in the lifeboat for several people. Certainly more than enough for her needs, though the selection and taste left something to be desired. The carton of Tootsie Rolls was a surprise and she downed several of those early in the day. Her mother might not approve, but then she wasn't here, was she? It was just as well, for Jessica was considerably thinner, having lost weight while imprisoned in Jordan and in Fardusi's Iranian compound. She needed the quick energy that the candy provided.

Freedom.

It was hard to know just how to feel about it. Jessica understood that her future was far from resolved, but for the first time in months she felt totally free. No one guarded her door. No one even knew she was here.

I did it. Oh, thank you, God. I'm free. I wonder where this ship is headed? Do you suppose the people on board are friendly?

She lifted the water bottle to her lips.

Don't trust anybody.

How am I going to get in touch with my parents? And what about all those children that the man with the scar said he was going to kill? I need to tell somebody. But who? Who would believe me?

She shifted uncomfortably as she became aware of a more pressing concern. Her perpetual problem as a hostage had not changed in her new status as a stowaway

I need to go to the bathroom!

By now, the blueness of the sky had begun to darken, and Jessica knew that it must be getting on toward evening. Finally, she could wait no longer and she decided that risking capture was preferable to the other option. Her heart raced as she crawled out of the lifeboat and climbed down the ladder to the deck. Her legs were stiff from inactivity and her bladder was so full that it hurt.

The first passageway was only a half-dozen feet beyond the ladder. She peeked around the corner. A dark-haired man in blue overalls was walking away from her. At the same time, she noticed the doorway to one of the ship's restrooms. It was wide open. There was no mistaking it. That was where she desperately needed to go. Jessica took one more look at the man and then slipped into the passage behind him and through the open door, closing it quickly.

Safe!

Moments later, she stood in front of the mirror and stared with shock at the reflected image. It was the first time she had seen herself in weeks. Her hair was matted and sweaty. Her face was smudged with dirt, sweat, and grease.

Where did that come from?

Spying a bar of soap, she washed her hands and face. It felt so good that she pulled off all her clothes and indulged in a "sponge bath," finally rinsing off with handfuls of water scooped from the sink and poured over her body. Soaking wet and naked, she dried as best she could with paper towels, crushing each one tightly before dumping it into the trash basket. Reluctantly, she put her dirty clothes back on.

The floor was covered with soapy water and dirt. It wouldn't do to leave it in this condition. Someone might wonder how it got that way and become suspicious. Using more paper towels, Jessica wiped up as much as possible. It didn't look as good as it had, but with any luck, once the door was open and fresh air let in, it would dry before the next person came to use it.

Cautiously, she unlocked the door and peeked out. The passageway was clear. She stepped out, leaving the door ajar. Four short steps carried her to the exit to the deck. She quickly looked both ways. No one. Rushing outside, she scuttled up the ladder and into the lifeboat. Once she had caught her breath, she arranged the flotation devices so that she could lie down on them like a mattress. Thus situated, she gazed upward at the emerging stars.

Her body felt really clean for the first time in a long time.

Her mind was as clear as the night sky.

Her last thoughts before sleep were of home.

98

Saturday, 03 December, local time 1230
Abu Dhabi, United Arab Emirates

John could hear the phone ringing. Once, twice, three times. He'd put off the inevitable as long as he could.

"Hello." The voice sounded drowsy at the other end. John glanced at his watch.

Nuts!

In all that had transpired during the last few hours and days, he had completely lost track of time back home. Now, he realized that it was past midnight in California.

Oh, well.

"Hello, sweetheart."

"John?" He could almost see her throwing back the covers and rising up in bed. "John? Is that you?"

"Yes, hon, it's me. Sorry to wake you. I forgot the time difference."

"Don't be silly." She was wide awake now, he could tell by the sound of her voice. "Are you all right? Where are you?"

"Yes, I'm okay. We're in the United Arab Emirates. I'm calling from the U.S. embassy."

"Were you . . . were you . . ." He heard the catch in Esther's voice.

"We weren't able to get her out," he said huskily, "but we do know she is still alive."

There was a long silence. He heard Esther clear her throat. His eyes filled with tears as he thought of the struggle she must be going through to keep her feelings together.

"What . . . what happened? What can you tell me over the phone?" Esther's presence of mind made him suddenly cautious. She was right. Who knew who else might be listening in?

Is this paranoia or what?

John recounted enough information—leaving out certain details, names and places—to let Esther at least have some hope. It was not the phone call he had dreamed of making. It was simply the best he could do for now.

"Will you be coming home soon?"

"I'm not sure just when. Hersch is not feeling well."

"He's sick?"

"In a manner of speaking, yes. He has to spend a few days in the hospital here in Abu Dhabi. When he's better, we'll head back."

More silence.

"Is it serious?" Esther's voice was low and filled with concern.

"He's going to live, if that's what you're asking. It hit him suddenly, without any warning. But he'll be okay."

"Thank God."

"We are, believe me."

"And Jessica?"

"She's out on her own somewhere. I'm not quite sure where to look. She decided to get out and see some of the countryside, I guess."

"She's . . . by herself?"

"Yes. But she has a number of Christian friends who are keeping an eye out for her. I'm sure we'll hear something soon. Honey, I hate to break this off, but I have to go. I'm going to visit Hersch."

"John . . ."

"Yes?"

"I love you."

"I love you, too."

"Be safe."

"Count on it."

—~—

LOCAL TIME 0245

Esther replaced the receiver and dropped back onto the bed, a feeling of hollow emptiness inside.

They weren't able to get her. She's still alive and must have escaped. But where are you, honey? What's happening to you now?

For a long time, Esther's eyes were closed—not in sleep but in prayer.

She prayed for John.

He sounded so disappointed and lost, Lord. And he wants so desperately to bring our little girl home.

She prayed for Herschel Towner, too.

He's a good man, Lord, but John says that he's angry at you over the death of his wife. Now something has happened to him. Whatever it is, be with him in that hospital. Let him experience your healing touch and let him find your peace.

Most of all, with feelings that fought for release from deep inside, she prayed for her baby.

"Mom?"

Her eyes opened with a start and she caught her breath.

"Mom, are you okay in there? I heard the phone ring."

Esther got up and felt her way around the edge of the bed in the dark. When she opened the door, Jeremy was standing there in his shorts.

"I'm okay, Son."

"It was so late, . . . I thought maybe . . ."

"You thought right. It was your dad. Come on; let's go make a pot of coffee. I don't think I'll be able to get back to sleep anyway, so why should you? Besides, you want to know, and I need some company. Okay?"

Jeremy followed his mother into the kitchen, reaching past her to turn on the light.

SYNAGOGUE BOMB KILLS THREE
Dozens injured in Sabbath blast

CHICAGO—A bomb exploded in downtown Chicago yesterday, destroying part of a synagogue as worshipers gathered for Sabbath services. Three people were killed and thirty-two injured in the blast, which shattered windows of nearby buildings and ignited a fire that was quickly extinguished by firefighters. Among the injured were thirteen children, ranging in age from nine to fourteen.

An anonymous caller took credit for the attack on behalf of the Palestinian Islamic Jihad, an extremist group attached to Hamas. The group has declared itself in opposition to the proposed Israeli-PNA Accord and has demanded that the UN rescind its 1948 affirmation of the State of Israel. . . .

"MYSTERY VIDEO" DENIED BY CNN

NEW YORK—Senior executives at CNN denied reports yesterday that a videotape related to the recent rash of terrorist attacks across the nation had been received by the network. Other networks also issued denials. Unconfirmed reports circulating on the Internet had indicated that a "mystery video" containing terrorist demands had been mailed to several major networks. The Office of Homeland Security issued a statement advising citizens to remain on heightened alert in the wake of recent attacks on public gathering places. The terrorist alert for the nation remains at Code Red.

In the past five days, a Chicago synagogue, a Roman Catholic church in Baltimore, a Baptist church in downtown Atlanta, and schools in Racine, Wisconsin, and Santa Fe, New Mexico, have been the targets of terrorist bombs. In all, seven adults and twenty-three children have died and fifty-two others have been injured. Telephone callers claiming to represent the Palestinian Islamic Jihad have claimed credit for each of these attacks.

JESSICA CAIN VIDEO RELEASED

ATLANTA—A videotape received two days ago, but withheld at government request, was aired on all the major news networks yesterday. The tape, featuring Jessica Cain, the missing twelve-year-old daughter of Wailing Wall hero John Cain, presented demands from the terrorist group known as the Palestinian Islamic Jihad. The State Department had asked the networks not to release the video while a search for the missing girl was under way in several undisclosed Middle East locations. That request was rescinded early yesterday.

On the tape, an obviously shaken young girl, reading from a prepared statement, indicated that her abductors were demanding the equivalent of one dollar for every boy and girl in the United States and Israel as a ransom for her life. The list of demands also included the abolition of the State of Israel and the repatriation of any and all Palestinian political prisoners held by Israel and the United States.

Jessica Cain has been missing since September 18, when her father and a group of Christian pilgrims from California were abducted by the Palestinian Islamic Jihad, the same group now claiming responsibility for the current rash of terrorist incidents ravaging America and Israel. Her whereabouts remain a mystery. Unconfirmed sightings have been reported in cities from Rio de Janeiro to Tehran. Sources have verified that her father flew to New York on November 30, but his present location is unknown and the family remains in seclusion, unavailable for comment.

Demands for military intervention are being presented by both parties on the floor of Congress. The White House has ordered all National Guard reserve units to report for active duty, in cooperation with local police and the FBI. The president will make a special televised address to the nation at 9:00 Eastern time tonight, to explain the administration's non-negotiation stance regarding terrorist organizations.

Meanwhile, schools continue to close in many communities, and retailers have reported a sharp decline in sales due to shoppers staying away in large numbers this Christmas season. Last weekend, many churches and synagogues reported that attendance at weekly worship services had dropped by as much as half.

99

Wednesday, 07 December, local time 2145
Arabian Sea

For three days, all that Jessica had been able to glimpse from her lofty perch was the open sea. On one occasion, well off in the distance, she had seen another ship steaming in the opposite direction. But that was it. At least during daylight hours.

Daytime temperatures were warm, though the ocean breezes mitigated what otherwise would have been unbearable heat. Still, Jessica knew that she was burning under the intense sun. By the time she had discovered the protective sun lotion included in one of the survival packs, it was almost too late: her face and arms were an angry red. As a countermeasure, Jessica spread out two of the waterproof covers from the foodstuffs, and laid them over the exposed parts of her body. It was hot and uncomfortable, but there was no other protection available.

Her only excursions from the lifeboat consisted of nighttime visits to the ship's head. Always well after dark, before she slept, and before dawn—if she was awake, just for good measure. In the evening, putting cool water to her face was a luxury to look forward to as she removed the sweat and grime. However, though the days were hot, the nights were cold, and Jessica found herself shivering in her lightweight clothing. In addition to the one blanket she had found, she tried wrapping the food parcel coverings as tightly as she could around her shoulders, and tucked her feet together under another package to stay warm. It usually was not quite enough to do the job.

Tonight, after more fruitless attempts to ward off the cold, Jessica decided to take a chance. Throwing off the wrappings, she slipped over the side and down the ladder. Once her feet hit the deck, she checked out the passageway where the head was located. No one was there. She glided past the entrance and continued along the deck, careful to stay away from the rail and in the shadows as much as possible.

Seeing a set of steps leading to another deck, she glanced around and then started up. At the top she walked about twenty feet to another open doorway and peered in. The room was full of instruments, glowing in the dim light. She made out the figure of a man in a white shirt and blue jeans, standing by a console, talking over what looked like a telephone.

It must be a radio.

The man put the receiver back on its hook and turned toward her. She pulled away quickly, hoping he had not seen her, and ran back along the deck toward the steps, pausing in the shadows to check behind her. A minute passed, though it felt more like an hour to Jessica. No one followed after her, however, and she took her time making her way back down the steps.

On the main deck, she jogged back to the doorway behind her lifeboat. Sliding the door open, she discovered another empty passageway, with several doors on the right side.

Maybe that's where the crew lives.

To the left was an open door, beyond which she could see cooking stoves and a food preparation table. No one was about as she tiptoed in. A fluorescent light lit up the stove area and a cooking pot sat off to one side of the grill.

Looks like the restaurant is closed.

Her stomach rumbled at the thought of something to eat besides hardtack and Tootsie Rolls. She opened the refrigerator. Inside were two cartons of milk and some chicken left over from the crew's evening meal. She lifted the milk carton to her mouth and drank deeply.

Oh, gooood.

With her free hand, she stuffed two of the five pieces of chicken in her pants pocket. Then she drank almost all of the rest of the carton.

Better leave some.

With milk dribbling down both sides of her face, she replaced the nearly empty carton, closed the door, and turned to leave. Out of the corner of her eye, she saw a pie. It had been cut and served, but three pieces remained. Jessica scooped up one of the pieces.

Cherry pie. Hallelujah!

Holding onto the pie, she pushed the chicken pieces deeper into her pocket, so as not to lose them. Then she slipped out and made her way back to the ladder. Balancing the pie in one hand, she pulled herself up with the other. It was awkward, but she didn't want to eat the pie until she had devoured the chicken. This was, after all, going to be a genuine feast.

100

Sunday, 11 December, local time 0705
Red Sea

In the early morning light, Jessica saw land from her lifeboat hideout. It was low and well off in the distance, but it marked the first time since leaving Iran eight days before that she had seen land from this side of the ship. The sun was in a different position as well, and she surmised that they must have changed course. After watching the sun rise for a while, she concluded that their course was almost due north.

She was curious as to their whereabouts, though she had already acknowledged to herself that it would make little difference if she knew. Wherever the ship finally docked again would be better than being in Iran. She would get off and try to find help. She had no money and that would be a problem. What worried her even more was something that should have been simple enough, but she knew that it really wasn't.

How do you go about making an international phone call? I've got no money. No credit card. And what if the operator doesn't speak English?

These thoughts were troubling her as the *Evvoia* passed along the African coast of Eritrea until it disappeared from view. Seeing land had given Jessica hope that they were nearing the ship's destination. When it faded from sight, and did not return again, her spirits fell.

Her face was beginning to peel from overexposure to the sun and salt air. Her cheeks were dry and burned, and even the tips of her ears had become tender to the touch. The sun had also worked its way through the matted strands of her long hair and singed the top of her head. She knew that she needed some lotion in addition to the sunscreen she had finally discovered in the lifeboat supplies.

Oh well. Better to be worried about this than to be back in that room with those awful people.

She suddenly shivered at the thought. It had been another world. One she would like to forget but couldn't.

—∾—

The day stretched out, hour by tedious hour. The monotony of ocean travel, accentuated by the discomfort of the lifeboat and the tension surrounding her need to remain hidden, was wearing thin. Finally, as the afternoon wore on, she curled up on the shady side of her lifeboat roost and fell asleep.

—∾—

Jessica awoke to a change in the ship's forward movement.

She listened intently.

The engine vibration had decreased. The ship's motion was different.

Something was happening.

Crawling out from under her makeshift shelter, she peeked over the edge of the lifeboat.

What she saw caused her heart to skip a beat.

As far as she could see in any direction were the shadowy outlines of ships, like a city of watery skyscrapers, rising from the sea.

101

LOCAL TIME 1715
SUEZ BAY, EGYPT

Captain Callimachus never tired of passing through the Suez Canal. It interrupted the tedium of long ocean journeys like this one. As far as he was concerned, this was what made being the captain of a ship worthwhile. This part of the voyage did not happen often enough for him.

Mindful that an armada of ships was already anchored in the area, at twelve miles out he ordered a decrease in speed, first to three-quarter, then to half. The three men on the ship's bridge were quietly and efficiently busy now, as was the rest of the crew scattered throughout the vessel.

Five miles out, they spotted Separation Zone Buoy #1. Captain Callimachus spoke with Port of Suez officials via ship-to-shore radio, informing them of the *Evvoia*'s current latitude and longitude readings, the vessel's name and call sign, the draft of the ship, and the type of cargo being transported.

First Mate Morales paid close attention now to the position of the *Evvoia* relative to the many other vessels gathering in the bay. All three men kept an eye out for the two light buoys marking the canal's south entrance. Callimachus saw them first, pointing to the eleven o'clock position. The buoys each had a visible height of seven meters. Eastern, at Hm. 3.00, was black, cone shaped, and showing one occulting green light every four seconds. Western, at Hm. 1.00, was red, similarly cone shaped and with a comparable occulting red light every four seconds.

"Engine back three-quarter."

"Engine back three-quarter, aye." Morales nodded and smiled. Reaching into his shirt pocket, he proceeded to ceremoniously lay a one hundred drachma note on the panel in front of the captain. The helmsman glanced over at the captain and grinned as he saw him pick it up, touch it to his lips, and stuff it in his pocket. It was a game they played, seeing who would make a particular sighting first. Morales made sure the captain won more times than not. He knew that at the next opportunity, the captain would take the note and combine it with some of his own for a bottle of wine to be consumed together with his friends.

"Steer two-one-zero," the captain ordered.

"Two-one-zero, aye."

The helmsman made the necessary course adjustments so that the *Evvoia* was headed directly between the two entrance markers. Callimachus stepped back into his office to quickly review the instructions related to port plans and mooring diagrams in the *Guide to Port Entry*. Minutes later, he was back in the captain's chair, observing their progress. Finally he gave the order.

"Engine back full."

"Engine back full, aye!"

The ship eased into its appointed place and slowed to an all-stop. A short while later, the sound of the anchor could be heard as its massive bulk splashed into the water and the *Evvoia* came to rest for the night.

Most of the crew members were out on deck after dinner, smoking and relaxing, trying to count the number of ships around them that were waiting to enter the canal. The moon looked cold and pale, the stars bright against the black velvet of the night. The lights of the ships in the bay added a feeling of holiday festivity to the evening.

The captain and first mate joined with the others in leaning against the deck rail, trading stories, and answering questions about tomorrow's transition through the canal.

—∾—

Jessica listened to the men from her overhead hiding place about twenty feet away from where most of them were standing. They sounded normal enough to her. They could have been boys on the play yard at school, only in grown-up bodies. There were words she could not understand in a foreign language. It sounded like Spanish, but she wasn't sure. Several spoke English. From her perch, she luxuriated in one of the things she had missed most during the past months. Laughter.

Since being kidnapped in Israel, she could not remember a time when she had heard people laughing. Everything had been so intense, so extreme. The laughter, the sounds of frivolity, and the occasional guffaws at the punch line of a joke washed over her like warm water. Even a ribald discussion concerning the physical attributes and sex appeal of Egyptian women brought a guilty smile to Jessica's lips, though she was certain her face was burning a time or two from more than overexposure to the sun.

More importantly, she had overheard the captain's answers to questions posed by his crew. As a result, for the first time in eight days, she knew where she was. At least she remembered what it looked like on a map in her classroom. She had seen maps of the area in the back of her Bible as well. This was Egypt. They were on the Red Sea. The one Moses parted with his rod so that the Israelites could escape their bondage.

Bondage. I've heard the story of Moses so many times. I wish he were here right now. I could use a little deliverance myself.

—w—

It was nearly midnight when the launch with the port officials finally arrived alongside the *Evvoia.* Captain Callimachus welcomed them on board and ushered two men into his office. Within minutes, crewman Timothy Marcos entered, bearing a tray containing a pot of coffee, cups, and slices of cake from the galley. Callimachus nodded to Marcos and continued answering questions as the young man served their Egyptian guests. One of the officials was going through the crew member's passports.

Approximately thirty minutes after their arrival, the port officials returned to the launch and chugged off into the darkness.

—w—

The *Evvoia* was eighth in line as it joined the convoy at 0600 hours. The sun's early light was waking up the day, but as yet it had not made an official appearance. Meanwhile, a crew member hoisted the "Q" flag, the International Quarantine Signal signifying a healthy ship.

Morales had the radiophone in his hand, talking ship-to-shore when the captain came onto the bridge. Northbound messages had to be repeated to agents at Suez. Otherwise, the *Evvoia* would not receive any advance information. Port Said agents passed messages to Suez agents, but Suez agents did not repeat them to the ships. It was one of those procedural idiosyncrasies that Captain Callimachus had previously suggested to officials would be helpful if it could be changed. Of course, nothing ever was.

Today on Suez Bay, as was true every day here, ships from many nations queued up to form a one-way parade to the north. The waterway was deemed so important that canal operations were permitted to continue at night, even on Fridays and other religious holidays, including Ramadan, Islam's holiest fast, which lasts for thirty days.

As the bay came to life, enterprising merchants in small boats putt-putted about, selling fresh fish, poultry, cigarettes, candy, and well-worn paperbacks, as they dodged back and forth among the vessels. Lines, or flimsy ladders, were occasionally dropped over the side to permit these young entrepreneurs to come on board. Dickering and the transfer of cash and purchases took place on deck. Now and then, a ship's captain even permitted these Egyptian nationals to stay on board until the opposite end of the Canal was reached.

Convoy speed today was 14 km/hour. Progress remained steady and orderly as the awesome parade of ships passed El Shallufa and proceeded on into Little Bitter Lake. The flotilla then snaked through Kabret Bypass and the Great Bitter Lake before venturing along Deversoir Bypass, into Lake Tinsal, and finally exiting the canal at Port Said. Often there was a wait of several hours in the Bitter Lakes area while ships traversed the canal from the opposite direction. Today was no exception.

By nightfall, however, the *Evvoia* was churning through the waters of the Mediterranean, the Suez Canal rapidly fading from view in its silvery wake.

102

The nights grew colder as the *Evvoia* steamed northward. No amount of waterproofing material from the remaining lifeboat provisions was able to keep the chill from numbing Jessica through and through. Her teeth chattered and she shook nonstop, hunkered down in the bottom of the small craft.

The third night brought a chilling rain, complete with lightning and gale force winds. Finally, out of desperation and soaked to the skin, Jessica knew she had to get inside.

With hands so cold she could barely hang onto the ladder, Jessica climbed down to the slippery deck. Leaning into the wind and rain, she fought her way to the passage entrance. The heavy door was closed tonight, and it took all her strength to slide it open. A quick look assured her that no one was in sight. She stepped inside and let the door roll back into place.

At that same instant, halfway down the passageway, a cabin door opened and a man stepped out. His back was toward Jessica as he closed the door. Frightened, she sprinted the now familiar four steps she had taken so many times before on her way to the head, but as she reached for the door both feet suddenly slipped out from under her. Jessica fell with a hard thud that left her momentarily stunned. The man in the hall turned as she scrambled to her knees and tried crawling into the head. It was too late. He was on top of her in a flash, pinning her helplessly to the floor.

She struggled desperately, fear releasing a fresh flow of adrenaline, With an almost maniacal strength, she wriggled and kicked and tried to bite the man's arm, but it was to no avail. She heard him shout for help. Seconds later, three others were out in the passageway with them.

"Hey, stop it, kid. Give it up!"

It was impossible. Jessica knew she had no chance. Suddenly, and as totally as she had fought back, she surrendered. Tears filled her eyes and spilled down her face, mixing with the dampness caused by the rain. The man who had yelled at her gradually released his grip from around her body. Completely spent, Jessica fell back in a wet heap on the passageway floor.

Timothy Marcos stared at the skinny child slumped in front of him. It had all happened so fast. He had spotted her out of the corner of his eye. By the time he had fully turned around, she had panicked and was scrambling to get out of the passageway. He was on top of her before he knew what or who she was. He only knew that this person was not one of them.

"What did you catch there, Tim? Looks like you got yourself a stowaway," Angel Ramirez muttered. "Where do you suppose we got him anyway? In the Suez?"

"It's not a 'him,' Angel," Marcos responded, breathless from wrestling their uninvited stranger to the floor.

"What?"

"It's a 'her.'" Marcos looked down at the sopping wet child, hair strewn across her face and clenched fists wiping at her eyes. "This is a girl."

"Are you serious?" Ramirez leaned down and lifted the stowaway's face so that he could see it. Green eyes blazed back and he quickly moved his hand away. "She's a feisty one, that's for sure. Be careful with her, though. She looks like she might have rabies."

The others laughed.

Timothy Marcos crouched down and spoke with a gentle tone. "Who are you? Do you speak English?"

The strange girl looked up, but said nothing.

"Hey, we aren't going to hurt you," he smiled reassuringly. "Just tell us your name."

Jessica shivered uncontrollably, whether from fright or from the freezing cold rain, she couldn't tell. She was angry at having let this happen and fearful of being locked up again. The man kneeling in front of her now was the one who had tackled her moments before.

His voice was soothing, though, and sounded kind. "Who are you? Do you speak English?"

Jessica watched him through narrowed and hostile eyes but did not answer.

"Hey, nobody is going to hurt you," the man repeated. "Okay?"

He was young. His hair was jet black and straight. Bronze skin. Dark eyebrows and a mustache. No shoes. Faded blue jeans and a white T-shirt imprinted on the front with the word *Nike*.

He doesn't look like an Arab, but he's not an Iranian either. And he has a nice smile.

Watch it, Jessica. You can't trust anybody.

"Just tell us your name."

His accent reminds me of . . . someone . . . Madeline! When he talks, he forms his words like Madeline did.

Just then, one of the crew led another man in out of the storm. He walked over to where Jessica sat shaking in a puddle of rainwater, wishing that she could stop, but finding it impossible to do so. She looked up and recognized him immediately.

"Who is this?" asked Captain Callimachus. "Where did we get her?"

"I was just leaving my room, sir, and caught her by surprise," Marcos answered the captain. "I think she was trying to get in out of the storm. She hasn't said anything yet. I asked if she understood English. I think she does, but she's not talking."

The captain stared at her for a long, disconcerting moment.

"She's cold. All right, Marcos, you caught her so you take charge for now. Get her some dry clothes and a shower." The captain glared at the sound of a snigger coming from one of the crew that crowded around to view the spectacle. Word spreads fast on board ship. "You know what I mean. Guard the door until she's finished."

"I've got an extra shirt, Tim," one of the crew volunteered and ran off to get it.

"I have an old pair of jeans she can wear."

"She'll need a rope to keep them up, Freddie."

"Nah, these have an elastic waist. They'll work. She's about my height, too."

"What about dry underclothes?"

There was an embarrassed silence, then raucous laughter filled the passageway.

"Hey, any of you guys wearing women's underclothes?"

More laughter.

"Actually, gentlemen," the captain spoke softly and the passageway became instantly quiet, "I do have some female undergarments in my cabin."

He looked around to see who might say something crude, but no one dared open their mouth.

"They were left there when my daughters visited me just before school began. Jimmy, come with me and I'll get some things for you to give to the girl."

He turned back to Jessica.

"Get up and go with these men."

Jessica continued shivering, but made no move to respond.

"Do it now, young lady," the captain's voice was suddenly gruff, his eyes narrowing. "You're in a lot of trouble. See to it that you don't get into any more by pushing my patience too far."

The young man with the Nike shirt held out his hand to her. Slowly, still shaking involuntarily from head to toe, Jessica reached out and took it. He helped her to her feet.

"Ramirez, you go with Marcos. See to it that she doesn't overpower him and try to escape."

More sniggers could be heard as the crew parted for Marcos to pass. Jessica followed after him, shivering, sullen, and defeated. Angel Ramirez brought up the rear.

"She looks hungry, Marcos," the captain called out after them. "When she's cleaned up, take her to the mess and give her something to eat. Let me know when she decides to talk and I'll join you later. Now, as you were, gentlemen. Paulo, swab this area down before someone gets hurt."

103

Jessica stood in the doorway and watched as the young crewman, whom the captain had called Marcos, entered the shower room ahead of her. He pulled a towel down from a nearby rack and placed it on the edge of one of the sinks. Reaching into the nearest shower stall, he turned on the water, testing it with his hand until it felt warm.

"It's all yours," he said with a smile. "Get warm. And get clean. There's soap in the dish. Oh, wait. Here's the shampoo. Your hair looks like it could use some. Come out when you are finished. If you're not out in fifteen minutes, I'm coming in to get you. Understand?"

Jessica didn't answer. Just then, two men came up and handed over the spare clothing she had heard them talking about. Marcos handed them to Jessica. She looked at them and then at the young man.

"It's this or nothing," he said finally, in exasperation. "Take it or leave it. The wet stuff is coming off."

That was enough of a threat for Jessica. She snatched the clothes away from the young man and closed the door as fast as she could. She fumbled for a lock. There was none.

"There's no lock." The young man's voice could be heard clearly through the door. "Don't worry. You're safe. But this door opens in fifteen minutes. I'll be coming in to get you if you're not out here already. So, get busy!"

What choice do I have?

Without a word, still shivering and dripping water on the floor, she stripped off her clothes and stepped into the shower. That's when she made her second discovery. There were no shower curtains.

Men!

The water was warm. She turned it up even more. It felt unbelievably wonderful.

How long has it been?

Jessica couldn't remember. Eyes closed, she stood still, absorbing the warmth, as water cascaded over her body. Reaching for the shampoo, she soaped her hair and rinsed it. It still felt dirty and matted, so she shampooed again. For the first time in weeks her hair was beginning to feel clean. She lost track of time as she shampooed and rinsed her hair thoroughly for the third time.

"Two minutes and I'm coming in."

Jessica stopped, riveted with consternation as water continued to spray over her naked body.

"No!" she shouted back. "I'm not ready. Give me ten more minutes. Please!"

Outside the door, Timothy Marcos chuckled. Angel Ramirez leaned against the opposite wall, arms folded, grunting his amusement.

"I guess she does speak English after all. All she needed was a little motivation, Tim."

"Okay," Marcos called through the door. "You get ten more minutes. Then out you come."

Exactly eight and a half minutes later, the girl opened the shower room door and stood there, looking for all intents and purposes like the waif she was. The shirt was several sizes too big, but the pants fit surprisingly well. Her feet were still bare. She clutched her wet clothes in a rolled-up bundle with one hand, while gripping her sodden shoes in the other. Her long hair was still damp, though obviously she had rubbed it as dry as possible with the towel.

"Feel better?"

She did not answer.

"Look," admonished Marcos. "We've got to talk to one another sooner or later. It's only a matter of time. You can make it much more difficult by being uncooperative, but it won't do you any good. I'm not the enemy. I want to be your friend, okay?"

Still, the girl said nothing.

"You look hungry, so let's go find something to eat. If you promise not to give me a bad time, Angel will go back to his cabin. He's got to go to work in an hour. Will you promise?"

The girl shrugged and stepped through the door, then waited for Marcos to lead on.

"You be okay?" Ramirez asked.

"I think we'll be fine,"

"Okay. If you need help, just holler."

"Will do."

Ramirez turned and headed away from them. Halfway along the passageway, he rounded the corner and disappeared from sight.

"Let's go . . . what did you say your name was?"

Still no answer.

Like I'm going to fall for that one!

At the end of the passageway, they turned left and entered the seamen's lounge. The galley and mess hall was next door.

"This is the lounge. We come here to read and watch television when we're not on duty. Come on through here and I'll get you something to eat."

He led Jessica through the small lounge and into the mess area, turning on the light as he entered. He stopped, but she moved up beside him, still holding her worldly goods in each hand.

"Let me take your things," Marcos said, reaching out his hands.

Jessica shrank back.

"Hey, whatever-your-name-is, it's okay. Your clothes need to be washed and your shoes need to dry out. I will put them over here next to the heater and we'll turn it on. Before too long, these sneakers of yours will be warm and bone dry. All right?"

Her eyes never left his face as he spoke to her. Without a word, she held out her clothes and shoes. Marcos took them and smiled again.

"Good. I'm glad that you're finally starting to trust me. I want to be your friend. It looks to me like you could use one right about now." Marcos watched his charge out of the corner of his eye as he dropped her clothes on one of the tables and moved away from her toward the wall heater with her shoes in hand. He was ready to drop them and catch her if she made a break, but the girl did not move. He flipped the heater switch and adjusted the thermostat. Bringing a chair around to face the heater, he turned over her shoes to check the bottoms. The tops were dirty and beat up, but the soles appeared relatively new. There was lots of wear left on them.

Where is this kid from? And where do you suppose she's been?

"Hey, nice shoes," he said, holding them up next to the imprint on his shirt. "Nikes."

He placed them on the chair and walked around the table, opposite Jessica.

Next test. If the kid was going to run, this was her chance, with the table between them. He saw her eyes flicker, but she made no move to attempt an escape. *Good.*

Marcos motioned for her to follow. "Let's see what we have to eat."

Her eyes. They are like emeralds, they're so green. And when she called out from the shower. . . . I wonder. . . .

They went into the galley. Marcos moved past the range and opened the refrigerator.

"I've got some cold chicken. Here, you like some?" He held the plate of leftovers out to the girl.

She nodded and took two pieces, unconsciously licking her lips as she did.

"Here's a piece of watermelon, too. Straight from Egypt. Some bread. And a Coke to drink. Okay?"

The girl nodded again.

"Let's go back to the mess and sit at a table."

Marcos grabbed another Coke and followed her through the door to the first table. He watched her hesitate for an instant, as if she didn't quite know what to do. Then she sat down, eyeing the food, but made no move to begin eating. Marcos was certain she was hungry. He started to say something, but checked himself just in time, dumbfounded at what she did next.

The girl closed her eyes. Her lips moved.

What's this? Is she praying?

The moment passed. She opened her eyes and reached for a piece of the chicken. There was no doubt about her being hungry. She consumed it like there was no tomorrow. First, the chicken, both pieces interspersed with huge bites of plain bread and gulps from the bottle of Coke. Finally, she swooped down on the watermelon. It had no chance of surviving the attack.

Marcos was amused at the sight of the hungry stowaway putting down her dinner.

I wonder what you've been living off of, kid? And where have you been hiding all this time?

But there was one other question that needed to be asked first. He waited until the watermelon had disappeared. The girl carefully wiped her face clean with a paper napkin that she pulled from the holder next to the salt and pepper shakers. Finally, she looked up at Marcos. It was the first time she'd made eye contact since sitting down at the table. Her gaze was steady, even defiant, as if she were thinking, *All right. I've eaten your food. Now what?*

"Hey, kid," asked Marcos softly, watching carefully to see what her response would be. "Are you a Christian?"

Jessica stared at the man across the table.

Are you a Christian?

Of all the questions he might have asked, that was absolutely the last one Jessica had expected. Her response was one that Timothy Marcos did not expect either.

104

"Are you a Filipino?"

Timothy Marcos's mouth fell open in surprise. He was glad that the girl had finally said something, but he was totally caught off guard by her question.

"Yes, I am. Why?"

"Do you know Madeline?"

"Madeline who?"

"I don't know her last name, but she works in Iran. She's a maid. And she is from the Philippines."

"No, I don't know any Madeline. I'm sorry."

"Me too. She's nice."

"Is she? I'm glad."

"Are most Filipinos Christians?"

"Well, I don't actually know how many. But there are a lot of them back home."

"Is that where you're from? The Philippines?"

"Yes."

"Is it nice there?"

"Very."

"It's a bunch of islands, right?"

"Right."

"Are you a Christian?"

Marcos hesitated.

What is this? And when did I lose control of this conversation? Truth is, I probably never had it in the first place.

He decided to go with the flow.

"Yes, I am," Marcos responded.

"Have you been one very long?"

"For about three years."

"What's the fourth book in the New Testament?"

Marcos chuckled.

She's checking me out.

"It's the Gospel of John."

"That was easy. Anybody could know that."

"Oh? Well, then, what's the sixth book in the Old Testament?"

The girl thought for a moment.

"Joshua."

"And the one after that?"

"Judges."

Marcos had now regained the role of questioner.

"And the shortest verse in the Bible?"

"'Jesus wept.' And do you know John 3:16?"

Getting the upper hand in this conversation was one thing. Keeping it, Marcos decided, was proving to be quite another.

"Yes, I do. 'For God so loved the world that he gave his only begotten Son, that whosoever believeth in him should not perish, but have everlasting life.'"

"That's from the King James Version, isn't it?"

This girl is full of surprises.

"Yes, it is," he replied.

"How come you know so much about the Bible?"

"We have a Bible study on board, three other guys and me. And I read a lot. I'm working as a member of the crew in order to earn enough money to go to Bible college. Someday, I will be the pastor of a church."

He saw the girl's eyes blink with surprise as she leaned back in her chair. Her hands went down to her lap and she stared at them for a long time, biting her lip. When she looked up at him again, he could see that she was fighting back the tears.

"What's the matter, kid?"

Her lip quivered.

"Did I say something?"

She pushed her chair back from the table, but didn't get up. Marcos was touched as he watched her. Not defiant any longer. Not angry. Instead, she looked pathetically scared and alone.

"It's my dad."

"Your dad? What about him?"

"He's a pastor."

The answer stunned Marcos, and now he leaned back.

"Your dad is a pastor?"

The ship's prize stowaway nodded.

"Where?"

"California."

Once again, Marcos was startled. He studied the youngster sitting in front of him. *Who are you anyway?*

"How old are you?"

"Twelve."

The girl did not look up, but continued staring at her hands, watching them slowly curl and uncurl in her lap.

"How did you get here, anyway? You're a long way from home, aren't you?"

She remained silent, while Marcos realized that he'd asked two questions instead of only one. Was she deciding how to answer them? Or was she retreating back into her earlier refusal to communicate? Just when he was beginning to wish someone else had been put in charge of this little ragamuffin, she looked up, her eyes darting about cautiously, as if she were inspecting the premises for unwelcome visitors. Then she looked straight at Marcos.

"I was stolen," she answered finally, her voice subdued.

Startled by her response, Marcos studied her suspiciously for some sign that would indicate she was lying.

"Stolen?"

"Yes. Kidnapped, by terrorists."

The girl's eyes remained steady, looking straight into his.

"When were you kidnapped? And where?"

"September 18. I was in Israel with my father."

Hmm. This sounds so familiar. Wasn't that when . . . ?

"Hey, kid. I know you've got a name. Mine is Timothy Marcos. Do you think you can trust me enough to tell me what your name is? Look, I want to help you, okay? And, nobody on board this ship is going to hurt you. I can promise you that. So, what is it?"

The girl sat still now, her eyes fixed on the table.

"Your parents don't know where you are, right?"

She nodded, pressing her lips together.

"Then help me get you back together with them. I can't do anything unless I know your name."

"Jessica." She said it softly, her hands clenched into small, tight fists. Her body tensed. Marcos saw that she was prepared to bolt. He remained quiet and did not move. Waiting. The moment passed and girl seemed to relax slightly, though she had scooted to the edge of her chair. Her eyes were on him, searching to see what might happen next.

"Jessica Cain," she said at last. Her body was rigid once more, the earlier dullness in her green eyes now replaced with an uneasy look of apprehension.

"Jessica . . ." Marcos suddenly sat up straight and leaned forward. *Cain. Green eyes. Long, reddish-brown hair. Twelve. Israel. Even the date makes sense.*

"You are—"

Before he could get the words out of his mouth, the doorway opened. At the sound, the girl leaped to her feet and whirled around.

"Wait, Jessica, it's okay. It's the captain."

She remained frozen in place, realizing that there was nowhere to run. The captain had stopped in place as well, aware that his entrance had frightened the young stowaway.

"Captain Callimachus, this is Jessica Cain," said Marcos, introducing the wary child to his boss.

The man smiled, extended his hand toward the girl, who hesitated briefly, then grasped it with surprising firmness.

"And now would you like to tell me what are you doing aboard my ship, Jessica Cain?" he asked, smiling as he released her hand.

The girl licked her lips hesitatingly but did not answer.

"Jessica says she was kidnapped."

The captain glanced over at Marcos and then at the girl once again.

"Sir, she fits the description of that American girl who's been missing since last September. She says her father is the pastor of a church in California and that she was 'stolen' in Israel. It all fits, sir."

Captain Callimachus looked at the dismal, joyless face peering back at him.

"Are you certain, Marcos?" asked the captain, incredulously.

"I believe her. Look at her eyes, how green they are. The kidnapped girl has green eyes. All the news reports mention that. And I remember seeing a picture of her, together with an article, in one of the news magazines that we have on board. Just a minute. I think I can find it."

Marcos started for the crew lounge.

"You won't find it."

He hesitated, turning toward the voice that had spoken up so unexpectedly.

"It's not there," she said with assurance.

Both men were watching her curiously.

"It's in the lifeboat."

They looked at each other and then back at Jessica. Suddenly, both the young man and the captain broke out into laughter.

"Young lady . . . Jessica . . . whoever you are," Captain Callimachus chortled, "I think we had better have a nice, long chat. It seems you may have some stories to tell me about your passage on my ship. You have apparently made yourself at home . . . where? In one of our lifeboats? And you have even helped yourself to our library. I must admit that I am impressed."

The captain shook his head, still chuckling as he envisioned the pluck and courage of the young girl standing in front of him. He looked at Marcos.

"Are you done here?"

"Yes sir."

"Then, Jessica, gather up your things and come with me. I am taking you to my cabin. There is still an extra cot there that one of my daughters slept on while visiting me this summer. You must be tired. Tim, you come along, too. You can prepare the cot while I get some more information from our young passenger." Turning to Jessica he said, "I'll need your parents' names and address. Then, we'll call my company, the people who own this ship. They'll let your parents know that you are here and that you are safe. You are safe, you know. No one on board this ship will hurt you. We only want to get you home where you belong. In fact, you should be there for Christmas."

Home. Where I belong. For Christmas!

These men were different from the others. It was still too quick to shed all the distrust and the fear of the past few months. But at least the cloud was lifting a little. The young man who questioned her seemed nice enough, and he even claimed to be a Christian.

She followed the captain up the steps, but hung back as he opened a door and passed through.

"Come on," he urged, his voice not at all threatening as he waited for her to follow.

Cautiously, Jessica stepped into a large room. The walls were finished with panels of light oak. One held a calendar with a picture of beautiful white buildings clinging to the sides of cliffs rising serenely out of the sea. On another wall, near a curtained-off area, two pictures appeared to be etched in wood. Each face depicted was that of a man, obviously from ancient times, and what looked like a cross rose from behind one of them.

A massive, wooden desk filled the center of the room, and on the side opposite where they stood was the captain's leather chair. In front of the desk were two steel-framed chairs without armrests. Underneath them was a rich-looking rug, its unfamiliar design woven with colors of beige, dark blue, and orange.

The room had a warm feeling about it, Jessica decided, kind of like her father's office at the church. Her trepidation was gradually easing. Anyway, there were no Playboy pictures on the calendar, and the other pictures looked kind of religious, although Jessica was not at all sure who the men depicted might be.

Maybe that one in front of the cross is supposed to be Jesus. Sure doesn't look like him, though.

Timothy Marcos was busy making up the cot, which the captain directed should be placed at the far side of the room. Clean sheets and a blanket were put in place as Jessica watched silently, her eyes recording all there was to know about this place. The curtained-off area, she concluded, must be where the captain slept.

"All right, Jessica," the captain said, pulling one of the steel-framed chairs around so that it faced the other, "sit here, please."

Jessica sat down, nervously rubbing her fingers together.

The young man smiled and turned to go.

"Wait," she blurted out. Marcos stopped and turned as she slumped back into the chair, embarrassed at having called out. The men looked at each other with a slight shaking of their heads. Marcos walked back and knelt down on the rug beside her.

"Jessica," he said, his hand gently touching her arm, "we don't know where you've been or what has happened to you. But it's safe here. Captain Callimachus is a fine man and he will not hurt you. Take my word . . . as a fellow Christian. Okay?"

Jessica sat still for a long moment, then nodded.

"Okay," she whispered, fighting to maintain the invisible barrier that held back a reservoir of unshed tears.

Marcos patted her arm as he rose. A moment later, she was alone with the captain. She looked up, her fingers now twisting at a corner of her recently acquired, oversized sweatshirt. The captain smiled.

"Now," the man said, "I must know some things about you. Your parents, where you live, how to reach them. I will let them know that they can pick you up at our next port. We will be at Split in approximately thirty hours, so we had better get to it."

For the next few minutes, the captain jotted down information as Jessica responded to his questions.

"It is late now," Captain Callimachus concluded at last. "You should go to bed and to sleep. There is a toilet connected to my sleeping area, but perhaps you should use the one out on the passageway. I'm sure you know where it is?"

Jessica yawned as she nodded.

"You are free to come and go," the captain continued. "I'll be on the bridge for a while. If I am not here when you awaken, come out and I'll let you steer the ship."

Jessica's eyes widened at the prospect.

"Well, not really. This ship is steered in a manner different from a small boat like you may have taken out on the bay in California. I have been there, you know. About a year and a half ago. Anyway, I'll show you how it is done after you have rested."

"Thank you, sir," Jessica said, as the captain turned to leave. "I'm sorry I've caused you so much trouble."

Pausing at the door, the captain looked at Jessica. "It is not necessary for you to apologize. In fact, your presence makes our journey just that much more interesting."

"Good night, sir."

"Good night, Jessica Cain."

105

WEDNESDAY, 14 DECEMBER, LOCAL TIME 2345
NORTHERN MEDITERRANEAN SEA

"Yes, that is all the information we have at the moment."

Captain Callimachus watched as raindrops hurled themselves from out of the darkness, pounding against the windows on the bridge. The roll of the ship made him switch hands with the radiophone and grasp for a nearly empty coffee cup that was sliding away.

"That is all we know," he continued. "I think you should contact the U.S. State Department. She has no identification papers, but her personal knowledge and physical description seem to confirm that she is the missing girl. . . . That's right. No, let me give it to you again. It is *J* as in John. The first name spelling is J-e-s-s-i-c-a. You have the last name. . . . Yes, that is the correct spelling. *C* as in Christopher.

"She says she boarded in Bandar-é Abbâs. . . . No, I'm certain it could not have been the Canal. . . . That's right. What? Oh, it was purely by accident. She was trying to get in out of the weather when one of the crewmen spotted her. . . . No. . . . All right. I understand . . . Yes. She will be ready when we arrive at Split. You will let us know if you are successful in reaching the girl's parents? Yes, thank you. And to you as well."

Several hundred miles to the east, somewhere deep in Lebanon's Bekaa Valley, a dark-haired woman pulled a set of earphones away from her head and placed them on a makeshift table by the radio receiver. Glancing over her hastily scribbled notes, she pushed back her chair and hurried from the warmth of the tiny room into the cold night air.

Her lungs felt the bite of each breath as she ran up the steep path. Regulations forbade the use of a light lest their location be discovered by the enemy, whose military outposts were only a few miles away, and whose eyes never seemed to close in sleep. Her only illumination was that of the pale sliver of moon and the pinpoints of distant stars. Stumbling on a stone, she reached forward, catching herself. The note papers dropped to the ground. With a curse, she ran her hands across the dirt and stone until she had recovered them all before hurrying on.

The path ended in front of a dilapidated wood and stone building, set against the side of the hill. Breathless, she pounded on the door until a man, still rubbing sleep from his eyes, opened it and motioned her inside. The nineteen-year-old freedom fighter was not aware of the importance of her information, only that a vital secret plan was at risk unless the American child who had escaped in Iran was found and eliminated. She did know, however, that an otherwise boring night spent monitoring the transmissions of vessels that had sailed from Bandar-é Abbâs during the last eleven days had finally paid off.

106

Thursday, 15 December, local time 0745
Northern Mediterranean Sea

The room was dark when Jessica awakened. There were no windows or portholes, only a dim light emanating from the captain's sleeping quarters. Jessica slid out of bed and padded across the floor on bare feet until she could see that the captain's bed was empty. She made her way to the door and cracked it open, peeking out into the passageway. An open door at the far end revealed bright sunlight. Last night's storm had evidently passed, leaving the decks washed clean.

She closed the door and turned on the light, stifling a yawn as she raised her arms, stretching out the muscles in her back and legs. She slipped into the borrowed jeans and pushed the socks she had been given into her pocket. She would put them on later when she found her shoes.

Leaving the room, she strode down the passageway with greater confidence than she had felt in a long time. She wasn't hiding. Outside, the sun was bright and the sky clear, even though seas were running high enough to cause her to hold onto the door in order to maintain her balance. Carefully, she made her way to the bridge and stepped inside.

"Good morning, Miss Cain." First Mate Morales smiled with his greeting.

"Hello," she replied. She had seen this man before, but only at a distance from the lifeboat.

"Hello, Jessica," Captain Callimachus emerged from behind a bank of navigational and communication instruments. "You seemed to have slept well, yes?"

"Yes sir," she replied, still intensely conscious of not being at the center in a hostile environment. "Sir, do you know what happened to my shoes?"

Captain Callimachus looked at her feet and smiled. "I suppose the floor is pretty cold without them. You'll probably find them in the galley. I believe the seaman you were talking to last night may have left them there to dry."

"You mean Marcos?"

"Yes. Why don't you run down and get them before you catch a cold?"

Jessica turned to go.

"By the way, I made contact with our company headquarters last night. I explained to them who you were and instructed them to contact your State Department. They will notify your parents. I have suggested that we place you in the custody of an officer of our company or someone else who has the ability to care for you until your parents arrive. We'll be dropping anchor in Split tomorrow."

"Can't I stay on board until my parents come for me?"

"Unfortunately, that is not possible. We must anchor offshore overnight and wait for a berth to open for my ship. That may be the next day, but the docks are at capacity at the moment. It could be even longer. My orders are to take you off by tender as soon as we arrive. That's a small boat that will come out from the docks to pick you up. A representative from our company will meet you. You'll be well cared for, I assure you, and your parents will be here soon. Okay?"

"Do I have a choice?"

"Not really. We're under company regulations with regard to stowaways. I'm sorry."

"Okay, then. Thank you, Captain Callimachus. You've been very kind to me. I'll write to you when I get home."

"I will look forward to it. It has been a pleasure, Jessica. You remind me of my own daughters. God forbid that it would ever be, but I would wish that under similar circumstances, someone would help them in the same way as I am able to do for you."

Jessica blushed as the captain, in the gallant fashion of European gentlemen, took her small hand in his and gently kissed it.

107

THURSDAY, 15 DECEMBER, LOCAL TIME 0800
WASHINGTON, D.C.

"Are you serious? In a thousand years, I never would've thought it."

Whenever he became excited, Charles Rodeway's unmistakably southern drawl became even more pronounced, causing each syllable to drift into the next like ocean waves rolling toward the beach. His words slowed, prolonging each vowel with lengthened tones.

The door was open to the side office where his secretary usually worked. But this morning it was empty. She had called in sick at eight o'clock. Rodeway was alone.

He had been clearing security sensitive papers from his desk and placing them in a small safe when the phone rang. He dropped the remaining folder on the edge of the desk as he listened to the news coming from his counterpart in London.

"Yes. . . . Yes. . . . Are we absolutely certain it's the girl? No kidding. . . . Man, I'll tell you what, I can't believe it. First, that video. I figured she was dead before they . . . Yeah, now this. Okay, thanks, we'll get right on it. . . . No, nothing more for now, but I'll let you know how it goes. . . . Yeah. Thanks again. . . . What? . . . Yeah. . . . Yeah. . . . Well, I'll check with the boss. We should probably get somebody down there from Zagreb to pick her up. . . . Right. . . . Okay, I'll be in touch."

Rodeway ran his finger down a list of frequently called numbers, copying several of them onto a stray sheet of yellow paper. Then he picked up the phone and went to work.

108

THURSDAY, 15 DECEMBER, LOCAL TIME 0715
BAYTOWN, CALIFORNIA

The telephone began ringing at the house on Jefferson Drive, just as Esther and Jeremy were sitting down to breakfast.

"Wouldn't you know it," Esther muttered under her breath.

"I'll get it," said Jeremy, stabbing a warm biscuit with his fork as he rose from the table. "Allison said she was going to call this morning."

"Ask her to call back, Son. Breakfast is ready."

"Hello. This is Jeremy. . . . Yes, Jeremy Cain. . . . Yes, may I say who's calling?"

Esther looked up in time to see Jeremy's face grow serious. "Just a moment. She's right here."

Jeremy placed his hand over the phone and took a deep breath.

"It's Mr. Rodeway, Mom, from Washington."

For one terrifying instant, Esther couldn't move. The normal rituals of life that had been there moments ago while she was preparing their meal had suddenly vanished. In their place now was a frightening sense of disorder and confusion. A wave of apprehension threatened to overwhelm her calm demeanor as she took the phone from Jeremy.

"Yes?" Her voice shook while she cleared her throat. "This is Mrs. Cain."

"Mrs. Cain, this is Charles Rodeway at the State Department. I have good news. We believe we've located your daughter."

Esther's hand was shaking so that she gripped the receiver with both hands. "Are you . . . ? Is she, is she all right?"

"Yes, she is. A young girl that fits your daughter's description was found stowed away on a cargo ship bound from Iran to Croatia. She has no passport, but we are certain that it is Jessica."

Tears streamed down Esther's face as she looked up at Jeremy.

"It's Jessica! They've found her," Esther whispered to Jeremy.

Jeremy came and stood behind her, his hands on her shoulders. "Is she okay? Is she safe? Where is she?"

Esther nodded, suddenly unable to speak.

"Oh, thank you, Jesus," Jeremy breathed, his eyes moist. He buried his face on his mother's shoulder as she turned her attention back to the telephone.

"I'm sorry, Mr. Rodeway. You'll have to forgive us, but your news is more than overwhelming. It's all we've ever dreamed of hearing and we're trying to get it together here."

"No apologies are necessary, Mrs. Cain. You've been through a terrible ordeal, and now you're on your way back. I understand that Reverend Cain is still out there somewhere. Last I heard, he and a companion were recovering from the effects of an unofficial visit to some of our friends. Do you know how to reach him?"

"I certainly do. As soon as we are finished talking, I'll call him at his hotel."

"Is he still in the UAE?"

"Yes. The embassy has informed him that they will issue temporary passports, but will only approve travel back to the States. He's not very happy with that arrangement, I can tell you."

"Well, we can change that now, Mrs. Cain. State just didn't want those two single-handedly declaring war on an entire nation."

"Where can we go to get her?"

"That will not be necessary. I've been authorized by the head of consular affairs to take her off the ship at its next port of call and repatriate her as rapidly as possible. We'll have her home in three or four days, maybe sooner."

"Wait a minute, Mr. Rodeway." Esther was wiping away tears with a napkin from the table. Breakfast had grown cold, forgotten in the excitement. "That's our daughter you are talking about. Of course we are going to meet her. Where will she disembark?"

"She'll be taken off the ship at the port in Split."

"Split? I don't know where that is."

She thought she noted a slight hesitation. She heard him clear his throat.

"Split is a port city of about a hundred and fifty thousand people located in Croatia, along the Dalmatian coast."

"Croatia? You mean near Bosnia and those places? Oh, Mr. Rodeway, she can't be getting off there. Won't that be too dangerous? I saw on the news that terrorist activity has started up again in Croatia."

"It will be all right, Mrs. Cain. It's been weeks since even one shell has been fired into that locale. It's very calm right now. There is a large port there that is visited by ships from many nations, including the United States. Lots of loading and unloading of cargo and supplies. There's a strong UN peacekeeping presence there as well. I assure you, it will be perfectly safe. Besides, we really have no choice. She has to be taken off the ship at its next port of call. We'll send someone down from our embassy in Zagreb to pick her up and bring her out."

"When will she arrive there?" Esther asked, calmer now as she sat down on the chair that Jeremy had pulled over for her.

"The *Evvoia,* that's the ship she is on, is scheduled to get in sometime early tomorrow evening. They tell me around five o'clock their time. That's about eight tomorrow morning on the West Coast."

"Mr. Rodeway, I intend to meet my daughter." Esther's tone changed, a sound of resoluteness permeating her voice. "I know that as soon as I contact John, nothing you can say will stop him either. Now, you can help us get there or make it that much more difficult, but John and I will not sit and wait for her to come to us. We've worked too hard and it's been too long for that. Am I making myself clear?"

There was a long silence at the other end of the line.

"Mr. Rodeway?"

"Yes, I'm still here. Just thinking. I'm a parent, too, Mrs. Cain, and I understand. It's not what I think best as a State Department official, but I figured this would probably be your reaction. Actually, it would be mine, too. That's why I've already checked the airlines to see what might be available. United has a flight to New York out of SFO at eleven o'clock. I was able to get you a seat in tourist. From there you take Alitalia to Rome and Zagreb, which is the capital."

"I'd like to take Jeremy, too."

"Sorry. No can do. I had to pull some strings just to get the one seat. It's full to New York. Besides, we don't need any more citizens in there than necessary."

"But you just said it was safe."

Rodeway's voice changed and became very businesslike.

"I know what I said, Mrs. Cain. Now, please. We don't have much time. If you are determined to go through with this, you will have to take what I'm offering. It's the best I can do. You need to call your husband and get to the airport. Have your son drive you. Are you okay with that?"

"Yes," she answered, realizing that she might have pushed him a little too far. "We can do that."

"Tell you what. Have your husband meet you in Zagreb if he can make connections in time. Tell him that Rome or Zurich is probably the best entry point. He should be able to get to one of those. I'll pass the word to our embassy in the UAE, asking them to provide whatever assistance they can. Your connecting schedule is tight in New York, but you should be okay. In Rome, it's even tighter and I'll make arrangements for them to hold for you, in case your plane is delayed. Here is your flight info."

Rodeway called off the names and numbers of each flight as Esther scribbled them down on the kitchen notepad.

"All right," she said, after repeating the numbers back to him. "I'm on my way."

"Be careful, Mrs. Cain. Don't forget your passport. And good luck."

"Thanks for your help, Mr. Rodeway. I hope we will be able to meet one day."

"It will be my pleasure. Sorry to rush now, but I've got some other calls to make."

She heard the phone click as she put the receiver back and turned to Jeremy. They hugged each other and laughed and cried as Jeremy lifted his mother and whirled her around the room. Esther answered Jeremy's questions, filling in parts of the conversation with Rodeway that he had not been able to piece together. His face dropped at the realization that she was going without him, but the disappointment quickly passed.

"Jeremy, I'm giving you the day off from school. I'll write a note for you on the way to the airport. And I need you to get your dad on the phone while I throw some things into a carry-on. After you get back from the airport, I want you to call your grandparents, too. Okay?"

"Okay."

"Ask them not to say anything to anyone until we have her."

Esther started for the bedroom, then stopped and turned back.

"Honey?"

He paused, phone in hand.

"When you reach him . . . let me tell him. Please?"

"You got it," Jeremy smiled, as he reached for the directory containing the numerical sequence for international dialing.

109

THURSDAY, 15 DECEMBER, LOCAL TIME 1750
ABU DHABI, UNITED ARAB EMIRATES

John could hear the telephone ringing as he hurried to unlock the door to his room. He had been downstairs in the hotel lobby, catching up on the world with a day-old edition of the *International Herald*. Now, he willed the phone to keep ringing as he fumbled to get the key card in the lock. This far from home, every call was important. He didn't want to miss it. The card was left in the door lock as he rushed to lift the receiver.

"Hello?"

"Hello, Dad?"

"Hey, is that you, Jeremy?"

"In living color. Say, this is a really good connection. You sound like you're right next door. Are you okay?"

"I'm fine. How about you and Mom?"

"We're doing great. I'm really glad I caught you. It must be tonight where you are, right? What time is it there anyway?"

"It's nearly six. I just walked in from the lobby. It's good to hear your voice, Son. I miss you."

"Miss you too. Wait a minute. Here's Mom."

"Nice talking to you," John replied, not knowing whether or not Jeremy had heard.

"Hello, sweetheart," Esther's voice sounded fresh and warm. "Are you okay?"

"I'm fine. Hersch is on crutches, but doing well. We're about ready to bail out of here."

"Good. Honey, listen. I've just talked with Mr. Rodeway from State."

John's hand tightened on the receiver with a sudden apprehension, waiting to hear what came next.

"He said they've found Jessica. Honey, she's alive, on a ship somewhere in the Mediterranean. Can you believe it?"

John felt with his hand for the bed and sat down.

"Are they sure?" he asked, his voice hoarse with emotion that threatened to break loose from some unknown, subterranean place. John wanted desperately to believe, but was unprepared to weave his way through one more disappointment, unwilling to face one more near miss. "Are they really sure?"

"Mr. Rodeway says it's her. She stowed away on a ship that will be in port by tomorrow night. I'm going to meet her. Can you join me?"

"Where?"

"She's going to be taken off at Split."

"Split? Isn't that in Yugoslavia, or what used to be Yugoslavia?"

"Yes. Now, I guess it is part of Croatia. I am flying New York to Rome to Zagreb. That's Croatia's capital city. Mr. Rodeway says we have an embassy there. Embassy people from there will take us to Jessica. Can you do it?"

"Can I do it? Of course I can do it. I'll meet you there tomorrow at the airport. I can hardly believe it. After all of this . . . she must have sneaked onto a ship at Bandar and slipped out of the country on her own. What a kid!"

"You said it, darling. I still can't believe it. Oh, and Mr. Rodeway said that he would contact the embassy there and ask them to help you. By the way, what will Hersch do?"

"I'll find out, but my guess is that he'll want to head for home. He's been gone from his job longer than he'd planned. He's out of the hospital, as of yesterday. I managed to get him a room next door to mine."

Esther proceeded to give John the flight numbers that Rodeway had left with her.

"Okay, darling," she said at last, "I've got to run to catch a plane. I love you."

"Wait," John said, a note of sharp tension in his voice. He closed his eyes and then opened them again.

"What is it?"

For a moment, it was as if an invisible hand had swept away his elation over the news about Jessica. It was gone. Vanished. All that was left was a sudden feeling of hollowness in the pit of his stomach. He stared at his hand. It was shaking. He forced himself to concentrate on steadying it.

"John, are you all right?"

"Yes, but . . ."

"Something's the matter, I can tell. What is it?"

"Listen, you've got to go. But have Jeremy contact Jim Brainard. See if he can join you in New York."

"What?" Esther sounded perplexed. "Are you serious?"

"Never more so, hon."

"I can't imagine that he could get a ticket at this late date. My plane is full from San Francisco. I'm sure it will be the same in New York."

"I understand. Look, I'm not sure why, but all at once I've got this strange feeling. I think Jim is supposed to come, too. No questions. Just get going. If I'm right, Jim will be there. If not, well, we'll chalk it up to too much time in the Arabian sun."

"Okay, if you're sure."

"I'm sure."

"All right, I've got to run now. It's morning rush hour, and I have a plane to catch."

John could hear the excitement in her voice.

"See you in Zagreb tomorrow," he said. "Be careful, sweetheart. I love you."

110

THURSDAY, 15 DECEMBER, LOCAL TIME 1055
WASHINGTON, D.C.

"Ready on your call to Mr. James and Mr. Henderson, sir."

"Thank you," Rodeway responded, picking up the phone. "Hello, gentlemen."

"Good morning, Charlie. Why don't you hang it up for a day and go home to your wife and kids. That way you'd give the rest of us a break so we could catch up on our work." Harold Henderson, head of Consular Affairs in Washington, D.C., laughed as he spoke.

"What's up, Charles?" The clipped New England intonation of Deputy Undersecretary of State Roland James always brought a smile to Rodeway, who swore jokingly to others that he was the only one at State who *didn't* talk with a regional accent.

"Some good news for a change. I might have waited, but I need some direction here."

For the next few minutes, the Political and Diplomatic Security Section's senior officer updated the other two on the Jessica Cain case. Both men were enthusiastic and surprised that the girl had been found. Each of them had privately written her off weeks ago. They listened as Rodeway pointed out the concerns over what her return home might mean in relation to recent terrorist threats and the subsequent rash of bombings, attributable to Hamas and the Palestinian Islamic Jihad.

"I think we should keep her under wraps until we catch this Dosha fella or until the FBI runs these misbegotten fanatics back into their holes," Henderson declared emphatically. "No publicity."

"Do you seriously think we can keep her recovery a secret, Harry?" queried James, his raspy voice ending in a high, squeaky pitch, forcing Rodeway to pull the receiver away from his ear.

"Well, at least there should be no publicity until she is safe," Henderson insisted. "They're dropping her off in a red area, you know."

There was a moment of silence as each man mused over the truth in this added ingredient of danger.

On a regular basis, the State Department distributed a travel report on one hundred sixty-seven countries to its staff members. Each country was listed under one of four designations: *status green* = modest risks; *status yellow* = some precautions warranted; *status orange* = essential travel only and with rigorous precautions; *status red* = highly volatile, travel strongly discouraged. This month, status red included seventeen countries, including Croatia, with the exception of Zagreb, the capital city.

"Is there any other place to get her out?"

"Not really," answered Rodeway. "Not unless we run a chopper in and pick her right off the ship's deck. She's on a cargo vessel bound for that port. It's headed for Marseille after that, with no stops in between."

"Why don't we take a different tack?" asked James. "This thing has had so much publicity, let's go ahead and grab some of it for ourselves. God knows the State Department could use a few kudos for a change."

"I say no press," Henderson proclaimed adamantly. "The rule is, be prudent. Play it safe. Deal with publicity like the enemy it usually is. We all know publicity is a fickle friend, even on a good day. What if something goes wrong?"

"What could possibly go wrong?" James exclaimed, his voice once again taking on that irritating nasal sound that Rodeway detested. "We send someone down to meet her. She gets off the boat, into a car, and onto an airplane. Look, we could even send the CG himself to pick her up, along with, maybe, a consular officer and a network pool reporter and cameraman. Get the parents and take them, too. Make a party out of it. Give her a heroine's welcome home and all that. Americans love this sort of thing. The world will love it, too. It's so Rockwellian, what with shots of the family being reunited and all. State will look as though we're doing our job for a change. Maybe we can turn it into such a setback for Dosha and his crowd that they'll back off, at least for a while. What do you think, Charlie?"

"There are always risks attached to any operation, but I tend to agree with you, sir," Rodeway answered. "The level of risk here seems minimal, and this could well be the year's biggest story. Better to feed on the inevitable publicity than be eaten by it."

"I still disagree," growled Henderson, "but if you both think it's the best thing, okay, I'll go along. Just keep a lid on it, Charles, until you've got her. No pictures released until she's out of the red area and home where she belongs. Good grief, think of what that kid must have been through. How old is she?"

"Twelve," responded Rodeway.

"Twelve," Henderson muttered. "She should be home packing up her dolls and thinking about boys."

"That's where she'll be in a couple of days, sir."

"Okay, Charlie," said James. "Make it happen. See you in the papers."

"Thank you both for your time," Rodeway began moving to wrap up the conference call. He had covered his backside, always an important thing to do in this business, and gained approval for what he had already started. That had been the main purpose for calling his boss and the undersecretary. Now he needed to get the rest of the pieces in place. "I've got an hour's work ahead of me, and my assistant is sick today, so I'd best get to it."

"Give my love to that wife of yours, Charlie," said James. "Maybe when this is done you could come over for dinner."

"Thank you, sir. We will look forward to it."

"Good luck, Charles," echoed Henderson.

"Thank you, sir. I can always use a truckload of that."

111

THURSDAY, 15 DECEMBER, LOCAL TIME 1110
SAN FRANCISCO, CALIFORNIA

United's late morning flight to New York rose from the runway at exactly ten minutes after eleven, its right wing lifting a salute to the sun-kissed city of San Francisco. In a matter of minutes, the "City by the Bay" had disappeared, and Esther Cain was settled back in her assigned seat: tourist section, aisle seat, next to last row, right side.

Esther leaned out into the aisle and scanned the cabin in front of her. From the looks of things, every seat was full. The woman seated next to her, obviously a well-seasoned frequent flyer, was already engrossed in a hardback copy of Mary Higgins Clark's latest mystery novel.

That was good.

Esther was not in the mood for conversation.

Her thoughts were focused on tomorrow.

—∾—

THURSDAY, 15 DECEMBER, LOCAL TIME 2015
JFK INTERNATIONAL AIRPORT, NEW YORK CITY

By the time the flight reached New York, Esther had stolen just enough sleep time to make her feel miserable. Her eyes were burning so badly that she stepped into a restroom to rinse them with Visine. Then she hurried out of the domestic terminal and onto a bus. She had enough time between connecting flights, but little to spare. Looking out the side window, she was amazed at the glut of traffic pushing its way through what seemed to be perpetual gridlock.

This driver needs a medal or something. How in the world does she manage to get this big bus through these narrow spaces? Maybe God, in his infinite wisdom, knew from the beginning that some New Yorkers would need the "gift of driving" in order for the rest of us to survive the experience. She smiled at the thought.

At JFK's international terminal, Esther stepped down from the bus, hiked the strap from her carry-on onto her shoulder, and walked toward the sign marked Alitalia. A uniformed woman inspected Esther's bag at the door and pointed her toward the gate—"up that way"—with a look on her face that said, *How could anybody be so stupid as not to know their way around here?* Esther was about halfway to the next door when a man fell into step beside her.

"What's a pretty thing like you doin' in a place like this?" he said.

Startled, Esther glanced over—into the twinkling eyes of Jim Brainard. Without missing a beat, she said teasingly, "Lookin' for an older man," in her finest imitation of Brainard banter.

"Well, look no further, lady. Just hand me your bag and give me a hug and let's find out where we queue up. Hey, now, isn't this somethin'? Our little girl is comin' home at last. I tell you for sure, I'm lookin' forward to meetin' her. I think we're over this way, Esther. Through that door, it looks like."

"I'm so glad Jeremy managed to reach you in time, but I still can't believe you're here. Say, do you suppose there's a place to get some mineral water around here? I'm desperate for a drink. During the last few hours, I seem to have acquired a first-class case of traveler's indigestion. I think the water and a couple of aspirin might help."

"We'll keep a lookout. They just announced boardin' will begin in about fifteen minutes, so, we have to keep movin', but . . . *there.* . . . I think I see somethin' down that way. Follow me." Jim led the way past people standing around in sleepy-eyed groups of twos or threes, along with others sprawled uncomfortably in chairs, heads back, mouths open, eyes closed. He purchased a bottle of water for Esther and eventually found a chair where she could sit and rest. He sat down across from her, listening as she told him of her conversation with Charles Rodeway and what she knew of the plans for Jessica's recovery, reiterating John's sudden request for Jim to come with her.

"John will be so glad. He seemed to think that your being here is very important. I can't believe you got a seat with no more notice than this."

"A friend in high places," Jim answered simply.

Esther shook her head. Weariness and the gradual release of tension were catching up to her. Just then, a woman's voice came over the loudspeaker, announcing the initial stages of boarding for their flight.

"Time to go," he smiled sympathetically. "Once we get on the plane, maybe you can get some serious shut-eye."

A few minutes after ten, Alitalia's Boeing 767, bound for Rome, backed away from the terminal and turned slowly toward the runway. Charles Rodeway had managed to upgrade Esther to first class, which was a new experience for her. She sighed as she sank down into the soft leather seat, but immediately felt guilty knowing that Jim Brainard was wedged into a middle seat halfway back in tourist. When comparing seat assignments earlier, she had tried to exchange with him, but he would not hear of it.

After they were off the ground, Esther spoke to the flight attendant, pointing back toward the rear of the plane. The woman nodded understandingly, and in a few minutes returned, saying she had found one open seat in business class. Moments later, Esther had offered her first-class seat to the man who was sitting in the aisle seat next to the empty one in business class. He quickly realized his good fortune and was delighted to trade up. With the transaction accomplished, the flight attendant disappeared into the tourist section. Minutes later, a surprised and very pleased Jim Brainard was seated next to Esther, giving instructions for changing their watches to "Italy time," and enjoying a beverage that was served in a real glass.

PART EIGHT

They [the apostate rulers] tried, using every means and seduction, to produce a generation of young men that did not know anything except what [the rulers] want, did not say anything except what [the rulers] think about, did not live except according to the rulers' way, and did not dress except in the rulers' clothes. . . . The bitter situation the nation has reached is a result of its divergence from Allah's course and his religious law for all places and times. That bitter situation came about as a result of its children's love for the world, their loathing of death, and their abandonment of jihad.

— "Declaration of Jihad Against the Country's Tyrants, Military Series," recovered by police, Manchester, U.K., from home of Nazihal Wadih Raghie, May 10, 2000

Muhammad said: No Muslim should be killed for killing a Kafir [infidel].

—hadith 9:50

Pride goes before destruction,
a haughty spirit before a fall.
—The Holy Bible
Proverbs 16:18

112

THURSDAY, 15 DECEMBER, LOCAL TIME 1225
ZAGREB, CROATIA

Milton Creston had been busy making arrangements ever since arriving for work this morning at the embassy. He was young and new in Zagreb and a little nervous about all of this. It wasn't the complexity of the assignment that worried him, or even potential danger. It looked like a very simple operation. Fly to Split; get the girl; fly back—a piece of cake, really.

The conundrum for Creston centered on the realization that there would be international publicity surrounding the journey. Not that he minded what it might do for his career. Throughout the morning, he had grown increasingly excited about the prospect of seeing himself on television for the first time. His new bride would be thrilled, as would his parents and friends back home. He thought about the millions of people who would tune in to watch the unusual outcome of this kidnapping story that had gained worldwide notoriety—including the secretary of state and probably the president himself.

None of that troubled him. In fact, he was elated. His frustration had surfaced, however, about an hour ago, when word came that his boss, Daniel Banks, the consul general, would be joining the welcome party, which until then had included only Creston, a two-person network pool crew chosen from CNN, and the girl's parents. Not that Banks was a bad guy. In fact, he was well-liked by the embassy staff and had as good a rapport with the Croatian community as could be achieved during such stressful times.

It was this very popularity that caused Creston to see the handwriting on the wall. His personal moment of glory would now likely be neutralized by his boss, whose presence would relegate Creston to the level of an assistant—which, in fact, he was. All morning, he had been mulling over this dream assignment that was certain to lift his diplomatic career out of obscurity and place him on the fast track, lack of life experience and professional seasoning notwithstanding. Now, his "moment" was being stolen by the consul general, and that knowledge birthed a wintry resentment in Creston.

He pushed back from his desk, opened an attaché case, and stuffed a handful of papers inside, mostly official forms to be passed along to the appropriate people, authorizing CNN's team and the girl's parents, along with himself—and now Daniel Banks—to board this afternoon's C-130 UN supply flight to Split.

On any other day, Creston would have looked forward to getting out of the gray grimness of winter in Zagreb. There was no snow on the ground, but it was definitely overcoat weather. Had he taken a moment to consider things, he would have realized just how skewed his thinking was. Instead, he waited dejectedly in the doorway to the consul general's office, listening as Banks gave last-minute instructions to his administrative assistant.

It was an opportune time to rehearse the details of the journey, to make certain in his mind that nothing had been overlooked. That was what he was trained to do. That was what he was paid to do. His usual alertness, however, had given way to feelings of rancor and depression.

113

Friday, 16 December, local time 0800
Washington, D.C.

"That's right, sir, everyone is in place. The CG and an attaché named Creston are personally handling the matter. Both her mother and father are flying into Zagreb. CNN has a news team on site and ready as well. . . . Yes sir, a pool team. They've agreed to share the footage with all the major networks. . . . The mission should be completed and the family back in Zagreb tonight. . . . No, not a hotel. They've been invited to stay with the CG and his wife. . . . I look for them to be in Frankfurt sometime Friday afternoon. . . . Well, we want to debrief the child and check her out medically and psychologically there, before they come home. . . . Okay. Thank you, sir. I'll keep you apprised. . . . Yes. . . . Good-bye, sir."

Charles Rodeway hung up the phone and turned his chair to face out the window. An icy rain was falling on the nation's capital, but a good feeling warmed his "father" nature.

Otherwise, he thought, *this would be a truly miserable day.*

—∞—

John and Hersch's connecting flight from the United Arab Emirates had taken them through Zurich. After a four-hour layover, they were headed south again, proving once more, according to Hersch, that "the shortest distance between two points is not necessarily a straight line."

"Zurich. Zagreb. Isn't it odd that the cities we land in today both have names beginning with the letter *Z*?"

Hersch pushed his crutches farther down until they were jammed against the bulkhead. The embassy had thoughtfully requested business-class seating so that Hersch could stretch his leg and be as comfortable as possible. He eyed John quizzically. "Are you okay, Cain?"

"I think about things like that," John chuckled. "Especially when I'm flying. I mean, think about how many cities have names that begin with the letter *Z*."

"Zonguldak."

"Get out of here."

"It's a port city in Turkey."

"Really? Are you pulling my leg?"

"I don't do legs right now," Hersch grimaced, shifting his own to a more comfortable position.

"Are you sure you feel up to this?" asked John. Concern creased his brow as he watched Hersch trying to ease his discomfort. "I still think you should have gone straight home."

"I wouldn't miss this reunion for anything. It's payback for the pain."

Just then the flight attendant brushed against John's shoulder on his way forward with the drinks cart.

"Zhdanov."

"Zhdanov?"

"In the Ukraine on the Azov Sea."

"Okay, okay, enough already," John exclaimed in mock exasperation. "You've made your point."

Hersch gave a satisfied smirk, leaned back, and closed his eyes.

"The only other one that I can think of is Zion."

Hersch peered at John out of the corner of one eye. "Illinois?"

"Jerusalem."

"Doesn't begin with *Z*."

"In ancient times, it was the site of the Temple. Now it's a hill in East Jerusalem. The most important hill in the world," said John.

"I know a few senators who might not agree with you on that," Hersch replied.

"That's true," John chuckled. "But when was the last time you felt confident that our nation's leaders knew how to agree on anything that was really important?"

"Get some sleep, Cain. You're starting to sound too much like me. You need to catch some Zs so you'll be sharp when you see your daughter."

"I don't usually sleep and fly at the same time."

"No? You mean I have finally discovered something that puts a little fear in you?"

"Flying is worse than Iran, Hersch, and I was scared to death there most of the time."

"You shouldn't let a little plane ride get you down," Hersch chided.

"Isn't that the idea?"

"What?"

"After they get you up here, don't you want the plane to get you down again? Gently? And in the right place?"

"Rev, you're okay for a preacher. A little fear never really hurts. In fact, it sharpens us up. There's a huge difference between fear and cowardice. And a coward, you ain't, John. After what we've been through, I'd go with you anywhere. And there aren't many guys I'd say that to."

"Thanks," John said. Just then, he felt the plane start its gradual descent. Instinctively, he closed his eyes and his hand tightened on the armrest.

Hersch shook his head and settled back, turning his attention out the window where one frozen field after another was disappearing under the wing.

—⁓—

FRIDAY, 16 DECEMBER, LOCAL TIME 1335
ZAGREB, CROATIA

John and Hersch were the final passengers to exit the aircraft. John led the way down the steps to the tarmac, looking back once to check on Hersch. He saw Esther standing to one side, hands tucked inside her coat pockets. She was being protectively surrounded by two strangers in overcoats and two uniformed UN soldiers, each cradling an M-16. He guessed that the men in the overcoats were from the embassy. Standing just behind the others was Jim Brainard. John waved as Esther came forward to meet him. They embraced, then looked at each other and began to laugh.

"Your eyes are red," said John. She closed them as his lips touched first one, then the other. "When did you get in?"

"You've lost weight," she replied, running her hand over the stubble that was sprouting on his chin. "Less than twenty minutes ago."

"Arabic food has been very good to me," he answered with a thick accent. "In and out. Doesn't stick to the ribs. Very tasty on its way through, though."

They laughed and hugged again. Then Esther pulled away and moved toward Hersch. He paused and smiled as she hugged him and kissed his cheek.

"Herschel Towner, I am so pleased to finally meet you. We will never forget what you have gone through to help us," she said, standing back at arm's length, eyeing his crutches. Her words became husky with emotion. "John was careful in what he told me on the phone, but I was certain that you'd been wounded. Thank you, Mr. Towner, for all you've done. And for bringing John back to me like you said you would."

"The name's Hersch, and hey, it was nothing," he said feigning brusqueness. "When the Iranians got a good look at John, they decided to throw him back. The rest was easy."

He grinned as the others laughed. "Truth be said, it was your husband that got us out of there. He's quite a guy, Mrs. Cain."

"Esther," she corrected, glancing over at John, a look of pride on her face. "Yes, actually, he *is* quite a guy."

She took John's arm and wrapped hers through it tightly.

"Let me introduce you to our friends. Hersch, this, of course, is your father's old soldier buddy, Jim Brainard." Then she turned to acknowledge the two men in overcoats. "And this is Consul General Banks and Mr. Creston, an attaché from our embassy. Gentlemen, my husband and Mr. Herschel Towner, a dear friend from Seattle, who has been helping us try to find our daughter."

"It's a pleasure to meet you both," Banks responded as the men shook hands. "I regret that we don't have time to offer you our local hospitality, but that will come later."

"Dear, these gentlemen have indicated to me that Jim's presence, and now I suppose yours as well, Hersch, is a problem for them," Esther interrupted. "We are flying to Split by special dispensation from the UN, and they are not prepared for extra passengers."

"Yes, if we had known, Creston might have arranged for it," Banks explained. "Unfortunately, we had no knowledge that you two were joining us here. And our flight is warming up over there even as we speak."

All eyes turned in the direction Banks was pointing. The motors on a gigantic, olive-green C-130 were just beginning to turn over. It was then that John first noticed the man with a television camera balanced on his shoulder, film obviously rolling. To one side stood an attractive woman, dressed in ski pants, boots, and a heavy wool jacket. She was saying something into a handheld microphone.

Hersch started to speak when John suddenly interrupted. "I appreciate the imposition, Mr. Banks, but you must understand our circumstance. These two have been deeply involved in getting Jessica back, and in fighting against the acts of terrorism that are now being directed at our country." He spoke loud enough for the news team to be able to pick up his words. "I regret that we were unable to inform you that they would be joining us, but I assure you that their presence is essential. We cannot go on without them."

"But Mr. . . . Reverend Cain," protested Creston. "This sort of thing takes advance preparation. We'll be flying into a dangerous area."

"Mr. Rodeway, at the State Department in Washington, said that it would be quite safe," responded Esther sweetly, picking up on John's strategy. "That's a very big plane over there, Mr. Creston. Don't you think we could manage to squeeze these two in with the rest of us?"

Creston exchanged looks with Banks. The CG shrugged his shoulders, glanced at the whirring camera, and nodded. Without a word, Creston turned and jogged off toward the airplane to talk to the man in charge. They had not even gotten off the ground, and already he was being called upon to smooth things over so that the CG could look good on camera.

114

Friday, 16 December, local time 1615
Split, Croatia

As Jessica emerged from the passageway, she was surprised to see the crew of the *Evvoia* standing single-file, shoulder to shoulder, along the deck rail. Captain Callimachus was at her side, and behind her was Mr. Hatzimustafovic, the shipping company's local representative, who had come aboard a short while earlier. His shirt was open at the collar and Jessica noticed his pants showed signs of wear, as did the navy blue suit jacket underneath his raincoat. The man seemed okay, though. Besides, what choice did she really have? She had come to trust the crew of the *M/V Evvoia.* Why not Mr. Hatzimus . . . whatever?

The overcast sky was dark, hiding the sun's final attempt at providing some cheer for what had been an otherwise dreary day. She felt the sting of raindrops as a biting breeze snapped across the deck. It was cold enough to make her pull the wool jacket that the captain had insisted she take from his closet up under her chin. It was several sizes too large, but she was glad to have it on as the raindrops pelted her face.

In fact, everything she was wearing had been given to her by the captain or by members of the crew. Fresh underclothes and socks, thanks to the captain's daughters. The jeans and pullover that she had been given the night before were officially hers now. Their rightful owners had insisted. Only the Nikes she wore had been hers before last night.

As she started past the line, the first crew member reached out and took her hand, smiling.

"Have a safe trip," he said in accented English.

Jessica suddenly felt embarrassed, but there was no time to recover. The next sailor had his hand out now.

"Godspeed," he said, shaking her hand firmly.

The tiny procession moved on slowly, each man shaking her hand and wishing her well, until she reached the end of the line. The last person, standing next to the steps leading down to the waiting transfer boat, was Timothy Marcos. He held out his hand.

"God bless you, Jessica," he smiled broadly. "I hope to see you again someday."

Jessica's eyes filled with emotion she could no longer contain. She brushed past his hand and threw her arms around the young man, holding on to him as tightly as she could.

"Thank you for everything, Timothy Marcos," Jessica wept, her face buried in his chest. Then she looked up. "I will never forget you. Never. I will tell my father about you . . . that you want to be a pastor someday. Maybe he'll be able to help you."

Now it was Marcos's turn to be embarrassed. He glanced up at the crew's faces, but they were all nodding or smiling their approval. He looked at Captain Callimachus. The captain reached over and touched Jessica's shoulder.

"It's time to go, Jessica."

She released her hold on Timothy Marcos.

"Perhaps," said the captain, looking at Marcos, "we could offer up a prayer for Jessica?"

"Yes sir. That would be wonderful. May I?"

The captain nodded, motioning to the crew with his hand. Those with hats snatched at them respectfully as they bowed their heads. The stiff breeze had let up, at least for the moment, but large drops of cold rain started falling in earnest as Marcos cleared his throat.

"Lord Jesus," he began. "We want to thank you for our captain and the ship's crew. We thank you for our families back home, our health, and our jobs. But most of all, today, we thank you for Jessica Cain. You chose us, out of all the ship's crews in the world that you could have picked, to be the ones to carry her back to her family where she belongs. Keep her safe, now, as she leaves us. Watch over her and help her always to know how much she is loved. In Jesus' name we pray. Amen."

A chorus of "amens" echoed from the crew.

"Thank you," said Jessica, smiling appreciatively. With Mr. Hatzimustafovic following her, she waved her hand and started down the same steps on which she had surreptitiously boarded the *Evvoia,* some thirteen days before in Bandar-é Abbâs.

"Good-bye, Jessica," the crewmen shouted out as she stepped over onto the wooden tender bobbing up and down on the water's surface.

"Bye," she called out happily, waving again. "Thank you. I love you all."

The motor chugged into action and the tender moved out from under the *Evvoia*'s long hull. Jessica glanced over at the shipping company's representative. He was busy talking to the boatman. With a final look and a wave at the *Evvoia,* she turned her attention to the direction in which they were headed.

It was a big harbor. She had noticed that upon their arrival. Bigger, at least, than the one at Bandar. Now, as they churned along through the sea, past several cargo vessels anchored offshore, she could see other ships lining the docks. *This place is definitely bigger.* Small fishing boats, trawlers, a barge, even two ominous-looking warships were scattered about, some in motion, most patiently waiting their turn for whatever came next. It was part of a world and a life that now seemed both familiar and foreign to her at the same time.

Huddled against the cold wind, in the bow of the boat, she tried to guess which dock they were headed toward. Captain Callimachus had said he was certain that her parents would be at the dock when she arrived. If for some reason they were delayed, Mr. Hatzimustafovic had promised to stay with her until they came. Even though they were still too far out, Jessica kept peering over the edge of the boat, scanning the docks in hopes of seeing some sign of them.

It's been so long. How many weeks?

She couldn't remember for sure.

A million years. At least!

115

16 DECEMBER, LOCAL TIME 1620
SPLIT, CROATIA, AIRPORT

The news team was the first on the ground.

Milton Creston smiled for the camera as he led the way out of the airplane and down the steps to the tarmac, followed by Consul General Banks, then Esther, John, and Jim Brainard. Herschel Towner was last and the others waited as a crew member tried to assist him. He was having none of it, however, exercising his independence by carrying his crutches in one hand, while limping down each step and balancing with his other hand on the railing.

He grinned sheepishly upon arriving at the bottom step.

"Ain't life grand?" he grimaced ruefully. The others laughed, huddled under umbrellas, in the drizzling rain.

Two mud-spattered jeeps roared around the corner of the terminal building, headed in their direction.

"Methinks yon chariots are ours, my dear," John whispered in Esther's ear.

"I'll go in a wheelbarrow, just so long as there's room in it for one more," she answered, watching as the vehicles came to a stop in front of them. Each one was clearly marked with the letters *UN* across the hood.

"Hop in, folks," invited Daniel Banks. "And hang on. We're a few miles away yet. Our drivers will take us straight to the harbor. We'll pick up your daughter and come right back here. By that time, they'll have the plane unloaded and be ready to take us back to Zagreb."

Esther wasted no time climbing into the nearest jeep.

"Which dock do we go to, sir?" asked the first driver.

Banks looked at his attaché, waiting for the answer.

"Pier 12," Creston answered, fumbling through the sheaf of official-looking documents in his hands. He looked up. "Take us to Pier 12."

Both drivers nodded as the others finished settling into the close confines of the jeeps. The camera crew was the last to climb in.

Where is that fax with the pier number?

As unobtrusively as possible, Creston sorted through the file once again, in case he had passed over it by mistake. No. It was not there among the other papers. The cold rain stung his face as they bounced along the two-lane highway toward Split's harbor. He thought back to when he had left his office, frowning at the realization that he must have misplaced it on the desk. No problem, however. He remembered clearly.

Pier 12.

—~—

LOCAL TIME 1645
SPLIT, CROATIA

The boatman held the tender steady while Jessica climbed over the side and onto a small platform. Mr. Hatzimustafovic joined her and pointed up the narrow, wooden steps to the top of the dock. Jessica nodded and began climbing, pausing briefly to look around. There was no sign of her parents. She continued up the steps and waited on top for Hatzimustafovic to join her.

"Your parents are not here yet?" he asked in heavily accented English, out of breath from the climb.

"No." She couldn't keep the disappointment out of her voice.

"Do not worry." He patted her shoulder and then pointed toward the opposite end of the dock. "They will be along any minute. Come, let us go over there and wait."

The rain had let up for the moment, although the chilling breeze was back again, whipping at the collar of Jessica's jacket as she walked toward a long row of warehouses situated along the shore. Just beyond the dock, a loading crane squatted like a giant Jurassic Park insect, waiting to gobble up its prey. Not far from the crane, several dock workers were huddled in front of a large building to get out of the weather. Jessica's eyes darted back and forth, sharp with excitement and anticipation.

Where are they?

116

LOCAL TIME 1645

Esther glanced impatiently at her watch.

Where is she?

She and John and the others huddled together at the pier's edge, staring out into the harbor. Esther was surprised by the amount of shipping traffic in the harbor.

"Split has served for some time as a major loading and unloading point for goods and supplies bound for Bosnia," explained Banks to anyone listening. "Many of the units attached to the UN Protective Forces have landed their heavy equipment here. Their most important logistics line runs to the interior from this location."

Five more minutes passed and small talk decreased as the cold dampness and the feeling that nothing was happening set in.

"Are you sure we're in the right place?" Esther asked, her concern growing the longer they waited.

"This is Pier 12," Creston answered. "The fax we received from the *Evvoia*'s home office said they would deliver her to Pier 12." As soon as he had mentioned the fax, he wished he had not.

"May I see it?" asked Banks, absently holding out his hand as he stared into the distance.

"Sir?"

"The fax. May I see it, please?"

Creston hesitated, desperately wishing he was somewhere else. Anywhere but here. But he stubbornly bucked up and decided to make the best of it.

"I'm sorry, sir. I didn't think it was necessary to bring it."

Banks gave him a sharp look.

"She should be here by now, John," Esther said, looking first at John, then at Daniel Banks.

"I'm sure they were just delayed a bit," said Banks. "Still, it won't hurt for us to double-check. Right, Milt? In case there was a last-minute change that we don't know about?"

Creston felt the edge in his boss's tone. *I should have brought the fax. He knows it. I know it. I'm sure about the pier number though.*

But Creston knew he was no longer as sure as he had been.

"Yes sir. I can contact the embassy from the jeep."

Esther felt John's arm around her, drawing her close. She watched as Creston hurried away, then turned her gaze back to the sea. *Please, God. Let her come quickly.* She closed her eyes to ward off the apprehension gnawing at her stomach.

Minutes crept like hours. She watched as the attaché put the phone back on the jeep's front seat and hesitated for a moment. Was that uncertainty she saw on his face? He jogged back and drew the CG aside. She observed Banks's hand grip the attaché's arm. Then, quickly, it fell back to his side. Banks turned and walked toward them, a look of concern and apology on his face.

Something is wrong.

"I must ask you to get back into the jeeps. It seems that we have a small hitch in things," Banks said, his voice calm and reassuring.

"What's the matter?" John asked guardedly.

"It's nothing really. We've just been waiting at the wrong pier. It looks like she is coming into Pier 21, not Pier 12."

"What?" Esther's tone was anxious and tinged with frustration. "We've been standing here waiting for our daughter at the wrong dock?"

"So it seems, Mrs. Cain," Banks answered, conscious that CNN's faithful reporters were filming away. "I'm truly sorry for the mix-up. But let's be off. Pier 21 is only a short distance from here. We can be there in five minutes."

Esther glanced up at John. His face flushed with unvoiced anger as they ran to the jeeps. As soon as everyone was in, they roared off into the gathering darkness. A short distance farther, they noticed lights coming on, apparently automatically, along the docking area. Ships tied up for loading and unloading dwarfed the jeeps and their occupants as they sped by.

All Esther could think about was the need to hurry.

117

LOCAL TIME 1655

Jessica dropped a half-step behind her Croatian escort. It allowed the man's body to act as a shield from the cold breeze. As they neared the land's end of the dock, she looked again at the men standing near the building. She presumed that it must be a warehouse. There were four. No, there were five. She had not seen the one squatting in the shadows until he stood up.

"Over here, Jessica," Mr. Hatzimustafovic said, pointing away from the men toward a stack of large wooden crates. She breathed a sigh of relief. She didn't like the idea of being here, outnumbered by five strangers.

Remember, Jessica, you can't trust anybody.

The familiar sound of that inner voice surprised her. The past twenty-four hours on board the *Evvoia* had dulled her sense of universal distrust and the animal alertness that had been so essential for survival. The closer they came to the workmen huddled near the building, however, the more her cautionary instincts resurfaced. Mr. Hatzimustafovic veered to the left, moving laterally away from the men. Jessica's anxiety dwindled slightly. But not entirely.

The crates provided shelter from the wind while still allowing the scene to remain in full view. Jessica backed against the crates, hands in her jacket pockets, waiting.

Come on, Mom and Dad. Hurry.

A chill sent a shiver through her body.

As they waited in the growing darkness, lights began to come on along the dock area. They were not powerful enough to illuminate the entire area, but it was comforting to know that they did not have to wait in complete darkness.

At last, from a narrow opening at the opposite end of the nearest building, two figures emerged from the shadows, walking rapidly toward Hatzimustafovic and Jessica.

It's them.

She felt Hatzimustafovic's hand on her shoulder and looked up. He was looking at her and smiling.

"Your parents?" he asked.

Jessica's face lit up with excitement as she watched the approaching couple. She started jumping up and down. Then, as quickly as she had started, she stopped as the pair walked beneath a dock light.

She saw them clearly now.

Inside her, something crumbled as longing gave way to shocked disbelief.

These two were not her parents, but she knew who they were.

From deep inside her throat, a cry of terror began to rise.

The next five seconds ran like a B-movie in slow motion.

The man with the scar withdrew his hand from his coat pocket. Jessica saw the flash a millisecond before the muffled popping sound reached her ears. In the same instant, Hatzimustafovic groaned, falling back against the crates. Another flash. She heard the sickening impact of the second bullet as it, too, found its mark. Out of the corner of her eye, she saw the Croatian slide to a grotesque sitting position on the pavement beside her, his back against the crates.

Frozen with bewildering fear, Jessica watched the handgun swing ever so slightly until it pointed directly at her. Behind the dark barrel, the man with the scar was smiling. Leila Azari's face was a mixture of dark fury and hatred.

BOOOM!

The force of the explosion threw her backward, slamming her body against the stack of crates.

118

LOCAL TIME 1705

John, Esther, and the others had just passed Pier 19 when they heard the explosion. Dead ahead, a flash of light and flames shot upward into the sky, then disappeared, replaced by an eerie glow.

"What was that?" exclaimed Esther.

"I don't know," John replied, instinctively tightening his grip on her shoulder.

Cars and trucks were parked haphazardly along this section of the pier, partially blocking the narrow street and causing the drivers to slow as they weaved their way through. The street continued to narrow, until it became impassable, completely blocked by an ancient Volkswagen that acted like the cork in the neck of a bottle.

"Come on," said John, scrambling out of the jeep.

"Wait, let's stay together," admonished Banks, looking around to check the quality of their position. He didn't like it. There was not room enough to turn their jeeps around without backing up for at least a block or more. "Be careful, everyone. We don't know what's happening. It could be an accident. A gas explosion. It might also be shelling or a bomb, so stay close. Remember where we are, people."

The cameraman from CNN stood by, shouldering his camera and chewing gum, looking like he did this every day. For all John knew, maybe he did. The female reporter appeared a little more anxious. Jim Brainard and Milton Creston stood quietly nearby. Hersch was the last to join the circle.

"Mr. Towner, you wait here. You'll only be in the way. I would suggest Mrs. Cain and Mr. Brainard do the same. I'll leave a driver. He's well armed. The other one goes with Reverend Cain, Creston, and me, for a look around."

"In a pig's eye," Herschel grunted.

"I'm serious," Banks said firmly.

"So are we," Jim retorted emphatically. "Now, son, you can waste your time and everyone else's by standin' here arguin.' It ain't goin' to change a thing. We're stickin' together. You all go on ahead, and I'll be along with Hersch here.

Take these boys who've been drivin' us with you. They look like they can handle themselves okay. We'll catch up."

Without waiting for orders, the drivers had placed themselves at the front and rear of the small contingent, facing out, M-16s at the ready. They listened to the discussion, smiling slightly as the old man put the CG in his place, but their eyes never stopped searching out the darkened rooftops, windows, and alleyways.

Banks stared disapprovingly, but he knew he was not in control. Not completely, at least. The circumstances he had started out with a few hours earlier were not the same as those facing him now. It was time to reconnoiter and make the best of it.

"Okay," Banks sighed in resignation. "Let's go. But stay together."

"Sir," one of the drivers touched Jim's arm.

Jim looked at him questioningly.

"Do you know how to handle one of these? You may need it."

The soldier held out a handgun that had been strapped to his waist a moment before. Jim took it gratefully, turned it over in his hand, and smiled. "Thank you."

The others struck out with Jim walking behind Herschel Towner III, who limped along after them.

"You want to stick that thing in my belt before you hurt one of us with it?" Hersch asked.

Jim chuckled. "Son, I was shootin' these things before you were ever a gleam in your daddy's eye. But yes, I don't mind if I do stick this in your belt. I'm a senior citizen with enough weight to carry around all by myself. I don't need extra."

He reached over and pushed it through Hersch's belt and they walked on, with Hersch trying to move faster. The others had disappeared on ahead. The two of them were alone.

—w—

Stunned and breathless, her ears ringing painfully, Jessica tried to focus her eyes. Less than a dozen feet away, she saw Leila Azari lying facedown, not moving. The man with the scar had pushed himself to his knees and was shaking his head. He looked behind him in the direction of the blast. An old building at the end of the pier was now a blazing inferno. Broken timbers were still falling from the force of the detonation. Shattered pieces of glass littered the roadway and the land end of the pier.

Jessica raised her head at the same instant that the man looked back at her. She saw him glance over at his fallen partner. He was looking for something.

The gun.

The explosion and the fall had knocked the gun out of his hand.

Jessica saw it at the same time he did. It was far enough out of reach that he had to get up or crawl for it. He chose to get up. In the same instant, Jessica forced herself up from the pavement. The man with the scar was moving to his left, toward the weapon. Jessica began running in the opposite direction, away from the pier.

Her body ached from having been thrown against the crates by the explosion. Still, she managed a few quick steps before darting behind another stack that had survived the blast. As she did, she heard the first bullet tear through a wooden crate, just above her head. A second shot buried itself deep into whatever the crates contained.

She could hear footsteps behind her now, and the sound ignited adrenaline from a reservoir that Jessica had thought long since depleted. She ran faster than she could ever remember. Faster than any race on the school track back home. She ran for her life.

Past the huge crane.

Across some steel tracks.

Alongside a brick building.

Still more rail tracks.Running under one of the pier's lights she felt, as much as heard, the sound of another bullet ricochet off the bricks slightly above and in front of her. *That was close.* A chip from one of the bricks stung her cheek, creating a small but painful cut just below her eye. She rounded the corner and immediately faced a decision. Either take the street that stretched along the waterfront or one of two alleyways close at hand. She chose the nearest alley. It was narrow and dark, but thankfully clear of the usual debris. She ran as fast as she could, fueled by the fear of what was behind her. A jog in the alleyway appeared so suddenly that Jessica bounced off the wall and fell backward to the ground. Scrambling to her feet, she dodged around the corner and ran on. Her hand was bleeding from having scraped against the wall. No matter. She ran on, desperate to put distance between her, the man with the scar, and the evil woman who had kept her a prisoner. How had they known where to find her? *And where are Mom and Dad?*

119

LOCAL TIME 1717

Sirens could be heard somewhere behind them as John and the others ran out of the narrow street into the open and stopped to stare at the scene. As they had dreaded from the outset, a sign on the side of the building nearest them identified this as Pier 21. Or, what was left of it. The main warehouse at the end of the pier looked to be a total loss.

There was shouting as men rushed down the gangplank of the nearest large ship, heading toward the blaze. They stopped well short, however, in the realization that there was nothing they could do. For the moment, at least, confusion and bedlam were sovereign rulers of this scene. A short distance away, John saw a woman struggling to her feet. She looked small in stature, and at first he thought it might be Jessica. He started forward, but a second look made him hesitate. It was a grown woman. He could see her clearly now in the firelight. She seemed dazed but was walking and appeared to be okay. John turned his attention away from her and back to the question foremost on everyone's mind.

Where is Jessica?

—~—

LOCAL TIME 1722

Leila Azari was badly shaken from the effects of the blast. As she stumbled to her feet and instinctively moved away from the direction of the fire, she saw Marwan Dosha walking hurriedly toward her out of the shadows. He grasped her elbow and began to guide her toward the narrow street leading back to their rental car.

"What happened?" Leila's first words came as she stumbled along beside Dosha.

"An explosion," Dosha growled in reply. "Some stupid Serbs."

Another boom was heard in the distance.

"They must be firing on the city now," said Dosha as he half carried, half dragged Leila out of the lighted area. "We should have been warned about it. They picked a fine time to resume their war on this place."

"I'm okay," Leila declared, pushing away from his grasp. "Are we going back to the car?"

"Yes."

"And the girl?"

Dosha's silence was her answer.

They were almost to the street when two men emerged from a nearby alley, headed in the direction of the fire. One was on crutches. The other one was older. Dosha glanced over his shoulder. The old man had stopped and turned, staring after them. He pushed Leila forward.

120

LOCAL TIME 1725

"It's him," Jim whispered hoarsely.

"What?"

"It's him," Jim said again, his voice low. "I'd recognize that face anywhere."

"Whose face?"

"It's Dosha! Give me that gun, Hersch."

"Wait . . ."

"The gun. Give it to me."

Jim fumbled with Hersch's belt as he groped for the handgun, all the while never taking his eyes off the man and woman who were walking quickly away.

"Are you sure?"

"Positive. He lived at my house for a week."

Now it was Hersch's turn to gape.

Jim took the gun. He stepped forward, uncertain what he should do about the two figures receding into the darkness.

"Stop!" he called out.

—∾—

Dosha hesitated, uncertain whether to obey or run.

"Can you run, Leila?" he whispered.

Leila nodded.

"I know who you are, Marwan Dosha, and I have you covered with this gun. Don't either of you move or I'll shoot."

Dosha was dumbfounded. That someone would actually call out his name was the last thing he had expected. *How could that old man possibly* . . . He shook his head in disbelief. It was the old man who ran the inn in Booth Bay, Maine, where he and his team had planned the ill-fated attack on Boston in September.

But how did he get here*? . . . No time for that now. He's here, that's all that matters. And he knows who I am.*

"Run, Leila," he ordered in a low voice, pulling his pistol from the belt holster hidden under his jacket. Without another word, he turned and fired.

Pffft!

The bullet hit close enough to send Jim and Hersch diving for cover. Dosha fired again. Jim threw himself down behind a garbage barrel and got off a round in return.

Hersch had hit the deck and tried to ignore the intense pain in his injured leg as he rolled behind the cover of a stone wall. Looking around to see if Jim was all right, he noticed one of his crutches lying in the middle of the roadway, between them. The second bullet zinged as it glanced off the stone wall right above his head.

Jim peered out from behind the barrel. The street looked empty. There was no one there. *Where could they have gone so fast?* He stood to his feet, the gun still dangling from his hand.

"Here, give me that," Hersch limped over to where Jim was standing and reached around to take the gun.

"What happened?" One of the jeep drivers ran up to them. The news team was right behind them.

"Mr. Brainard here thinks he saw a man he knows."

"Do you always shoot at people you know, sir?" the young soldier asked.

"What's going on? Are you both okay?" John was out of breath as he ran up to the others.

"It was Marwan Dosha," answered Jim.

John stared at Jim. "Are you certain?"

"I said that I'd never forget that face. And I didn't."

"When he called out to him," Hersch added, "the guy fired at us and took off. There was a woman with him."

"A woman?" John repeated. "Dark hair? Jeans and a jacket?"

Herschel and Jim both nodded.

"Then, I must have seen them, too. There was a woman, over in that direction," John continued, pointing excitedly. "It looked like she had been knocked down by the explosion, but she was getting to her feet when I saw her. She looked dazed. At first, I thought she might have been injured by the blast, but then she began walking away with a man helping her, so I didn't pay any more attention."

"Ol' Doc Brainard here," Hersch continued, "called this guy out by name and told him not to move. Just like the O.K. Corral. Only this fellow didn't listen very well. The woman ran and the guy got off a couple of near misses. Doc fired back. Me, I dove for cover. Nearly broke my neck on these crutches doing it, too."

Hersch's half-joking description failed to elicit a response.

"I'm sorry, John. I don't think I hit him. Now they're gone."

"It's okay," John said. "This is all starting to make some sense. Let's get back to the jeeps and drive around."

"Why?" queried Banks. "What good can that do?"

"Stop and think," said John. "If that was Marwan Dosha—"

"It was," Jim interrupted emphatically.

". . . then he was here for the same reason we are. Jessica. Somehow, he found out that she was coming here and he wants his hostage back. Or worse." He glanced over at Esther, noting her ashen look. "As long as he has her, she's worth millions. Provided the world comes up with the ransom he's demanding. Or it could be he thinks she knows something. At any rate, she's important enough to Dosha that he came here personally tonight to find her."

Another boom echoed in the distance. Everyone was listening to John now.

"All right," he went on. "We've looked, and she's not here. However, there is a man over there by those crates, where that policeman is now. He's dead, but not from the blast. I found him just a couple of minutes ago. He's been shot. But there was no sign of Jessica. If she was not with Dosha when you saw them, and she's not around here, that must mean she escaped again. Somehow, in all the confusion, she managed to get away."

John looked next at Milton Creston. The attaché, whose name could well have been changed to Crestfallen, stared gloomily at the pavement in front of him, both hands jammed into his coat pockets. He looked miserable.

"Creston, I know you feel terrible," he continued. "Maybe if we hadn't waited at the wrong pier, we would have been in time to get her. But it's also possible that we could have shown up just in time to get us all killed, either by the blast, or by Dosha. Maybe God had a hand in delaying us this way. Either way, you need to get it together now, because we need—all of us—to begin searching."

Creston looked up, glancing at Daniel Banks.

Banks said nothing.

"Okay, let's get out of here," John said. "We have to assume that Jessica is close by. She hasn't seen us, but she has seen Dosha. That means she'll be hiding. Staying in the shadows, and alleyways, and whatever. Trying to get as far from here as possible without giving herself away."

"Do you really think a twelve-year-old would do all that?" Banks asked skeptically.

John turned to face the consul general, controlling his emotions now with great difficulty. "Sir, with all due respect, last September I left my daughter in Israel in the hands of terrorists. That was three months ago. Since then she's made it all the way to Iran and from there to here and she's still alive. I don't know how, but with God's help, she's done it. Don't doubt for one minute that this 'twelve-year-old would do all that.' Dosha believes it, too. That's why he's here. So, let's stop standing around. We've got to find her before he does."

John strode off down the narrow street, the others hurrying to catch up. Banks was still the consul general. Creston was still his attaché. The two UN soldiers still carried their automatic weapons. But it was clear to everyone who had taken charge.

121

LOCAL TIME 2135

Jessica pressed against the side of the building, trying to stay under the narrow overhang and out of the rain. It was not coming down as hard as it had earlier, but she was still soaked through and shivering from the cold. Directly beneath her, she could hear the past hour's runoff coursing through one of the city's ancient drainage channels. She could not stop shaking.

If you stay here, you'll freeze to death, Jessica. You've got to keep moving.

She pushed away from the brick wall and walked on to the end of the alley.

Be careful, Jessica.

Another big boom sounded in the mountains somewhere above the city. This time, she felt the ground shudder as the shell hit less than a block away.

This is unbelievable. In the movies, yes. But this is real life and those are real guns.

Jessica shrank back.

What kind of place is this? Why is everyone bent on killing everyone else?

She winced as she thought back to the shipping company's Croatian representative.

He died standing right there next to me, and I can't even remember his name. Hats . . . something. The poor man. . . .

Jessica came around a corner, climbed three low steps, and began walking along the sidewalk, making sure to stay close to the buildings. The street was empty of traffic. She tried each door she came to. They were all locked. Some windows had glass and she thought about breaking one in order to get inside. Others were already broken and long since boarded up. She shied away from the idea of breaking and entering, not so much because she felt it would be wrong, as from a sudden sense of claustrophobia at the thought of being trapped inside one of those buildings. As long as the man with the scar and Leila Azari were around, she wanted to be free to run.

She came upon a large hole and stared at the muddy water that had collected in it.

Strange . . . why would that be here? They should put some construction barriers around it.

As the sound of another artillery shell being fired from the mountains echoed across the city, a sudden comprehension coalesced in Jessica's mind. She hurried on, suddenly anxious to get away.

As she continued, half running, half walking, trying to reason out some sort of plan for the rest of the night, she saw the telltale spires of an old cathedral, looming straight ahead on the opposite side of the street. She also saw that the stretch of buildings on her side of the street came to an end, opening up onto a small city square. It looked as if the cathedral faced out on the square, as well, although from where she stood, she could not be absolutely certain. As she came closer, it appeared to be one of the few buildings in the area that had not suffered the wounds of war.

Jessica started toward it when she heard a noise behind her. Glancing back, she saw a small, dark-colored sedan round the corner and move slowly in her direction.

Maybe it is the police. What if it's Mom and Dad, and they are looking for me?

Jessica halted, bone weary from the constant tension of running and hiding, desperately wanting this car to be the answer to all her prayers, unsure as to what to do next. Feeling hollow inside, her emotional resources spent, she leaned against the nearby building. She knew she was not thinking clearly, but for the moment it no longer seemed to matter.

This has to be a policeman. Who else would be out here tonight? But what if they're like the policemen in Iran? What if it's not a policeman? What if it's . . . them?

The car suddenly sped up, heading toward her.

Something snapped inside.

Run, Jessica, run. You can't trust anybody.

Fantasy gave way to reality. She was back on the streets again, running for her life.

She sprinted to the next opening between buildings, about half the distance to the corner. It was another narrow alley and she dashed into it, feet splashing in the mud and water. A car door slammed.

Someone has gotten out.

As the car sped off she knew, instinctively, what was happening. Whoever had gotten out would follow her on foot. And whoever was inside the car was turning at the corner. She could hear tires squealing in the distance. The driver was racing around to where this alley opened onto the next street. Gauging the distance in her mind, she knew she was going to lose. The car and driver had the advantage. She was trapped!

Jessica ran with her left hand out, keeping her balance by feeling the wall. Otherwise, she would have missed it. For a brief instant, there was no building to touch. She stopped so fast that she slipped and fell. Quickly, she got up and investigated, feeling with her hands in the dark. It was a small opening between two buildings. She dodged into a space that turned out to be barely wide enough to stand in without twisting around. Pausing for a moment to catch her breath, she heard footsteps. She had been right. Someone was coming down the alley after her. She held her breath, afraid to move, and watched through the narrow opening as a sinister-looking shadow passed briefly across her line of vision and disappeared out of sight.

Releasing her breath slowly, she pushed on through the passage, which was really nothing more than a place for stray cats to run. The farther she went, the tighter it became. Looking up, she could see nothing but walls that appeared as if they ran together high overhead. Beyond where she stood, she could see a narrow opening, outlined by a lighter shade of darkness. She pressed forward by turning sideways, hands at her sides, sliding her body between the two concrete block walls. Finally, not more than six feet from the end, the crevasse became too tight even for her willowy figure. She pulled back, at the same time fighting off another panicky wave of claustrophobia. In frustration, she pounded against the wall with her fist, fighting back tears that persisted in rolling out onto her already rain-dampened cheeks.

What was that?

Jessica looked back toward the wider end of the passageway. Her pursuers had not seen her come out. They must have concluded that she was still somewhere in the alley. She felt it.

Someone is in here with me!

"Jessica," the voice called out softly, almost musically.

A man's voice. One she would never forget. The man with the scar. Jessica froze. He couldn't see her if she didn't move. Could he?

"Jessica, I know you're in here."

He was getting closer. Taunting her. Frantically, Jessica looked back at the opening.

Your jacket.

What?

Take off your jacket.

The voice was real. Or was it? Jessica was so frightened that she wasn't sure what "real" was or wasn't anymore.

Take off your jacket.

There it was again.

"Jessica . . ."

The second voice was real enough. *And he's closer than before!*

Jessica slid her hand up and quietly unbuttoned the front of the wool jacket she had been given on board the *Evvoia.* She was almost out of it when . . . he was there!

"Come here, you little—"

Jessica screamed and pressed farther into the narrow crack. The man's hand brushed against her shoulder. All at once the jacket was gone. Without its bulk, Jessica was able to squeeze farther forward in the crevasse than before.

"Come here," the voice snarled again.

He was close enough for her to see the shadowy outline of his face, even the scar that ran along his cheek. She screamed again.

"Give it up, kid," he growled, reaching in after her.

Jessica could feel his heavy breathing and hear the scraping of his feet in the mud as he pushed his way farther into the crack between the walls. She pressed forward again, her body scraping against the rough concrete as she tried to stay away from him. His hand was there again. He grasped at her arm.

"No!"

Desperately, she twisted forward, as hard as she could, scratching her forehead on the rough wall, but also smashing the man's hand against the concrete. He grunted in surprise as much as in pain, but it was enough. For a split second, his grip loosened.

All at once, she was moving. A few inches. Just beyond his reach. A few more. And suddenly, like a cork out of a bottle, she popped out onto the street, stumbling against a lamppost as she caught her breath. Her shirt was torn both in front and in back. Looking down, she saw scratches on her chest and supposed they were repeated on her back from having wedged through the cramped space. She felt a small trickle of blood run down her forehead into the corner of her eye, and she dabbed at it with the back of her hand.

She could hear the man cursing now and calling for Leila, his voice growing more distant with each shout as he made a hasty retreat through the narrow passageway. Jessica looked around, knowing that she had to do something.

Run. Just run.

But where? She spied the cathedral again. Instinctively, she saw it as a sanctuary, a place of refuge and safety. The church had been that to her all her young life. Now she needed it more than ever. As fast as she could, Jessica sprinted toward the old building.

Bounding up the steps, she threw herself against the large wooden door, crying, "Oh please be open!"

The door yielded on creaking hinges, and Jessica slipped gratefully into the darkened entryway.

122

"You didn't get her?" Leila said, standing by the open car door at the far end of the alley. "What happened?"

"Never mind. She's like a cat, that one; but her nine lives are about to end. Turn around and go back to the other street. Hurry, before she gets away again!"

Leila threw the car in gear. With one foot on the brake and the other on the accelerator, she turned the wheel and skidded until the car was facing in the opposite direction. An instant later, they slid around the corner and drove out into the open square.

"Easy, easy," Dosha motioned with his hand, his eyes quickly scanning the scene before him. Good news and bad. The good news was that the streets and the square were empty. People were inside tonight, protecting themselves as best they could from the stupid gunners up in the hills. It meant that he and Leila could move about in their search with relative ease. The bad news was the same: The streets and the square were empty. The girl had disappeared again.

"Where could she have gone so quickly? Would she retrace her steps into the alley?"

"No," Dosha answered. "She's out here somewhere. She knows better than to go back into that alley. The only question is, where?"

They drove slowly around the square and returned to the location from which Jessica had emerged. Dosha cursed as he stared at the tiny open space that she had slipped through. Then his eyes darted around the square.

"She's here, Leila. I can feel it. She has got to be hiding here somewhere. Drive up to the corner and park. You take that side, and I'll take this one. Try all the doors. See if any are unlocked. If you find one, signal, and I will come to you. Keep an eye on me, and I'll do the same."

Dosha got out and quietly closed the car door. Leila motored up to where the street entered the square, parked, and began walking back on the opposite side of the street, testing doors as she went. The rain was coming down hard again, pelting them both until they were thoroughly drenched. Leila's dark hair glistened as she hurried up the steps of the church two at a time and pushed on the door. It opened.

She turned and waved at Dosha. When he saw her signal, he stopped what he was doing and ran the remaining distance across the square to join her on the steps.

"It's unlocked?"

"Yes."

"Then she's inside. She's got to be."

Dosha pushed the door open and they stepped inside.

"We need some light," Leila whispered quietly, as she felt along the wall for a switch.

"No!" Dosha put a hand on her arm. "We'll use my flashlight. Light up this place, and we'll attract attention. Everything else has been blacked out since the shelling began, and we don't want anyone coming in while we are here. We certainly don't want to offer those artillery nuts up there in the mountains a real target."

"Who do you think it is up there?"

"Who knows? Some renegade Serbs, most likely. I don't care. We have more important matters to concern us." He moved stealthily across the entryway of the cathedral. "Now, let's find our little friend. You take the stairs up to the balcony. Wait at the top until I give you some illumination."

Dosha switched on the light, grunting his approval at its surprisingly powerful beam. It lit up the large, solid oak doors that on Sunday would open wide to welcome those few parishioners daring enough to leave their homes and venture out to the house of God. He stepped forward into the center aisle, slowly moving the light back and forth between well-worn pews.

Pausing at the center of the building, he turned abruptly and flashed the powerful beam toward the rear balcony. The light illuminated the cathedral organ, its long, slender pipes poised like sentries overseeing the house of worship. He moved the light across the balcony and then back again as Leila surveyed the area from her position at the top of the stairs. Finally, she shook her head and disappeared back into the darkened staircase.

Dosha shifted the light onto the tall, carved wood pulpit that towered above the empty pews, near the center right-hand side of the sanctuary. He climbed up the steps until he was standing in the pulpit, moving the light in random, twisting patterns, across the cavernous room, revealing only an esoteric mix of stone gargoyles and radiant Madonnas. The beam passed across a large, circular rose window, located in the nave above the baptismal font.

Standing on opposite sides of the room, with the long rows of empty pews between them, Marwan Dosha and Leila Azari continued to move slowly, checking under each row, testing each of two remaining side exits and confirming that the only unlocked doors had been those at the main entrance. Having reached the front, they paused, silently listening for any telltale sounds. Then, stepping up to the chancel area, they examined the altar and two small rows of pews situated off to one side, facing three high-backed chairs on the other. Nothing.

Puzzled, Dosha motioned to Leila and they retreated from the chancel, down the center aisle, until they reached the large doors through which they had entered. He switched the light off and whispered, "Stay here. Don't move."

Then his voice cut through the darkness. "I must have been mistaken. She's not here. Let's go."

Opening the door, he glanced down at his wristwatch in the half light. Then pushed the door shut. The sound of its closing reverberated through the sanctuary. They stood quietly, hardly breathing, and listened for some sound of the girl. Eventually she would have to come out this way. It was the only available exit.

Five minutes passed.

Then ten.

Then another ten.

Finally, Dosha broke the stillness as he shuffled his feet. He switched on the flashlight, pointing it away from him while checking his wristwatch.

Twenty-nine minutes.

"She's not here," he said at last with a heavy sigh, "or she would have shown herself by now. She must have hidden in some other place. Let's go back to the car."

He returned the small flashlight to an inside pocket, pulled the damp collar of his jacket up around his neck, and opened the door. Leila stepped through first, while Dosha took one final glance back into the darkened interior of the old church. Then he walked out into the night. They jogged across the square to where Leila had parked the car. She slid in behind the wheel and looked inquiringly at Dosha. He said nothing, hands pushed deep into his jacket, a dispirited and gloomy demeanor on his face as he stared, without seeing, at tiny rivulets of rain running down the window.

Leila waited, nervously, for some signal.

"Do you think that she might try returning to the docks?" she asked, breaking the silence at last.

Dosha's eyes closed for a moment, as if he were pushing the question away from his thoughts. When he finally looked at her, it was with a dark smoldering rage that caused her to bite her lip and wish she had remained silent.

"It's too dangerous down there for us to go and see," he said at last. "You can count on policemen being there through the night, thanks to whoever blew away that warehouse. If she does go back, well, that's that."

There was resignation in his voice as he glared out the window.

"May she die first from pneumonia!" He spit the words out like bullets, suddenly banging his fist against the dashboard.

The pair sat silently for several minutes as the rain beat down on the roof of the car.

Finally, Dosha shifted his eyes back to Leila Azari.

"When presented with an unexpected problem," he said, "as is often the case in my business, you learn to punt."

"Punt?"

"An American football term. It means that we are still in the game, but we must readjust our game plan by playing defensively for a while, before taking over the ball once more to score the winning touchdown."

"How will we do that?" Leila asked, not at all sure that she understood what he was talking about.

"Instead of waiting until Easter, we're going to cut the timing of our American project short. It will mean a smaller payoff," he continued, his words sounding every bit like the evaluation of an investment downturn on Wall Street, "but no matter. I'll have my contact in Zurich arrange to gather up the gifts so graciously donated by our public thus far, and then we'll wish them all 'Merry Christmas.'"

"Merry Christmas?"

Dosha smiled grimly, the inner rage already stemmed and stored away, as thoughts of the next few days replaced it.

"Come. We need some rest. At daylight, we'll cross over to Italy. The ferry should be running. If not, I saw some fishing trawlers that will be easy enough to hire. Once we are in Italy, you and I will begin wrapping a special present. Or perhaps I should say *unwrapping*."

Leila looked at him curiously. Pushing in the clutch, she turned the ignition and twisted the wheels away from the curb.

Seconds later, the square was empty and quiet.

123

Jessica wasn't certain exactly how much time had passed. It felt like at least an hour. Slowly, she raised herself from the prone position in which she had been lying. Every muscle in her body was quick to remind her of having been abused. Finally, sitting in an upright position, she paused to stretch her arms and legs. Hunching her shoulders and leaning forward as far as possible, she both felt and heard her back pop twice, giving some additional relief.

Her eyes had long since grown accustomed to the darkness, enabling her to discern, with a fair degree of certainty, the details of her hiding place. She let her legs dangle freely now, on either side of her twelve-inch-wide perch, while the circulation of blood worked its way into her body's extremities.

Are they really gone?

Desperate with fear when first she entered, she had darted first to the left then back to the right. Almost instinctively, she found a set of stairs and climbed up to the balcony. Quickly recognizing that it would be an easy matter to discover her there, she surveyed the nearest of several beams that spanned the width of the sanctuary. The only possibility for reaching the nearest one had been a narrow ledge that ran along the wall. Jessica's mind flashed back to another place and another ledge, another impossible chance. Then, taking a deep breath, she started to climb.

Once over the balcony railing, she found handholds and toeholds that carried her four feet higher until she reached the ledge. Pressing her body against the cold concrete wall, she eased herself along. It was a distance of only about six feet, but it felt like forever until her right hand touched the wooden beam. Twisting around, she pulled herself onto the rough surface.

No sooner had she gotten settled than she heard the doors open below. Lying flat, she checked the beam's edges, making certain that no part of her slender form was exposed. They would have to throw a light on her directly from the balcony, or from the very front of the church, before she could be seen. It was a chance she'd have to accept.

She prayed. *Jesus, I need you once again to save me. Blind their eyes. Don't let them see me up here.*

Now, Jessica waited. As time passed, she found herself fighting off exhaustion from lack of sleep. To fall asleep up here would be inviting disaster. She had to get down. From her sitting position, she scooted back to the wall and then twisted around until she was facing it. At this point, she did not want to look down. Getting off the beam and back to the balcony was going to be harder than getting on. Every move had to be slow and precise.

Carefully, she worked her way off the beam and onto the ledge, pausing to catch her breath and gather up the courage necessary for the remainder of the return journey. Releasing the stored-up air in her lungs, she tried to relax as she inched away from the wooden beam, never taking her eye off the balcony.

Easy does it. One more step and you're there.

As she put her foot down and shifted her weight onto it, the aging cement crumbled and broke away, throwing her off balance.

There was nothing to hold on to.

Her body teetered backward.

In sheer desperation, as her foot broke through, she instinctively pushed away from the wall as she had done many times from the side of her swimming pool back home. She came off the ledge so strongly that she hit the balcony railing full force, knocking the wind out of her. Fighting to catch her breath, she began sliding backward off the rail. Frantically, she groped for some way to stop.

The inside of her upper left arm, just above the elbow, finally caught the rail, bruising the tender skin as the weight of her body shifted to it. Her fall slowed just enough for her to twist around and grasp hold of the top edge of the rail with her right hand, while her feet dangled helplessly in space. It felt as if her arm was tearing away from its socket as she drew on every remaining ounce of strength to pull herself up and over the rail, crumpling in a heap on the wooden floor.

When she was finally able to move, Jessica crawled on hands and knees, shaking and crying all the way to the organ bench. She tugged and pulled until it came far enough away from the bass pedals for her to get underneath. The bench offered paltry protection, but for the moment it satisfied a little girl's desperate need to be covered by something.

124

SATURDAY, 17 DECEMBER, EARLY MORNING

The rain clouds continued to break apart against mountains that in turn seemed to vanish mysteriously into the murky mist. It was a dismal morning. The sun never really rose; the day just grew lighter somehow, revealing the city of Split stretched along the Dalmatian coast like a fat, dark snake.

The five- and six-story high-rises, favored by the socialists of another era, were clustered in the center of the city that once had been a favorite of the Roman emperor Diocletian in 284–305. The remains of his palace still attracted history buffs and visiting tourists.

At either end of the "snake" were hundreds of small houses, most with red tile roofs that bleached lighter in the hot summer sun, then returned to the color of red wine under the winter rains. In front of the city, the dark blue Adriatic Sea had donned thousands of tiny whitecaps that now dotted the surface as far as the eye could see. Behind it all stood the mountains.

Raindrops fell gently this morning on the vineyards and gardens that stretched down the mountains all the way to the sea. These same mountains had spewed forth a barrage of mortar and artillery fire just the night before. At this moment, however, all was quiet.

—~—

At Pier 21, weary firefighters dragged water hoses and other gear through the rain-soaked debris as they began their retreat from the ruins of what had once been a warehouse containing food and medical supplies destined for Sarajevo. The building and its contents were a total loss. The fire had spread rapidly, causing additional damage to the warehouse next door. It was too early to calculate the losses there, though they were expected to be severe, as well.

—~—

In front of one of the red-roofed houses that dotted the northern edge of town, a rain-spattered, dark blue, two-door sedan, with a small rental sticker on the rear bumper, straddled a dirt path leading up to the door. Except for the car, the house looked abandoned. Curtains were drawn over its two small windows. The houses on either side of this one were devoid of any signs of habitation, as well.

Inside, wrapped in separate blankets on a single bare mattress, a man and woman stirred restlessly. Some pieces of clothing were draped over the top of an open door. Still others had been spread out to dry on two metal chairs and a small table in the only other room in the house.

Marwan Dosha and Leila Azari had not given up the search until after two o'clock, even though random shelling and mortar fire on the city had made driving or even walking the nearly empty streets a life-threatening experience. The fact that few people dared to venture out had made searching simple. Anything that moved might be the girl. But there was no further sign of her. She had vanished once again.

—w—

Split's small international airport terminal had taken a direct hit from random artillery fire three months before. A gaping wound near the north end of the building had been patched over with pieces of wood and plastic to keep out the rain and cold. It worked as well as most things in this beleaguered part of a once proud nation, keeping out most of the rain and letting in most of the cold.

Actually, airport officials had stopped heating the building anyway.

This morning, a scruffy-looking old character, eyes haunted by having seen a thousand days of war, whose job in better times had been to handle airline passenger baggage, busied himself by passing hot cups of coffee to each of his visitors, compliments of an earlier UN supply run.

Handing the phone pack to a nearby soldier, Consul General Daniel Banks walked over to where the others huddled together in a vain attempt to get warm.

"Word has it that intermittent shelling has begun again. It looks like insurgents have surrounded almost the entire city. Apparently, they've got mortars and some armor. They fire and move; create havoc and fear. They're concentrating on the central district, but air observers have identified light artillery movement and mortar fire not far from here. The airport has been closed to all commercial traffic and workers sent home.

"Spotters have seen at least one MLRS 227mm moving closer to the airport. It's a mobile rocket launcher, of British origin, and has a range of about 30 kilometers. They expect that by this afternoon, the airport could go. There's one more UN flight on the way in right now. It should be here in an hour. When it turns around, we've got to be on it."

"No!" Esther fairly shouted. The inflection of her voice mirrored the distressed look she gave Banks. "Not without our daughter."

"Mrs. Cain, I understand how you feel, but we have no choice but to—"

"No!" she exclaimed again, starting to cry, her hands clenched tightly at her sides. "You *don't* understand, Mr. Banks. You just don't. There is no way that you can understand how I . . . how we . . . feel. Our daughter vanished three months ago. John and Mr. Towner here have risked their lives to try to reach her. We stood there yesterday on the wrong dock while Jessica was being stalked by a killer, a half mile away. She's out there, Mr. Banks, and she's by herself. I know that she's alive. Now you want us to just fly away and leave her here? You've got to be out of your mind to think that we could ever do such a thing."

John put his arm around Esther and drew her close. He could feel the rigidity in her slender body, electric with pent-up emotion. He sensed that she was near the breaking point, and truthfully, he wasn't far from it himself.

How much more disappointment can we take without coming unraveled?

"We understand that you may have to leave, Mr. Banks," said John. "And Mr. Creston here, too. I won't speak for Jim or Hersch, but Esther and I stay until we find her."

The consul general looked at Jim Brainard and Herschel Towner. They glanced at each other and nodded.

"We're in with John and Esther," Herschel affirmed solemnly, "until this is over."

Banks sighed and turned away, but not before glancing over at the CNN news team. They had said very little, but Banks thought they would probably opt for getting out at the first chance. The others, he knew, would not come without force, and he was not prepared to go that far. He had expected as much anyway, when first he broached the subject.

What a mess!

125

Jessica crawled out from under the organ bench. When she stood up, she felt shaky on her feet. The rose window at the far end of the nave could be seen clearly now, the gray light from outdoors filtering through the ancient leaded glass.

How long have I been sleeping?

She let herself drop back onto the bench and reviewed again the events of the night just past.

Especially that final frightening moment.

She looked up at the transverse beam on which she had hidden. Her eyes trailed back across the ledge along the wall, heart beating faster as she traced the nearly invisible path to her hideaway.

How could I have done that?

She easily made out the spot that had given way underfoot on her return. She stared for a long time, swallowing once again the feeling . . . *the incredible feeling of falling. . . .*

Getting to her feet now, Jessica pushed the frightening images out of her mind and tugged the heavy bench back to its original place, though not entirely certain why she thought that so important. Maybe it felt like she was straightening up her room or something. Like so many other things in her life right now, it just didn't make sense.

She walked slowly down the steps until she stood in front of the doors through which she had entered the night before. Taking hold of the ornate handle, she pushed until it opened just enough for her to peer out through the crack. Everything looked clear. The square was empty.

Jessica emerged from the cathedral into a fine drizzle. The temperature had dropped during the night. Her clothing felt cold and stiff with dampness. She wished for her jacket, but it was gone, abandoned in an alley she had no intention of returning to. That, together with the sounds of shelling that continued intermittently until just before dawn, had made it a disturbing and restless night.

She stretched again, jumping up and down a few times to encourage circulation. It had been almost as cold inside the church as it was outside. She looked down at her hands. They were a bluish white and the tips of her fingers and toes were numb. She rubbed her hands together and stomped her feet vigorously until at last they began to tingle.

Walking stiffly, she moved across the cobblestones in front of the church, working sore muscles as she went. Nobody was around. For the first time, she became intensely aware of the quiet. The shelling had stopped, at least for now. She hoped it was for good. It looked like a ghost city, though Jessica was sure that behind the shuttered windows, above the empty shops and offices that surrounded much of the square, people had lived through the terror of the night with much the same fears as she had. How could they not?

There is no way anyone could ever get used to this.

Jessica stayed in the alleys, walking aimlessly, unsure of what to do next. After a few blocks, she happened upon another small public square where she observed signs of human activity. Shrinking back, she watched for a while, wondering if it was safe to venture out.

In front of a five-story building, with its first-floor doors open onto the square, Jessica watched people of all ages, including several small children, milling about. Some carried old, worn suitcases, while others had simply wrapped their few remaining possessions in blankets. Two buses, both painted white, were parked in front of the doorway. Near each bus, men in military uniforms, wearing white helmets, were shouting out names and giving directions as the people crowded around. Jessica moved closer, staying along the edge of the nearby buildings until she saw the letters *UN* written on the sides of the buses.

UN. Mom and Dad were coming here on a UN airplane. That's what Captain Callimachus said. Do you suppose these people are from the United Nations?

The soldier closest to her was attempting to help an old man and woman who had shuffled up to the door of the bus, each bent under the weight of a blanket-wrapped bundle. She heard the soldier say something to them. He pointed to the blankets. The man protested and the old woman tried to climb into the bus with her full blanket. The load was too heavy, however, and the first step was too high for her to navigate. A young man, next in line, stepped forward to help her. She pushed him away. He stood back protectively alongside his wife and two small children and waited as the soldier continued trying to communicate with the old couple.

By this time, Jessica could see that at least one of the problems was that the soldier was not speaking the same language as the old people. They either could not or did not want to understand. The soldier pointed to a small pile of suitcases stacked along the side of the bus. The old woman shook her head violently and tried to get on once again, her best efforts resulting only in blocking the entry for others. The soldier lifted his hands in exasperation, saying something to the young man standing by with the family. The young man shook his head. Jessica was shocked by what she heard next. Not by what was said, but by the fact that she understood it!

"Do you speak English, then?" the soldier asked.

"A little," the young father replied.

"Will you explain to these people that they must leave their things here by the bus? There is not room inside. We will put as much as we can underneath, in the baggage compartment, but tell them that people are more important than possessions. Do you understand?"

He nodded.

"They are my parents. I will try to speak to them again. They are very upset."

"Tell them that the most important thing is for us to get them out of here and to a safe place. If they don't cooperate, I'll be forced to leave them here."

The young man nodded again as a look of concern flashed across his face. Then he turned to talk to the old couple in their own language. When he had finished, it was clear to Jessica that they had understood. Slowly, they turned and walked over to the pile of suitcases and boxes and dropped their load next to it. With cold and wrinkled fingers, the old woman fumbled over the knotted blanket until it opened. Reaching down, she withdrew two items and then stood back as the young man retied the bundle for her.

Jessica watched, curious to see what the old woman had retrieved. She was crying. The old man shuffled over to her, and tenderly put his arms around her, whispering something in her ear. They turned away, and Jessica watched them disappear into the bus.

She wiped at her eyes. She had seen what the old woman had in her hands and was moved by it. Out of all her worldly goods, she had chosen two framed pictures. That was all.

Who is in those pictures? Are they wedding pictures? Her parents, perhaps? Or her children? Who?

Jessica shook her head. What things in life were ultimately too dear to lose? Right now, she could think of only one thing.

Life itself.

Jessica desperately wanted to stay alive. To go home. To be with her family. She continued watching as the young man, together with his wife and the two children, moved closer to one of the buses.

Shall I take the chance? It looks like they're treating these people okay. Maybe they'll help me. She started toward the buses.

You can't trust anybody, Jessica.

The words reverberated in her mind and she stopped.

You can't trust anybody.

Jessica hesitated, uncertain of her next move.

What should I do?

Suddenly, Captain Callimachus's face flashed across her mind, along with Timothy Marcos and the other members of the *Evvoia* crew.

I wonder if I could get back to the ship? No. If the man with the scar and Leila are still looking for me, wouldn't they be thinking the same thing? They could be waiting for me to show up there. Besides, even if they aren't, how would I ever get off the dock and back out to the ship?

The buses were almost finished loading. The young man was ushering his wife and children up into the bus that the older couple had boarded. If she was going to do anything, she had to make her move now.

Jessica swallowed.

Jesus, please take care of me now.

She ran across the cobblestones and up to the soldier. He turned when he felt her pull on his arm.

"*Qui va lâ?*" he said, with a friendly grin.

"Are you with the United Nations?" Jessica asked, her heart pounding.

"Oui," he replied.

"Mister, I know you speak English," she blurted. "My name is Jessica Cain. I'm an American citizen, and I need you to help me. Will you? Please?"

126

LOCAL TIME 0925

The mood inside the Split International Airport waiting area was painful, to say the least. Looking around the small circle, John took note of the mood of each of the others. Daniel Banks appeared to be keeping his gaze diverted away from the Cains, but every now and then John caught him staring at them. He glanced over at Creston, who was sitting slightly apart from the rest, hands folded in his lap, looking positively miserable. He noted that Hersch was resting his leg on a pair of steel folding chairs. His back was against the wall and eyes were closed.

Sleeping? I doubt it. He looks uncomfortable. I'll bet that leg is hurting.

Esther, however, was sleeping pretty soundly. About an hour ago, she had finally succumbed to the insistence of the others and curled up on a straight-back vinyl sofa. Her head rested on John's lap.

After giving up the search earlier that morning, John had convinced the others that they should all return to the airport and wait until it was light before doing anything further. It ran counter to what he had really wanted to do, but it had been the best choice.

Banks had advised them all to get out of Split right away. Things were seriously coming apart. The word from the UN peacekeeping force was not good. The rebels appeared to be closing in for the kill. Split was teetering in the balance and looked as if it was going to fall, probably in a matter of two or three days, maybe sooner, if help did not come. But John had meant it when he said they were not leaving. And nothing was going to change his mind.

He watched Jim Brainard turn a page in the small New Testament in his hand. The older man's on-the-spot identification of Marwan Dosha had doubly confirmed John's decision to ask him to accompany Esther. How fortunate—no, providential—it was that Jim had been here. He was the only one among them who could have recognized Dosha. Who knows what might have happened if he had not?

"Mr. Banks, sir. Phone message."

The soldier with the phone pack called out from the far side of the room. Out of the corner of his eye, John saw a frown on the consul general's face. Banks got to his feet and crossed over to where the young man waited, taking the receiver in his hand.

"This is Banks. . . . Yes. . . . what?" Banks turned away from the others and lowered his voice. John was able to hear only snatches of the conversation.

"Repeat that, please. . . . Are you able to verify? . . . All right. Can you bring her in? . . . I see. Well, then, we're on our way. I'm giving you back to our driver."

He handed the phone back to the soldier.

"He's going to give you directions. Before you hang up, be absolutely certain you know how to get to where he is. I don't want us winding up someplace else. Got it?"

"Yes, sir."

The consul general stared out the window, apparently gathering his thoughts as he watched several soldiers loading a shipment of food and emergency medical supplies onto trucks. He motioned to the CNN team to follow him, and then walked over to where the others were seated. Esther had awakened when the soldier had shouted. She was sitting up now, brushing hair back from her face.

"John," Daniel Banks spoke quietly. "Mrs. Cain."

Hersch lifted his leg from off the chairs.

Jim Brainard closed the New Testament.

John and Esther sat side by side, absolutely still, her right hand clenched onto his left.

There was something in the tone of the consul general's voice. Everyone knew. Something had happened. Good or bad, this was it.

"Your daughter has been found," Banks announced quietly, unable to keep the emotion from choking his words, "by UN soldiers."

No one moved, silently waiting to hear his next words.

"She's alive."

The next sixty seconds were sheer pandemonium.

John and Esther leaped to their feet and threw their arms around each other.

"Oh, thank you, Jesus, thank you, thank you, Jesus, thank you," Esther cried over and over, gratefully clutching onto John as he held her tightly.

Herschel Towner limped over and pounded John on the back with one hand. With the other, he was wiping his eyes.

"I knew we'd get her," he exclaimed excitedly. "I just knew it."

Jim Brainard wrapped his arms around John and Esther. In a voice husky with emotion, he said, "Congratulations, you two. You've persevered and now God is answerin' your prayers. And I'm lookin' forward to finally meetin' this new 'granddaughter' of mine."

"Where is she?" John asked Daniel Banks.

"How did they find her?" Hersch chimed in.

"Are you sure that she's all right?" Esther said, her voice quivering with excitement mingled with fear.

"That's all I know for the moment," Banks said. "Our driver has the instructions. They don't have a way to bring her in right now. It's an area where they're moving out refugees." He paused for a moment, scanning the expectant faces of the group. "So, what are we waiting for? Let's go get her. Get into the jeeps. I'll follow."

As the others rushed to leave, Banks pulled Creston aside.

"It was you who contacted the refugee points with word about the girl, right?"

"Yes, sir," answered Creston with a sheepish grin, the kind seen on a child's face when caught in the act of doing something good.

"Excellent. I should have thought of that, but I missed it."

"You've had a lot on your mind, sir."

They walked outside together, toward the others, who were settling themselves in the jeeps.

"Sir?"

"Yes?"

"I'm really sorry I messed up yesterday. I . . . there's no excuse, sir. I just blew it."

"I know you did. It surprised me, because you're better than that. But we all make mistakes. The key is never to make the same one twice. Besides, with a few well-placed phone calls, you've made a more than adequate recovery. You're a good man, Milt. Don't ever forget it. I'm glad to have you on my staff."

127

LOCAL TIME 1010

In most European cities of one hundred fifty thousand people, downtown streets at midmorning are filled with the sounds of automobiles and buses, streetcars and trucks. Intersections bustle with pedestrians and workers walking smartly in every direction. But not in Split. Not this morning.

As the two jeeps raced into the city's central district, the streets were eerie, almost ghostlike, in their absence of traffic. Only a few trucks, filled with armed men, hurried along the city's main boulevard. A lone pedestrian ran across the street, carrying a loaf of bread under each arm, and disappeared inside a building. The shutters on a third-floor apartment window opened and an old woman leaned out to survey the city below. John thought that it must be an unusual sight. Surely it wasn't like this every day. He wondered if the city's docks were deserted this morning, as well, but the route they were traveling did not take them close enough to see.

"The man I talked with said they were located near the city center, so it shouldn't be much farther," Banks said, leaning over to John. "Strange to see an entire city hunkered down like this, isn't it?"

"Exactly what I was thinking," John replied, hanging on as they rounded a corner. "Have you noticed that no streetlights are working?"

"Yes. This is not a good day for the people of Split, and they know it. I think we're getting out of here without any time to spare."

"It should be just ahead, sir," the driver called out, as they sped past a cobblestone square.

"Look at that old cathedral, John." Esther pointed with her hand as she spoke. "Isn't it beautiful?"

"It is indeed."

"When you see something like that, it is so hard to believe there's actually a war going on around us."

John smiled and drew her close. As he started to answer her, their vehicle turned the corner into yet another square. No sooner had they driven into the open area than the driver slammed his brakes, coming to a sudden stop. The second jeep almost rammed them from behind.

"Back up, back up!" shouted the lead driver.

Both vehicles were already retreating by the time the scene before them fully registered on John's mind.

"Get out. Take cover!" the soldier was shouting again, waving them out of the jeep and under a narrow building overhang. John saw the young man drop down by the jeep, M-16 ready, as he scanned the windows and rooftops of the buildings opposite them. Satisfied that they were safe for the moment, the soldier ran beyond the jeep to the edge of the square, not more than twenty feet away. Then he doubled back to where they huddled in horror and disbelief.

"Sir, it's a mess out there. They've taken out a busload of people. Probably refugees. I see one of ours down. Bodies everywhere."

"Can you tell what happened?"

"Could be a bomb, but my guess is an RPG, sir. Probably from up there somewhere." He pointed his rifle over their heads.

"Any signs of life?"

"It's hard to say, sir. I thought I saw someone moving off to one side, but I'm not sure."

"RPG? What's an RPG?" Esther said.

"That's a rocket-propelled grenade, ma'am," the soldier replied.

John had already turned loose of his grip on Esther and was walking out onto the sidewalk.

"Come back, sir," the soldier ordered. "You can't go out there."

"And you can't stop me, soldier. I've got to find my daughter."

"Sir, I can't let you go. It's too dangerous."

"Leave me alone!" The look on John's face caused the soldier to hesitate. He looked over at Banks.

Banks shook his head. "Let him go. Can you get across the street and watch for snipers?"

The soldier nodded and ran off toward a boarded-up office building.

"You, son," Banks motioned to the other soldier, "cover us. I'm going with him.

"I'm going, too," said Esther, a determined look on her face.

"No, Mrs. Cain. There may still be someone up there. If there is, he's ready to shoot anything that moves."

"Mr. Banks, I expect that I've already been shot more times than any man here. Now, step aside or go with me. My daughter is out there. Dead or alive, I'm going to look for her."

They could hear sirens now, wailing in the distance. Help was apparently on the way. Esther ran after John and grabbed onto his hand. He wanted her to stay protected, far from the horror just around the corner. But he knew Esther.

"Stay close, hon. Let's go."

"I'm coming, too," declared Jim Brainard. "Might as well give them as many targets as possible."

He looked over at the soldier. "If he drops one of us, son, you nail him before he gets anybody else. Okay?"

The soldier blinked and nodded, looking as if he found it hard to believe what he was seeing and hearing.

"That's an order, son," Jim called over his shoulder as he ran after the others. "Hersch, get ready to bring one of those jeeps out in a hurry."

Hersch moved as quickly as he could, falling into the driver's seat of the lead vehicle and forcing the foot on his wounded leg to rest on the accelerator. All the while, he scanned every window and rooftop in his line of vision for some sign of snipers, wishing desperately to be able to lay his hands on a weapon. A quick glance around told him that none were available.

"Stay as close to the buildings as you can," shouted Jim Brainard to John and Esther as they moved toward the square. "Spread out and we'll make poorer targets than if we're close together."

At the corner, they stopped to survey the scene. The bus was a burning hulk. The missile had apparently hit the gas tank as it exploded. It was hard to imagine that anyone could have survived. A second bus had managed to pull away into the street at the far side of the square. It was damaged, but had not sustained a direct hit. The occupants had managed to get out and were standing about, crowded into small groups, stunned and horrified by what had just happened.

John's first feeling was one of nausea at the sight of so many human bodies and body parts scattered across the cobblestones. He reached for Esther to shield her from the trauma of what he saw, but it was too late.

"Oh, dear Lord, these poor people," she cried out, stopping to stare in revulsion at the slaughter.

Just then a shot rang out.

The huddled refugees screamed and scattered, leaving behind one of their own lying in a pool of blood. John saw the CNN news team running for cover. Seconds later, they stopped behind a stone wall, within fifteen feet of the sniper's victim. Without a pause, they continued filming.

In that same terrible moment, John heard several bursts to his left. He glanced over to see the driver of their jeep firing from a kneeling position, his arm resting on the edge of a bench that had been placed there for pedestrians to enjoy on a sunny day in Split.

"He's out of it, sir," the soldier shouted. "But we had better hurry. There may be others."

All at once, John saw what he was looking for.

"Over here. She's over here," he shouted, waving to the others.

He ran to where Jessica was sitting, partially hidden behind a wheel that had been blown completely away from the devastated bus.

"Daddy?" Her eyes were big and green and dry. "Is it really you?"

"Sweetheart," he exclaimed. Dropping to his knees, he stared at the sight of her. "Oh, sweetheart."

"I knew you'd come," she said simply, making no attempt to move.

Esther ran up, followed closely by Daniel Banks and Jim Brainard.

"Oh, Jessica, my darling sweetheart," she cried as she pushed past the bus wheel and halfway reached for her, then hesitated in shocked disbelief at the same sight that John was trying to absorb.

"Hi, Mom," Jessica said softly. Still, there were no tears. No outward emotion at all. And, still, she did not move.

Jessica's shirt was not really a shirt anymore. It hung on her in tattered strips, barely covering the upper part of her body, with portions of borrowed underwear, now stained and soiled and bloody, peeping through. Her face was puffy and bleeding from a deep cut high on her forehead. Her lips were bruised and bleeding as well. There were scratches on her arms and one pant leg was torn almost entirely away. Dirt and grime covered what remained of her clothing. Several open scrapes and bruises were visible as well. Esther could see where tiny rock fragments had cut into the skin's surface.

"Are you all right, honey?" asked Esther, so stunned by her first sight of Jessica that now she was afraid to do what she had dreamed and yearned of doing for so long.

As her rescuers peered down at Jessica, their gaze was drawn to what she was holding. With a tender stroke, she brushed the cheek of a little child that cuddled silently in her arms, staring up at them.

"Sir, we've got to get out of here." Both drivers had joined the group, M-16s at the ready, warily scanning the nearby rooftops and windows.

"I know," replied Daniel Banks. He turned to John and said, "Is your daughter able to walk? We've got to move it. We're targets here."

"Can you walk, honey?" John asked, reaching out to Jessica.

"Yes, I can walk."

John and Esther helped her to her feet. Her legs were wobbly and she started to sag. John put his arm around her waist.

"Here, sweetheart," Esther said, reaching for the child. "Let me take her."

"No," Jessica's voice was sharp as she tightened her hold on the girl.

"But we need to give her to someone."

"No, I can't give her to anybody. I promised."

"Come on," Banks shouted, waving the group back toward the jeeps. "We've got to get out of here. We can sort everything out later."

Hersch crawled into the back of the lead jeep, along with Jim Brainard and Milton Creston. Daniel Banks settled in alongside his driver. Esther helped Jessica and the child into the back of the second jeep. The news team crowded in as well, while John joined the driver in front. They were on their way almost before John had time to climb in.

They were halfway across the square when another rocket-propelled grenade hit the top corner of the building directly in front of them. Seconds later, another craterlike hole erupted in the cobblestones, lifting the severed wheel of the demolished bus high in the air before dropping it harmlessly twenty feet away. Esther looked over her shoulder in horror as mud and rock rained down on the place where, only moments before, they had all been standing. Wrapping her arms around Jessica, she hung on as the jeep skidded past the corner, leaving the square and its horrible carnage behind.

Esther could not turn her eyes away from Jessica. She could hardly believe that, at long last, her precious daughter was right here in her arms. A wave of tears ran down her cheeks. Jessica looked up at her mother and smiled weakly.

"I'm sorry, Mom," she said.

Esther wanted to speak, but was too overcome with emotion. She opened her coat and tried to wrap part of it around Jessica's shoulders. Her arm tightened around Jessica and with her other hand she hung on for both of them as they sped through the city. Every few seconds now, artillery shells, mortar rounds, and rocket fire rained down on the city's central district. Straight ahead, dirt, brick, and pieces of roof tile sprayed in all directions from a solid hit on an apartment building. Esther ducked her head, covering Jessica and the little child with her body as they passed by.

Each minute felt like an hour, until the sounds of the shelling gradually faded behind them. At least, Esther hoped they were in the clear. John kept looking back, smiling and every once in a while giving a reassuring "okay" signal with his hand. Esther noticed him looking at the child in Jessica's arms and was sure that he had as many questions as she did. There would be time enough for that later.

A sigh of relief escaped her lips as they turned off the main road toward the airport parking lot. But the jeeps did not stop there; they kept going around to the back of the terminal, pulling to a halt near the waiting room exit they had left an eternity ago. In a matter of seconds they were inside the empty building.

Daniel Banks was instructing the old baggage attendant to heat water for some tea. Milton Creston was busy talking on the field telephone to someone. The others had crowded around Jessica, while the film crew kept on doing what film crews do.

"How is your daughter?" Banks asked, pushing in alongside John and Esther.

"She looks very thin," answered Esther. Her voice filled with greater concern now that she had a chance to really look at her. "She has several cuts and bruises. There do not seem to be any broken bones or life-threatening wounds, though. I think she's in shock. And wherever she got this little girl . . . she won't turn loose of her."

Creston tapped his boss on the shoulder. "The plane is coming in now, sir. They figure to be on the ground just long enough to release their load. Thirty minutes max, maybe less. We've got to be ready when they are. It's our last chance to get out."

Banks turned to Esther. "Mrs. Cain, ask her about the child. We've got to decide what to do with her."

Esther nodded and moved in close, kneeling in front of Jessica.

"Honey, are you feeling okay?"

Jessica nodded.

Esther looked at her daughter carefully. Her green eyes were dull, lacking the luster and snap that Esther remembered.

"Who is this child, sweetheart? How did you get her?"

Jessica stared at the floor without responding.

"Honey, our plane is due in a few minutes. We've got to know more about the girl so that we can help find her parents."

"They're dead."

"What?"

"They're dead. So is her brother."

"Were they . . . in the bus?"

Jessica nodded, her countenance sober as she looked at her mother. Her eyes flickered at the mention of the bus. The little child in her arms never once whimpered or made a sound.

"Her name is Jasmina."

Esther saw the child blink at the mention of her name and look up at Jessica.

"How do you know that? Did you know her parents?"

Jessica shook her head.

"I was talking to the . . . soldier?" Jessica spoke deliberately, as if questioning her own memories as they replayed in her mind in slow motion. "I took the chance . . . and talked with him, and asked if he would help me."

The others were listening silently, encircling her as she recounted what had happened. Esther wondered what she meant by "took the chance," but said nothing. Her awareness was intensifying with the realization that she had no idea what her little girl had endured.

"And he did help you, didn't he?" coached Esther, her hand lightly touching Jessica's bruised knee.

"Yes. He was French, but I knew he spoke English because I heard him."

Esther wanted to ask when and where, but bit her lip. *Later perhaps. Let her go on now.* She waited.

"I told him my name, and he looked surprised. He said that someone had called earlier and asked them to watch out for me."

The others in the group looked over at Banks questioningly. This was news. He motioned with his head toward Creston and smiled.

"We were standing back, away from the bus, when her daddy got off. He was holding her in one arm, you know, like Daddy used to do Jenny? It reminded me of that exactly—of Daddy and Jenny." She looked up at John, and then back to Esther. Her words were coming more rapidly. "He waved to us. I guess he wanted to tell the soldier something. He was only a little ways away when the bus blew up. There was no warning or anything. It just . . . blew up." Jessica looked away, biting her lip at the memory.

The newsman peered through the eye of his camera, taking everything in. His lens even caught his coworker brushing away an unanticipated tear.

"He . . . and the soldier . . . were between us and the explosion. I was knocked backwards, but I landed on my side, I think." She glanced down at her leg, with its cuts and scratches.

"There was this heavy weight on top of me. It was . . ."

Her voice cracked and she cleared her throat. Tears spilled down onto her cheeks now as she looked at Esther. "It was . . . the soldier, Mom. He said he would help . . . and then he got killed."

No one moved, mesmerized by what they were seeing and hearing.

"When I pushed him off of me, I saw the bus. Pieces of it were still falling all around. And there was her daddy. He was . . . hurt very badly. But he moved, so I crawled over to him, to see if I could help. And that's when I saw her. She was still in his arms. I guess he protected her like the soldier did me.

"I knelt beside him and asked him what I could do, and he spoke to me in English. He said, 'We are all dead now. No one is left. Please take my little girl. Her name is Jasmina. It is her grandmother's name. You must care for her now. Get her out of here,' he said. 'Will you do this for me?' I didn't know what to say. So, I said, 'Yes.' Then he . . . he pushed her over to me, and he made me promise. 'Please,' he said, 'you must promise.' Those were his words. So, I picked her up, and I promised."

Her voice quivered as she looked up at her parents.

"And then he died."

Jessica lifted the little girl until they looked into one another's eyes. Tears ran freely down Jessica's cheeks now, causing others to look away in order to gather in their own emotions.

"I promised. Daddy, I promised."

128

LOCAL TIME 1055

Milton Creston was torn between the mesmerizing scene unfolding before him in the airport waiting room and the status of the C-130, sitting on the tarmac as indefensible as the last bald eagle in a forest full of trophy hunters. It was against the rules of engagement for either side to target a UN plane, because they were known to be ferrying only emergency food and medical supplies as part of an agreed-upon humanitarian relief mission. But Creston was sure that the "hunters" were not interested in the "rules" of war and would not be able to resist bagging such a "trophy" once they had it in range.

His eyes moved from Jessica and the solemn little Croatian girl to the window at the precise moment the first rocket shell hit, about two hundred yards away, throwing dirt and brush high into the air.

"Sir," Creston tugged at Banks's arm, "that round was meant for us. Has to be an MLRS in the area."

The consul general's brow wrinkled with concern as he walked to the window. He saw the men who had been unloading supplies hurrying to the waiting trucks. One of the UN drivers, who had been speaking over the radio pack, began motioning to Banks and pointing to the airplane. Banks nodded and turned to the others.

"Excuse me for interrupting," he said, almost apologetically but with a tone of urgency that made everyone look his way. "It is time. I must ask you all to follow our drivers to the vehicles you were riding in a little while ago. Move quickly and don't leave anything behind, because, ladies and gentlemen, we are not coming back."

Everyone stood and began shuffling toward the exit. Esther wrapped a protective arm around Jessica, who in turn was wrapping a protective arm around Jasmina.

"What about the little girl?" Esther asked, looking up at Banks.

"Bring her along. We'll see what we can do for her in Zagreb."

John turned to follow the others. As he did, the old man who had served them tea extended his hand. John took it, looking first at his wrinkled face, then questioningly at Banks. Banks shook his head. John's gaze returned to the man again, not knowing what to say. The old baggage carrier's eyes said it all.

"Thank you," John said finally, gripping the man's hand tightly. "We are all in God's hands. I will pray for you."

The old man lowered his eyes and nodded, a pathetic smile of resignation flashing briefly across his face, as they released their handshake.

"John?" It was Banks who had called him. The rest were following Esther and Jessica through the door.

"I know," John responded, walking swiftly to catch up with the others. "I know that we can't save the whole world. It's just that, right this minute, the whole world seems to be living and dying in that old man's eyes."

"Unfortunately, you're right. The difference is that he knows."

"Knows what?"

"Wait. Let me show you something." Banks turned back to the old man. "Would you like to come with us? We will take you to Zagreb on the plane. Come on."

The old man licked his lips, as if savoring the idea, then motioned with his hands and bowed his head. Finally, eyes glistening with sadness, he looked up and shook his head, lifting his shoulders in a helpless shrug.

Banks waved understandingly and pushed John forward through the exit.

"He doesn't want to come?" John said, his voice filled with disbelief.

"I can't answer that. Probably, under other circumstances, he might enjoy the ride to Zagreb. But Split is his home. It is the only life that he knows. And this is his war," Banks answered. "You have just won yours. So let's get you out of here while we still can."

A second artillery round fell in the parking lot on the opposite side of the terminal building. John, Hersch, and Jim joined Creston and Banks with quick handshakes and a "thank you" to the two UN drivers, who were staying behind. Moments later, the group hurried up into the belly of the C-130, unable to hear anything but the scream of the plane's powerful engines as the pilot prepared for takeoff. The plane began moving even before the cargo door was fully closed.

"Welcome aboard," two UN soldiers said politely but without smiling. They were all business as they directed their human cargo to fold-down seats attached to the sides of the plane, and helped them secure their safety harnesses. There were no windows to look through, nothing to see, only the movement of the huge bird as it picked up speed, and finally the moment of liftoff. No one spoke.

At first, everyone was holding their breath, as if not breathing might somehow thwart the unseen hunters who were no doubt taking aim at the eagle in its moment of final flight.

As they reached altitude and began to level off, there was a collective sigh, but still no one spoke. They stared across the empty void, each one replaying in silence the events of the past few hours.

Finally, Daniel Banks broke the silence.

"Well, my friends," he said, unfastening his harness and standing up, "this has been a most interesting day at the office."

129

SATURDAY, 17 DECEMBER, AFTERNOON
ZAGREB

At the airport in Zagreb, John and the others said good-bye to the CNN news team, who were anxious to be off to file an amazing story. The rest of the group climbed into a pair of waiting automobiles and was whisked away along a main highway leading into the city.

When they arrived at the consul general's house, Dorothy Banks welcomed them inside and shooed them all toward a crackling fire in a large stone fireplace. The rest of the afternoon was spent relaxing, bathing, and conversing quietly. Later, a small buffet was served by a Croatian maid in the dining room.

A local physician was called to examine Jessica and the child. While John and Esther watched, he carefully removed bits of dirt and stone that were embedded in the skin of both children. He cleaned the small wound under Jessica's eye and the deeper cut along her hairline, advising them that stitches might be necessary. He offered to do the work at the emergency room in a nearby local hospital, but when Daniel Banks informed him that they would be transferred to Germany the next morning, the doctor encouraged them to wait. Supplies and personnel were extremely short in Zagreb's medical facilities and better care could be anticipated in Germany.

It was six o'clock by the time Jessica had eaten part of a sandwich and finished drinking a glass of cold milk. Esther saw to it that she was tucked in for the night, sitting awhile on the edge of her bed, answering questions about friends at home and filling in a few details about events there over the past months. Jessica offered little about her own harrowing experiences, and Esther wisely chose not to press for information. She knew that would come later. Instead, Jessica insisted on sleeping with Jasmina, who had yet to utter a word or sound but clung to Jessica.

Retreating from the bedroom, Esther joined John in front of the fireplace, where he was talking to Daniel and Dorothy Banks. Jim stood by the sofa on which Hersch stretched out his leg. They were laughing and talking like old friends after a second pass at the potato salad, fresh bread, and cheese.

"How are the children?" asked John, taking Esther's hand.

"They are resting. I'll check on them in a few minutes. Jessica insisted on sleeping with Jasmina." Esther looked questioningly at the others. "What is going to happen to her?"

"I will arrange for a local orphanage to take her tomorrow," answered Daniel Banks. "They are overcrowded, but given the circumstances, it is the best we can do for her. If there are any relatives, we'll try to find them."

"Jessica says that there are not."

"Perhaps an aunt or a cousin will surface after this is over."

"If that were possible, which seems unlikely, when would it happen? How long will she have to live in an overcrowded orphanage?"

The consul general hesitated a moment, his eyes steady on Esther.

"What are you suggesting, Mrs. Cain?"

Esther gave John an imploring look.

"I think what Esther is suggesting," said John, placing his arm around her shoulders, "is that maybe the child could come live with us."

"You mean take her to the States?"

"That is where we live," John responded with a smile. "I think it's a good idea. What do you say?"

Esther sighed with relief. "Are you sure, dear?" she asked.

"I'm sure," he answered, enfolding Esther in his arms. They told Daniel and Dorothy Banks of the loss of Jennifer, their youngest daughter, who had been gone for well over a year. "No one will ever take Jenny's place in our hearts, you understand, but this girl, . . . well, we're in a position to help her. She needs a home and we can provide her with one. After all, Jessica did promise her father. And besides, she belongs."

"Why do you say that?" asked Daniel Banks.

"Her name begins with the letter *J*, just like the rest of our children."

The four of them laughed at this bit of reasoning.

Daniel Banks looked over at his wife. "Didn't I tell you that these people are truly amazing?"

She smiled and nodded, taking Esther's hand.

"I'm with you," Dorothy said. "If you really want to take her, then I think you should do it. You can work it out, can't you, Dan?"

"I'm not sure that I can on such short notice, but I do have a very competent attaché. If anyone can get permission to let this child out of the country with you in the morning, Creston can. I'll call him right now and get the process started. Excuse me." He turned and headed for a small den that opened onto the hall.

"You've been through a great deal during the past day or two, to say nothing of the past few months," Dorothy Banks said to the Cains. "Would you like to retire early? I overheard Dan say that a NATO plane will be here to pick you up first thing in the morning."

"That sounds like a good idea, Dorothy," agreed Esther. "Actually, I'm exhausted. I think my nerves are finally catching up to reality and are starting to ask, 'Where have we just been?'"

The others laughed again as Herschel Towner and Jim Brainard joined them in front of the fireplace. Just then, the consul general returned from making his call.

"Creston is working on it, even as we speak," he said reassuringly.

"What's this that he's workin' on?" asked Jim. John quickly explained what was being attempted.

"I'm going to repeat my suggestion that you all retire early this evening," said Dorothy Banks, setting her teacup down on a small table. "Your beds are ready and you will need to be up . . . how early is their flight, dear?"

"Six o'clock takeoff. We couldn't get you out before then."

"Then that means getting up at four. I'll have the coffee made."

"Please," Esther protested. "You've done more than enough already."

Dorothy Banks smiled. "It's been our privilege to have you as our guests. Now, you will be awakened at four o'clock. Coffee will be ready at four-thirty. You will leave here at five and be at the airport in plenty of time. In any event, I'm sure they won't leave without you."

130

SUNDAY, 18 DECEMBER, LOCAL TIME 0400
ZAGREB

At four o'clock sharp, the Cains, Hersch, and Jim Brainard were gently awakened by the maid. A half hour later, one by one, they straggled out into the dining room where Dorothy Banks was scurrying about in housecoat and slippers, setting out coffee and cups alongside what looked like home-baked breakfast rolls.

Jessica looked strained, a hint of dark circles under her eyes, as she stood in the doorway holding Jasmina's hand.

"Here, honey," said Esther, offering her a breakfast roll. "You need something to eat."

Jessica shook her head.

"You have to eat something, darling,"

"Mom, what's going to happen to Jasmina?"

Esther started to answer, then stopped, glancing over at John. Just then, Daniel Banks strode into the room.

"Good morning, everyone," he said cheerily. "Your plane has arrived and is refueling even as we speak. We'll leave for the airport in thirty minutes. Okay?"

He poured himself a cup of coffee and walked over to where Jessica and Jasmina were standing.

"Good morning, young lady," he said to Jessica. "How are you and your little friend here?"

"Much better, thank you."

"Jessica, your mother and father talked last night about the possibility of taking Jasmina with you to America. What would you say to that?"

Jessica stared in disbelief at the consul general for a long moment, then at her mother and father.

"What a cool idea," she exclaimed excitedly. "Can we really do that?"

"We've been working on it and have been able to arrange for temporary custody and an exit visa. That's no small miracle, let me tell you. Things are so chaotic around here at the moment that the powers that be seemed glad to be of service. It was too late last night to do very much, but we've gone that far, with the proviso that if other family members are discovered still alive, they will be given opportunity to ask for her. Do you know her last name?"

"I'm sorry, sir. Her father didn't tell me her last name."

"That makes it more difficult. Maybe even impossible. We'll do the appropriate things here to try to locate living relatives, but my guess is that this little lady needs a new family. And from the looks of things, it appears she has one."

"All right!" Jessica exclaimed. Kneeling down, she rested her hands gently on the child's shoulders. "Jasmina, Mr. Banks says that you can come home with us, okay?"

The little girl stared, uncomprehendingly, into Jessica's sparkling green eyes.

"You probably don't understand a word I am saying, do you?"

The girl's eyes never wavered from Jessica, as if there was no one else in the room. Slowly, she lifted her hand until it touched Jessica's face. She held it there for a long moment, then lifted her other hand until both were pressed against Jessica's cheeks. Everyone watched with interest as she moved her hands away and took a step forward, laying her head against Jessica's chest, reaching as far around her as her little arms could.

"I think Jasmina understands you just fine, Jessica," Daniel Banks said, clearing his throat. "I think she is looking forward to having an older sister like you. Now, let's all get something to munch on before we have to leave. You have a date at our army hospital in Frankfurt."

Jessica looked inquiringly at Esther and John.

"They're going to give you a physical checkup and take care of the rest of these cuts and bruises," John said reassuringly.

"And they're going to want to ask you some questions, Jessica," Daniel Banks said. "Lots of them, I'll bet. We're all interested to know where you've been and how you have managed these past months."

Something flashed over Jessica's countenance for an instant. A shadow. John saw it and wondered.

"Dad, can I talk to you and Mom for a minute?" There was something in her voice, a confessional tone that John recognized. Whatever it was, she felt that it was important.

"Sure, sweetheart," he responded gently, glancing over at Daniel Banks. "May we use your den?"

"Of course, right over here," he said, leading them to the open doorway.

Jasmina held onto Jessica's finger and padded along beside her. "I'll shut this and let you have your privacy. But don't be long."

"Thanks," John nodded appreciatively.

Jessica sat down on the sofa. Jasmina crawled up beside her and laid her head on Jessica's lap. John and Esther turned two chairs around and sat facing the girls.

"What is it, hon?" asked John.

"I . . . I'm not sure where to start. But I guess I should tell you the most important thing. I haven't told this to anyone else, because who would believe me? I'm only a kid."

John and Esther listened without responding.

"Do you know about the tape?" Her voice quivered at the memory of that helpless moment in front of the camera.

"Yes, we do, honey," answered Esther. "I've seen it, but your dad hasn't. It was something they forced you to say, though, honey. There was nothing you could do about it."

Jessica sat quietly. A tear dropped onto her cheek. "Thanks," she said simply. "It was hard."

She paused again, arranging her thoughts carefully, trying to recall exactly what had been said in her presence on that last night in the house in Iran.

"I didn't want to, but . . . this man . . . his name is Dosha. He was there and made me do it in front of a camera. Then, afterward, I overheard their conversation. I think they thought I had passed out, but I hadn't. Well, almost, I guess. But I was able to overhear some things, too. They were speaking in English, which was kind of unusual, so I could understand what was being said. There was a group of people there. Maybe it was the only language they all knew. I heard them talking about plans for killing a lot of people."

"Jessica, honey, if you are about to tell us something that involves the welfare of people or the security of our nation, maybe we should invite Mr. Banks to come and listen."

"I don't know if he'll believe me."

"I'm sure he will believe you," John said. "And it sounds like he needs to hear what you have to say, so that he can tell the right people what you know."

"Okay," she said, shrugging her shoulders.

John opened the door and motioned to Daniel Banks. A moment later, the consul general was inside, listening carefully as Jessica reiterated what she had already told John and Esther. Then she continued her story.

"The man with the scar, the guy named Dosha? He talked about how they would spend the ransom money, and that he wanted even more money. When they asked him how he was going to follow through on the things he made me read, he said that their freedom fighters—that's what he called them—were already inside the country and prepared. I guess some of them are college students, as well as others who have gotten into America illegally. What was it he called them? Politics silent?"

Banks smiled. "Was it political asylum?"

"That's it. Political asylum. Oh, yes, and he said some of them were businessmen or shopkeepers or something, too, but he didn't say any names or anything. At least not that I remember. He said that they did not have a nuclear bomb—'not yet' was the way he put it, but that they do have a secret weapon of some sort. This secret weapon is supposed to make thousands die when they destroy an entire city somewhere.

"They asked him questions about what city it was . . . but he never mentioned it by name. This guy said it would be destroyed, though, and tens of thousands—those were his exact words—tens of thousands would die. I guess they had been talking about this place before they came to my cell."

"You were in a cell?" asked Esther, horrified.

"Not like in the movies, Mom. It was really a room with a cot where they kept me by myself. I could never leave. I was guarded all the time, so, I called it a cell."

"You were right in doing so," Banks said. "It helps you keep the right view of things in your mind."

"Did they say anything more about this city?" questioned John. "Anything that would help identify what location they have targeted?"

Jessica shook her head.

"I've tried to remember, since then. Like, you know, the exact words that I heard them say? I didn't pass out, but I guess I was close to it. I sort of faded in and out for a while. I'm sorry."

"That's okay, young lady," Banks said, patting her shoulder. "You are a heroine of the highest order in my book. Now, let's get you out of here and on your way to Germany."

"There is one other thing. I don't know if I mixed it up or if this is what that Dosha guy really said. He said something about the secret weapon being simple and silent. Those were his words. Then he said something like 'that which flows from under the temple will poison the earth.' I remembered that one because it was so weird. It didn't make any sense."

The others were silent, absorbed in their thoughts.

"That's all you remember?" asked John, taking her hand in his.

Jessica shrugged again. "I wish there was more, but that's it."

"Okay. Time to go, everybody," Banks's voice took on an authoritative tone. "We don't want to keep the pilot waiting. As soon as I get back to the office, I'll call Washington and bring them up-to-date. And, Jessica, you are an incredible young lady. You make me proud to be an American. I hope that I'll see you again someday soon. Let me warn you, though. They are going to ask lots of questions in the hospital at Frankfurt, so be prepared. I know you'll do your best and that's all anyone can ask. You'll do fine."

"Thank you, Mr. Banks. And, thanks for coming to get me yesterday. I . . . I didn't know what to do. When the bus blew up . . . I thought I was finally going to die. I was so scared. How could I keep running, now that Jasmina was with me. I couldn't go off and just leave her. So, I was praying and asking Jesus for help again, to give me more courage and tell me what to do, you know? And when I opened my eyes, there was Daddy and Mom and the rest of you. It's still hard to believe. I really thought I was dreaming."

Daniel Banks smiled and put his hand on Jessica's shoulder. "Well, it's no dream, young lady. It's real. You are finally back where you belong, with your mother and father. You also have a brother back home, I understand?"

"Yes, and I can't wait to punch him out."

"I'm sure he's looking forward to that," Banks laughed. "Okay, let's get on with it."

Each of the guests thanked Dorothy Banks again for her hospitality as they stepped into the two waiting automobiles. Twenty-five minutes later, they were boarding a U.S. military plane at the Zagreb airport. A flight attendant in military uniform greeted them as they entered and introduced them to an army physician and a registered nurse who had been awaiting their arrival as well. They offered Jessica a place to lie down, which she declined, wanting instead to sit between her parents during the flight. Maybe later, if she became tired, she would lie down.

Jessica sensed that once again she had become the center of attention, only, this time it was different. She was surrounded by family and friends who loved her, not by the enemy. Her body was sore literally from top to bottom. She had slept fitfully through the night, her nerves still on edge, still tense, ready to run at the first sound of danger. But it didn't matter. She had never felt better in her life.

PART NINE

We—with God's help—call on every Muslim who believes in God and wishes to be rewarded to comply with God's order to kill the Americans and plunder their money wherever and whenever they find it. We also call on the Muslim ulema [community], leaders, youths, and soldiers to launch the raid on Satan's U.S. troops and the devil's supporters allying with them and to displace those who are behind them so that they may learn a lesson.

—Declaration of War by Osama bin Laden,
together with leaders of the World Islamic Front
for the Jihad Against the Jews and the Crusaders
(Al-Jabhah al-Islamiyyah al-'Alamiyyah
Li-Qital al-Yahud Wal-Salibiyyin),
Afghanistan, February 23, 1998

Those who disbelieve, among the People of the Book and among the Polytheists, will be in hellfire, to dwell therein (for aye). They are the worst of creatures.

—The Qur'an
Surah 98: Bayyinah:6

"Then neither do I condemn you," Jesus declared. "Go now and leave your life of sin."

—The Holy Bible
John 8:11

GUNMAN TERRORIZES LOCAL MALL

SEATTLE—A mall security guard, four other adults, and three children were killed yesterday when a gunman ran into the Tall Pine Shopping Mall, spraying bullets from two automatic weapons into a crowd of patrons waiting to see Santa Claus. The man also detonated two grenades in the center of the mall, shattering windows and wounding twenty-four bystanders, two critically. Miraculously, no one was killed in the grenade attack.

Witnesses reported that the lone assailant drove up to a mall entrance and ran inside, carrying two AK-47 rifles and the two grenades. The security guard was shot while attempting to stop the attack. Police arrived on the scene within minutes and tried to take the gunman into custody as he ran from the mall. When he refused to surrender and pointed his weapon in the direction of the officers, they opened fire, killing him instantly. Authorities were unable to identify the gunman, who was carrying no identification.

Within an hour of the attack, a caller claiming to be affiliated with the Palestinian Islamic Jihad claimed responsibility and threatened even greater violence if the U.S. government does not cease its financial and military aid to Israel.

131

TUESDAY, 20 DECEMBER, LOCAL TIME 1015
FRANKFURT, GERMANY

After two days in the U.S. Army hospital in Frankfurt, Jessica was beginning to feel stronger. The army doctors were thorough in their examination of the former hostage's physical condition. They confirmed, among other things, that she had not been sexually assaulted, nor had any bones been broken. She had lost at least fifteen pounds during her ordeal, however, and required several stitches to close the wound along her forehead, as well as three small sutures to close the cut under her eye. There were bruises on her back, left arm, and leg; a cut along the left knee that required stitches; as well as numerous scrapes and abrasions on her back and chest. Several more bits of stone were removed from her leg and the wounds were carefully cleaned and dressed.

Esther was escorted to the nearby PX, where she purchased clothes for Jessica and Jasmina. Both girls were provided beds in the same room, but Jasmina slept most of the time with Jessica. Jessica remained in bed during the first day, except for short walks along the hall, and beyond to the counseling center. During the second afternoon, she went with her parents for a walk outside on the hospital grounds while Jasmina was taking a nap.

The psychologists who examined Jessica were pleased and somewhat surprised by her strong and stable mental condition. There were signs of anger and depression, which the doctors deemed appropriate and normal behavioral responses, considering what she had been through, but no signs of anxiety attacks, inordinate fear, or withdrawal. She spoke thoughtfully, and seemed at ease with the mental probing.

During these interviews, John and Esther were silent witnesses, sitting near the window, as two doctors, a female FBI agent, a male member of the CIA, and a representative of the State Department, posed questions and recorded answers regarding the harrowing story of their daughter's last three months as a hostage. The Cains could hardly believe it was their little girl who was sitting across from them, recounting her agonizing experiences with such calmness and candor.

Each interview was immediately transcribed and sent to intelligence analysts in Washington, D.C. Of particular concern was the information that had already been forwarded to the State Department by Consul General Banks in Zagreb regarding another city about to be targeted by terrorists. After the incident in Boston, no one was willing to write off the possibility as simply the overactive imagination of a twelve-year-old.

Of special interest was the cryptic phrase attributed to Marwan Dosha by Jessica: "*That which flows from under the temple will poison the earth.*" The intelligence analysts were busy trying to decipher the code.

Israeli authorities increased security around Jerusalem's volatile Temple site, in anticipation of a possible attempt by the Palestinian Islamic Jihad to finish the job that had been thwarted in September. In the United States, security was also increased around the Mormon Temple in Salt Lake City.

The State Department arranged to fly the Cain entourage back to the United States on a military aircraft. But then Lufthansa, Germany's impeccable national airline, offered the group free first-class accommodations back to San Francisco on one of its flights. John, who had never flown first-class, was eager to accept the offer.

"Just think of the money we'll save the taxpayers," he said.

John and Esther agreed to give the news media a thirty-minute press conference at the hospital. They thanked people around the world for their generous outpouring of love and compassion during Jessica's ordeal. It was agreed that Jessica would not be granting any interviews before returning home.

132

By the time their plane touched down at San Francisco International Airport and began taxiing toward the terminal building, John and Esther and the others had been informed that a contingent of local and national news teams was waiting in the airport, jockeying for position to get pictures of the twelve-year-old escaped hostage, the tiny Croatian refugee, the former member of the Navy SEALs who had led the Iran rescue attempt, the man who had helped to save the city of Boston from disaster in September, and John and Esther Cain, the parents who had faced overwhelming odds to bring their family together again. Put it all together with Christmas just around the corner and it was just too good of a story to pass up.

As they were ushered off the plane and into the VIP lounge, John was the first to see Jeremy standing off to the side. Jeremy and Jessica spotted each other at the same time. With a squeal, Jessica ran toward her brother, leaped into his arms, and wrapped both feet around his legs.

"Oh, Jeremy!" she shrieked. "I am *so* happy to see you!"

"Hey, sis," Jeremy said huskily, both arms around her in a bear hug. "You are a piece of work. We send you off on a little vacation and look at you. You don't come home for three months. Some people will do anything to get out of school."

"Oh, you . . . man, you!" she exclaimed, releasing her grip. Standing up in front of him, she pounded his chest with her fist. "I missed you so *much*, big brother."

"I missed you, too, sis," Jeremy's eyes were wet as he blinked back tears and hugged her again. "I wish I could have been there for you."

"Yeah, me, too."

After a long moment, they released each other again.

"Hi, Mom. Hi, Dad." Jeremy hugged each of them. "You guys are looking good. And Mr. Brainard, you made sure they all came home, didn't you?"

"That's right, young fella," Jim responded with a hug of his own. "They couldn't have done it without me. 'Course this fella here helped a little, too. Jeremy, I want you to meet Herschel Towner."

"Hi, Mr. Towner. I'm pleased to meet you. I've heard Mom and Dad talk about you."

"Well, don't you believe anything your dad says. I'm really a nice guy."

"And look what we brought home," Esther said. "Well, actually, what Jessica brought home. This is Jasmina."

Esther held her up so that Jeremy could see her.

"She's beautiful, Mom."

Jeremy held out his hands, but Jasmina buried her face in Esther's neck. "She'll come to you in time. All this is just too much too soon. It wasn't until the second day in the hospital in Frankfurt that she finally left Jessica and sat in my lap. She still hasn't said anything. Not a word . . . since her parents . . . died."

Jeremy put his arm around Jessica's shoulder and John saw Esther's countenance turn suddenly sober. He knew what she was thinking by the expression on her face.

So much pain in the world. So many who have lost so much. And yet, here we are, together again, with lots of love and hope for the future. God is faithful and good.

John shifted his gaze and nodded at an airline employee who waited patiently by the door. "Okay, gang, the sooner we face the music outside, the sooner we can all go home," he admonished genially.

At the door, he paused.

"Here, honey," he said, taking Jessica's hand. "You go first."

"No, Dad, please."

"It's okay. I'm right here with you. We're all here with you."

Jessica looked plaintively at the others, but no one offered to argue on her behalf or take her place. She took a deep breath and brushed her hand nervously along the length of her hair. Exhaling, she looked up at her father and nodded. He smiled and opened the door.

A cheer went up and flashes went off from cameras everywhere. A sudden, unexpected panic took Jessica's breath away as she stared into the abundance of lenses and smiling faces. For a brief instant, she was back in her cell again. Voices shouting questions. People pushing and shoving.

John raised his hands above his head, signaling for quiet. It took at least a minute, but eventually the noise subsided.

"This is all very overwhelming," he began, stepping up to a phalanx of microphones. "We're happy to see you here . . . again. But as far as I'm concerned, we've got to stop meeting like this."

The laughter was spontaneous, followed by applause.

"On behalf of Jessica," he continued, "who has something she wants to say in a moment, and Esther, my wife, and my son, Jeremy, we want to thank you all for not letting our daughter be forgotten. You kept her face in print. You told her story on radio and TV, and followed us all the way. Without you, we might never have known this happy occasion. So, God bless you all, and thanks again for everything you've done."

The crowd cheered and applauded. Several bystanders held up hastily scrawled signs that read, "We love you, Jessica," and "Welcome home, Jessica!"

"Now I think our daughter, Jessica, has something she'd like to say."

The crowd cheered again as Jessica stepped up to the microphones.

"All right, Jessica!"

"Welcome home!"

"America loves you!"

The reporters began shouting questions all at once.

"How do you feel, Jessica? What was it like in Croatia? Tell us how you escaped."

Finally, John lifted his hands, once more signaling for quiet.

Jessica paused, gathering her nerve, then spoke in a quiet but steady voice.

"I want to say thank you, as well," she began. "I've been scared a lot during the last three months, but you guys are probably the worst."

There was more laughter but it quickly grew quiet again.

"I still don't know all that has been done to help me get home. I know my parents and my brother, Jeremy, worked hard. I guess a lot of other people did, too. I know that lots of people prayed, and I think that is what really did it. Jesus was with me all the time, though I have to confess that sometimes I felt so alone I wondered if he had forgotten where he put me."

Just then, Jessica saw two of her school friends, Amy Foster and Shawna Pickett, standing off to one side along with their parents. She waved to them.

"Hi, Amy. Hi, Shawna. I missed you guys so much. I just can't believe you're really here." Then, remembering where she was, with an excited giggle she turned her attention back to the camera. "These are my best friends at school. Before I left, I just took them for granted, like a lot of us do with our family and friends. That's one thing I will never do again. Family and friends are too important. Anyway, I just want to say thank you again to everyone. It feels so good to almost be home . . . I'm going to sleep in my own bed tonight, everybody, and it's going to feel *wonderful*."

The crowd erupted in applause, which went on for several moments. They grew silent again as Jessica remained in front of the cameras and microphones.

"I guess . . . well, there were times when I wasn't sure . . . it would ever happen again, you know? I know I'm a preacher's kid and all, and I'm only twelve, so I've got a lot to learn. But I want you all to know how much God has meant to me while I was a hostage. I thought I was a Christian before I left on this trip, and I guess I was. But I'm a different Christian now. And I hope that someday my life will make a difference in this world, even if it's only a little one.

"There is someone new in our family that I'd like to introduce to you and then I'll shut up. Once I get going, I'm quite a talker, as you can tell, and there hasn't been much opportunity to do it recently. It feels so good to be free to talk, that once I get started, it's hard to stop."

More laughter.

"This is Jasmina," said Jessica, turning and taking the little girl from Esther's arms.

Flashbulbs created a brief strobe effect as dozens of cameras clicked at once.

"Tonight," Jessica continued, "I'm going to my old home and my old, familiar bed. But Jasmina is going to her new home and a new bed, one that she's not seen before. Her family was killed by terrorists in Croatia, in the city where my parents found us.

"I have a little sister who died in an accident. Her name is Jenny. She was so beautiful. No one can ever replace her, and we'll never forget her. The fact is, we all still miss her a lot. But Jasmina is going to sleep in my little sister's bed tonight. We're really happy for that to be able to happen, but I think that Jenny will be the happiest one in our whole family when she looks down from heaven and sees her there. Maybe Jasmina is why I had to go through all of this. God knows when people need him. He knew when Jasmina needed someone and he let me be there for her, don't you think?"

The crowd was silent, totally focused on the winsome youngster and the small child she held in her arms. It was no longer a typical news conference or a media circus. People had become reflective. There were sniffles and damp eyes as those who were standing about considered Jessica's words.

Off to one side, a veteran reporter for a local news station summed up the scene for his viewers.

"Here in the international terminal at San Francisco Airport, a courageous young lady stands holding a little child. Defying the coercive forces of evil, her faith and fortitude refused to give up. Two children that evil intended to harm, but God intended it for good, in order to accomplish what needed to be done. These two youngsters have given back the gift of hope to at least one cynical, old newsman. I think I'll go to church this Sunday."

133

Wednesday, 21 December, local time 1530
San Mateo County, California

At exactly three-thirty, the rental car turned off Cañada Road, and drove through a gateway opening onto a small parking lot. Two men dressed in jeans and sport shirts got out of the car. One pulled a cardigan sweater over his head, the other a black jacket to ward off the chill in the air. They headed toward a tall monument that looked, for all purposes, like a well-preserved but displaced artifact from the ancient Roman Empire.

As they strode through the parklike setting, they were careful to observe everything about this place. To their right was a small but colorful garden of flowers, tiered above a series of circular steps. Between the garden and the monument lay a rectangular pool of water, lined with eight cypress trees on two sides and surrounded by lawn, giving the entrance to the area a soft, yet majestic appearance.

At the far end of the grove, directly in front of a high wire fence, stood a monument flanked by magnificent live oaks. A perfect circle of concrete and brick formed the platform surrounding an inner wall. Ten Corinthian pillars, each one reaching upward from identically carved bases, were separated from the cornice by handsomely carved capitals depicting the leaves of the Mediterranean acanthus herb.

High up inside the circular cornice, there had been carved the familiar Greek "key" design, together with a series of flowering wreaths. Because there were no corners on which to place a cornerstone, a tablet had been shaped into the inner wall, bearing the message:

ERECTED
MCMXXXVIII

The two men leaned over the wall and examined the scene below. Water ran steadily from a large tunnel into a simple, blue-green enclosure, and then out again along an above-ground concrete canal, finally disappearing over the weir, about a hundred yards beyond the fence. A locked gate in the fence held a large *No Trespassing* sign.

"It won't be necessary," the man in the sweater said, jerking his head toward the sign. "This will be perfect right here. Can you believe this? No security. Their most valuable natural resource and not even one guard."

The other man shook his head. "How do the Americans say . . . 'a piece of cake.'"

The first man chuckled and turned back to the wall for another look. He pointed to the opposite side of the monument. His partner nodded as they read the words engraved in stone,

"I GIVE WATERS IN THE WILDERNESS
AND RIVERS IN THE DESERT
TO GIVE DRINK TO MY PEOPLE."
ISA. XL

"Okay, let's go," he said, stretching away the initial tension he had felt in his back muscles. "We can do it all right where we are standing. It shouldn't take more than fifteen minutes to turn San Francisco back into a wilderness and a desert."

The pair returned along the gravel path to the car. As they backed up to turn around, another vehicle, carrying a man, a woman, and a child turned into the lot. The driver smiled and waved as he coasted past them toward a parking space. Both men waved back, pausing at the gate to read the sign one last time.

PULGAS TEMPLE
TERMINUS
HETCH HETCHY AQUEDUCT
SAN FRANCISCO
WATER DEPARTMENT

SCHOOL BUS IS TERRORISTS' LATEST TARGET

JERUSALEM—A busload of Israeli schoolchildren returning from an outing to Masada came under fire in an ambush yesterday afternoon on the outskirts of the city. Terrorists shot out the bus' tires and then raked the vehicle with heavy gunfire from automatic weapons. The driver, an armed guard, and fourteen children were killed in the attack. Nineteen children were wounded, two critically. Of the survivors, the most seriously injured were two thirteen-year-old boys who were shot trying to escape the bus. Both boys were taken to Hadasa Hospital's critical care unit and are expected to survive.

After the attack, the six assailants fled in a white minivan toward the city. Law enforcement units searched the area, but by nightfall no arrests had been made and no one had claimed responsibility for the attack. An Israeli spokesman said that the Palestinian Islamic Jihad is suspected of instigating the attack, and that Israel's military has been placed on standby alert.

SUICIDE BOMBER STRIKES MIAMI

MIAMI—A suicide bomber killed herself and eight passengers on a downtown Miami bus last night, the seventh act of terrorism inside the United States in the past week. Suicide bombers have also struck twice in London and four times inside Israel over the past eight days. All attacks have been attributed by authorities to the radical Palestinian Islamic Jihad. The group appears to have stepped up its efforts to terrorize Israeli, American, and British citizens in an all-out effort to win support for their demands.

In a statement released by the White House, the president again vowed that the American people would not bow to acts of terrorism by any individual or group. He is expected to address the nation this evening in a televised speech from the Oval Office.

134

FRIDAY, 23 DECEMBER, LOCAL TIME 1625
SAN MATEO COUNTY, CALIFORNIA

John merged from the on-ramp into the right lane on Highway 101 and headed in the direction of the San Mateo Bridge. Esther leaned back in her seat, scanning the handwritten list one last time. She creased it once and dropped it in her handbag, glancing over her shoulder at the array of boxes and bags in the back. It had been the only one-day Christmas shopping experience that she could remember since their first Christmas together. Hectic but efficient.

She closed her eyes. A nap would be nice. Before she could doze off, however, she felt the car slow and finally come to a stop.

"What's the problem?" she asked, sitting up to look around.

"No problem. Just the world's longest parking lot," John replied, drumming his fingers on the steering wheel. "We've caught the commute traffic. Plan on a late dinner."

Esther sighed and settled back, reaching for the San Francisco *Chronicle* they had picked up on the way out of the Stanford Shopping Center. "I'm really glad you don't have to drive in this mess every day, honey. Can you imagine?"

"I still like your idea that employers ought to let their people go home in alphabetical order, according to their last names," John said, laughing. "And I still say you should send your idea to the governor."

Esther punched him playfully on the arm and went back to reading the paper. John reached down to tune the radio to the all-news station, but turned it off again when a reporter began an in-depth analysis of the recent terrorist attacks.

"I don't need to hear any more about that right now," he grumbled. "And I guess I don't need their traffic reporter to tell me I'm stuck in a backup."

"John, look at this," Esther said. As the car continued to creep along the freeway, John glanced over at the newspaper page that Esther held out for him.

"Right here. Look."

John's eyes darted back and forth from the picture to the on-again, off-again taillights immediately in front of them. It appeared to be a monument of some kind.

"What is it?"

"The San Francisco Water District is preparing for a celebration next year commemorating the Hetch Hetchy water project."

"So?"

"So all the big California names are being invited to an event over here behind Redwood City. According to this article, it will happen 'at the place where San Francisco's citizens first cheered the long-awaited arrival of water as it spilled out into the waiting reservoir. It was a momentous occasion, the culmination of twenty years of politics and engineering. Today, pure mountain water still flows from under the Temple to the people of the Bay Area.'"

"Flows from where?" John asked.

"That's what this gazebo-like monument is called. The Pulgas Water Temple. Ever hear of it?"

"No."

"Well, apparently it marks the end of the line for water being transferred from the Sierra runoff into the San Francisco Water District reservoir system. According to this article, there are several reservoirs in the area. It doesn't say whether or not they are connected to each other, but I suppose they are. Anyway, the Hetch Hetchy water flows into Crystal Springs Lake. It's strange, though, don't you think?"

"Strange? How do you mean?"

"Doesn't the similarity strike you as being odd? Jessica quoted Marwan Dosha as saying 'that which flows from under the temple will poison the earth.' This article talks about water that 'flows from under the Temple.' You don't suppose . . ."

John gripped the steering wheel and stared straight ahead as they picked up speed.

Marwan Dosha. It's Christmas and still we can't forget about that clown and his crowd of terror merchants.

"John," said Esther, finally breaking the silence as she watched the lines around his eyes tighten, "what do you think?"

"I think it may be totally off the wall, but it's worth a call to the FBI. They've been covering everything from Jerusalem to Salt Lake City. Maybe we were wrong in thinking that Dosha was going after some holy site. Everybody has been concentrating on the 'temple' idea and passing up on the part about 'that which flows from under it,' because we've had no idea what it meant. I've wondered if maybe Jessica got it mixed up somehow, in the stress of what she was going through. But what if you're right? Maybe Dosha is planning to poison the city's water supply. How many cities do you suppose have 'water temples'?"

Esther was thoughtful for a moment. "I know of at least one," she said finally, staring at the picture on page three.

"Dosha said that his bribery program was going to last until the end of December," she continued. "At that time, if we had paid up, he would release Jessica. Of course, now we know that he had no intention of letting her go."

"So, thinking after the fact that Jessica might remember what he had said in her presence, he tried to kill her in Croatia," John interrupted, looking over at Esther. "Failing that, if you were him, what would you do?"

Esther pondered the question for a moment.

"For starters, if I really had a time frame that I intended to work within, I might toss it out and move the clock up so that I could accomplish what I'd set out to do before somebody figured it out and stopped me."

"Exactly," exclaimed John, gripping the steering wheel with growing excitement. "Now, we have no idea whether New York or Washington or Boston or wherever has their own 'water temple.' But here is one, right across the Bay from the place where Dosha struck once and failed three months ago. Maybe the attack on our church was just the opening phase of a coordinated, diabolical plan and not simply an isolated terrorist incident."

"And maybe we're just crazy with speculation," said Esther, folding the paper so that the picture was on top as she laid it down in her lap. "What if we blow the whistle and we're totally wrong?"

"On the other hand, perhaps . . . just perhaps . . . the Holy Spirit is prompting and guiding us in this," answered John. "What if God led you to read that article? If that were the case, then it is no coincidence and it is certainly not our paranoia, either. If this is the Lord giving us a warning, then we've got to contact the FBI."

Esther gazed silently into the growing darkness outside the car. All vehicles had their lights on now and she had to hold her watch up closely, in order to check the time.

"How long before we get home?" she asked, finally.

"In this traffic? Probably forty-five minutes. Why?"

"Because if I was Marwan Dosha, and I was hurrying to do something that would strike fear and gain the most worldwide attention, I think I know when that would be."

John looked across at Esther, waiting.

"Christmas Day might be a good time, don't you think?"

John nodded thoughtfully, letting the impact of her reasoning work its way in.

"And," she added reflectively, "Christmas Eve might even be better."

135

"Hello, Federal Bureau of Investigation. How may I direct your call?"

"Hello. My name is John Cain. I am the senior pastor at Calvary Church in Baytown."

"Oh, yes, Reverend Cain, and congratulations on your daughter's safe return."

"Thank you. Would it be possible for me to speak to Special Agent Duane Webber?"

"I'm sorry, sir. Agent Webber left about two hours ago and will not be returning until after the holiday."

"Is there someone else that I might speak with? This is in regard to the terrorist Marwan Dosha."

"Paul Danversen is the Assistant Special Agent-in-Charge. I'll see if he's available. One moment please, while I put you on hold."

John waited. An eventual look at his watch told him that a minute had passed while he listened impatiently for some human response.

"Hello," a voice boomed suddenly into his ear. "Danversen here."

"Hello, Agent Danversen. This is John Cain, from Calvary Church in Baytown."

"How do you do? We've not had the pleasure of meeting, but congratulations on getting your daughter home safely."

"Thanks."

"I understand you want to discuss our friend, Mr. Dosha."

"Yes, my wife and I have come up with a theory that we think is worth troubling you about."

"Before we continue, Reverend Cain, would you please give me your social security number and your driver's license number. I think that I recognize your voice from television, but we've had a rash of calls in the last few days, what with all the recent problems around the country. It's only a formality, but I need to confirm that I am indeed speaking to the right person."

"I understand," replied John, reeling off the memorized numbers.

"Okay, thanks. Now, what is it you have for us regarding Dosha?"

John began laying out his and Esther's suspicions. Danversen listened attentively, breaking in twice to ask questions.

"You were reading a newspaper? And all this just sort of came to you?"

"I know it may sound far-fetched, Mr. Danversen, but we can't help but think that there may be something to this. If we are correct, and Dosha is plotting to do something to our area or to one of our nation's other water supplies, then someone needs to act right away."

"Okay, I hear you. Tell me again what that phrase was that your daughter heard him say?"

"'That which flows from under the temple will poison the earth.' Those were Dosha's exact words, according to Jessica. And this statement was made with regard to a specific city."

"But no city was named?"

"None that she remembers."

"All right, Reverend Cain. I'm going to be in touch with Special Agent-in-Charge Duane Webber and tell him about your idea. If I need you, how can I be in touch?"

John gave him the phone number and thanked him for his time. When he hung up, Esther looked at him expectantly.

"I don't know if he bought it or not, but he promised to get in touch with his boss and talk it over. We've done all we can."

They sat together on the sofa and watched Jeremy and Jessica finish decorating the tree that Jeremy had purchased that morning at a nearby tree lot. It was late to be preparing the house for Christmas, but the occasion was too special not to, no matter how close to Christmas it was.

Esther watched Jasmina running back and forth between the tree and the piano.

What do you suppose is going on inside her little head right now?

The girl had still not spoken a word, nor was there any sign that she ever would. The doctors believed it was a temporary condition, resulting from the shock of the battle and the deaths of her family members. Still, Esther was beginning to worry. How long would it be before Jasmina would open up the doors that had slammed shut inside her little mind?

136

Saturday, 24 December, local time 2035
Baytown, California

"I think those were the best Christmas Eve services we've ever had, sweetheart, and you did a great job."

"Thanks. The choir's songs were wonderful, weren't they?"

"However," said Papa Stevens, grinning from ear to ear, "I think Jessica's return was the Christmas present everyone looked forward to seeing, don't you?"

"I thought we would never get settled down again after she was introduced," Esther acknowledged. "We didn't want her homecoming to divert people's attention from the service itself, but it didn't seem right to keep her away, either."

"Of course not," Grandma Stevens chimed in, running her hand down the length of Jessica's hair. "And the way they stood and applauded for so long was not just for Jessica. It was really for Jesus, don't you agree? I felt such a spirit of thankfulness there tonight."

"Yes, I did, too," agreed John.

"I'm so glad it's finally over and everything can get back to normal," said Grandma Cain. "It seems like 'normal' has been such a long time coming to our family."

John lifted Jasmina onto his lap. It was the first time, since arriving home, that she had been content to let him hold her like this. On other occasions, she had wriggled away and run to Esther or Jessica. But not tonight. It warmed John's heart to feel her there, snuggled quietly in his arms, yielding to the sleepiness that had finally overcome her vigil in front of the tree lights. She had not touched the presents stacked underneath, but it had been a constant challenge to keep her fingers away from the lights.

The television was tuned to Channel 20's annual Christmas Eve Special. Two hours of uninterrupted music, with the only picture on the screen being that of Yule logs burning in a fireplace. The first time John had seen it, he had thought, *Only in California would people sit around and watch a log burn on television.* However, the music selections were always good and the program had proven to be a comforting addition to their Christmas tradition.

John stared at the image of the flickering log fire. *Thank you, Lord, for making this the most special Christmas ever. I remember how hard it was last year. When Jenny left us, so did the spirit of the season. We were here together, but we couldn't seem to come together. It feels so different tonight, Lord, a priceless feeling. Thank you for making us a family again. Stronger than we've ever been. And, merry Christmas, Jenny. There must be a wonderful celebration going on in heaven right now. Enjoy!*

Jeremy had gone to his room for a package to put under the tree, and Jessica was in the kitchen helping Esther put dishes in the dishwasher. The grandparents had gone off to bed, in preparation for what was always an early Christmas morning at the Cain household. John noticed a crawl line begin to make its way across the bottom of the television screen.

"Esther!"

The tone of John's voice caused her to put the soup pot back on the stove and hurry into the family room. Jessica followed after her.

"Look."

John was leaning forward, Jasmina asleep in his arms, watching as the crawl line message repeated itself.

Channel 20 News Bulletin: Explosion reported inside 29-mile Coast Range Tunnel, part of the Hetch Hetchy Aqueduct, San Francisco's primary water source. Extent of damage unknown, but believed to be massive. No casualties reported. Stay tuned.

The crawl line started to repeat itself for the third time. Esther stared at the screen.

"Do you think. . . ?" She stopped in midsentence.

John was up now, handing Jasmina over to Jessica. "Put her in bed, hon," he said as he opened the drawer by the telephone and took out his book of numbers. Thumbing down to *F*, he opened it and punched in the ten-digit number.

"Hello, FBI." The voice was brusque on the other end.

"Hello, this is Pastor John Cain, of Calvary Church in Baytown. I need to speak to Agent Webber or Danversen, please. It is very urgent."

"I'm sorry, sir. They are not available. May I take a message?"

"Look, it is absolutely essential that I—"

"Sir, it is Christmas Eve. I can take your message if you'll give it to me. I'll forward it to the appropriate desk."

John's irritation was building.

"Have you heard about the bomb blast along the Hetch Hetchy Aqueduct?"

The voice on the other end changed, becoming suddenly cautious. "Yes sir. Do you have information that might help us?"

"Tell Webber or Danversen that the tunnel is a diversion."

"A diversion?"

"Yes. Tell them that the real action will be at the Pulgas Water Temple, near Redwood City. Get the police or somebody over there right away!"

"Sir? How do you know this? Can you confirm this information?"

John was ready to explode. It was the one time this week that he wanted to be recognized, yet the agent apparently did not know who he was.

"This is the work of Marwan Dosha and his band of terrorists. They are waging war against America. And the longer you keep talking to me, the less time you have to stop them. San Francisco's water supply is in grave jeopardy. You need to hurry!"

"Sir, would you tell me your name again, please?"

John pulled the receiver away from his ear in exasperation, just as Jeremy entered the room.

"What's going on?" he asked, looking first at his dad and then at Esther.

"They've blown up the Hetch Hetchy Aqueduct," said Esther.

"The what?" Jeremy said, with a puzzled look.

"It's the water supply system for several Bay Area counties," John explained, handing the receiver to Esther. "Here, give the agent whatever he wants. Only make sure that he contacts Webber or Danversen."

She took the phone, a worried look on her face. "What are you going to do?"

"I'm going to the Pulgas Water Temple."

"No, John, please . . ." Her tone was pleading.

"I have to go. It may be too late already."

"I'm going with you, Dad."

John hesitated for an instant. Then he motioned to Jeremy with his hand. "Okay, get our jackets. I'll be with you in a second."

John ran down the hall and into the master bedroom, while Jeremy went to the hall closet for their jackets. His mind racing on ahead, John fumbled with the key that unlocked the drawer where he kept the Colt .45 ACP. Moments later, he reappeared, the handgun tucked into the leather holster that Carla Chin had presented him at his concluding lesson.

"How far is this place, Dad?"

John thought for a moment. Like most Californians, he automatically measured freeway distance in terms of time, not actual mileage.

"My guess is thirty minutes, at this time of night. Less if we hurry."

Esther was still busy on the phone. John blew a kiss in her direction and mouthed "*I love you*" as he went out the door, with Jeremy right behind.

—m—

SATURDAY, 24 DECEMBER, LOCAL TIME 2205
SAN MATEO COUNTY, CALIFORNIA

"It can't be far from here," said Jeremy, looking up from a map that lay crumpled in his lap. They had reached speeds of eighty miles per hour while crossing the San Mateo Bridge and making their way up the long hill on Highway 92. Amazingly, John thought, there had been no patrol cars to hinder their progress. He didn't know whether to be relieved or chagrined that no one had stopped them. A glance at the dashboard clock told him they had been gone from home exactly twenty minutes.

"There! Turn left!" Jeremy pointed, as the car skidded into the left turn lane and onto Cañada Road. "My guess is that it's about a mile from here. According to the map, it should be on the right-hand side."

"Good navigation, Son. You got us here. Now, when we see some sign of this place, I'll drive past slowly. If the police are there, I'll pull in. If not, we'll go on by, turn out the lights, and double back until we get close. If that's the way it goes, you stay with the car while I check things out."

"No way, Dad. I'm going with you."

"No." John's voice was sharp. "You stay here."

"But—"

"No buts, Son. Don't argue. As far as this operation is concerned, I am in charge. Just do as I say. Everything is going to be okay." John's thoughts flashed back to a dark street in Bandar-é Abbâs, and Hersch's words to the same effect as they had stood outside the Fardusi compound. Then he saw it. "There. Up ahead. This is it!"

The sign was illuminated by the car's headlights.

PULGAS TEMPLE
TERMINUS
HETCH HETCHY AQUEDUCT
SAN FRANCISCO
WATER DEPARTMENT

John slowed the car as they drove past the gate. It was shut, with a sign on the gate indicating the hours it would be open to the public. There did not seem to be any cars in the parking lot, though in the darkness he could not be sure. They kept going until well past the gate. Then John switched off the lights, turned the car around and coasted back until they were about a hundred feet from the entrance. He pulled over onto the shoulder and stopped.

"All right, Son, get behind the wheel and lock the doors. If you hear or see anything out of the ordinary, get out of here. Go find the police. If they show up before then, tell them that I'm inside. I don't want to get shot by mistake. If there's nothing suspicious, I'll be back in a few minutes."

"Be careful, Dad."

"Thanks. You can count on it."

John opened the door and stepped out, shutting it quietly. He felt for his gun as he walked up the road, but left it in the holster. At the gate, he hesitated, peering into the darkness. There did not seem to be anything unusual. He looked at the chain on the gate. It was wrapped around the gate frame and the padlock was in place.

Wait.

He bent down to look closer.

The lock is open! There wouldn't be a padlock here if they didn't lock it after hours. It could be that the caretaker had forgotten to set it, but that's doubtful. Someone has picked this lock, and there's a good chance that person may be in there right now.

Careful not to make any noise, he removed the chain and pushed the gate open just far enough to get past. Stepping through, he glanced around the parking lot again. Nothing. The night sky was filled with twinkling stars and a three-quarter moon edged its way from behind a passing cloud. He felt the chill of a light breeze through his jacket. As his eyes grew accustomed to the semidarkness, he saw something in the distance. Was it the monument? As he came closer, the shadowy outline took the same shape as the one pictured in the newspaper.

John continued moving forward, then stopped suddenly at the sound of voices. At that moment, the moon began to move out from behind a cloud, illuminating the scene. A tanker truck was backed up to the monument, and two dark figures could be seen standing nearby. *Wait.* A third man emerged from the shadows and strolled over to the others.

This is it. They are putting something in the water! "That which flows from under the temple will poison the earth." Whatever it is, they've got to be stopped.

John moved slowly. The men suddenly stopped what they were doing and turned in his direction. John halted his movement, watching, waiting. He heard them speaking in low tones, but couldn't make out what was being said. He looked for the third man but he had disappeared. *Where did he go?*

"Whoever you are, come forward slowly, with your hands where we can see them." The voice was low and threatening, coming from the passenger side of the truck.

Well, at least now I know where you are.

The moon was all the way out from behind the cloud now and John knew he was a sitting duck once they saw his shadow. He ducked and dove laterally, off the path and onto the grass. At that precise moment, he saw the flash and heard the echo of a gunshot. Instinctively, he scrambled toward a mound and dropped for cover behind it. A second shot zinged past his ear. He hit the grass hard and kept rolling until he was behind what looked to be a tiered step-garden of some sort. Fumbling for his gun, he drew it from the holster.

—∾—

Jeremy was standing by the car, with the door open, listening and watching.

Dad must have found something or he would be back by now.

Then his heart did a double skip and leaped into his throat at the sound of gunfire. One shot; then another. Quietly, he closed the car door and ran up the roadway toward the Pulgas Temple gate.

—∾—

There were shouts.

John thought it still sounded like three men, no more than that. Someone was running off to the right now. He saw the shadow and fired. *Missed. He's still moving. Where are the others?*

Quickly, John surveyed his situation.

I'm much too much out in the open here. But there's nowhere to go. He'll see me if I move. I still don't see the others. Maybe they're circling around the opposite way.

The shadow he had fired at was gone. John began inching his way along the grass on his stomach, trying to gain some additional protection from the small garden mound.

Boom! Another flash and simultaneous report.

Over there. To the right of that live oak.

John scrambled back the way he had come, as the gunman fired another round. John grunted involuntarily as the bullet chipped the cement step, just inches above his head. He turned his attention back to the live oak, watching for some movement.

What I wouldn't give for a tritium night sight.

"Don't move. Drop the weapon or I'll kill you right now."

John froze. It was a male voice, slightly accented, and it came from directly behind him. Somehow, the first man had managed to circle around behind him, and John knew he had no chance. He lowered the gun to the grass.

"Stand up slowly. Keep your hands away from your body. Do not make any sudden moves or you are a dead man."

Deliberately, John drew himself to his knees. Then he pushed up to a standing position, watching as a shadow moved toward him from the live oak. It was the second assailant.

"Keep your hands high in the air. I am right behind you," declared the voice. John felt the muzzle of a handgun in the small of his back, as the man ran his hands up and down John's body, confirming there was no other weapon than the one being picked up at that moment by the gunman's partner.

"Turn around slowly," the voice ordered.

John turned around until he could face the man. Off to the right, a third man walked toward them. With the moon behind them, it was impossible to distinguish their features. His guess was Middle Eastern, given the nature of things.

"Who are you?" the first man asked. "Police? FBI?"

John said nothing.

"Listen, my friend," the voice of the second man was oily slick, and it too carried an accent, more pronounced than his partner's. "You have rather rudely interrupted our work here tonight. That being the case, it will cost you dearly.

I can assure you of that. We are well away from any populated area, and no one will have heard shots being fired. So, you have a choice. You may die swiftly and cleanly, or slowly and with great pain. It matters little to us which way you choose. If you wish it to be quick, however, then you must cooperate. Understand?"

"I understand," John said, concentrating on keeping his voice from showing the fear that stuck like a dirt clod in his throat.

"Once again, what is your name?"

"John Cain."

He saw the men glance at each other.

"You are *the* John Cain? The one who was in Israel last September?"

"That's me."

"Hand your wallet over. It is in your jacket. I felt it a moment ago. But move very slowly, please."

John reached inside his jacket and withdrew his wallet.

"Throw it over here."

The man caught it in midair and opened it with a flick of his fingers. Holding it up to the moonlight, he briefly examined the driver's license behind the plastic window, before handing the wallet to his partner.

"Well, well. The great cleric, John Cain, has indeed paid us a visit tonight. This is certainly much more than we could have possibly hoped for. Allah must truly be smiling upon us. We'll keep the wallet, thank you. It will be enough to prove to our friends that you have been eliminated once and for all. You have been a real nuisance to our cause, John Cain, you and that daughter of yours, and it will be a distinct honor to send you to an infidel's hell."

"That is the one thing I am absolutely sure the two of you will not do to me," John responded, as an unexpected calmness settled over him, causing him to wonder if God was preparing him for the inevitable final journey. "You cannot send me to hell. Jesus Christ, God's Son, has made certain of that."

The man holding the wallet stepped forward and drove his fist into John's stomach. John doubled over in pain, just in time to catch a second blow on the side of his head. He toppled like a freshly cut tree. His only sound was a low moan as he tried to suck in air.

"Get up!" the man ordered, propelling the toe of his boot into John's ribs with such force that it lifted him partially off the grass. John fell back on his side, rolling over as he gasped for breath.

"I said, get up, Mr. Cain. You should enjoy watching what we are about to do."

Every attempt to breathe brought with it excruciating pain. John struggled to his feet, half anticipating another felling blow, but none came. His eyes focused again gradually, as the one whose boot had done the damage pushed him forward, past the reflecting pool and toward the monument.

137

Jeremy slipped past the open gate and ducked behind a cluster of bushes, listening all the while for something that would tell him what was happening. He caught his breath as more gunfire erupted. He saw a shadow darting from one tree to another. Finally, he recognized his father, lying in the grass. At first, he thought he had been hit. But no. He saw him stretch out his arms, gun in hand, looking in the other direction. He opened his mouth to call out a warning, when he heard the man behind his father shout. He saw John rise to his feet as the man moved closer. He waited, listening from his hiding place, wincing as he watched his father's beating.

What should I do? Dad said to get the police.

Jeremy turned and headed back to the gate.

—~—

John stepped up onto the platform surrounding the inner wall of the Pulgas Temple. Curious, he glanced over the side. Far below the wall it was dark, but he could hear water running in the cistern-like cavity. In the distance, on the other side of a wire fence, moonlight shimmered on water flowing along an above-ground aqueduct and disappearing into the darkness.

"Have you any idea what we are doing? Is that why you have come, Mr. John Cain? It must be."

John now saw there were actually two additional big black trucks off to one side, away from the cistern's concrete wall.

"Having had some taste of the diabolical way your kind thinks, I must assume that you are going to try to poison the water."

"Not 'try.' That is where you are wrong. No, we *will* poison the city's water system. Of that, there is no doubt. Our fellow warriors have by this time destroyed the tunnel that brings water to this region from the mountains. We in turn are about to pollute the reservoirs with plutonium nitrate. It is a plan that has taken many months to bring to fruition. And somehow, in the process of it all, you and your daughter, have managed to be a constant mosquito buzzing about our heads. But we are patient. And now we succeed in spite of your meddling.

"I would kill you now, just to be rid of you. But it gives me pleasure to know that you, of all people, will be witness to this great victory in our holy war. A few more minutes to watch as we kill thousands." He turned to his companion. "Rehan, let us begin releasing the plutonium."

The one called Rehan opened the door to the nearest truck cab and climbed in. The engine growled its protest before finally rumbling to life. Rehan leaned out of the open door and shouted something in Arabic. The man holding his gun on John answered. Rehan's head disappeared inside the cab and the truck began moving backward, picking up speed as it went. John watched in horror as it broke through the wall, its momentum continuing until the truck's rear wheels ran off the edge of the cistern and the belly of the tank dropped at a crazy angle against the platform floor.

The second man slipped on rubber gloves and leaned over the edge to press something onto the tank's outer surface.

"Stand back," he ordered, recovering his balance and stepping back toward the others. "Behold, the shaped charge of C-4 plastic. When it explodes, it will rupture the bottom rear of the tank."

John felt sick as he thought of its lethal contents spilling out into the water below.

"Quickly," the leader motioned to the others. "Move the other trucks into position. Set the remaining charges and we'll release the contents all at once. We won't need a tractor to escape in. I'm sure that John Cain has been kind enough to provide us with a vehicle, have you not?"

John said nothing, calculating the distance between himself and the man holding the gun, realizing at the same time he had no real chance.

"And when you finish, Rehan, go and check just to be sure he didn't come here on a motorcycle."

The second truck roared to life and slowly began moving backward toward the cistern. With a grinding crunch of metal against concrete, the second tanker soon hung precariously over the cistern beside the first. The man with the rubber gloves was holding a small flashlight between his teeth as he bent over a bag containing more explosives. Meanwhile, the leader prodded John ahead of him with the barrel of his gun until they stood near what remained of the cistern wall.

"I assume you know something about plutonium nitrate? It comes in liquid form, is completely soluble, and mixes quite well with water. Your fellow infidels will soon be drinking, straight from the tap, millions of tiny subatomic particles known as alpha radiation. We brought along enough here to contaminate the entire water supply. Those who manage to escape death will leave the area in panic. San Francisco will become a ghost town. So will the surrounding communities. It will be months, maybe even years before an alternate water source can be created. Meanwhile, who will want to live near our little plutonium ponds? I predict the total collapse of the area's economy, John Cain, what do you think?"

"How did you manage to get this stuff?" John inquired, stalling for whatever amount of time he could get.

"We have gone to great lengths to establish connections with the scientific community in what used to be the mighty USSR. This purchase was made from reactors there that were using the PUREX refining process. To their discredit, the Russians are very poor record-keepers and never quite seem to know the exact amounts of plutonium at their disposal. Their scientists are also very poor since the breakup of Russia's research industry. It has been easy for our leaders to make these two conditions work for us.

"Ooomph!"

Out of the corner of his eye, John glimpsed a dark object hurtle past him and slam into the side of the man holding the gun.

Jeremy!

The force of Jeremy's full-body tackle knocked the gunman against the waist-high Temple wall. A gunshot reverberated and the bullet ricocheted wildly off the brick platform. The man's arms flailed at the air as he tried to regain his balance, but it was too late. He pitched over the side and disappeared into the darkness.

The man with the gloves looked up in surprise as John sprang forward and fell on top of him, pummeling him with his fists as they rolled off the edge of the platform and onto the ground. With surprising agility and fueled by a burst of adrenaline, John regained the upper position as he and the other man rolled back toward the platform. With a move that shot pain through his side, he banged the terrorist's head against the concrete slab. The man went limp.

John looked up to see the one called Rehan running away from the trucks. Before John could stop him, Jeremy darted off in pursuit. John sat gasping for breath as another searing flash of pain shot through his chest. He heard a commotion out in the darkness, but he couldn't see anything.

"Jeremy!"

There were only sounds of grunting and gasping. Finally, all was still.

"Jeremy!" John looked around for a weapon. There was none.

He saw a shadowy figure coming slowly toward him, and he breathed a sigh of relief at the sight. He would recognize that rolling gait anywhere, even in the semidarkness. It was Macarthur High School's starting point guard.

"Are you okay, Son?"

"Better than you, I think," Jeremy answered, with a grin.

"Where is he?"

"Resting in the grass by the path. But we'd better see if they have some rope or something in the truck. He'll come around pretty soon. What about the other guy?"

"I don't know."

Inside the glove compartment of one of the trucks, Jeremy discovered a roll of electrical tape. Quickly, he tied up the one beside the platform and then ran off to take care of the man he had knocked out.

John found a flashlight on the truck seat. He limped back to the inner wall of the Temple and turned the beam downward. Ten or twenty feet below, he saw the third man's body lying face up, arms outstretched in the shallow water. It appeared that he had struck the concrete bottom and either broke his neck or knocked himself out and drowned. Either way, the man was clearly dead. John looked at his watch. Forty-five minutes had elapsed since they'd left home. He went to find Jeremy.

Just then, a car swung through the open gate and came to a stop in the parking lot. Two men dressed in police uniforms got out. One of them had a flashlight. Its beam caught John just as he walked up to Jeremy.

"Police!" the man shouted, as he drew his weapon. "Down on the ground. Now! Both of you! And keep your hands where we can see them!"

John groaned, with a fresh stab of pain, as he dropped obediently to the ground next to Jeremy.

"Been there, done that once already tonight," John said, grinning at Jeremy. "But somehow it isn't the same this time."

Epilogue

SUNDAY, 25 DECEMBER, LOCAL TIME 1400
BAYTOWN, CALIFORNIA

"Yes, we're all fine, Jim," Esther said in reply to the concern in Jim Brainard's voice. "We're opening our presents a little later than usual this year, but otherwise things are as normal as they ever seem to get in the Cain household. . . . Yes, John is taking it easy on the sofa. Three cracked ribs and a small fracture in the left cheekbone. His eye is black, he's taped up pretty good, and he looks like the loser of a barroom brawl. Other than that, he's fine. . . . What? . . . Yes, I'll tell him that Hersch offered his crutches. . . ." She raised her voice to make sure that John could hear the last line.

"Well, the problem was, it took awhile for me to convince the FBI that I was for real. John ran out of the house and left me to give out his driver's license and social security number. Only he took them with him. . . . I know, what else can you expect from a preacher?

"I finally had to call Lieutenant Randle of the Baytown police. I met him last September and remembered that he was a personal friend of FBI Agent Webber. When I explained the situation to him, he got things going. He contacted the FBI and local authorities in Redwood City or Belmont, I'm not sure just where. They sent a patrol car out, but by that time, my men had everything under control. . . . Yes, you heard it right on television. Jeremy saved their bacon. . . . What's that? . . . Oh, I wouldn't worry, I think he still wants to work for you next summer. Hopefully, he's had enough excitement for a while."

Jeremy, listening from across the room, grinned and winked at his dad.

"Yes, the police handcuffed them both and hauled them in with the terrorists. One of the men had John's wallet in his pocket, so it took a while to sort the bad guys from the good. . . . No, I'm not sure about that. The reservoir has been shut down and tests will be made right away. Everyone has been notified to conserve on water usage.

"There are lots of people afraid to use any tap water, even though it does not appear they were able to insert any contaminants in any of the reservoirs.

But they were *that* close! Bottled water is being shipped from L.A. and Portland. I think that's what we'll be drinking until we hear for sure. It's all you see on television and it's pretty scary, all right, but officials are promising to let the public know everything. I guess we'll wait and see.

"They have engineers out at the tunnel, too. They will check out the extent of the damage and also submit a proposal for a temporary alternate water source that will give them time to reopen the tunnel.

"Dosha? Unfortunately, nobody seems to know where he or that Azari woman disappeared to. Our guess is they are somewhere in Europe or the Middle East. We don't think either of them is here in the States, but who knows? . . . Yes, it is a bit unsettling to think about it. I hope they are caught soon. We'll certainly feel a lot safer. . . . Okay, I'll tell them. Merry Christmas to both you and Hersch. I'm so glad he was able to spend Christmas back there with you. We love you both very much."

Esther put down the telephone and smiled at the others. Everyone had crowded into the family room. The grandparents sat on chairs that had been placed in a semicircle together. Jeremy was on the floor with an arm around Jessica, who in turn had her arm around Jasmina. The young girl seemed at home today, more relaxed and contented than usual. John, careful not to move any more than he had to, lay stretched out on the sofa, a little groggy from pain medication, but otherwise alert and enjoying the scene. Esther walked over and knelt down by him, pecking his forehead with a kiss.

Esther shifted to get more comfortable. As she did, her eyes caught movement in the pool outside the family room door. It was the pool sweep; John's *beloved ghost* that had haunted them ever since Jenny's death. She looked again. Its ethereal qualities seemed to have vanished. She smiled.

It's just a pool sweep now.

Esther ran her hand across John's chest.

"I love you," she whispered.

"I love you, too," he replied with a smile.

"Why do you suppose God has allowed all this to happen, John? And how did we find ourselves in the middle of it?"

John shook his head. "I don't know, darling. I honestly do not know."

Esther's gaze turned back to Jasmina, standing next to the tree, touching a Christmas light with her delicate fingers. No one said anything to stop her.

We live in two different worlds, don't we, little lady—at least one with two different parts. Maybe God is teaching us that there is more going on here than meets the eye. Maybe this is not just a war on America. Could it be that this is "spiritual warfare" made visible? The thought sent a shiver down Esther's spine.

Suddenly, Jasmina whirled like a ballerina, one hand held high and the other pointing out, away from her. It was magical, like a scene from *The Nutcracker.*

Has someone taught you that? Esther mused silently. *What other secrets are hidden inside your little mind and heart? Will we ever know?*

Jasmina stopped and began walking purposefully toward Jeremy and Jessica, carefully planting one foot directly in front of the other, arms stretched out, as if she were walking an invisible high wire. Finally, she looked up, pointed, and smiled.

"*Jes-see-kah.*"

—ʍ—

"If you, then, though you are evil, know how to give good gifts to your children, how much more will your Father in heaven give good gifts to those who ask him! So in everything, do to others what you would have them do to you."

—Matthew 7:11–12

—ʍ—

Where it all began . . .

When ancient hatreds explode, John Cain is thrust into the middle of a precise, coordinated jihad where he will look straight into the abyss and discover whether or not his God is big enough to see him through.